Richard Laymon wrote over thirty nov[...]
May 2001, *The Travelling Vampire Shou*[...]
Best Horror Novel, a prize for whic[...]
shortlisted with *Flesh, Funland, A Goo*[...]
and *A Writer's Tale* (Best Non-fiction[...]
books of the Beast House Chronicles: *The Cellar, The Beast House* and
*The Midnight Tour*. Some of his recent novels have been *Night in the
Lonesome October, No Sanctuary* and *Amara*.

A native of Chicago, Laymon attended Willamette University in
Salem, Oregon, and took an MA in English Literature from Loyola
University, Los Angeles. In 2000, he was elected President of the Horror
Writers Association. He died in February 2001.

Laymon's fiction is published in the United Kingdom by Headline,
and in the United States by Leisure Books and Cemetery Dance
Publications. To learn more, visit the Laymon website at: http://
rlk.cjb.net

'A brilliant writer' *Sunday Express*

'Incapable of writing a disappointing book' *New York Review of Science
Fiction*

'No one writes like Laymon and you're going to have a good time with
anything he writes' Dean Koontz

'One of the best, and most underrated, writers working in the genre
today' *Cemetery Dance*

'This author knows how to sock it to the reader' *The Times*

'This is an author that does not pull his punches . . . A gripping, and at
times genuinely shocking, read' *SFX Magazine*

*Also in the Richard Laymon Collection published by Headline*

*The Beast House Trilogy:*
The Cellar
The Beast House
The Midnight Tour

The Woods are Dark
Out are the Lights
Beware!
Dark Mountain*
Flesh
Resurrection Dreams
Funland
The Stake
Darkness, Tell Us
One Rainy Night
Alarums
Blood Games
Endless Night
Midnight's Lair*
Savage
In The Dark
Island
Quake
Body Rides
Bite
Fiends
After Midnight
Among the Missing
Come Out Tonight
The Travelling Vampire Show
Dreadful Tales
Night in the Lonesome October
No Sanctuary
Amara
The Lake
The Glory Bus

*previously published under the pseudonym of Richard Kelly
Dark Mountain was first published as Tread Softly

# Night Show

and

# Allhallow's Eve

headline

NIGHT SHOW first published in Great Britain in 1984
by New English Library

ALLHALLOW'S EVE first published in Great Britain in 1986
by New English Library

First published in this omnibus edition in 2006
by HEADLINE BOOK PUBLISHING

A HEADLINE paperback

2

ISBN 0 7553 3170 2

Typeset in Janson by Avon DataSet Ltd, Bidford on Avon, Warwickshire

Printed and bound in Great Britain by
Mackays of Chatham plc, Chatham, Kent

Headline's policy is to use papers that are natural, renewable and recyclable
products and made from wood grown in sustainable forests. The logging and
manufacturing processes are expected to conform to the environmental
regulations of the country of origin.

HEADLINE BOOK PUBLISHING
A division of Hodder Headline
338 Euston Road
London NW1 3BH

www.headline.co.uk
www.hodderheadline.com

# Night Show

# Chapter One

A car slowed down, keeping pace with Linda. She didn't look. She walked faster, hugging the books more tightly against her chest.

She wished, now, that she had accepted her father's offer to pick her up. But she'd hoped to run into Hal Walker at the library. She had waited at a table near the entrance, trying to study, her heart racing each time the door opened. Betty came in. Janice and Bill came in. The nerd, Tony, came in and made a pest out of himself until she told him to get lost. But Hal never showed up.

'Hey, Linda, want a ride?'

Her head snapped toward the car. A dumpy old station wagon. Tony's car. She might've known. She counted three vague figures in the front seat.

'How about it?' a boy called through the open window.

'Bug off.'

'Aw, come on.'

She picked up her pace, but the car stayed beside her.

'Think you're hot shit.'

She ignored the remark, and tried to place the voice. Not Tony. This had to be one of his jerk-off friends. Maybe Joel Howard, or Duncan Brady, or Arnold Watson. A bunch of scuzzy misfits.

'Get out of here!' she yelled.

'Don't think so,' said the boy at the window.

'Look guys, you're gonna be in big trouble if you don't cut it out.'

'Cut what out?'

'Her tongue?' asked a different voice.

She reached the corner and stepped off the curb. The station wagon swung in front of her.

'I'm warning you . . .'

Her voice stopped as the door flew open.

Two boys leaped out. In the streetlight, she glimpsed their twisted, flattened faces. She whirled around to run, but even as she sprang for the curb an arm hooked her waist. Her books tumbled. She was yanked backwards. She tried to yell. A hand clutched her mouth, mashing her lips into her teeth. She squirmed and kicked. A boy lunged against her legs, grabbed them and lifted.

She was carried to the car. The third boy swung open the tail door. The other two wrestled her inside, and the door thunked shut.

She was in darkness, one boy under her back, one on top of her legs. She tried to pry the arm loose from her belly. The hand on her mouth pinched her nostrils shut. She couldn't breathe. The car lurched forward. She tugged at the smothering hand. The other arm eased its clench, and a fist hammered her belly. She felt as if a bomb had exploded, bursting her lungs and heart.

'Lay still.'

She grabbed her chest, struggling to breathe. The boy's hands, she realised, had moved down to her hips. He was holding her firmly, but no longer crushing her.

'You okay?' asked the boy on her legs.

She couldn't answer.

'You weren't supposed to hurt her, asshole.'

'She was fighting me,' said the one beneath her. She recognized his whiny voice – Arnold Watson – and decided she might be better off keeping the knowledge to herself. At least until she got away.

Arnold held her steady as the car took a corner fast.

She found that she could breathe again, though her lungs still ached. 'Let me go,' she said. 'Please.'

Arnold laughed, his belly shaking under her back.

'What do you *want*?'

'You,' he said. 'And we've got you, haven't we? The one and only Linda Allison.'

'Please, just let me go. I promise I'll never speak a word. Honest.'

'You had your chance.'

'Huh?'

'Should've been nice when you had the chance. Think you're hot shit, always dumping on us.'

'I don't either. I never . . .'

'We've got feelings, you know. The question is, do *you*?'

'Of course I do. For godsake . . .!'

'You're gonna get it, now.'

'What are you . . .?' She couldn't bring herself to finish, this time; she didn't want to hear the answer.

'We've got plans for you.'

'No. Please. Just let me go. Please!'

'Real interesting plans.'

'Tell her,' said the boy on her legs.

'Hell no. Let her worry about it. Right?'

'Right,' said the driver. 'She'll think of all kinds of neat stuff.'

3

Though the voice was low and husky, apparently to disguise it, she knew it came from Tony. 'What do you think we'll do to you, huh, bitch?'

'Please. Just let me go. I'm sorry if I hurt your feelings.'

'Too late for sorry.'

'Please.'

'Who knows?' Tony said. 'Maybe you'll get yourself raped, or tortured. Maybe your pretty face is gonna get all fucked up with battery acid or a knife. How would you like that?'

Linda started to cry.

'Maybe you'll get cut up into little tiny pieces: first your toes and fingers, then maybe those nice big tits . . .'

'Come on, stop it,' said the boy on her legs.

Tony laughed. 'Bet you can feel that knife, right now, slicing into your . . .'

'Don't listen to him. We're not going to hurt you.'

'Don't count on it.'

'Hey, you said we'd just . . .'

'I know, I know.'

'Go ahead and tell her,' Arnold said.

'Okay okay. Here's what's really gonna happen. You know the old Freeman house?'

'Yes,' she sobbed, and wiped the tears from her face.

'It's still deserted. Nobody'll touch the place. It's supposed to be haunted. They say the ghosts of all those bodies moan inside the walls where crazy Jasper plastered them up, and that Jasper himself walks the house at night looking for fresh young girls to chop. Girls just like you.'

'He's dead,' Linda muttered.

'It's his ghost,' Arnold whispered. 'And he wants *you*.'

'Fun, huh?' asked Tony. 'Nice place to spend the night.'

'You're not . . .!'

'Oh yes we are.'

Her dread was mixed with relief. Tony had talked of rape and torture just to scare her. All they really intended was to leave her alone in the Freeman house.

All.

Oh God!

But Jasper'd hanged himself in jail. No reason to fear him.

No such thing as ghosts.

But to be alone in the very house . . .

'You're crazy,' Linda muttered.

'Yeah,' Tony said. 'Real crazy. But not half as crazy as old Jasper.' She felt the car slow down and turned. 'Here we are. Your home away from home.'

It stopped. Tony climbed out. He opened the tailgate, and Linda was dragged feet first from the car. The boys stood her up and held her steady. Their faces, in the darkness, were weirdly stretched and distorted, their hair flat as if painted on. She realised, now, that the effect was caused by nylon stocking masks. Knowing the cause, however, didn't help. She felt as if the boys were grotesque strangers only pretending to be Tony and Arnold and – who was the other, Joel?

'Let's go,' said the one with Tony's voice. He started toward the gate of the low, picket fence. The other boys, one on each arm, forced Linda ahead.

The Freeman house looked similar to many of the older homes in Claymore, a two-story frame structure with a front porch, and a picture window looking out from the living room. Someone had kept it up. The lawn was trim. Only the shuttered upstairs windows and the FOR SALE, LELAND REALTORS sign hinted that it stood vacant.

The hinges groaned as Tony pushed open the gate. 'Wonder if Jasper heard that,' he whispered.

Arnold laughed softly, but his fingers dug into Linda's upper arm. He's frightened, she thought. He doesn't want to go in there any more than I do.

She looked to the right. In that direction was only the golf course, deserted now, a sprinkler hissing on the nearest green. To the left was the abandoned Benson house.

No help from the rear, either. Across the street, she knew, was only the bait and tackle shop – closed for the night.

The boys forced her along the walkway, up the wooden stairs, onto the porch. She expected the front door to be locked, but Tony turned the knob and pushed it wide open.

They must've been here before, forced their way . . . They'd planned all this. No spur of the moment decision. They'd plotted, made preparations.

'Anybody home?' Tony called, leaning into the darkness.

'Just us ghosts,' Arnold said, and gave a nervous laugh.

Tony entered. He waved the boys forward, and they guided Linda into the house. The air was cold, as if some of the winter's frost had been trapped inside, the heat of the warm June days kept out. The cold moved up Linda's bare legs, seeped through her thin blouse, brought goosebumps.

Arnold nudged the door. It banged shut, its crash resounding through the house.

'Loud enough to wake the dead,' Tony whispered.

Arnold laughed again.

'Let's hurry up,' said the other boy.

'Nervous?' Tony asked.

'Damn right.'

They walked Linda through the dark foyer. She let each foot

6

down softly, heel first, rolling toward the toe, straining for silence. All three boys, she realised, were also treading softly. Arnold, holding her right arm, cringed when a floorboard squeaked under his weight.

At the foot of the stairway, Tony stopped. His head tilted back as if he were studying the darkness at the top of the stairs. 'Jasper's bedroom was up there,' he whispered. 'They found one of the bodies on his bed. He'd been . . . snacking on it. They say the head was never found.'

'Come on,' said the boy on Linda's left. Joel. She was sure of that, now. 'Let's get out of here.'

''Fore we freeze our nuts off,' Arnold said.

Tony turned around. He slung the coil of rope off his shoulder. 'Bring her here.'

They tugged Linda's arms. She stamped on Arnold's foot. He grunted and his grip loosened. She jerked her arm free, spinning toward Joel, and drove her elbow into his face. He staggered backwards, letting go. She lunged through the darkness. Her hands clawed the door as footfalls raced toward her. She found the knob. Turned it. Then her back was hit. She slammed forward, her head exploding with pain as it crashed against the door.

A dull ache pulsed behind her eyes. She grimaced, her forehead burning as its skin pulled taut.

She bunked her eyes open, and saw her hands on her lap. They were bound together. The pale rope angled upward to the banister.

She was seated on the third stair, leaning awkwardly against the bars of the railing, her legs sloping down, her feet resting on the floor. Her ankles were tied together.

So, they'd done it. They'd tied her up, and left her here all alone.

Or had they left?

From her position on the stairs, she could see little of the house: the front door, a set of closed doors to the left of the foyer, a corner of the living room and some of its picture window through the entry on the right, and a narrow hallway that ran alongside the staircase. The only light was a pale spill across the living-room floor: moonlight slanting in through the window.

No sign of the boys. They'd either left the house or hidden themselves.

'Guys?' she asked, her voice no more than a whisper. 'Hey, look, I know you're here. You're just hiding on me.'

She waited. The house was silent.

She started to shiver. She raised her arms and pressed them tightly against herself for warmth.

'Guys?'

They're probably just out of sight, she thought, huddled together in the living room, nudging each other, trying not to giggle. Sooner or later, they would jump out at her.

'Okay,' she muttered. 'Have it your way.'

The rope, she saw, was looped around the banister and knotted at her wrists. She twisted her arms. Straining her head forward, she found that her teeth could just barely reach the bundle of knots. She bit into it, and tugged. The rope didn't give. Her tongue explored the mass of swirls, felt knot piled upon knot.

Her throat tightened. Her chin started to tremble and she blinked tears from her eyes. She lowered her arms in frustration.

'Come on, guys,' she pleaded. 'You've had your fun. You've taught me my lesson. Now let me go, please.'

Somewhere above Linda, a board creaked. With a gasp, she snapped her head around and looked up the stairway. She stared for a long time, afraid to move.

There was only darkness.

It's just them, she told herself. They didn't hide in the living room, they hid upstairs.

*Fuck off!* she wanted to yell.

But she kept her mouth clamped shut so hard her teeth ached.

She heard another quiet moan of wood. Above, but off to the left. As if someone were sneaking very slowly through the upstairs hallway.

The thought of it raised a whimper in her throat.

She flung herself away from the railing. The tether pulled taut. Ignoring the pain in her wrists, she tugged furiously. The banister squeaked and wobbled a bit. But it held. The rope held.

She drew her legs up, planted her tied feet on the next stair down, dropped to a crouch and sprang at the railing. Her shoulder smashed against the banister. Pain blasted through her body. She recoiled, and fell until the rope yanked at her wrists. It swung her sideways. Her other shoulder slammed into the newel post.

She hung there, numb with pain, her feet still on the second stair, her side against the post, all her weight tugging at her wrists. As she tried to pull herself up, the rope snapped. She dropped. Her back and head pounded the floor.

She lay there, stunned at first. As the pain started to fade, she realised she was free.

Free of the banister!

If she could just untie her feet . . .

Opening her eyes, she raised her head. Her skirt was rumpled around her waist, her panties pale in the darkness, her bare legs angling up to the second stair.

She drew her knees forward. She spread them, reached between them with her tied hands, and felt the knotted rope. As her fingers picked at the coils, a movement drew her eyes to the top of the stairs.

A dim figure stood in the darkness.

Linda's breath burst out as if she'd been punched in the stomach. Her bladder released. She clawed at the knots as the warm fluid spread down her buttocks.

Her eyes stayed on the motionless form. It just stood there.

She jerked a knot loose and kicked her feet. The bonds held. Another knot! She grabbed it, picked it, winced as a fingernail tore off.

An arm of the figure swung forward. A pale object seemed to break off. It hung in the air, fell, and hit the stairs midway down with a harsh thud. Gazing through the gap in her upraised legs, Linda watched it tumble down the remaining stairs. She saw trailing hair, a blur of face. She heard herself whimper again. She ached to throw herself out of its path, but the knot was pulling loose. She tore at the rope. The knot opened as the thing thumped off the final stair and rolled against her rump. A single, wide eye peered through the crevice between her legs. With a shattering scream, Linda kicked her legs free and rolled aside. She flipped over. On her belly, she glanced from the severed head to the stairway.

The figure was halfway down, walking slowly as if he had all the time in the world. He was naked, boney, and dead pale. A dark beard hung to his chest. He held a long object in his hands – an ax!

Linda shoved herself to her feet. She staggered back, whirled around, and raced for the door. She hit it with her shoulder. She swept down her tied hands, seeking the knob.

Found it!

Her sweaty hands twisted the knob. She dropped back, jerking the door open, crying out as it hammered her knee. Her leg buckled. She dropped hard to her rump, losing her grip on the knob.

The door swung open wide. In the dim light from the porch, she saw the man striding slowly forward. His head was tilted to one side, his face ragged with open sores, his tongue drooping out.

'No!' she shrieked.

He raised the ax high.

With her good leg, Linda thrust herself backward. She slid over the doorsill, and tumbled onto the porch. She rolled, forced herself to her knees, and scrambled for the porch stairs. She hurled herself off them. Clearing the three steps, she caught the walkway with her knuckles and landed flat with an impact that slapped her breasts and thighs and slammed the breath from her lungs. Dazed, she flopped onto her back.

She sat up, and peered into the porch.

The front door of the Freeman house swung shut.

Inside the house, Tony lowered his ax and leaned back against the door. He started to peel the makeup and false beard from his face.

In spite of the chilly air, he wasn't cold.

The tremors that shook his naked body had nothing to do with cold.

They had to do with excitement.

He'd scared himself silly. His heart was thundering, his guts

11

knotted. Touching himself, he felt his goose-flesh, his stiff nipples. His penis was shrunken as if to hide. His scrotum was shriveled the size of a walnut.

My God, what a charge!

Hefting his ax, he made his way across the dark foyer. He stooped, picked up the mannequin head by its hair, and eagerly started up the stairs toward the black upper story of the house.

# Chapter Two

Dani Larson leaned forward, bracing her hands on the sill, resting her forehead against the window pane. 'I'm so afraid,' she said. 'Margot, Julie, Alice – all dead.'

She flinched as Michael touched her bare shoulders. 'It's all right, honey,' he whispered. 'You're safe here.' His lips brushed her shoulders.

'Michael, no.'

'I'll help you forget.'

'I don't want to forget. He's out there somewhere, looking for me.'

'Worrying about it won't help.' His hands slipped around to the front of Dani, held her breasts gently through the thin fabric of her nightgown while he nibbled her ear.

She arched her back, moaning as if with pleasure. Suddenly,

she gasped. Her eyes bulged. Her mouth jerked open, ready to scream.

'Cut, cut! Beautiful! That's a print!'

'Aw shit,' Michael said. 'Just when I was starting to enjoy it.'

'Should've blown your lines,' Dani said, peeling his fingers off her breasts.

The window flew up, and Roger Weston poked his head inside. 'Beautiful, gang. Lovely. Ready for the splash scene, Dani?'

'We'll set it up.'

'Good kid.'

She turned away, caught Jack's amused look, and shrugged.

'Let's go to it, kid,' Jack told her.

Dani bared her teeth.

'Should've done that to Rog,' he said.

'I don't like to abuse short people. They've got enough troubles.' She picked up her blue windbreaker with MIDNIGHT SCREAMS printed across the back, slipped it on to cover the top, at least, of her sheer nightgown, and snapped it shut.

Then she followed Jack to a corner of the set, where Ingrid stood with her mouth agape and terror in her eyes. The mannequin was a duplicate of Dani: five foot six and slim, with shoulder-length auburn hair, gelatin eyes the same emerald color as her own, and lightly tanned latex skin. It was exact to the tiny scar on its chin, the slightly crooked upper front tooth.

Dani noticed, as she approached, the blatant dark thrust of its nipples through the gown.

She hoped that her own hadn't been so apparent.

They must've been, though. Identical nightgowns, identical breasts. She'd cast them, like the rest of Ingrid, from molds of herself. She'd taken great care, sitting half-naked in her work-shop, comparing, trying to find a perfect match of the flesh tones even though she hadn't known the nightgown would be quite so revealing.

If she hadn't made them so well, maybe she and Ingrid might have both been spared the embarrassment . . .

'Problem?' Jack asked.

'Huh?'

'You look upset.'

'No, it's all right. Just wishing the negligees weren't so transparent.'

'She looks great. You did, too.'

'You're not supposed to notice those things.'

'I'm a man.'

'I'm your boss.'

Jack laughed, and clawed fingers through the side of his dark beard. 'Gonna be the pits, blowing her away.'

'I don't need the competition.'

He wrapped an arm around Ingrid's waist. With a hand bracing her head, he tipped her sideways. Dani grabbed the legs, and lifted.

They carried Ingrid to the window. Dani lowered her feet to the chalk marks, and they set her upright. As Jack left to fetch the other mannequin, the continuity girl held a Polaroid snap-shot through the window: Dani's final moment with Michael. Using the photo as a guide, she arched Ingrid's articulated back and placed her fingertips on the sill.

Jack set down the Michael mannequin behind Ingrid.

Dani hadn't bothered to rename it, hadn't needed to. Constructing Michael's duplicate, she'd felt none of the eerie discomfort she'd experienced in making her own. Even giving her model a rather silly name like Ingrid hadn't been enough to dispel her uneasiness. At one point, she'd gone so far as to cover Ingrid's terrified face with a paper bag.

This morning, she'd let Jack do the dirty work on Ingrid while she worked on Michael: stuffing the hollow skulls with blood packs and calf brains fresh from the butcher. Jack had seemed reluctant, too. But he was a good fellow, always followed instructions.

Now, they adjusted Michael so he pressed against Ingrid's back, his lips against her neck. They raised his arms, placed his hands over her breasts.

Ingrid, at least, would have no cause for modesty.

Dani checked the final positions against the Polaroid. 'All set,' she called through the window.

Roger strode forward. Dani handed the snapshot out to him. He stared at it through his oversized glasses, then studied the set-up. 'Beautiful, beautiful. Okay, shut the goddamn window.'

Jack lowered the window. He stepped back. He looked at Ingrid. For an instant, Dani saw a hint of sorrow in his eyes. It vanished, and he winked at Dani. 'This is gonna be good,' he said.

'Hope so.'

They walked around the wall. From the front, the façade appeared to be the side of a small, woodframe house. The young couple looked frozen behind its window.

The set was crowded, people standing around with coffee cups, others busy adjusting lights, the sound man in headphones fiddling with dials like a HAM operator tuning in to exotic bands, Roger peering through the Paniflex and turning away to instruct the weary-looking cameraman.

'I'm off,' Jack said.

'Give it your best shot.'

He laughed, and headed away.

While she waited, Dani made her way to the coffee machine. The aluminum container was nearly empty, the fluid black and grainy as it trickled from the spout. In her styrofoam cup, it looked like watery mud. She took a sip and winced at the bitter taste. As she set the cup down, someone reached from behind and squeezed her breasts.

'Hey!' She flung up her arms, forcing the hands off, and whirled.

Michael grinned.

'Don't you *ever* do that again,' she said, barely able to control her rage.

'Whoa!' He raised his open hands as if to ward off an attack. 'So sorry. I just couldn't help myself. My hands have been burning ever since . . .'

'Don't be a jerk.'

'Come on. You enjoyed it.'

'See how you enjoy a punch in the face if you ever try that again.'

'The lady doth protest too much, methinks.'

'Think again.'

'Quiet on the set,' announced a nearby voice. 'Scene forty-four, take one.'

The studio went silent, and a red dome light began to spin. Dani stepped silently away for a better view. Michael stayed at her side.

She spotted Jack near one of the cameras, dressed now in jeans and a parka, a blue ski mask over his head, a shotgun in his hands.

'Action,' Roger said.

Jack ran forward, hunched low in front of the window, brought up the shotgun. But he didn't fire. Instead, he looked over bis shoulder. He stood upright and turned around, lowering the weapon.

'Cut, cut, cut!' Roger snapped. 'What the fuck's going on!'

Jack shook his head.

'*Jeezus*! Dani?' Roger twisted to face her. 'Dani, did you tell your boy what's going on? We're making a goddamn movie here. This ain't fun and games, it's the real thing. If he can't pull it off . . .'

'He's fine,' Dani said.

'Bull-fuckin'-shit! You said he could handle it. Nobody touches the goddamn trigger but your boy here. Requires precision, all that bullshit. All right. Okay. Christ! Now let's get it together, huh? That too much to ask?'

'You okay, Jack?' Dani asked, burning from the tirade, embarrassed for herself and Jack, furious with Roger.

Jack nodded.

'Okay,' Roger said in a calm, almost cheerful voice. 'Let's try it again.'

Dani blew out a long breath. She felt drained, as if Roger's tantrum had shaken out all her energy.

'Feathers a bit singed?' Michael whispered.

She glared at him, then turned her attention to Jack.

'The gun loaded?' Michael asked her.

She ignored him.

'Quiet on the set. Scene forty-four, take two.'

Jack was crouched off-camera, waiting.

'Action.'

He ran forward, crouched in front of the window, shouldered the shotgun and fired. The blast stunned Dani's ears. She saw the window blow in. Buckshot slammed into the right side of Ingrid's face, into Michael's forehead as he kissed her neck. Their latex skin disintegrated into pulp. Ingrid's eye vanished. Red, clotted gore exploded from both heads as the two figures flew backwards and vanished from the window.

'Cut, cut! Beautiful!'

'Not bad,' Michael said.

Dani realized she was holding the side of her face, covering her eye. She quickly lowered her hand. It was trembling.

She hurried toward Jack. He was bending down to pick up the spent, red cartridge.

'Great shot,' Dani said. 'Right on the mark.'

He straightened up, and turned to her. He dropped the shell into a pocket. 'Like I said, the pits.'

He handed the shotgun to Bruce, the prop master.

'You did fine,' Dani told him. She took his arm, and led him off to the side.

'Sorry I screwed up,' he said.

'Roger's a bastard.'

'No, he was right. I screwed up.'

'That's no reason for him to fly off the handle. He's a spoiled baby.'

Jack pulled the ski mask off his head, and rubbed his face. Stroking his ruffled beard, he shook his head. 'I am sorry. It made you look bad.'

'Hey, we're doing great work for that turkey. Our efforts are the only saving grace in his stupid, harebrained movie, and he'd better realise it.'

Jack appeared, for an instant, as if he might laugh. Then his face darkened. He gnawed his lower lip, and looked into Dani's eyes. 'That first time, when I was taking aim . . . Hell, you'll think I'm crazy, but I got the feeling it was you in the window. Really *you*. A switch got pulled, or something. I just couldn't shoot. I had to make sure . . . and then I saw you standing over there with Michael, and I was all right.'

Dani stared at Jack. She remembered the day, only two months ago, when he had entered her house for the job interview. His size and shaggy beard had intimidated her, at first; he looked like a wild mountain man. But his mild, intelligent eyes and quiet voice quickly won her over. She liked him, hired him over thirty-two other applicants who'd responded to her ad in the *Reporter*. He soon proved himself to be a competent employee – better than competent: energetic and eager, a fast learner, innovative and usually cheerful. But he'd been an employee, nothing more. They'd kept their emotional distance, stayed safely impersonal.

Until now.

Looking into his eyes, Dani felt a warm tremor of excitement.

'Guess it's out of the bag,' he said, a worried, glad look on his face.

'I guess so,' Dani said. 'What'll we do about it?'

'How about a kiss?'

She stepped close to Jack, felt his arms wrap around her, pull her snugly against his parka. Hugging him, she tipped back her head. He smiled down at her. His lips and beard pressed her mouth.

She knew that others might be watching, but she didn't care. It only mattered that this man she had worked with, joked with, had wanted her all along and kept it to himself. If he hadn't hesitated to shoot Ingrid, the masquerade might have gone on and on.

She eased her mouth away. 'How come you never . . . said anything?'

'Didn't want to get canned. Look what happened to Al.'

She winced at the mention of her previous assistant. 'He was a turkey.'

'A turkey who put moves on you.'

'How'd you know that?'

'Just a guess. His work was good: he went straight from you to the Steinman Studios. So it had to be something else.'

'He tried to . . .' Dani's face burned. 'He thought I was being coy when I told him to lay off. He tried to force the issue.'

'Bastard.'

'Well, it's over. He got canned and you got the job, so it all worked out for the best.'

'Indeed it did,' Jack said.

Dani grinned at him. 'Indeed, indeed.'

# Chapter Three

'To Ingrid,' Dani toasted.

'May she rest in peace.'

Dani clinked the rim of her vodka and tonic against Jack's, and took a sip. They were sitting outside at Joe Allen, the restaurant where she'd been fêted several months ago by Roger and the producer of *Midnight Screams*. She remembered listening to their eager descriptions of the effects they envisioned and finally, over coffee, signing the contract. The contract led to Ingrid, to Jack's revelation. It seemed only fitting that she should bring Jack here tonight.

A starting place, of sorts.

She stared at him, nervous and excited, wondering if he felt the same way. He certainly didn't look nervous. Puzzled, maybe, studying her eyes as if searching for answers to the same questions that whirled through Dani's own mind: where will this lead, to joy and fulfillment and an end to the loneliness, or to a bitter parting? The alternatives seemed too big, the chances of failure too great. She suddenly felt overwhelmed and afraid. She set down her glass. It left her hand cold and wet. She rubbed her hands together, squeezed them, pressed them to her chin.

'Dani?'

She tried to smile. 'I'm not sure if I'm ready for this.'

'Me, too. Let's forget the whole thing.'

His response shocked her into laughter. 'You creep!'

'See how easy it is, now that we don't have to worry about a serious relationship, a commitment, the heartache of rejection?'

'Much easier,' she admitted. 'But I think I prefer it the other way.'

'I do, too.'

'We'll give it a try.'

'At least till something better comes along.'

'You *are* a creep!'

'See?' Jack said. 'You're already starting to plumb the depths of my being.'

The waiter came and they both ordered ribs. When the meal came, Jack said, 'Be messy. Don't make me look bad.' Dani found that she didn't have to try. The juices and tangy sauce clung to her fingers, trickled down her chin. Fortunately, the table was well stocked with napkins. She used plenty, but Jack used more. She watched him, amused, as he swiped at his dripping mustache and beard.

'You should feel honored,' he said. 'I wouldn't humiliate myself, this way, in front of just anyone.'

'You look like a bear in a honey jar.'

'Please. It's hard enough to maintain dignity eating bones without comparisons to Gentle Ben.'

'I was thinking of Winnie the Pooh.'

'Gasp. Groan. How *could* you?'

When the stripped bones lay heaped on their plates, Jack said, 'I'm gonna need soap and water. Back in a minute.'

He left. Settling back in her chair, Dani looked around the restaurant. She saw waiters hurrying to crowded tables. She saw men gesturing at each other with forks, a late arrival greeting his companion with a shoulder slap, a hollow-cheeked beauty sipping wine at the table of two older men who talked vigorously and ignored her, a slick young man with an open shirt and gold necklaces, holding the hand of a girl who looked sixteen and awe-struck.

The man seemed too earnest, a sure sign that he was handing out a line. The girl looked innocent. She would buy the line, whatever it might be, and probably live to regret it. She would lose some of that youth, that innocence. Next time around, she would be more cautious.

But not too cautious, Dani hoped. You've got to take chances.

Her stomach fluttered. Jack would be returning any minute. Dinner was nearly over. Then they would drive to her house, if only because Jack's car was parked there. A great relief to just kiss him goodnight at the door, postpone the tense, wonderful time of intimacy. Perhaps they would both be better off waiting.

But she knew it wouldn't happen that way. Now that she'd found him, discovered the truth, she wanted him too much.

They would go to her house and make love.

She reached for her wine. The surface of the Sauvignon. Blanc shimmered as she lifted the glass to her lips.

'Danielle Larson?'

Startled, she jerked her head to the right. A man on the sidewalk waved. Dani stared, trying to recognise him: tall, so skinny he looked as if his black turtleneck was all that held his bones together, hairless and pale. With his back to the lights of the street, however, shadows concealed the features of his face.

He looked like no one Dani knew, or wanted to know.

But he'd called her name. She didn't want to snub him, so she waved.

He began to run toward her. Dani caught her breath. Goose-bumps stiffened her skin. This is a put-on, she told herself. Nobody runs like that, on tiptoes, hunched over, arms up like a goddamn boogyman ready to grab a throat.

It's a joke.

But he was plunging straight for the patio railing, straight for Dani.

Someone screamed.

Dani shot her chair back and leaped away. Her shoulder caught a passing man. He started to fall. Their feet tangled and Dani dropped onto him. 'Geez. I'm sorry, I'm sorry,' she muttered, scurrying off.

'Quite all right. Any time.'

She looked toward the railing. No sign of the intruder. But a crowd had gathered there as if everyone in the restaurant had raced over for a look at the phantom. They talked in a rush.

'Some kind of nut.'

'Run, you bastard!' a man yelled.

'Matters are coming to a pretty pass when one . . .'

'Probably freaked out on Angel Dust.'

'Certainly sparked things up.'

'Where's the manager?'

As the commentary continued, Dani pushed herself to her feet. Her skirt was twisted awry, her green silk blouse untucked. She was trying to straighten herself when Jack came out. His mouth dropped open. She saw alarm on his face. It changed to relief when he spotted her. He eased his way through the throng of guests returning to their tables.

Then he reached Dani and took hold of her shoulders. 'You all right?'

'I'm okay. Just a bit rumpled.'

'What *happened*?'

She shrugged. 'I'm not really sure. Some guy on the sidewalk called my name and waved. Next thing I knew, he was running for the patio like a madman.'

Jack frowned. 'Did he say anything?'

'I didn't stick around to find out.'

'But he was coming for you?'

'Sure looked that way.'

'Let's get the hell out of here.'

Against Dani's protests, Jack paid the bill. On the sidewalk in front of the restaurant, she kissed him. 'Thank you for the dinner. It was supposed to be my treat, you know.'

'I'm a chauvinist.'

'I'd better raise your salary.'

'Feel free.'

He took her hand and they headed for her car. Dani wished she hadn't parked so far away. During her eight years in Los Angeles, she'd developed the habit of taking the first parking place within walking range of her goal. It saved her from crowded, expensive parking lots, from the intimidation of valet parking, from circling blocks in a frustrating search for an empty stretch of curb. Sometimes, the practice backfired. She would walk three blocks only to discover a parking space directly in front of her destination. Tonight, she wondered if the strange, skinny man might be lurking nearby, ready to spring out at them. The sanctuary of the car remained a block away, around the corner on Robertson Boulevard.

She held Jack's hand more tightly.

'It's all right,' he said.

'I hope so.'

'Do you have *any* idea who it might've been?'

'Not the slightest.'

'But he knew you. Did you tell anyone you'd be here tonight?'

'Nobody,' she said, and heard the quiet tread of footsteps from the rear.

They both looked back. The lone man, far behind them, waddled along in a pale suit and Stetson, a cigar poking from his mouth.

'That him?'

Dani smiled with relief. 'Not unless he's a were-oaf.'

'A *were*-oaf?'

'By day, a cadaverous vegetarian. But when the full moon rises, a strange sensation grips his body. He pulses with throbbing corpulence. His clothes burst at the strain and he sags out, four hundred pounds of shimmering obesity, driven by an insatiable need to stalk the night in search of lasagne.'

'Wow,' Jack said, 'you oughta run that by Roger.'

'Yeah, he'd probably go for it. He went for *Midnight Screams*, didn't he? Call it *An American Were-oaf in Sardi's*.'

'Or *The Slobbering*.'

They rounded the corner, laughing, and Dani spotted her white VW Rabbit halfway up the block. She started to walk faster. Freeing her hand from Jack's, she reached into her purse for the keys.

Across the street, the brake lights of a car glared red. The car stopped.

'Oh boy,' Dani muttered.

'Hope it's not stopping for us,' Jack said.

The car was a black hearse. It didn't move.

'Maybe he needs directions to Forest Lawn.'

'Funny,' Dani said.

The hearse began to creep along, keeping pace with them as they hurried to the Rabbit.

'Want me to check?' Jack asked.

'No!'

Dani rushed into the street and unlocked her door. She climbed in, jerked it shut, and locked it. Then she leaned across the passenger seat to unlock Jack's side. As he lowered himself into the car, the hearse sped away.

Dani twisted around to watch it. At the end of the block, it turned onto a sidestreet. 'Well, it's gone.'

'For now,' Jack said.

'Bite your tongue.' She started her car and pulled away from the curb, keeping her eyes on the rearview mirror. The road behind her was clear for a moment. Then headlights pushed into the intersection. The long, dark body of a car swung onto the road. 'Oh shit,' Dani muttered.

Jack looked around. 'Is it the hearse?'

'I couldn't tell for sure. I think so.'

'Well, don't worry.'

'Tell that to my stomach.'

'Don't worry, stomach.'

With a nervous laugh, she flicked her turn signal on. At least the traffic light was green; she wouldn't have to stop and let the car catch up and find out, for sure, that it was the hearse.

She made her turn, and the car vanished from her mirror. Speeding up Third Street, she continued to watch. The traffic light changed, and a line of waiting cars started through the intersection. Dani sighed as if given a reprieve. 'That should hold him,' she said.

'It probably wasn't the hearse, anyway. And if it was, there's still no reason to think it's following us.'

As they passed Joe Allen, Dani's eyes moved from the lighted, bustling patio to the deserted sidewalk where the stranger had called to her.

Her scalp suddenly prickled. 'It's him,' she whispered.

'What?'

'It's him! I know it. The guy in the hearse, it's the one who ran at me. He hung around, followed us to the car.'

'No. Come on.'

'Yes!'

'Come on, this isn't one of Roger's splatter movies, it's real life.'

'I don't care.'

'It does make a difference, Dani. If we were characters in some damn thriller, I'd say sure, the nut hopped into his hearse, he's gonna follow us and treat us to a nasty death – special make-up effects by Danielle Larson.'

In the rearview mirror, the stream of cars was drawing closer.

'But this is real life. The nut was probably just a harmless space case. The guy in the hearse probably just stopped on the road to get his bearings, figured out his mistake, and turned around to get on the right track. Two unrelated incidents.'

'I hope you're right,' Dani said.

'So do I.' Jack looked over his shoulder. 'There it is,' he said without excitement.

'Where?'

'Second car back, in the other lane.'

'What should I do?'

'Just keep going,' Jack said, and faced the front.

'Toward home?'

'He'll probably turn off. Chances are that he's *not* following us. Really. I can think of several times I was absolutely convinced cars were tailing me. They stayed back there, turn after turn. But nothing ever came of it. They just happened to be heading the same way.'

'Yeah, I've gone through that, too.' She eased into the left-hand turn lane.

Jack looked around.

'Is it there?'

'Afraid so. Just behind this Mercedes.'

'Oh, Jack.'

'Everybody takes Crescent Heights from here.'

Dani knew he was right. The road led directly into Laurel Canyon Boulevard, one of the few routes over the hills to the western side of the valley. The knowledge, however, didn't ease her mind.

'When do we decide he *is* following us?' she asked. 'Our next turn-off's Asher. By then, it'll be too late.'

The signal changed, and she made her left turn.

Jack was silent for a few moments. Then he said, 'I think we'd better play it safe. We certainly don't want to lead him to your door.'

'That's for sure.'

'What's the road before Asher?'

'Dona Lola.'

'Okay, take that instead. If he turns there, we'll know.'

'Then what?'

'We'll worry about that when it happens.'

'Don't you mean *if* it happens?'

'Right, if.'

They continued up Crescent Heights. Though Dani kept checking the rearview, there was always at least one car between them and the hearse. Jack, sitting sideways, had a better view and sometimes spotted it.

'We're coming up on Sunset,' Dani finally said. She drove this route almost every day. Half the cars, she knew, would turn off at Sunset – a major boulevard and the last opportunity to leave Crescent Heights before it became Laurel Canyon and climbed into the hills.

She drove through the intersection. 'Is it . . .?'

'Still with us.'

'Oh shit.' She wiped her sweaty hands on her skirts.

'Just means he's heading toward the valley like the rest of us.'

'Yeah.'

The narrow road led upward, twisting and banking, the darkness of the wooded hillsides unbroken except for an occasional window light.

'Isn't that store up ahead?' Jack asked. 'That old-fashioned country store?'

Dani nodded.

'Pull into its parking lot. But do it suddenly, if you can, and don't signal.'

'What if *he* pulls in?'

'At least there should be some people around.'

'Okay,' Dani said. She didn't want to do it, wished she had more time to prepare herself. Dona Lola was five minutes away, but seemed like the distant future compared to this.

The road curved and she saw the well-lighted store standing among the trees. A man with a grocery bag was climbing down its wooden stairs. Half a dozen cars were parked in its lot.

Jack was right. A good place to confront the hearse. Certainly better than the lonely darkness of Dona Lola Drive.

She checked the mirror. The car behind her was a safe distance back. Suddenly, she jerked the steering wheel to the right. They hurtled into the parking lot and she hit the brakes.

Twisting around, she gazed back at the cars on Laurel Canyon.

The hearse sped by, along with the others.

Dani slumped back in her seat and sighed. She felt exhausted.

For a few moments, they sat in silence. Then Jack said, 'Would you like me to drive the rest of the way?'

'No, it's all right. We're almost there.' She turned the car around, waited for a break in the traffic, then accelerated onto the road. 'Anybody ever tell you you're brilliant?'

'Only my mother.'

'Well, you are.'

Jack smiled. 'The guy probably wasn't following us, anyway.'

'Probably not,' Dani said. 'After all, this isn't one of Roger's splatter movies. This is real life. Hearses don't tail you in real life.'

'Right.'

'Right.'

She wanted to believe it, but couldn't. She doubted if Jack really believed it, either. She wasn't terribly surprised when, at the crest of the hill where Mulholland intersected Laurel Canyon, they came upon a black motionless shape on the road's shoulder.

The hearse.

It had waited for them.

It swung onto the road behind them.

Dani wasn't terribly surprised, but she wanted badly to scream.

# Chapter Four

She swung onto Dona Lola. The hearse followed. 'Now what?'

'Stop the car,' Jack said.

'Here?' The street was dark and deserted. A few cars were parked along the curbs, and light shone in the windows of nearby houses, but nobody moved about.

'Let's see what he does.'

With a nod, Dani slowed the car, stopped it. She shifted to neutral and set the emergency brake.

In the rearview mirror, she watched the hearse creep closer. A few yards behind them, it stopped. The driver was alone. His face was a dim blur, craters of darkness where his eyes should be. His head was hairless.

'It's him,' Dani whispered. 'The guy from the restaurant.'

Jack looked through the back window. 'Are you sure?'

'I think so.'

The high beams of the hearse went on, shooting light into the car. It glared off the mirror. Squinting against the painful brightness, Dani shoved the mirror. It tipped upward, shining at the ceiling.

Jack faced the front. 'Obnoxious s.o.b.'

'What does he want?'

'Obviously, he wants to scare you.'

'At least,' Dani muttered.

'You know, it might be a practical joke. Maybe someone hired this guy to throw a little fun into your life.'

'It's a *prank*?'

'I wouldn't rule it out. After all, look at the irony of it: the queen of horror effects pursued through the night by a creep in a hearse.'

Dani nodded. 'It *could* be someone's idea of a joke.'

'Someone with a rather cruel and tasteless sense of humor.'

'Michael?'

'What about your old friend, Al?'

'My God, do you know what film he's on now? *The Undertaker*.'

Jack whistled. 'I believe the mystery is solved.'

'Not quite. How did he know we'd be at Joe Allen tonight?'

'Could've followed us from the studio. He'd recognise your car, wouldn't he?'

'Sure.'

'The weirdo didn't show up till we were done eating. Al probably phoned, let him know where to find us, and the guy hustled on over.'

'Al's certainly capable of it,' Dani said. 'I wouldn't put it past him, but . . . I don't know.'

'It's the only solution that makes sense.'

'Don't!' she cried as Jack pushed open the door.

'I'll be right back.'

'Jack, for Godsake!'

He flung the door shut and marched toward the hearse. Dani sprang from the car. She took a step toward the hearse, but fear hit her like an icy gale, forcing her backwards against the open door.

'Jack, come on!'

He tugged at the handle of the passenger door. The hearse rocked slightly.

Then the driver's door flew open. The man leaped out and ran at Dani, arms out, mouth agape.

His pointed teeth, she knew at once, were plastic vampire fangs.

A gag. It's all a sick gag.

Jack was charging past the front of the hearse, trying to head him off. But Dani saw that he wouldn't make it.

The lunging, cadaverous man was already too close, his demented murmur loud in Dani's ears.

She jumped into the car and slammed the door. As she pounded the lock button down, he grabbed the outside handle. He jerked it, shaking the car.

Then he pressed his young face to the window. He grinned like a madman, his nose and chin mashed against the pane, his eyes rolling. His tongue darted out between his plastic fangs and licked the glass.

Jack reached for him, but he jumped back, whirled around and ran.

Jack dashed after him. They sprinted up the street. The boy had given up his weird, hunched gait. He ran, now, with amazing speed, his head tucked down, his arms pumping, his legs whipping out in long, quick strides. The gap between him and Jack slowly widened. He cut to the right and raced up a lawn. As he vanished behind the corner of a dark house, Jack wheeled around and ran back.

Leaning across the seat, Dani opened the door for him.

But he didn't get in. He rushed by. Twisting around, Dani saw him crouch beside a front tire of the hearse. He removed something, flicked it away. The air cap? His hand shoved into a pocket and came out with a small object Dani couldn't see. He pressed it to the tire.

She looked toward the house, studied the darkness at both sides. The boy was nowhere to be seen.

She turned around. Jack still crouched by the tire.

'Hurry,' she whispered.

Then she realised that she could help. She shoved the shift into first, swung the car into a driveway on the left, and backed out.

She stopped beside the hearse.

Jack stood up. He stepped away from the flat tire and slipped his key case into his pocket. Then he climbed in beside Dani.

In the dome light, she saw speckles of sweat on his forehead. He grinned at her, looking both angry and gleeful. 'That'll fix the little asshole,' he said, and swung the door shut.

Dani sped toward the rushing headlights of traffic on Laurel Canyon.

# Chapter Five

Driving up Asher Lane, Dani kept her eyes on the rearview mirror. Headlights pushed through the darkness on Laurel Canyon, but none swept onto the narrow road.

As a precaution, she killed her own headlights. The arc lamps along the lane were spaced far apart with dark gaps separating their pools of light, but they gave enough brightness to steer by.

'I think we're okay,' Jack said. 'Even if he had an air can, we got a big enough jump on him.'

'Hope so,' Dani muttered.

She pulled into her driveway and stopped beside Jack's Mustang. She turned off the engine. Leaning against the steering wheel, she let out a shaky sigh. Jack's hand stroked her back.

'It's all right now,' he said.

'Will you come in with me?'

'Sure.'

'I'm just . . . it really shook me up a bit.'

'I know. Me, too. But I'm sure . . . the guy was probably harmless, just doing what he was paid for. Al or Michael – whoever's behind this – probably dug him up at central casting.'

'Or Forest Lawn.'

Jack laughed softly. His big, warm hand continued to rub her back. 'I . . .'

Dani waited. 'What?'

'Well,' he sighed. 'I do think we've lost the guy, but we ought to play it safe.'

Dani raised her head off the backs of her hands and looked at him. His face was a pale smudge, his familiar features masked by darkness. Only the feel of his hand assured Dani that this was Jack and not a stranger.

'What do you mean?' she asked.

'He might . . . I don't think we should leave your car here.'

'Oh, Jack,' she said.

'Maybe I'm over-reacting, but we don't want this guy to find out where you live. If we leave it here, it's like a name tag.'

Her mind fought against the suggestion. Couldn't she even park in front of her own house? What about tomorrow and the next day? 'You could've gone all night without saying that.'

'I'm sorry.'

'He doesn't know which street we're on.'

'He's only one away.'

'Al knows my address. If he hired the guy . . .'

'What if he didn't?'

'Oh shit. Then who *is* he?'

Jack shook his head. 'Maybe we can get it into the garage.'

The garage was her workshop, crowded with shelves, a workbench and tables, lamps and stools, all the tools of her craft and the make-up appliances she'd created for a dozen different films. She considered trying to clear a space. 'That'd take . . . no, forget it.'

'Let's park it up the street, then.'

'In front of somebody *else's* house?'

'Got any obnoxious neighbors?'

She surprised herself by laughing. 'That's wicked.' The laughter seemed to nudge her fear aside. When she finished, she found herself almost calm. 'Look, let's go inside. We'll leave the car here. If this kid's so goddamn determined to find my house, he'll manage it one way or another, anyhow. Sooner or later.

I'm not, for Godsake, going to spend the rest of my life hiding from him.'

Jack squeezed her shoulder. 'Let's go in, then.'

They climbed from the car. As they walked over the cobble-stones toward the front door, Dani heard a car engine. Her knees went weak. Looking around, she saw a car gliding slowly up the street. It passed.

A pale Mercedes.

With a sigh, she hurried into the dark recess of the front stoop. Jack stood beside her as she unlocked the door. They stepped into the lighted foyer. She shut the door and secured its guard chain.

Jack's hands curled over her shoulders. He turned her around, pulled her gently against him. She held him tightly. The strength of his body felt safe and comfortable.

'Thank God you were with me tonight,' she said. She tilted her head back, and they kissed. The pressure of his mouth soothed her. The tension eased out. She felt peaceful enough to fall asleep in his arms.

Then his mouth went away. 'I think it's time to call the police.'

'Oh no.'

'If the guy's still in the neighborhood, they might pick him up.'

'Yeah. All right.' Reluctantly, she let go of Jack. He kept hold of her hand, and they walked away from the door. The living room was lighted by a single lamp. The black expanse of its picture windows, at the rear, made her nervous. Leaving Jack, she hurried across the carpet to the draw cords. She kept her eyes down, unwilling to look at the window, afraid of what she might see in the darkness beyond. As she closed the curtains, she heard Jack dialing.

'Yes,' he said. 'We have a prowler . . . 822 Asher Lane . . . Laurel Canyon Boulevard . . . Okay, thanks.' He hung up.

'A prowler?' Dani asked.

'Close enough.'

'How about a drink?' she asked, and turned on a lamp by the couch.

'Sounds good.'

She turned on another lamp while Jack walked down the long side of the L-shaped bar. He entered the kitchen and turned on a light. 'Ten twenty-five,' he said.

The doorbell rang at five to eleven, making Dani's hand jump. She set down her vodka and tonic.

'That was quick,' Jack said. 'Thirty minutes. Good thing we didn't *need* them.'

She followed Jack to the foyer. He slipped off the guard chain and opened the door. Two uniformed patrolmen were waiting on the front stoop. 'You reported a prowler?' asked the taller man. The other, an oriental, tapped his night-stick against the side of his leg and seemed to be staring at Dani's chin.

'That's right,' Jack said. 'He just took off, though. Two or three minutes ago. In a black hearse.'

'Did you get the license number?'

'Afraid not.'

'Can you describe the man?' he asked, raising a clipboard.

'A Caucasian, maybe eighteen or twenty, very thin, bald. He wore a black turtleneck and jeans.'

Without a word, the other patrolman strode away.

'Did he attempt an entry of the premises?'

Jack shook his head. 'He was around back, looking at the windows. Scared the hell out of us. I yelled at him, but he wouldn't leave. He stayed back there, walking around the pool and watching us. I wasn't about to go out. You know? I figured he might be dangerous. So I phoned you people. He finally ran off, and we saw him get into the hearse.'

The patrolman nodded and glanced up from his clipboard. 'May I have your names?'

'I'm Jack Somers. This is Danielle Larson.'

'Whose residence is this?'

'Mine,' Dani said.

'All right.' He jabbed the pen into his shirt pocket. 'We'll see what we can do.'

'We appreciate it,' Jack said.

'Yes. Thank you.'

He aimed a forefinger at them, making a snicking sound against the side of his cheek, and winked. Then he turned away.

Jack shut the door.

'Good grief,' Dani said. 'What'd you do?'

'What, the fabrication?'

'You lied through your teeth. To the *police*!'

'I know. Naughty, huh?'

'Jack!'

'They'll never be the wiser unless they catch the guy.'

'Why not just tell the truth?'

'The truth was too complicated. A prowler's nice and simple – and ominous. I figured it'd be more likely to catch the interest of the officers . . . *involve* them.'

'It'll certainly involve *us*, if they nab the guy.'

'They'll understand.'

'You're crazy.'

'Does that mean you don't like me any more?' His eyes widened slightly.

Dani gazed at him, suddenly feeling weak and shaky. 'Doesn't mean that,' she finally whispered. She stepped out of her shoes, moved forward and began to open the buttons of his plaid shirt.

'Guess not,' he said.

Her fingers trembled. Her mouth was dry. She was surprised to be taking the lead this way. She didn't understand it, but she couldn't stop herself. She spread open Jack's shirt, pulling sharply to untuck its front, then let her hands glide over the smooth warm skin of his belly, the soft mat of chest hair. She lingered over the firm mounds of his pectorals. Leaning forward, she found a nipple with her tongue.

Jack moaned. He pulled her blouse from her skirt, and she felt his touch on the bare skin of her back, bunching up the blouse as they moved higher. Its silken front crept up her belly, taut and rubbing. Its folds seemed to trap her breasts for a moment. Then it flipped over them, releasing them.

She eased her face away from Jack's chest, and raised her arms. For a moment, their eyes met. Jack looked like a boy, full of hope and excitement but worried that he might somehow lose out. Then his face vanished behind a translucent curtain of green. The curtain lifted, tickling Dani's back and breasts, sliding up her arms. She saw Jack's belly, his bushy chest, his beard and gleaming eyes.

He flung her blouse aside and gazed at her. 'You're beautiful,' he whispered. He touched her shoulders. His fingers trembled over her collar bones, down her chest. They traced the outlines of her breasts.

She sucked a deep, shaky breath, arching her back as his thumbs grazed her nipples.

She opened her skirt. It dropped to her feet and she stood before Jack naked except for her panties. Crouching, he kissed a nipple. He licked it, took it between his lips. Dani clenched his long hair, gasping as he sucked her nipple, as he slipped her panties down, as a hand eased upward between her thighs. It pushed against her. Every muscle flinched rigid. A ragged groan escaped her throat.

She forced Jack's head away, bent over and kissed him. She thrust her tongue into his mouth, shuddering as his fingers slipped into her.

Her legs trembled. She fell to her knees, Jack staying with her. In a frenzy, she tugged open his belt, unbuttoned the waist of his trousers, jerked his zipper down. His trim belly sucked in as she clawed at the band of his shorts. She pulled the band toward her. The shiny head of his erection sprang out. In a fever, she tugged his pants to his knees! Her fingers encircled him, slid down, feeling the heat and thickness of his shaft.

Jack's hand went away. It was slick on her back as he lowered her to the soft nap of the carpet. He braced himself above her, his open shirt hanging down, caressing her sides. She stroked his back. Her fingers dug in as she felt the touch of his penis. Then he was lower, pushing gently, easing into her, sliding in deeper and deeper.

Her fingers relaxed and she sighed, savoring the fullness. She felt possessed, as if the penis had penetrated her hidden center and made her somehow a part of Jack. Raising her knees high, she felt it move farther into her. She worked muscles, tightening herself around the shaft, wanting it to stay forever.

It withdrew, but only to push in again. And then it was thrusting, sliding almost out, plunging as if in need of a deeper connection, jolting her body as it rammed.

Jack lowered himself. His chest mashed her breasts. His mouth covered hers. His tongue shoved it. Dani felt it thick and wet in her mouth, probing while his erection filled her below.

It was suddenly too much. She jerked taut, gasping, and as her body quaked with release she felt Jack throb inside her, felt his spurting rush of semen.

He lay heavily on her as they both tried to catch their breath. When he tried to raise himself, Dani hugged him tightly and wrapped her legs around him. 'Stay,' she whispered.

'Don't want to crush you.'

'It s fine.' She lay motionless, comfortable beneath his weight, feeling him still inside her where he belonged like a part of her own body.

She felt incomplete when he finally withdrew, but his presence remained like a warm imprint and she still held his fluid like a gift left behind.

She sat up carefully. It rolled inside her. It trickled down her thighs as she hurried to the bathroom.

The rest of the house was dark when she stepped out. She stood near the door, staring down the corridor. Fear crawled up her back.

'Jack?'

A pale figure appeared near the foyer.

'Is that you?'

'I hope so.'

'Did you turn the lights out?'

'Do you want them back on?'

'No. It just . . . gave me a little scare.'

He came up the dark corridor, and Dani was pleased to find him still naked. She raised her arms. He stepped into them and pulled her gently against her body. His hands glided down her back, held her buttocks.

'Will you stay the night?'

'If you want.'

'I want.'

'Good.'

She turned off the bathroom light. Taking Jack's hand, she led him to her bedroom. Its curtains were open, letting moonlight in through the sliding glass door.

'I'll close that,' she said.

They crossed the room. She started to pull her hand away, but Jack kept his grip. 'Let me look at you in the moonlight,' he whispered.

Dani nodded. They stepped close to the glass and faced one another. Though all she could see of Jack's eyes were glinting specks, she felt his gaze like a soft caress. Her skin tingled. Her nipples rose erect. A warm rush surged through her.

She studied Jack. Naked in the moonlight, he looked like a bearded giant. His shoulders were broad, his arms and chest bulging with muscle, his belly lean. He stood with his sturdy legs slightly spread. His dark sac hung between them. His penis was pale and rising.

'You're quite a hunk,' she said.

His laughter burst out. He lunged at Dani, grabbed her arms and swung her toward the bed. The mattress caught her behind the knees, and she sprawled backwards, laughing. She yelped as he nibbled her thigh. Then they both were rolling on the bed. Straddling him, she pinned his arms down. He raised his head, licked her breast. No longer laughing, she relinquished her hold on his wrists and scooted down, rubbing his chest. She flinched with the shock of desire as her anus rammed the blunt stake of his erection. She raised herself, felt it slide along her other opening, and drove backwards, gasping as she impaled herself.

She pressed her face against Jack's chest. She nuzzled the matted hair with her cheek, listening to the thunder of his heart and suddenly she felt her insides shrivel.

A dark figure was pressed against the glass door, staring in. *Him!*

His fingers clawed the glass.

'Jack,' she whispered.

She scurried free, rolled aside, and Jack sprang for the door. Sitting up, she saw that the intruder had already vanished. Jack tugged the door. With a low curse, he clacked open its latch. Then he jerked it again. This time, it rumbled open. He stepped outside and looked both ways.

Dani raced forward. She stopped at the open door.

'Gone,' Jack said.

'Come back in. There's no point chasing him.'

'Fuckin' maniac.'

She stepped out, shivering as the cool night air wrapped her body, and placed a hand on Jack's shoulder. 'Come on.'

He suddenly flinched.

'What?'

Raising an arm, he pointed toward the swimming pool. The black rippling water was dappled with bright specks of moonlight. 'I don't . . .' Her guts knotted. 'What *is* it?'

'I don't know. Maybe you'd better go inside.'

She shook her head and crossed her arms over the gooseflesh of her breasts.

Together, they walked alongside the pool toward the deep end and the *thing* on the diving board.

They reached the corner.

'A paper bag?' Jack whispered.

'But what's in it?'

'Wait here,' Jack said.

Dani waited, shivering. She pressed her palms to her rigid nipples and closed her legs tightly against a need to urinate.

Jack hesitated at the foot of the diving board. He turned around, scanning the darkness. Then he climbed up. He walked out over the water, the board vibrating slightly. Then he crouched down. He picked up the bag. The weight inside made its paper pull and crackle.

Holding it away from his body, Jack unfolded the top. He peered in.

'What is it?' Dani whispered.

'Can't see.'

He reached inside.

'Don't!'

He gasped and his hand darted out. For a moment, he seemed to lose his balance. He waved an arm through the air, steadied himself, then reached again into the bag.

This time, he brought it out clenching a fistful of hair. At the end of the hair dangled a human head. Its face turned, as if by intention, toward Dani. She stared at its bulging eyes, its gaping mouth and lolling tongue.

Dani realised she'd been holding her breath. She let it out quickly and sucked in the fresh, night air. 'If you tell me it's real, I'll scream.'

# Chapter Six

Linda rolled on her bed and gazed at the luminous face of her alarm clock. One thirty-six. The minute hand crept toward the next dot. She planned to wait until two, but time seemed to pass so terribly slowly.

She turned onto her back and stared at the ceiling. Her heart pounded fast. She rubbed her sweaty hands on her nightgown. Beneath them, her belly throbbed as if her entire body was pulsing with the frenzied heartbeat.

The surging blood made her left leg ache, and once again she saw herself lunging into the street, sobbing, blind with tears but almost home, and suddenly caught in a glare of headlights. Brakes screamed. She felt the impact, the blasting pain, saw herself tumble over the hood as if in slow motion, and remembered wondering in the eternal instant before she hit the windshield if this was bad enough to kill her and would it qualify as murder?

In her mind, it qualified. She'd been murdered by Tony and Arnold and Joel and the horrible maniac in the Freeman house, and nobody would ever know.

Let me be a ghost, she thought, so I can get them.

And then she had smacked through the windshield.

She awoke from her coma thin and weak, with a throbbing head and a leg in traction. Her parents acted as if she had, indeed, returned from the dead. While they wept, the doctor questioned her. Did she remember her name, her address, her birthday? Her parents looked tense until she gave the answers.

Did she remember the night of the accident? Oh yes, she remembered it all. But a new, sly corner of her mind whispered not to tell.

I was walking home from the library, and then . . . and then . . . I don't know.

Perfectly normal with a trauma of this nature, the doctor assured everyone. Nothing to be concerned about. The mind's way of protecting itself.

The memory of her deceit thrilled her, pushed aside her fear, and she grinned at the ceiling.

She'd known, even then, what her mission would be. Her secret mission.

She glanced at the clock. Only three minutes had passed.

Folding her hands behind her head, she felt the soft brush of her hair. Her stomach knotted.

Don't you think about that.

She sat up quickly. No more thinking, no more waiting.

She swung her legs off the bed and carefully stood up. Though her left leg felt weak and achy, she knew it was strong enough. The cast had been off for two weeks. She'd exercised constantly to strengthen the slack muscles, and finally, today, decided she was ready.

She stepped to the open window and slipped her nightgown off. The warm night breathed against her, fragrant with summer, making her shiver with fearful delight. Her own breath trembled as she gazed from her high window. All the houses but one were dark. Nothing moved on the lawns, the sidewalks, the street. The neighborhood looked deserted, as if everyone had fled a terrible menace.

Linda turned away from the window. Easing open a dresser drawer, she took out her Yankee ballcap and put it on. Only then did she allow herself to look in the mirror. She grinned, her teeth pale in the dim reflections. Taking out an Ace bandage, she wrapped her chest. The elastic band was only long enough to circle her body once, but she pulled it tight, squeezing her breasts until they hurt. She fastened the bandage in place with its tiny clips, then took a dark, plaid shirt from the drawer. Her brother's shirt, filched that day from the back of his closet. She put it on and closed the buttons. Rolling the sleeves, up her forearms, she studied her image. In the large, loose shirt, her flattened breasts made only the slightest bulges. At a distance, anyone would think she was a boy.

From her closet, she took blue jeans and her Adidas running shoes. She slipped into them, and returned to the dresser.

She reached into the open drawer, pushed aside a neat stack of panties, and pulled out her father's .38 caliber Smith and Wesson revolver. Sucking in her belly, she pushed its barrel under the waistband of her jeans. The weapon felt big and cool. Its muzzle, tight against her groin, rubbed her as she stepped toward the door. She thought of moving it, but the sensation was hot and exciting.

She inched the door open. Leaning out, she glanced both ways. The hallway was empty and dark, no stripes of light showing beneath any of the doors.

She took long strides down the carpeted hall, silently rolling her feet from heel to toe just as she'd done that other night when three boys took her . . .

No, she couldn't let herself think about that.

In front of her brother's door, a floorboard groaned. She winced but kept walking, reminding herself that Bob slept like the dead.

She reached the head of the stairway and started down, one

hand on the banister, shifting her weight to it whenever a step threatened to squeak. When she reached the bottom, she breathed more easily. Down here, small noises would mean nothing.

She hurried into the kitchen. From a large brandy snifter on top of the refrigerator she took two books of matches. She slipped them into her shirt pocket and headed for the connecting door to the garage.

The garage, with its single small window on the far side, was much darker than she'd expected. She bumped against her father's Imperial. Feeling along its side, she found the door handle. She pulled. The door opened, triggering the car's interior light.

Enough to see by. She found the empty milk carton on the cluttered shelf where she'd left it.

In front of the car, she stopped at the power mower. Crouching, she reached over it and picked up the tin of gasoline. Its weight overbalanced her. She stumbled, the gun barrel digging in painfully, her knee ramming the top of the mower. But she caught herself without dropping either the can or the milk carton. She straightened up. There was a warm pain, and she wondered if the gunsight had cut her. She nudged the pistol butt with her wrist, felt the barrel move away from the tender place. Then she stepped to the clear area beside the car.

She filled the milk carton, the gas fumes scorching her nostrils, bringing tears to her eyes. She returned the can, wondering if Bob would notice the missing fuel when he mowed the lawn next Saturday. Probably not. The two-gallon tin hadn't been completely full, and plenty of gas remained for filling the mower's small tank.

She picked up the milk carton. She pushed the car door

shut, killing the light. Then she made her way through the darkness, one hand trailing along the car as a guide. She passed its rear, stepped across a gap to the trunk of her mother's Omni, felt her way up its far side, past the window, and found the garage's back door.

The night outside seemed almost bright, and cooler than the stuffy garage. Staying close to the shrubbery, she rushed across the yard to the gate. Its hinges squeaked, but in moments she was beyond it and striding down the alley.

Loose gravel crunched and scratched along the asphalt under her feet. A few nightbirds twittered, crickets sawed. Electricity hummed from the lines overhead. Linda listened for voices, for cars, for shutting doors or footsteps, ready to duck out of sight at the first hint of approach. But she heard none.

She began to wish for a human sound – even the far-off tinny voice from a television – or anything to assure her that someone, at least, remained awake, alive.

Nothing.

She walked alone in the night, vulnerable from every side, peering at the dark recesses behind garbage cans and telephone poles, between garages, often casting a glance over her shoulder.

At the end of the block, she looked up and down the street. Deserted. This is how I want it, she told herself, and hurried across. No people around, no witnesses. But her feeling of isolation grew like a hollowness inside as she entered the alley.

She thought about turning back.

No. She'd wanted this night since she first came out of the coma. Even before that, even while her broken body hurtled toward the windshield of the shrieking car. Wanted it, waited for it, prepared for it. Tonight was just the beginning. She couldn't quit now. Couldn't quit until she'd finished it all.

A rattling, metal noise startled Linda from her thoughts. She froze, gazing into the darkness ahead. Far down the alley, a dark shape broke away from the shadows and moved towards her. Linda's heart thundered like a fist trying to smash out of her chest. Gasping for breath, she squinted at the approaching shape.

What *is* it?

The clinking, rumbling sound grew louder as it moved. Then it entered a spill of moonlight and Linda saw a hunched figure shambling along behind a shopping cart.

She jerked the pistol free so it wouldn't hurt her, then whirled around and raced from the alley. She sprinted up the sidewalk At a lighted street corner, she stopped to catch her breath, and looked back.

No sign of the weirdo with the shopping cart.

She pushed the pistol into her jeans and started walking. Though the street was deserted, it seemed less forbidding than the alleys. She felt as if she'd stumbled onto humanity after a detour into a strange, desolate land. The parked cars, the streetlamps, the rare lighted porches and house windows gave her comfort.

Once, a car turned onto the road. She pressed herself tightly to the trunk of an oak until it passed.

Though she walked for blocks, no other cars appeared. She saw a three-legged dog hobble along, glance at her without much interest, and urinate on a tree with a twist of its rump as if lifting the lost leg.

She saw a few fireflies glowing and vanishing. She saw a cat dash across the street and vanish beneath a parked station wagon. And then she was in front of the Benson house.

FOR SALE BY OWNER.

After tonight, Linda thought, maybe someone will dare to buy the place.

*We heard strange sounds at night*, Sheila had once told her.

Like women crying.

In the Freeman house?

And laughter. Real creepy laughter. The police came out, but they never found anyone.

Ghosts?

Don't laugh.

I don't believe in ghosts.

I do. Now I do.

Linda stepped past the hedge and saw the Freeman house. Fear crept up her spine, prickled the back of her neck. For a moment, she was in darkness, roped to the banister, the bony, naked man staring down at her. She clutched the milk carton to her chest, the gasoline sloshing inside.

Don't wait. Don't think about it.

She hurried up the sidewalk to the gate of the low picket fence. Turning around for a final check, she saw nobody. She opened the gate and rushed toward the house. The wooden stairs moaned under her weight. The blackness of the porch engulfed her.

Her hand found the door handle – cold as if the house's inner chill had passed through it. She pressed the upper plate. It sank. The tongue snapped back. With a slight push, the door started to open. It stopped abruptly with a shake of metal, and Linda saw the dim outline of a padlock just above her head.

Someone, probably the realtor, had come by since the night she was here, secured the front door.

She yanked the lock, twisted it, determined that it was securely latched. Her fingertips explored the mounting. Six screws held it in place, three in the doorframe and three in the door itself.

She pulled the pistol from her jeans. She slipped its barrel through the hoop of the lock hasp, and was about to tug when she realised that using it like a crowbar would mar the finish. Her father would know someone had used it. So she freed the barrel. She pushed it into her jeans again, glad to feel the return of its hard warm pressure.

Leaving the porch, she hoped for a moment that she wouldn't find a way into the house.

No, she *had* to get inside.

Burn the heart of it.

Burn the stairway.

She ran alongside the house, keeping close to the wall.

Burn the stairway. Let the flames trap *him* upstairs, if he's still lurking there. Let them wrap his hideous flesh, make it blister and snap, boil his eyes.

She raced up three stairs to the back door. There was no padlock. Its four windows shone in the moonlight. She rammed the gun muzzle through the pane on the lower right. As she reached through the hole, groping for the inside knob, her hip nudged the door open.

Not locked at all! Not even firmly shut.

She withdrew her arm, pushed the door wide, and stepped into the kitchen. Bits of glass crunched under her shoes. She halted, listening, then realised *he* might've heard the shattering panel, might even now be rising stiffly, reaching for his ax.

She hurried through the empty kitchen, down a passageway as chill and black as a cave, her ears keen for a sound from above. The stairway slanted down to her left. She sidestepped, peering up through the bars of its railing. Saw no one. Rounding the newel post, she stared into the darkness at the top of the stairs where she'd first seen his pale shape standing motionless.

Linda pried open the carton. Holding her breath against the fumes, she began to splash gasoline on the lower stairs.

Somewhere above her, a floorboard creaked.

The quiet sound knocked her breath out. Numb with fear, she raised her eyes.

A dim shape seemed to grow from the top of the upper newel post.

A face.

Linda clamped her jaw tight to hold her scream inside. She swung out the carton, gas splattering the stairs.

The word 'No' floated down to her like a moan. Then the pale figure was lunging around the post. She flung the empty carton down. Clawing into her shirt pocket, she found her matches. She tore one free. The man was halfway down the stairs when it burst to life. She held its flame to the dark rows of match-heads. They flared, and she tossed the blazing pack at the stairs.

The gasoline erupted with a *whup* like a flag hit by a sudden gust. The fire reached up the man's naked body. Screaming, he shielded his face and staggered back. He twisted away from the fire, fell, and scurried up the stairs shrieking, slapping his blazing hair. He vanished into the corridor, and another scream mingled with his own – the high, piercing screech of a woman.

Confusion rolled through Linda's mind. She knew only that she had to get out. Covering her ears against the cries from above, she raced up the passageway to the kitchen, and outside.

She was a block away when the alarm began wailing to wake the volunteer firemen. She ducked into an alley, no longer afraid of the shambling creature with the shopping cart, no longer afraid of whatever else might lurk in the shadows.

She had burnt the Freeman house, burnt the naked specter that had haunted her nightmares.

It had to be him. He'd looked different, but it had to be him.

The woman's scream?

One of Sheila's ghosts?

No such thing. Nothing to be afraid of.

Not even the empty darkness of the alley. Nothing could touch her.

# Chapter Seven

Dani rolled over and opened one eye. Jack was missing. She smelled coffee, and smiled. Turning onto her belly, she pushed her face into the pillow and snuggled against the sheet.

There was no hurry. She wasn't needed at the studio today.

She writhed, stretching her stiff muscles, remembering how they got that way. Last night had been wonderful in spite of the creep.

Maybe she should thank the guy. He'd provided a certain excitement . . .

Excitement, my ass.

He'd scared the hell out of her. He ought to be caged, the damned degenerate.

She thought of him at the window, watching her with Jack, and her skin turned hot. The bed was no longer comfortable. She tossed aside the single sheet and climbed off. Taking her satin robe from the closet, she headed for the open door.

She found Jack at the bar, a coffee mug at his elbow, his fingers probing the mouth of the artificial head. He grinned around at her. 'Amateur night,' he said. Swiveling his stool, he rested the head on his lap. He flicked its red hair. 'Cheap wig. The eyes were marbles.' He pulled the tongue from its gaping mouth. 'A slab of liver.'

'Yuck.'

Jack flung it onto the counter. 'The guy has, at least, got a certain macabre ingenuity.'

He tossed the head to Dani. She inspected its waxy flesh, its eye sockets and mouth.

'Mortician's wax,' Jack said, 'on one of those plastic skulls you can buy at a hobby shop.'

Dani inserted her forefinger in an eye hole. It pushed against a soft, rubbery substance. She pulled it out, glanced at the gray crescent under her nail, sniffed it. 'Modeling clay.'

'To give it some weight, I suppose.'

'Well, Al obviously wasn't involved. No one with any knowledge of the business would turn out this kind of work.'

Jack raised a forefinger. 'Unless, Sherlock, he did it that way to throw off suspicion.'

'Or as a joke,' Dani added. She set the head down on the counter, and kissed Jack. 'Good morning.'

'Good morning,' he whispered. 'Excuse me if I don't touch.'

'Me too,' Dani picked up the slab of liver and eyed it critically. 'Not enough for both of us. Would you rather have bacon?'

'I think so.'

She carried the liver into the kitchen, holding her breath against the stench, and put it down the disposal. Then she washed her hands.

Jack washed up while she took the foil-wrapped bacon from the freezer. She unwrapped the rigid strips, dropped them into a skillet, and turned on a burner.

Jack came up behind her. He stroked her hair away, and she squirmed as he kissed the side of her neck. He rubbed her belly. A hand slipped inside her robe. It glided up her ribs, closed over her breast. His other hand loosened the cloth belt. He spread the robe open. He held both breasts, squeezing gently. Then his big hands moved lower, touching her skin like a warm breeze as they drifted down her ribs and belly, caressed her hips, brushed over her thighs. She quivered as the hands curved upward between her legs. They stirred her tuft of hair. She waited, but they didn't seek deeper.

Turning around, she embraced Jack and kissed his open mouth. He held her tightly. Then his arms loosened and Dani stepped back. She stood motionless while he closed her robe and adjusted the belt.

'You have a nice way of saying good morning,' she whispered.

'When my hands are clean.'

'Two eggs?'

He nodded.

'Will you stay?'

'Let's see how well you cook.'

'No, really. I . . . I mean, aside from just plain wanting you here, I . . . I guess I'm chicken. That guy worries me.'

'I'll stay. At least for a while. We'll see how it goes.'

\* \* \*

Jack swabbed up the last of his egg yellow with a chunk of toast. As he finished chewing, he rubbed his mouth and whiskers with a napkin. 'Well, that was real good. I'd better get going, now. Want to come along?'

'No, you go ahead. I'll try to finish the machete work, and then we can have the rest of the day free.'

She gave him a key to the front door, and kissed him goodbye. When he was gone, she cleaned up the kitchen. Then she returned to her bedroom. Her chest tightened as she reached for the curtain cord. She hesitated, then pulled. The curtains skidded open, letting sunlight fill the room, and she quickly looked out.

Nobody there.

Of course not.

The back yard was deserted, the pool's surface pale blue and motionless, nothing on the diving board. Breathing more easily, she made the bed. She hung her robe on the closet door, cleaned herself up in the master bathroom, then got dressed in cut-off jeans and a baggy, sleeveless sweatshirt. She slipped into thongs, and made her way through the silent house.

The aroma of bacon lingered in the kitchen. She glanced out the window. Her Rabbit stood alone on the driveway, as if abandoned. Other cars were parked on the street.

No hearse.

She stepped to the side door, entered her garage, and turned on the overhead light. Shutting the door, she wished for a way to lock it from this side.

If he broke into the house . . .

She realised that none of her doors locked from both sides. You could lock someone out of the house, but not inside. You might secure yourself within a bathroom or bedroom, but there was no way to seal the doors from the other side.

Dani saw the workings of a benevolent, misguided hand.

No, no, no, thou shalt not lock thy child in his bedroom.

And thou shalt not take refuge in thy garage.

Probably a goddamn law against it. Probably in the building code.

Screw it, she thought. I'm gonna put a bolt on that sucker.

She would have to buy one, first.

Today.

But not just now. The first priority was business. Dani stepped over to her workbench and picked up the foam latex face of Bill Washington. He was to be the second victim, nonchalantly drinking a beer when the maniac leaped from the porch roof and whacked him across the forehead with a machete.

Jack would be wielding the machete, swinging it with enough force to penetrate the forehead of the appliance. The catcher's mask beneath would cushion the blow for Bill.

Dani pulled up a stool. The glass eyes seemed to watch her, as if mildly curious, as she fitted the face over the metal cage of the catcher's mask. She determined where it needed more padding. With an Exacto knife, she cut pieces from a mat of foam rubber. She glued them inside the chin, the cheeks, behind the eyes. She pushed blood-bags behind the forehead, then glued a patch of rubber over them. When the face fit snug against the tubing of the mask, she glued it in place.

With calipers, she measured the width of the forehead at the angle they'd decided the machete would strike. She marked off the distance on a sheet of poster board, and snipped out a crescent. She tried the cut-away cardboard on the face. The cut was too shallow. She took off another quarter inch, and again pressed it to Bill's brow.

Fine.

Stretching over the workbench, she picked up the two machetes. They looked identical, vicious weapons with worn wooden handles. But one weighed only a few ounces while the other dragged her arm down. Except for the handle, taken from a real machete, the lighter of the pair was constructed of balsa wood. Jack had done a good job. The paint gleamed like steel, shiny in the same places as the other, mottled with rust near the hilt, a few nicks on the edge.

A work of art.

Dani hated to tamper with it.

But if she didn't, Jack would have to take time when he returned. He'd be glad to have it done.

So she pressed the cardboard cut-out against the blade, and traced its crescent with a pencil. Carefully, she whittled down to the line. The machete looked as if a large bite had been taken out of it.

She pressed it, at an angle, against the mask's forehead.

It fit well.

After the real blow, the mask would be removed, the balsa machete glued to Bill's own forehead, and makeup applied. Cameras rolling again, he'd quiver and shake and slump.

End of effect.

With the proper camera angles, lighting and editing, it should look like poor Bill actually caught a blade in the face.

Smiling, Dani brushed the balsa curls off her sweatshirt.

She was out by the pool, stretched on a chaise longue with the sun pressing warm on her back, when the sliding door from the bedroom rumbled open. Her stomach jumped. She raised her head and saw Jack come out.

'Sorry it took so long.'

'That's all right.'

He walked forward, his swimming trunks hanging low on his hips, a towel under one arm. 'Had a couple of errands to run.'

'I just got out here. Finished up with Bill and the machete.'

'How do they look?'

'Just great.'

'So we're all set for tomorrow?'

'All set. The rest of the day is for play.'

With a grin, he flopped his towel onto the patio chair beside Dani. 'How's the water?'

'Let's find out.'

# Chapter Eight

'Bless my soul! How are you, honey?'

'Just fine,' Linda said, nodding pleasantly to the buxom, grinning woman behind the counter.

'Mighty good to see you up and around.'

'Thank you, Elsie.' She turned to the paperback rack, scanning the covers.

'You look real good. How's the leg?'

'Good as new, almost.'

'We were all just worried to death about you. 'Specially when we heard you was in one of them comas. I read me a book about a fella in a coma. He was dead to the world, oh, 'bout ten years.' Elsie leaned over the counter, her eyes widening. 'When he come to, he could see in the future. Gave him no end of trouble.'

'I wouldn't mind that,' Linda said.

'More a curse than a gift, you ask me.'

'Well, it didn't happen to me, so I guess I'll never know.' She slipped a book from the rack and carried it to the counter.

Elsie picked it up. 'Oh dear, that's a scary one. Did you read the other?'

'I sure did.'

'Them Bradleys, they had no end of trouble.' Elsie rang it up. 'You hear the news about our own haunted house?'

'The Freeman place?'

'Got burnt to the ground last night. Elwood Jones was in for his *Post*, told me all 'bout it. He's on the volunteers, you know.'

Linda nodded. She put a hand on the counter to steady herself.

'Yessir, burnt to the ground. That's three seventy-eight, with tax.'

Linda opened her purse. Her hands trembled as she took out her billfold.

In a hushed voice, Elsie said, 'There was two bodies in it, burnt to a crisp.'

'My God,' Linda muttered.

'They figure one's Ben Leland's boy, Charles. Couldn't tell by looking, but he's turned up missing and they say he takes his girlfriends in there for some foolishness – though, Lord knows, you wouldn't catch *me* in there after dark. Nor in broad daylight, neither.' She took the bills from Linda and counted out the change. 'Elwood, he says they don't know who the gal is yet. Larson, down by the morgue, he's gonna have to go by her teeth.' Elsie slipped the book and receipt into a bag. 'Real bad business, but that's what comes of fooling where you don't belong. Least the Freeman place is gone, now. That's a blessing.'

'Yes it is,' Linda said.

'You have a good day, now, and don't make yourself a stranger.'

'Thanks, Elsie,' She took the bag. With a wave, she turned away and headed for the door.

Outside, the heat wrapped her like a blanket. She stayed close to the store fronts, welcoming the shade of their awnings as she walked up the block.

Charles Leland. He'd been two years ahead of her in school, and she knew him only slightly. He wasn't the one who'd come after her with the ax, though. Not unless he'd been wearing weird makeup or a mask. That was too bad. She would've liked to burn up that man along with the house.

She realised she ought to feel guilty. Maybe she would, if she'd known him. But Elsie was right: he had no business being there. It was his own damn fault. Nobody to blame but himself.

Must've used a key from his father. That's why the back door wasn't locked.

Linda hoped the girl wasn't anyone she knew.

At the corner, she slipped the paperback out of its bag. She crumpled the bag and receipt, and tossed them into a trash bin marked KEEP CLAYMORE BEAUTIFUL.

Walking along, she creased the book's cover. She opened it to the middle and flexed the halves backwards. Turning to other sections, she bent the book again and again. By the time she reached the corner, the spine was streaked with white veins as if the book had been read more than once.

For good measure, she turned down a point of the cover. Then she slipped the book into her purse.

She turned at Craven Street. Passing Hal's house, she kept her eyes on the sidewalk.

If he'd shown up at the library that night . . .

But she couldn't blame him. He had no way to know she was waiting for him, wanting him.

A door banged shut and she halted, her heart racing. He'd seen her pass by! *I've wanted you so long, Linda*. His embrace would wash her clean and take away all the pain and she would be as she was before the Freeman house.

'Hi, Linda.'

She whirled around. Hal's smile pierced her. He was tanned and handsome in his T-shirt and faded cut-offs, a lock of golden hair falling across his forehead. 'Hi, Hal,' she said.

'How's the leg?'

'Fine, thank you.'

With a wink, he turned away. He hurried around the front of his Z car, and climbed in.

Linda's smile fell off.

The car lunged away from the curb. At the end of the block, it turned left and vanished.

Linda took a deep, shaky breath. She gritted her teeth to stop the trembling of her chin. The sidewalk blurred. She wiped the tears out of her eyes, but new ones came.

'Who needs him,' she muttered. She'd hardly given him a thought since the accident. If she hadn't been stupid enough to walk by his house . . .

He could've stopped all this.

He doesn't know. He'll never know.

Linda wiped her eyes dry and put on her sunglasses.

Two blocks later, she reached Tony's house. She turned up its walkway. A cat hopped onto the porch glider, setting it into creaky motion. From the back yard came the chatter of a lawn mower.

She walked in the shade between the side of the house and its garage. The air smelled of cut grass. She plucked her clinging blouse away from her back, but it stuck again. She wiped a hand on her skirt, then took the paperback from her purse.

From the rear corner, she saw a young man striding behind a mower. He appeared to be about twenty. He was taller than Tony, lean but not emaciated. His bare torso was glossy with sweat. His jeans hung below the band of his white underwear, and looked as if they might drop off.

Turning the mower for another sweep, he briefly faced Linda. His frown changed to a look of vague curiosity. He finished the turn and started away, his head swiveling to keep an eye on her.

Linda waved the book. 'Hey!'

He shut off the lawn mower, but didn't let go of it. He squinted at Linda over his shoulder.

'I'm looking for Tony,' she called.

'He ain't here.' Turning away, he bent down and grabbed the starter cord.

'Wait,' Linda said.

With a shrug, he straightened up. He watched Linda approach as if she were an odd species he couldn't quite identify. Before she got too close, he sidestepped to put the lawn mower between them.

'You're Tony's brother, aren't you?'

He nodded. His gaze lowered to the front of her blouse.

'I'm Beth Emory.'

He continued to stare.

'Tony let me borrow this book of his,' she said. 'I'd like to see that he gets it back.'

'He ain't here.'

'I know. I heard he left town right after graduation.'

'Hasn't come back.'

'Do you know where he went?'

The man's tongue darted out, lapped speckles of sweat from over his lip. 'Huh-uh.'

'If I had his address, I'd mail it to him.'

'Don't know where he went to.'

'Does your mother know?'

'Huh-uh.'

'Is she home now?'

His head shook slowly from side to side, his gaze remaining on Linda's breasts. 'Mom, she's been dead ten years this August.'

'Oh. I'm sorry. I didn't know.'

'You wanta leave that book, it's all right. Maybe he'll come back. You don't never know, with Tony.'

'I have to know where he is,' Linda said. She felt a sickening tightness in her chest, but didn't let it stop her. With trembling fingers, she flicked open the top button of her blouse. 'You can tell me.'

His shallow chest rose and fell. A hand went up to wipe his mouth.

Linda opened the next button. 'You know where he is, don't you?'

'Go 'way,' he whispered.

'Tell me.'

'I don't . . .' He shook his head sharply.

Linda opened the button at her belly, and spread the blouse wide. She squeezed the stiff cups of her bra. 'Tell me. Tell me and you can see.'

'He . . . he's in California.'

'Where?'

'Hollywood.'

'What's his address?'

'Don't know.'

She unhooked the front of the bra and lifted it away. 'Tell me. Tell me, and you can feel.'

He stared. He licked his lips. 'I don't knooow.'

'Yes you do.' She caressed her breasts, squeezed them.

'I . . . oh, *oh*! Go away!' Doubling over, he turned away and fell to his knees. He grabbed his groin. His forehead pounded the grass.

Linda stared, astonished and disgusted.

Clutching her blouse shut, she ran.

# Chapter Nine

Dani added a splash of milk, and set the pot back onto the barbeque grill. She stirred the creamy potatoes with a wooden spoon. After a few strokes, the heat became too much. She backed away, rubbing the hot skin of her belly.

'That hungry?' Jack asked.

'That burnt.'

He swung himself off the lounger, stepped up beside her, and sipped his vodka and tonic as he peered into the pot. 'Looking good,' he said.

'They're a real calorie bomb, but what the hell? We deserve it, right?' A few bubbles plopped to the surface. Dani reached out and stirred, the heat curling against the underside of her arm. 'I think we're about ready for the steaks.'

'I'm more than ready.'

'You want to keep an eye on this? Just stir it a bit.'

With a nod, he took the spoon in his free hand.

'Refill while I'm in?'

'Sure, thanks.' He tilted his glass back. The cubes broke loose from the bottom and dropped against his face, splashing him. He gasped with surprise. 'It fights back,' he said. He backhanded a drip off the tip of his nose, rubbed his wet mustache and beard.

'What poise,' Dani said.

'My specialty.'

She took his glass, picked hers up from the tray, and slid open the screen door to the living room. The carpet felt good after the rough concrete. The house was cool, almost chilly against her sun-heated skin.

She slid the glasses to the other side of the bar counter and wiped her wet hands across her belly, leaving dark trails on her skin. Rarely had she felt so fine: light and compact, glowing with the sun and two vodkas and her new closeness with Jack.

She stretched, sighing at the luxury of her aching muscles. They were tight and vibrant from so much swimming and from the long love-making earlier in the afternoon. The feel of Jack was still inside her.

Makes a lasting impression, she thought, and smiled.

Then she stepped around the counter to fill the drinks. She was carrying ice cubes when the telephone rang. She dumped the cubes into the glasses, flinched as she wiped her cold hands on her sides, and hurried to the end of the bar. She grabbed the phone.

'Hello?'

'Hello, Danielle.' The voice sounded young and ugly and almost familiar.

It made her stomach tighten. 'Yes?'

'Do you know who *this* is?'

'Not offhand,' she said, wondering if he were an acquaintance trying to be funny. 'Want to give me a clue?'

'Last night,' he whispered. In the pause, she heard him breathing. 'The restaurant. The death buggy.'

A cramp seized her stomach, and her legs went weak. She hunched over the counter, elbows bracing her. 'Who . . . who are you?'

'The Chill Master.'

'Huh?'

'I frighten people.' He spoke slowly, as if savoring the menace in his voice. 'I give them goosebumps. I make them wet their pants. I make them scream in terror.'

'You make them hang up,' Dani said, and hung up. She sagged off the bar top and crouched down, hugging her belly. The peal of the telephone jolted her. It rang again and again. She covered her ears. 'Stop,' she whispered.

And then she saw herself as if from a distance, huddled down and cowering.

Just what the Chill Master ordered.

She suddenly felt abused. Anger shoved her fear aside. She stood up straight and picked up the phone. 'Hello,' she snapped.

'Hello, Danielle.'

'What do you want?'

'Have I frightened you?'

'Yes. Happy?'

'Oh yes.'

'Good. How about getting out of my life?'

'But that's the whole point, Danielle. I want *into* your life. How did you like my surprise?'

'I don't like anything about you.'

'That's not nice.'

'I don't like being attacked at dinner, and I don't like being followed, and I don't like being spied on . . .'

'You're beautiful naked.'

'And you're gonna be in big trouble if you don't stop messing with me.'

'You shouldn't be mad, Danielle. You should be flattered that I chose you.'

'I'm not.'

'I could've chosen from so many others, you know. But I chose *you*.'

'What are you talking about?'

'I'm going to be your apprentice.'

It all suddenly fell into place. 'Last night . . . everything . . . it was your idea of an audition?'

'Yes, yes, *yes*! My way of introduction to the queen of horror makeup effects. Wasn't I brilliant?'

'Terrific,' she muttered.

'When do I start?'

'Start what?'

'Working with you. We'll be wonderful together. We'll set the world aflame!'

'I already have an assistant.'

'Fire him.'

'Not hardly.'

'But you admitted I scared you,' he said, his voice rising.

'That's not the point.'

'It *is* the point! I'm a genius! Nobody can frighten people like I can. I'm the Chill Master. You'll be famous for discovering me.'

'Sorry.'

'You don't think I'm *good enough*?'

'I don't need an assistant,' she said.

'You didn't like my head?'

'It was fine.'

'It was great!'

'Look, I have to go. I'm sorry I can't help you.'

'I want it back.'

'Okay. Give me your address and I'll mail it.'

'I'll come for it. Tonight.'

'No!'

'Scared?' he asked. Then he hung up.

Dani finished mixing the drinks, and carried them outside. The sight of Jack stirring the potatoes was comforting. He turned to accept his drink, and frowned. 'What's wrong?'

'The telephone.'

'I heard it ring.'

She took a swallow of her vodka and tonic. 'It was our friend from last night. He's apparently a horror freak who wants to apprentice under me.'

71

'Oh boy,' Jack muttered.

'Didn't know I was that famous. He called me "the queen of horror makeup effects." '

'He probably read the *Fangoria* article.'

'You're right. I hadn't . . . that'd explain how he recognised me, too.'

Jack shook his head, scowling into his drink. 'So, he followed us here so he could deliver a sample of his work . . .'

'And to prove how scary he is.'

'The bastard sounds like a mental case.'

'He really flew off the handle when I told him to get lost.'

'Did he say who he is?'

'Sure. He's the Chill Master. I tried to get his name and address, but . . . Ready for this? He's coming over tonight for his head.'

'Good.'

'Jack . . .'

'He'll have to trade in his hearse for a wheelchair.'

'Let's just leave the head out for him, and go to a movie or something.'

Jack shook his head.

'He's just a harmless nut.'

'He's a menace, Dani.'

'All he did . . .'

'Do you *realise* all he did?'

'He scared the hell out of me last night, and . . .'

'How did he get your telephone number?'

'I don't . . .'

'You're not in the book. It's unlisted, so he didn't get it from an operator.'

'Then how?' she asked, her voice a shaky whisper.

'It's on the phone labels.'

'Huh?'

'He read it off one of your phones. He's been inside the house.'

# Chapter Ten

'How about here?' Heather asked.

'Let's go one more,' Steve said. The movie theater wasn't crowded, so he thought it would be bad manners to settle down right in front of the couple already seated. They stepped to the next row. 'Is this all right?' he asked.

'Fine.'

'Do you want the aisle?'

'It doesn't matter.'

Steve preferred the aisle seat so he could stretch out his legs. If he took it, though, a stranger might sit down on the other side of Heather. He wouldn't like that. Heather wouldn't, either. Since both the seats in front of them were vacant, the view would be fine from either position.

He stepped into the row, giving the aisle seat to Heather. She smoothed her skirt against the backs of her legs and sat down. The skirt left her knees bare. She was wearing no nylons.

'Which show's first?' she asked.

'*Eyes of the Maniac*, I think.'

She drew up her shoulders and made herself shiver.

'Hope it's not too gory for you.'

'The gorier, the better,' she said.

He gave Heather one of the Pepsis and a straw.

'Did you see the one where the girl got scalped?' she asked.

'Yeah.'

'A real gross-out.' She tore off an end of the straw's wrapper, slid the thin paper sheath down a bit, and twisted the other end. 'I used to shoot these, did you?'

'Yeah.'

'It's so juvenile, though.'

Steve shrugged.

With a laugh, she blew the wrapper at him. It streaked past his cheek and landed on the next seat.

He held out his own straw. 'Try again?'

'Why not? You're only sixteen once, as Dad always says.' She aimed at Steve and puffed. He shut his eyes. The wrapper tapped his eyelid and fell. 'Oh *no*. You all right?'

'Sure.'

She lowered her head and gazed at him from under her curtain of brown bangs, sheepish but grinning. 'Sor-ry.'

'I can take it.'

She gave his straw back. He jabbed it through the X on the plastic top of his Pepsi. The tip had a pink smear from Heather's lipstick. He put his mouth on it.

Where her mouth had been.

It gave him a warm feeling. Almost like a kiss. He'd never kissed Heather, but tonight, when he took her home, he would try.

He sucked in a sip of Pepsi. When he slid the straw from his mouth, he could taste her lipstick.

Would she let him kiss her? It was their first date, and . . . yeah, she would. She must like him all right or she wouldn't be here.

She reached for a handful of popcorn, making the tub push down slightly on his lap. The feel of it made him want to squirm.

He took some popcorn. As he munched it, he watched her. She was bent over slightly, head down, eating out of her cupped hand.

Her blouse gaped like a slanted mouth in the space between two buttons. It showed a shadowy slope of skin, a lacey white corner of bra. Steve stared, suddenly dry-mouthed, his heart kicking, a hot surge swelling his penis.

Then the lights dimmed.

He looked away, relieved but disappointed, certain that nothing on the movie screen could match what he'd spied through the peephole of Heather's blouse.

She reached into the popcorn tub. The slight pressure was almost too much. Steve crossed his legs to ease the tightness. Pepsi washed the dryness from his mouth. He licked his lips, but the flavor of her lipstick was gone.

A preview for *Death Grin* came on.

'Oooh,' Heather whispered. 'That looks neat.'

'Yeah.' Maybe he would bring her back when it played here. A man dropped into the seat in front of Heather. The jerk. With all these empty seats . . .

'Can you see all right?' Steve asked.

'It's okay.'

'Want to trade places?'

'Well . . . Let's just move over one.'

They did.

The jerk scooted down and propped his knees against the back of the chair in front of him. A dark stocking cap covered his head. Steve saw no fringe of hair, and wondered if the guy was bald; he looked too young to be bald. Maybe shaves his head. Only a real jerk would shave his head.

Steve looked back at the screen as the film started.

A woman was taking a shower, humming as she soaped herself. Her back and rump were slick with streaming water. She turned round. Steve gazed at her small, glossy breasts, her nipples, the wedge of dark hair at her groin. He felt a warm stir, but it didn't compare with the jolt of desire at his stolen glimpse of Heather.

The woman turned away. She shut off the faucets. She slid open the shower curtain. Heather jumped as a shriek of music blasted through the theater and hands in leather gloves thrust a fireplace poker into the woman's belly. The point broke her skin, went in deep, hook and all. As the music screamed, she was rammed backwards against the shower wall. The gloved hands twisted the poker. Blood spilled from her mouth. Then the poker was pulled out slowly, the point of its hook stretching her flesh below the original wound, popping through, ripping open a flap of skin and dragging out slippery coils of guts.

Heather turned her head. Her eyes were squeezed shut. She opened one and looked at Steve. 'Is it over yet?'

'Just about.'

'Geez!'

'Okay, it's over.'

She turned her head, slumped low in her seat and sighed.

The man in the next row looked around, grinning. His face was pale and bony, his eyes hardly visible in the shadows of their sockets. 'Great effects, huh?'

'Yeah,' Steve muttered.

Heather nodded. She sat up straight and leaned away from the stranger.

'Know who did it? Danielle Larson.'

'A woman?' Steve asked.

'The queen of horror makeup. I work with her, you know.'

'You do?'

'Wonderful lady. Beautiful, too.'

'That's very interesting.'

'You think this is good, you should see our next film. It'll scare the shit out of you.'

Steve nodded. He took a deep breath when the young man turned away. The stiffness went out of Heather. She looked up at Steve, rolled her eyes, then settled her head against his shoulder. She kept it there while she sipped her Pepsi, ate popcorn, watched the movie. Sometimes, her hair tickled Steve's cheek.

On the screen, five young women were gathered for the funeral of their friend.

'They're all gonna get it,' Heather said.

'All but one.' The talking eased his nerves.

'Yeah. I bet it's the blonde with the freckles.'

'Yeah,' he said, wiping his oily hand on a napkin. His stomach fluttered. 'Okay if . . .?' he mumbled, and curled his arm around her shoulders. Her head returned as if nothing had happened. He squeezed her shoulder gently. Then, for a long time, he didn't move his hand. He'd made a big move, and needed time to get used to it.

'Uh-oh,' Heather said.

One of the five, a slim brunette, had let her boyfriend stop at a lover's lane.

'They're gonna get it now,' Heather said.

Steve gave her shoulder another squeeze as if to comfort her. The pair in the front seat were hugging, moaning as they kissed with open mouths. Then the man unbuttoned her blouse. She was wearing no bra.

Steve's thumb stroked the bra-strap through Heather's blouse.

Her breasts were blue-gray in the darkness of the car, her nipples almost black. The man quickly covered them with his hands.

They writhed against each other, gasping.

'Any second,' Heather said.

She flinched as something tapped the windshield.

Steve stroked her upper arm.

The woman raised her eyes to the windshield and screamed.

Heather jumped. She clutched Steve's leg.

A gloved fist smashed through the windshield, caught the woman by her hair, jerked her from the arms of her stunned lover and pulled her head through the jagged hole. The glass slashed bloody streaks down her face. The maniac, dressed in black and wearing a ski mask, leaped up and down on the car's hood like a frenzied gorilla, hanging onto her hair, tugging the head from side to side until finally the windshield cut it free. He hugged the severed head to his chest and ran off into the forest while the man inside the car stared at the pumping neck stump of his girlfriend and screamed.

Steve loosened his grip on Heather's shoulder. She let go of his leg, but her hand stayed there, a warm pressure.

The man in the next row looked back at them. 'Tore it right off, huh?'

'Yeah,' Steve said.

Heather reached for more popcorn.

'Yeah, right off. Can I have some of that?'

'Popcorn?' Steve asked.

'Let me have some. You don't need all that.' He reached over the back of the seat. His hand hovered over Heather's knees. She stiffened. Steve thrust the tub under it, and he grabbed a fistful. He shoved the popcorn into his mouth and dug into the tub again.

'Come on,' Steve said. 'We're trying to watch the movie.'

The young man made a mocking smile as he chewed. He reached in, took a third handful, then turned away.

Heather let out a shaky breath. She leaned closer to Steve and whispered, 'Let's move.'

He nodded. He felt shaky himself: angry and embarrassed and somehow frightened, just as he felt when accosted on the street by bums wanting handouts.

Heather took the popcorn tub. 'Want any more?' she asked.

'No way. Not after he's touched it.'

She set it on the uptilted seat beside her.

They stood up. Though their cushions squeaked, the man didn't turn. They stepped into the aisle and walked five rows back. 'This okay?' Steve whispered.

'Fine.'

They moved in, excusing themselves as they squeezed past a seated couple, and sat down near the center of the row. In front of them, two teenaged girls were slumped low, their heads well out of the way.

Heather sighed.

'Better?' Steve asked.

'A lot.'

'Me too.'

'What a creep,' she said. She finished her Pepsi and set it on the floor. Then she took hold of Steve's hand.

'Want me to buy some more popcorn?'

'No thanks. I had plenty.'

On the screen, one of the women was running through dark woods, whimpering, glancing over her shoulder. She was missing a sleeve. She stumbled and fell, scurried to her feet and kept running. Finally, she ducked behind a tree. She peered into the darkness, apparently looking for her pursuer.

The woods were silent. Nothing moved. The woman looked relieved. She stepped backwards away from the trunk. A vague blur appeared behind her shoulder – the masked face of the maniac.

Heather's hand tightened.

The woman continued backwards, gazing ahead, moving closer and closer to the waiting man.

People in the audience yelled warnings. Some squealed.

The woman kept stepping backwards. Behind her, an ax raised high.

Heather screamed and leaped from her seat, hands flying to the back of her neck, trying to pry loose the clutching fingers. The man, still hanging on, laughed like a lunatic. His stocking cap was gone, his hairless head gleaming like a skull.

Steve swung at his jaw. He connected, snapping the man's head sideways. A set of white fangs burst from the open mouth. He swung again. This time, he missed. The man grabbed his arm and bit it.

An usher hurried up the row, yelling.

The man sprang away. He hurtled over the seat backs, and raced up the next row. Yelling people rushed to get out of his way. He got to the aisle, turned on the charging usher, and bellowed a scream.

The usher stopped fast.

With a wild laugh, he bounded up the aisle and smashed through the door.

Heather threw herself into Steve's arms, sobbing. 'Take me home. Please I want to go *home*!'

# Chapter Eleven

Alone in her living room with the curtains shut, Dani tried to read. Though her eyes moved over the words, her mind strayed. Again and again, she reached the bottom of a page only to realise she knew nothing of what had happened on it. Finally, she shut the book.

She opened the front door. From where she stood, the aspen near the corner of the lawn was a vague, black shadow. She stepped outside. She toed the grocery bag, denting in its side. It hadn't been disturbed. She left it on the lighted stoop and walked toward the aspen.

'Jack?' she asked softly.

There was no answer.

More than an hour ago, just after dark, he'd crouched behind

81

the tree. 'A great place for an ambush,' he'd said, and smacked his open hand with a sawed off length of broomstick.

Dani's protests had been feeble. She wanted the boy punished, dissuaded from bothering her further, but she didn't like the idea of using violence against him. Jack had promised to hurt him only enough 'to get the message across.'

He was no longer behind the tree.

Dani looked down the hedge separating her lawn from the street. No sign of him. She peered along the dark shrubbery to the corner of her house where it met the redwood fence.

'Jack?'

No answer.

A cool trickle ran down her side. She rubbed it away with her sweatshirt and walked across the lawn toward the driveway. Jack's Mustang was still parked there beside her own car.

As she approached it, a pale blur appeared at the driver's window. She halted, staring at it, her heart pounding hard.

'Jack? Is that you?'

The window rolled down. 'What's up?'

At the sound of Jack's voice, she sighed. 'I thought you were by the tree.'

'This is better.'

'Why don't you come in now?'

'What for?'

'I don't think this is such a great idea.'

'Dani, we agreed . . .'

'I know, but I changed my mind.' She pulled open the car door. The ceiling light came on, and Jack squinted in its brightness. 'Come on, let's go in.'

He climbed from the car and pushed the broomstick into his back pocket. 'Why do you want to give it up?'

'I've thought about it a lot. It's a bad idea, Jack. Let's just go inside. He can take his head back, and maybe that'll be the end of it.'

'And maybe not. He needs a lesson.'

Dani shoved the car door shut. 'Look, if you beat him up, we could get into all kinds of legal hassles. He might sue . . .'

'For Godsake, he's the one who . . .'

'It happens. It's not worth it to me.' She took Jack's arm and walked him toward the house. 'Besides, that's just a minor thing. What really worries me is escalation. Suppose you *do* beat him up? It'd probably just make him mad. It'd make *me* mad. I'd want revenge. Wouldn't you?'

'I guess so.'

'I'm afraid he might come back again to even the score. Then *we'd* want to get back at *him*, and God only knows where it might end.'

'That's a risk involved, yes.'

'Well, let's just avoid it. So far, he hasn't done anything violent. As far as we know, he's harmless.'

'He broke into your house.'

'Maybe. But he didn't attack me. Hell, he doesn't want to hurt me, he wants a job. That could all change if we bash him around. We might *make* him dangerous.'

Jack shrugged. 'All right. We'll try it your way.'

'Thanks.' She squeezed his arm. They stepped around the grocery bag, and Jack pushed the front door open. Dani entered first, glimpsed the man pressed to the wall inside and jumped away with a gasp.

A low, mad laugh hissed through the mouth-hole of the ghoul mask. It stopped with a grunt as Jack's forearm rammed across the mask. His left fist jabbed hard into the boy's belly.

'That's enough,' Dani gasped. 'That's . . .'

Jack punched him once more, then stepped back. The boy slumped to a squat, clutching his belly and gasping.

Jack yanked the mask off.

Dani stared at the agonised face, the bone-white skin and tiny eyes, the lips peeled back over yellow teeth as he struggled for air. The head lowered. An eye, crudely drawn with marking pens, seemed to gaze at her from the center of his hairless crown.

'I'll watch him,' Jack said. 'You want to call the cops?'

Dani shook her head. 'What's your name?' she asked.

He looked up, glanced from Dani to Jack, to Dani again.

'If you co-operate,' she said, 'maybe we won't call the police. Now, what's your name?'

'Anthony.'

'Anthony what?'

'Johnson.'

'Let's see your driver's license.'

He started to get up, but Jack shoved him down by the shoulder. Reaching into a rear pocket of his black pants, he took out a wallet. He flipped it open and held it out.

Dani took it. 'You're from New York.'

He nodded.

'How long have you been out here?'

'Five weeks.'

'He's just eighteen,' she told Jack.

'Good. Old enough to be tried as an adult.'

'Let's go in the living room and sit down.'

'Dani . . .'

'We might as well be comfortable. It may take a while.'

'What?' Jack asked.

'We're going to defuse the situation.'

Anthony stared at Dani as if she were an intriguing animal. He got to his feet, and she gave his billfold back.

She led the way into the living room. Anthony followed, with Jack close behind him. 'You've been in here before,' she said.

'I didn't take anything.'

She nodded towards an easy chair. Anthony sat down.

'When and how did you get in?'

'This morning. You were in the pool, and left the back door open.' He seemed quite pleased with himself.

'The bedroom door?'

He nodded.

He must've passed within yards of her. While she swam, thinking she was alone, thinking she was safe even as he spied on her and sneaked into her house.

'Why did you do it?' Jack asked.

'Why not?'

'Wipe that smirk off your face.'

He wiped it off with his hand.

'Why?' Dani asked.

'I've got my reasons.'

Jack, tight with anger, looked at Dani as if asking permission to stomp the young man.

'Why don't you get us some drinks?' she asked. 'Anthony, would you like a beer?'

His head bobbed.

Jack's head tipped sideways and he regarded Dani with amazement.

'It's all right,' she said. 'I'm not crazy.'

'It's *your* party.' He made a smile at Anthony. 'Would you prefer Coors, Bud, or Dos Equis?'

'Coors.'

He glanced at Dani, rolled his eyes upward, and walked toward the bar.

Dani sat on the sofa. Elbows propped on her knees, she stared at Anthony. 'Did you do it to get my phone number?'

'Nooo.'

'You want to work with me, right? You want to learn the ropes, get started on a makeup career?'

He nodded.

'Then we have to trust each other.'

'You said you didn't want me.'

'Maybe I'll change my mind. You obviously have a certain talent for frightening people.'

'Oh I do.'

'Tell me about it.'

He leaned forward, bracing his elbows on his knees, his chin on his fists. The same position as Dani. She noticed the similarity, wondered if it was intended to mock her. But she didn't move.

'I've always liked scary films.'

'Why?'

'They're fun. People jump and scream.'

'In the audience?'

'On the screen, too. It's a blast.'

'These films, do they scare you?'

His tiny eyes widened. 'The good ones do.'

'How do they make you feel?'

'Tight and shaky. I get goosebumps all over and want to scream.' He lowered his hands, rubbed them, glanced toward the bar. 'I get that way when *I* scare people, too.'

'You frighten yourself?'

'It's fantastic.'

'Do you do that much, go around trying to throw a fright into people – and into yourself?'

'All the time.'

Jack returned. He handed a can of Coors to Anthony, then sat down beside Dani and gave her a bottle of Dos Equis. 'What'd I miss?' he asked, and smiled wildly as if eager to join the madness.

'Anthony was just explaining how he likes to frighten people.'

'That sounds like fun. It must be especially nice for his victims.'

'I never hurt anyone,' he whispered as if sharing a wonderful secret.

'You just like to make them squirm?'

'I like to make them *scream*.'

'Sort of a hobby.'

'Hobby?' He sniggered. He took a sip of beer, settled back and crossed his legs. 'I'm the Chill Master. Once I've become famous for my horror effects, I'll move into the production end. I'll make films that'll send audiences shrieking from the theaters.'

'Nice to meet a fellow with ambition,' Jack said.

Dani frowned at him, smiled at Anthony. 'Basically, then, you want someone to start you on the way.'

'Exactly,' he said. He took a sip of beer. 'Who better than the queen of horror makeup effects?'

'You read the *Fangoria* article?' Jack asked.

'Oh yes. And I've seen all Danielle's films. She's better than Savini.'

'Thank you,' Dani said.

'How did you find her?'

Looking pleased with himself, Anthony took out his billfold.

He removed a thick mat of paper from the bill compartment, and snapped off its rubber band. He unfolded the pack. 'My collection,' he said. He peeled off a color photo apparently snipped from a magazine, and held it up. At this distance, the bearded face resembled Jack.

'Rob Bottin,' Anthony said. He showed them another. 'Dick Smith. And here's Rick Baker. Tom Savini. Danielle Larson.'

Dani stared at the photo. It came from the *Fangoria* article.

Smiling, Anthony started to put his collection back together. 'I know all your faces. I've spent the last month keeping my eyes open, hanging around the studios and the "in" restaurants and bars. I knew I'd find one of you sooner or later.'

'You're very persistent,' Dani said.

'And innovative,' Jack added.

'I'm glad it was you I found. You're the best. And the most beautiful.'

*You're beautiful naked.*

'We'll make a great team,' Anthony said.

'I'm sure of it.'

Jack gaped at her.

Dani ignored him. 'We're busy tomorrow. Why don't you come over on Saturday? We'll show you a few things, get you started.'

'Honest?'

'Yep.'

'What time?'

'In the morning. How about nine?'

'Great!'

'There's only one condition.'

He sank back in his chair, looking suddenly dejected.

'No more bugging us. That means creeping around, following

us, trespassing, spying on us. None of that. Otherwise, it's all off. Okay?'

'Sure!' He grinned, pounded the arm of the chair, and raised his beer can high. 'To Danielle Larson. You're the greatest!'

In his boyish enthusiasm, he seemed almost human.

Dani leaned against the door and shut her eyes, relieved to be rid of the strange boy. But he would be back. 'Do you think I'm nuts?'

'Definitely. Haven't you ever heard the age-old adage?'

'Which one?'

'Don't feed it, maybe it'll go away.' Jack stepped close to her, held her by the shoulders, kissed her forehead. 'That guy,' he whispered, 'is a lunatic.'

'I know.'

She moaned as Jack's hands slipped inside her sleeve holes and rubbed her shoulders.

'Do you feel sorry for him?'

'Hell no,' Dani said. 'He scares me.'

'Then why did you encourage him?'

'I want him to be with us, not against us. You be nice to him Saturday, okay?'

'I'll be charming.'

The hands squeezed warmth into Dani's tight, aching muscles.

'I've got one request,' Jack said.

'Uh-huh?'

'Don't ever let him in the house when I'm not here.'

'You can bet on it.'

# Chapter Twelve

From her car parked across the street, Linda saw Joel leave his house. He started up the sidewalk, striding fast and swinging his arms high. His lips were moving. He was either singing or talking to himself.

Linda started her car. She pulled forward, turned around at the end of the block, and drove up beside Joel. He jumped at the beep of her horn, but kept on walking.

'Hey, Joel, want a ride?'

Turning, he ducked his head and raised his sunglasses. He squinted out from under the dark lenses. 'Linda?'

'Yeah. Where you going?'

'The pharmacy.'

'Hop in. I'll give you a lift.'

'Oh, that's all right.'

'Come on.' Leaning across the seat, she swung open the passenger door.

'Well ...' He shrugged, then loped over and climbed in. 'Thanks a lot,' he said. He slammed the door shut so hard the car shook. 'I don't want to put you out.'

'I was going that way, anyhow.'

'Well, thanks.'

She started the car forward. 'Besides, it's nice to have some company. I haven't seen many of the kids since the accident.'

'Yeah.' He nodded, staring straight ahead. 'That was too bad about your accident.'

'Those things happen.'

'You feeling all right, now?'

'Fine, thank you.'

'Good. That's good.' He rubbed his hands on his Bermuda shorts. He rested an elbow on the window sill. 'This sure beats walking.'

'It's hot out there.'

'Yeah. Sure is.'

'It'll be real nice over at the river.'

'Yeah, probably.'

'I'm on my way over there.'

'Yeah?'

Linda gestured over her shoulder. Joel glanced around at the back seat.

'Gonna have a picnic?'

'Sure am. I've got fried chicken in there, and beer in the cooler.'

'Beer?'

'I've got plenty. How would you like to come along?'

'Geez, I don't know.'

'Come on. It'll be great.'

'I'd better not. I have to pick up this stuff for Mom.'

'Oh. Is she sick?'

'No, but . . .'

'If it's nothing that urgent, you could just get it later, couldn't you?'

'I guess, but I'd still better not.'

'Thanks,' Linda said.

He frowned at his knees.

'What, have I got leprosy?'

'No!'

She shook her head and tried to look sad. 'You probably

think a girl like me has it made – a cheer-leader, good grades, popular as hell. Well, I've got news, I'm a human being. I get hungry, just like everyone else. I sweat. I worry. I get horny. I get depressed. Believe it or not, sometimes I even get lonely.'

'You?'

'Yeah, me. The marvelous Linda Allison. Do you know who always asked me for dates? Jerks who thought they were God's gift to women. They were the only ones with guts enough to call. Do you think they cared about me as a person? They didn't give a damn about what's in my head or heart. They just cared about what's under my clothes. If you want to know how lonely feels, you oughta find yourself parked in the woods with a guy who thinks you're a toy.'

'I'm sorry,' Joel said.

She stopped at the intersection. A right-hand turn would lead downtown, a left would take them toward the river. She stared at Joel. He looked confused and glum, but no longer nervous. 'Normal, nice guys – guys like you – never called.'

He shrugged.

'You thought I was too good for you?'

'Sort of.'

'You thought I'd laugh at you?'

'Maybe.'

Reaching out, Linda stroked his hand. 'Why would I laugh at you?'

He shook his head, and seemed to have a hard time swallowing.

'Come on, Joel. Let's go to the river. Please? I . . . I don't want to be alone.'

'Okay.'

She turned left.

The river, five miles north of town, curved through an area of dense forest. A portion of the woods had been cleared for the public, tables and barbeques set up, sand poured to make a small beach, a gravel parking lot laid. On summer days, it was usually aswarm with families, young couples, teenagers throwing Frisbees when they weren't swimming. At night, it became a place for romance.

Linda had been there often at night. Outside, on blankets. Inside cars. Usually as an eager participant. But she'd been with enough jerks to know how it felt being used – enough to convince Joel of her sorry plight.

As usual, the parking lot was crowded. She drove on by.

'Where's we going?' Joel asked, breaking the long silence.

'Up here a ways. I know a real nice place where there won't be a lot of people in our way.'

'Oh. Okay.' He patted his knees as if he needed to keep his hands busy.

'You don't mind, do you?'

'No. Wherever you want's fine with me.' He kept drumming his legs. He stared out the windshield, out the side window, down at his tapping hands. He looked everywhere except at Linda.

'No need to be nervous.'

'Me? I'm not nervous.'

'I don't bite, you know.'

'Just chicken?' he asked, and made a weak smile.

Linda forced herself to laugh.

Joel grinned and shrugged. 'Do you know why the chicken committed suicide?' he asked.

'No, why?'

'It didn't give a cluck.'

Linda laughed and shook her head.

'Wait. Wait, here's a good one. Do you know how to make a dead chicken float?'

'No.'

'First, you get a dead chicken. Add a little ice cream, a little root beer . . .' He started laughing.

'Oh, that's gross.'

'Yeah, isn't it? That's a good one. That's one of my favourites.'

Linda slowed down and swung onto the road's bumpy shoulder. 'Do you pluck it first?'

'No. The feathers are the best part.'

'Ish.'

They climbed from the car, Joel still laughing quietly. Linda opened the back door. She handed out the picnic basket and cooler. She grabbed her towel and faded red blanket, then led the way into the woods.

'Is the river very far?'

'Just two or three miles.'

He laughed some more. 'You know,' he said, 'you've got a good sense of humor.'

'Thank you. See, I told you I'm human.'

'Do you know what's green and red and goes thump, thump, thump?'

'No, what?'

'Kermit the Frog in a blender!'

He kept it up for the next fifteen minutes as they trudged through undergrowth, climbed over deadfalls, ducked beneath low-hanging branches. Then they reached the river. Linda found a grassy clearing a few yards from the bank. She spread out the blanket.

She sat down on it, kicked off her sneakers, and stretched out her legs. 'Can you tell the difference?'

He shook his head.

'Take off your sunglasses.'

He lifted them, glanced at her legs, and shook his head again.

'This is the one,' she said. She patted her left thigh. 'See? It's not as tanned.'

'They both look fine.'

'You should've seen it when they took off the cast. All shriveled and white.'

He wrinkled his nose, lowered his sunglasses, and sat down to the far side of the basket and cooler.

'You ready for a beer?' Linda asked.

'Sure.'

She took two cans of Genesee from the cooler. She popped them open and handed one to Joel. 'Did you ever hear how it happened? My accident?'

'You got hit by a car?' His hand trembled slightly as he raised the can to his mouth.

'That's it. The thing is, I didn't look where I was going. Stupid, huh? Just ran right out into the street and *wham*.'

'Gosh.'

She squinted as the top of her can flashed sunlight in her eyes. She took a long drink. 'Ready for some chicken?'

'Sure.'

She set aside her beer and opened the picnic basket. 'Sorry, I forgot the root beer and ice cream.'

He laughed a bit, sounding nervous again.

'What do you like: thighs, drumsticks, breasts?'

'I don't care.'

'I bet you're a breast man.'

He blushed, his pimply chin turning a deeper shade of red. 'Fine,' he told her.

Linda gave him a crispy breast and a napkin. She took out a thigh for herself. 'It's really nice here, isn't it?' she asked. 'So quiet and private.'

'Yeah,' he said through a mouthful.

'Are you glad you decided to come?'

He smiled, and wiped his slick lips with a napkin. 'I sure am.'

They ate and drank in silence for a while. Linda opened two more cans of beer, passed another breast to Joel, nibbled on a drumstick. 'I don't hold it against you, you know.'

He stopped in mid-bite. 'Huh?'

'My accident. I don't hold any grudges.'

His sunglasses slipped down his nose. He poked them back with a greasy forefinger. 'I don't get it.'

'Sure you do. You were just having some fun. How could you know I'd be dumb enough to run in front of a car?'

He frowned. 'I still don't . . .'

'You, Arnold and Tony? The Freeman house? Jasper the friendly ghost?' She shook her head and laughed. 'I tell you, it scared the hell out of me. I thought sure ol' Jasper was going to cut my head off.'

'That was Tony,' he muttered.

'*Jasper* was Tony?'

'Yeah. He, uh, stayed behind. He had all that stuff upstairs . . . the makeup and phoney head. And the ax.'

'Figures,' she said, and wondered why she hadn't figured it out for herself. 'The whole thing was Tony's idea, I bet.'

'Yeah. We had a ladder around the back. He was planning to use that, but then you got knocked out . . .' Joel's chin started to tremble. 'Boy, I'm really sorry. I was a jerk to go along with him. Tony gets these crazy ideas.'

'It's all right. Don't worry about it. I didn't bring you out here to get into all that. I just thought ... hell, you might be wondering about the whole thing, whether or not I recognised you. I just brought it up to let you know I'm not angry.' She took a drink of beer. 'Actually, it was a pretty neat idea. I wouldn't mind pulling it on someone, myself.'

'Really?'

'Someone like Tony.'

Joel laughed. Turning away, he took off his sunglasses and wiped his eyes. 'Tony deserves it.'

'Of course, the Freeman house is no more.'

'Yeah, wasn't that something?'

'The paper said it was arson. I wonder if Tony did *that*.'

'No. He's gone. Didn't you know?'

'He is?'

'Yeah. He left after graduation. He went to Hollywood.'

'What's he doing there?'

'Wants to get into horror movies. He's always been big on those things, you know, but after what we did to you ... I guess that made up his mind. He changed a lot, after that.'

'How do you know he's in Hollywood?'

'He keeps in touch with Arnold. They've been writing back and forth. He's trying to get Arnold to move out and join him.'

'Has he written to you?'

Joel shook, his head. 'I sort of had it out with him. After what happened.'

'It bothered you that much?'

He nodded.

'That's really sweet, Joel.'

'I shouldn't have let him do it.'

'He just would've done it without you. More chicken?'

'No thanks.'

'How about another beer? We might as well finish them off.' She gave him a beer, popped hers open, took a drink, and rubbed the cool wet can against her face. 'Oh, that feels good.' She opened the top two buttons of her blouse. Joel looked away as she slipped the can inside. It felt icy on her breasts, made her nipples rigid. Unfastening another button, she slid the can across her belly. Joel, facing the river, gulped his beer. 'You should try it.'

He shrugged, and kept on drinking. Linda crawled over to him. 'No, it's . . .'

'Lie back.'

'No, really . . .' But he didn't resist as Linda pushed his shoulder. He eased backwards, stretching out his legs and holding his beer can at his side.

Linda knelt beside him. Leaning over, her blouse gaping, she plucked off his sunglasses. He glanced at her breasts and quickly looked up to her face. He flinched as she worked open a button of his shirt. 'Wh . . .?'

'Won't hurt a bit,' she told him. Grinning, she continued to unfasten his shirt. His chest was hairless and pale. 'Ready?' He nodded: Linda pressed her beer can to his right nipple. He cringed, then laughed. 'See? Feels good, doesn't it?'

'Yeah.'

The can made a damp path down his skin. She slid it over his left nipple, then down his ribs. His belly sucked in at its cold touch. The front of his Bermudas bulged with the push of an erection.

'Roll over, I'll do your back.'

'This is weird,' he said.

'You like it, don't you?'

'Yeah,' he said, sitting up.

Linda helped him take his shirt off. Then he twisted around and lay down flat. He stiffened when she touched the can between his shoulder blades. She moved it slowly down his back, and up again, and then she upended it. Beer gurgled onto his shoulders.

'Hey!' he cried. He rolled away. Laughing, Linda pursued him on her knees, spilling beer onto his hair and face and chest. 'No! Don't!'

She stopped, and drank the final drops.

'Geez, you got it all over me!'

'Felt good, didn't it?'

'I'm a mess!' He wiped his chest, and glared at his hands. He looked as if he might cry.

'I'm sorry. I thought you'd like it.'

'I'm a mess.'

'You can do it to me,' she offered, and picked up Joel's can. She jiggled it. 'Half full. Come on.'

He shook his head.

'You want to, I can tell.'

'It's all right,' he said.

'Come on. Turn-about's fair play.'

'I don't want to get you messy.'

She set the can on the blanket near his knees. And then she took off her blouse.

Joel stared.

'Pour it on me,' she whispered.

Joel, looking dazed, picked up the can. He came forward on his knees.

'On my breasts,' she said.

Joel raised the can and tipped it. The cool beer splashed Linda's shoulder, washed over her breast, streamed around it, ran off the tip of her nipple. Joel gazed as if transfixed. He moved the can, and the beer spilled onto her other breast. It slid off, ran down her belly.

Moaning, Linda rubbed her breasts as if massaging the beer into them.

Joel poured until the can was empty.

Linda smiled and lowered her hands. 'Geez,' she said, 'you got it all over me. I'm a mess.'

His mouth twitched with something like a smile.

'I can't go home like this,' she said. 'I smell like a brewery.'

'Me too,' Joel said.

'We'd better wash it off,' she whispered.

He nodded, still gazing at her breasts. His eyes stayed with her as she stood up. They lowered, and his mouth dropped open when she unfastened her shorts.

'You gonna spend all afternoon catching flies,' Linda asked, 'or are you coming in?'

She kicked off her shorts and stood naked in front of him, feet apart, hands on hips, head tilted to one side. 'Well?'

He blinked. He licked his lips. He seemed to have a hard time breathing.

'Need help?'

He shook his head. 'Why . . . why don't you go on. I'll be there. In a minute.'

'All right, bashful.' She turned away and skipped down the grassy bank. Where the grass ended, the shore was rocky. She trod carefully over the stones, and waded into the water. It wrapped her legs, just cool enough to be refreshing. When it reached her thighs, she turned around.

Joel came down the slope, hunched over as if he were cold, hands shielding the front of his striped boxer shorts. He walked gingerly over the stones.

'Hey,' Linda said, 'you don't want to get your shorts wet. How'll you explain it to your mother?'

He groaned. Turning away, he pulled them down. He pinned them to the ground with a rock, then backed toward the water. When it reached his knees, he dropped. He swung around and paddled for deeper water. Two yards from Linda, he stopped. He stayed low, covered to the shoulders, and stared up at her. He looked frightened but eager.

'Come here,' Linda said. 'Rinse the beer off me.'

'Geez.'

'Come on.'

He waddled toward her.

'Don't hide from me. Stand up straight.'

He rose from the water, holding his cupped hands over his groin.

'Splash me,' Linda whispered. 'Rub me. Get all the beer off.'

His hands dipped into the water, and he flung it up at her. He splashed her again and again, as if giving up his attempts to cover himself. His penis stood upright and rigid. With open hands, he stroked Linda's body. At first, he was business-like as if actually concerned about washing off the beer. But his hands began to linger on her breasts, sliding over them, fingering her stiff nipples, gently squeezing.

'Now you,' Linda said. She eased his hands away. They hung at his sides while she threw water onto his chest. She caressed him, her hands roaming lower, and finally her fingers curled around his erection. He gasped as they slid down it.

She let go.

'There,' she said. 'All clean.' With a laugh, she sprang away and dived. She clawed from rock to rock, pulling herself along the bottom. Then Joel grabbed her foot. She kicked free and surfaced. Joel popped from the water.

'I don't think we got all the beer off,' he said.

'Well well.' She stepped toward him through the neck-high water, and felt his hands on her breasts. She moved still closer. His erection prodded her belly. Squirming against it, she hooked her arms behind his back, kissed him. She brought her legs up, wrapped them around him. 'Do you want me?' she whispered against his lips.

He only moaned.

Reaching down with one hand, she found his penis. It felt huge and warm. She held it, and lowered herself. It spread her, pushed into her, slid in deep. She hugged Joel tightly with her arms and legs, writhed, felt him penetrate even more.

His breath blew hard against her face. He held her more tightly and started to grunt, suddenly throbbing and pumping inside her, and jerked wildly, still coming, when Linda slammed the rock against the back of his head. He blinked, looking puzzled.

'That was your last wish,' Linda said, and struck again.

He tried to shove her away, but she clung with her legs and one arm, and pounded his head again.

He jerked at her hair.

The wig came off in his hand. He made a whimpering noise and she struck again, this time smashing the rock against his temple. His eyes rolled upward. He swayed. Linda shoved away from him, feeling an odd moment of loss when his penis left. She watched him go under. Tossing away the rock, she lunged for her floating wig. She shoved it onto her head, then went for Joel.

She found him a few inches under the surface, face down, arms and legs moving in a lazy way, hair stirring in the currents.

She curled her fingers through his hair, gripped it, and steered him lower. She rolled him onto his back. She guided him between her legs and clamped his head between her knees.

The river swirled around her. It pushed Joel, turned him slowly.

Finally, Linda opened her knees.

The body slipped away, feet first, and vanished in the murky water.

# Chapter Thirteen

'The machete has to go,' Roger said.

'What?'

'I know it's a drag, I know it's all set. We'll shoot around the splash scene and take it up on Monday.'

'What's wrong with the machete?' Dani asked.

'Not a thing. It's beautiful, beautiful.' He squeezed her shoulder as if to comfort her. 'But here's the thing, I caught

*Friday the 13th Part II* on *ON* last night and there's a guy catches a machete in the face.'

'I know. I told you that a month ago.'

'No big deal, right? Instead of a machete, our boy catches an ax.' He turned away and yelled, 'Bruce! The ax!'

The prop master, standing across the set by the coffee machine, nodded and hurried off.

'Wait till you see it,' Ralph said. 'It's a beauty. We'll give it to Bill right in the forehead, same as the machete, but nobody can say we're ripping off *Friday Part II*. Bruce!'

'Yo,' the prop man called. He rushed forward, carrying a shiny new ax at port-arms. He handed it to Roger.

'Wicked, eh?' Roger winked behind his tinted glasses, and tapped a finger against the cutting edge.

'It's a bit too wicked,' Dani told him. 'It's a lot heavier than the machete, and the weight isn't distributed the same way.'

'Yes?'

'It would chop right through the catcher's mask.'

'Have your man pull the blow.'

She shook her head. 'He'd have to strike hard enough to penetrate the face appliance. It's too risky. Besides, it wouldn't look right. An ax just isn't a machete, Roger. It wouldn't go in just a couple of inches. Not the way we'd want our maniac to swing it.' Dani drew a finger across her forehead. 'It'd pretty much take off everything from here up.'

Roger leered and nodded. 'Beautiful. That's what we'll do.'

'It'd take a full head appliance.'

'You'll have it ready for Monday?'

She nodded. 'Michael's about the same size as Bill. We can use his mannequin, attach Bill's head.'

'Fine, fine. Go to it, kid.'

She explained the situation to Jack as they left the sound stage.

'That means we're done for the day,' he said.

'Yep.'

'Nice. If you want to bring the car around, Bruce and I can take care of Michael.'

'That's all right. I love to see all those old props. Like a museum.'

Bruce smiled over his shoulder as he unlocked the door. 'Just watch out for the mice,' he said.

'Mice?'

He laughed. 'Cute little critturs, but they have a tendency to get under foot.'

'I'll watch where I step,' Dani told him. In her boots and jeans, she felt well protected. Still, she spent most of her time studying the concrete floor as she followed Jack and Bruce through the narrow aisles.

On both sides, the warehouse was packed with furnishings. She saw a dusty, roll-top desk, highboys, dining-room sets and sofas, floor lamps and table lamps and chandeliers. Then she watched the floor again, looking for mice but glancing at the framed paintings propped up on both sides of the aisle.

They turned a corner. She saw replicas of Venus and David, a statue of Napoleon, bird baths, fountains adorned with cherubs, naked women, a man balanced on one foot with his lips pursed to squirt.

She stepped on something small and soft. With a gasp, she jerked her foot up.

Only a scrap of thick-napped carpet.

'Here we are,' Bruce said.

Standing against the wall as if lined up for inspection were fifteen or twenty naked mannequins. Dani's eyes went directly to the life-like figure with the blasted face. Then she looked carefully up and down the row, pausing at each female.

She frowned.

'Where's Ingrid?'

'Ingrid?' Bruce asked.

'*Me!* Where is she?'

'Must be around,' he said.

'I don't see her,' Jack muttered.

Bruce shook his head, scratched his ear.

'You're in charge, aren't you?' Dani demanded.

'I put her there, right next to the fella. Had 'em both side by side.'

'She isn't there now.'

'I can see that, Miss Larson. Plenty of other folks have access here. Could be someone borrowed it.'

'I'd like to know.'

He scowled, looking puzzled. 'Ill sure look into it for you.'

Jack took her hand. 'I'm sure it'll turn up.'

'Yeah. Yeah, I suppose. I'm sorry, Bruce. I didn't mean to snap at you that way.'

'That's all right, Miss Larson.'

'I'm sure it's not your fault. It's just ... I feel a certain attachment to the damn thing.'

'Well, I'll see if I can't turn it up.'

'Fine. Thank you. Now let's grab Michael,' she said, forcing cheer into her voice, 'and get this show on the road.'

Dani drove slowly past the guard station at the studio gate, and turned left onto Pico. She searched the rearview mirror.

No hearse.

Of course not.

'Jack?'

He looked at her.

'About Ingrid. You . . . you don't think there's any chance that Anthony got her?'

'*Anthony*?' He sounded shocked. 'No. How could he?'

'He might've sneaked onto the lot. It's not impossible. It happens.'

'Sometimes. But look, how would he know Ingrid has anything to do with you? She hasn't got a face, and I don't think Anthony's seen the rest of you well enough to recognise her other features.'

Dani blushed. 'If he was on the set Wednesday . . .'

'Did you see him?'

'No. But that doesn't mean he wasn't there.'

'He didn't *find* you until that night.'

'If he was telling the truth.'

'I imagine he was. Nothing happened before then.'

'He could've been at the studio, watched the scene with Ingrid, and *then* followed us to the restaurant.'

'I suppose. Why don't we ask him tomorrow?'

'Lot of good that would do.'

'Really, Dani, I don't think . . .'

'But what if he *does* have her?'

'Long as he hasn't got the real article,' Jack said. Reaching out, he rubbed the back of Dani's neck.

His hand felt good on her stiff muscles, but there was a cold knot in her stomach as she thought about Anthony with the mannequin.

Ingrid, but Dani.

She saw him in bed with her headless body, fondling her, kissing her, sliding a hand . . .

'Look out!'

She stood on the brake pedal. Her car shrieked to a halt inches from the rear of a van stopped at the traffic light.

'Are you okay?' Jack asked.

'Yeah. Fine.'

# Chapter Fourteen

Cynthia Gable lifted her wine bottle toward the light and shook it. Through its tinted glass, she watched the cork toss like a tiny boat in a thrashing sea of Burgundy. She held the bottle steady. The tumult eased. The cork swayed back and forth, turning in a lazy way.

Murray had always been so good with corks. Plucked them right out. They never ended up in the bottom of the bottle when Murray did it.

Must be a trick to it.

Leaning over the coffee table, she stretched out her arm. The neck of the bottle hovered above her glass. She tried to hold it steady as she poured, but the bottle wavered. Some of the wine hit the rim and ran down the stem and made a shiny puddle on the table. Most of it, however, got into the glass.

She took a drink. A cool drop tapped her skin and trickled

down between her breasts. She followed it with her finger, wiped it away, and licked her fingertip.

Least it missed the nightgown.

She licked the wet base of her glass, slid her tongue up its stem, up the rounded underside, found the rim again and drank some more.

Her eyes met the TV screen. Sandy Chung was on, doing a news break.

What happened to the show? Must be over.

What show had she been watching? Oh yes. *Dallas*.

Must be over.

She finished her wine. She set down her glass near the puddle, picked up the bottle and upended it. A few drops fell into her glass. The cork slid up the bottle as if to get out, but stopped when the neck narrowed and dropped back to the bottom as she put the bottle down.

A dead soldier. That's what Murray called them.

Not the cork, the bottle.

A dead soldier with a cork in his stomach.

The telephone rang.

Moaning, she pushed herself off the sofa. She swayed over the coffee table. As she raised her hands for balance, she saw herself in the mirror above the fireplace. The image looked at her as if she were a stranger. It raised its eyebrows, grinned in a crooked way, and waved a hand.

'Hiya, gorgeous,' she said, and winked.

The gal in the mirror winked, too.

'Scuse me, scuse me. Gotta get the phone.' She sidestepped past the coffee table. In the dark dining room, she grabbed the back of a chair to steady herself. With three long strides, she made it to the doorframe of the kitchen. She leaned a shoulder against it and lifted the wall phone's receiver. 'Hello?' she asked, pronouncing it carefully.

A low, breathy sound whispered in her ear.

'Hello?' she repeated the word.

'Shhuh . . . Shhh . . . ahhh.'

'That's easy for you to say,' she said, and a giggle slipped out. 'C'mon, who's this?'

'Ssss . . . Cynthia.'

'No, *I'm* Cynthia. Who's this?'

'Sssso cold.'

The low murmur of the voice sent a shiver up her back. She slid a hand down the wall and found the light switch. The kitchen went bright. 'I'm not in a mood for jokers,' she said.

'I . . . miss you . . . Cynthia.'

'You be'er tell me who this is.'

'Have you . . . forgotten me . . . so soon?'

She hung up. 'Jerk,' she muttered. She rubbed her arms. They were pebbly with goosebumps. Her nipples stood rigid against the soft lace of her negligee. She would put her robe on. That would be snug and nice. Then maybe another sip or two of wine.

She tugged open the refrigerator and took out a long, slim bottle of Chardonnay.

The phone rang again, making her jump. She snatched it off the hook. 'Hello?'

'Cynthia,' said the same, low voice.

'Who the hell *is* this?'

'I . . . I want you . . . with me. So dark here. So cold.'

'Who *is* this?'

'Mmm . . . mmmm . . . Murray.'

The bottle slipped from her hand. It thumped the floor but

didn't break. It rolled a few inches and stopped. 'You're sick.'

'No, I'm dead.'

'You're a sick perverted bastard 'n I'm gonna call the cops.'

'Oh, Cynthia, I'm so cold. I want your warmth. I want to make love with you.'

'You piece of shit!'

'I'm coming for you.'

She slammed the receiver down. Then she tugged at the phone, unplugging it. She rushed into her bedroom, flicked on the light, and dropped to her knees by the nightstand. She jerked the telephone plug from the wall.

There.

The bastard! The shit! What kind of animal would *do* such a thing? Nobody she knew. Must be a stranger, got her name from the obituaries. Maybe goes right down the list, calling every widow.

Sick!

*I want to make love to you.*

*I'm coming over.*

No, he won't come over.

Just a sicko gets his kicks with the phone.

She rolled onto her back on the soft carpet beside the bed. The ceiling turned slowly.

Go over to Barbara's?

But it's twenty minutes on the freeway. I can't drive. Not like this.

Call Barbara, ask her over?

Maybe.

He won't come. Those types never do. That's what the cops say on TV, and he always ends up coming. But that's TV. He won't come.

Just a harmless sicko.

Sicko. Revolting word, sicko.

And suddenly she knew she would throw up. Clutching her mouth, she staggered to her feet and ran for the master bathroom. Her stomach tossed. Her throat filled. She cupped her hands under her chin and tried to catch the hot flood and then she was at the toilet. She hunched over it, vomiting and sobbing.

When she was done, she cleaned herself off with toilet paper. She turned on the bathroom light. The top of her nightgown was clotted with mess. She wiped some of it off. She considered throwing away the gown, but Murray had given it to her last Valentine's Day.

She turned on the shower. When the water was as hot as she liked it, she climbed into the tub and pulled the curtain shut. The spray hit her face, patted her eyelids, filled her open mouth. It soaked her nightgown, making it cling in a way that felt good, almost erotic.

She used a soap bar on the soiled places. She rubbed it over her breasts until the fabric was sudsy and slick, then put the soap away and rinsed.

Bending over, she lifted her gown. She peeled it up her body and struggled out of it. She wrung the water from it. Then she opened the shower curtain and tossed it into the sink, and thought she heard the telephone.

Impossible. Just her imagination playing tricks.

A faint ringing sounded through the house.

Her bowels shriveled. She hunched low and shut off the faucets.

There it was again – a long, insistent ring that crawled up her body like the fingers of a dead man.

This can't be, she told herself.

Silence. She waited, hanging onto the faucet handles to steady herself, drops of cold water hitting the back of her neck.

It's stopped, she thought. Thank God it's . . . it came again, this time in a series of quick shrills unlike any noise her telephone had ever made.

The doorbell!

Someone's at the front door.

*I'm coming for you.*

But not Murray. The caller hadn't been Murray. He's dead. The voice wasn't even his. Unless it had changed, somehow. Unless the accident . . . No, no, no. It was a sicko made those calls.

And now he's at the bell button.

He can't get in.

Maybe he can.

Maybe it's not him. Maybe it's Barbara or Louise or a neighbor or even the police.

Cynthia climbed out of the tub and ran, dripping, into her bedroom. She snagged her bathrobe off its closet hook. The ringing had stopped. Maybe *he'd* given up. Maybe he was making his way toward the back. But if it was a friend . . . She couldn't let a friend get away. Shoving her wet arms into the sleeves, she raced through the dining room. She pulled the robe shut and belted it.

In the living room, she grabbed an iron poker from the fireplace stand. She raced to the door. Her hand closed around the knob. The strength seemed to drain from her arm, from her whole body.

What if he's there, standing silent at the other side of the door, waiting?

Not Murray. It couldn't be Murray. He was in pieces from the accident, so even if . . . no, he's dead and in his grave and there's no way on God's earth it could be him.

It's the sicko who called, and he's standing just outside the door, no more than two feet away.

Cynthia's hand fell away from the knob. She stared at the door, wishing it had a peephole. But even if it did, she knew she couldn't bring herself to look out.

Water trickled down her legs, making the carpet wet around her feet. She swayed, taking deep breaths, and pressed a hand against her chest. Her heart pounded against it as if trying to smash through her ribs and escape.

*Go away!*

Maybe he's already gone.

I can't just stand here.

She gazed up at the guard chain. It was in place. She could open the door just a few inches, enough to look out.

No. No she couldn't.

But even as she told herself she didn't have the nerve, she saw her hand lift slowly toward the knob. Her numb fingers curled around it.

I can't do this!

She began to turn the knob and it pulsed against her palm as the door suddenly quaked. She jerked her hand away, lurched backwards. Blow after blow struck the door, shaking it in its frame.

Then it stopped.

'I . . . WANT . . . YOU!!!'

'No!' she shrieked. 'Go away!'

She heard the whisper of rushing footfalls.

He's leaving!

Somewhere outside, a heavy door thunked shut. A car engine sputtered to life.

Cynthia dropped her poker. She threw herself against the door, clawed the chain free and pulled the door open wide.

In her driveway stood a long, black hearse.

She shook her head, wanting to scream but feeling strangled. She stumbled forward one step. Her bare foot came down on something soft and crumbly. She raised it and grabbed the doorframe. In the porch light, she saw that the stoop was littered with fresh soil. Staggering backwards, she reached for the door.

She saw the hand.

Nailed to the outside of her door. A severed hand, filthy and blood-drenched. Red gore hung from the stump of its wrist.

She covered her mouth and screamed. The hearse sped backwards. She lunged into her house and screamed again as a glob dropped from the hand. She swung the door shut. Its bottom edge smeared the meat over her carpet.

Meat? It looked like ground beef. She crouched down for a closer look.

Raw hamburger!

Gasping for breath, she jerked the door open again. The wrist of the nailed hand was hollow. She touched it.

Rubber.

A rubber hand.

She almost laughed, but she cried instead.

# Chapter Fifteen

Lying on her side, Dani stared out at the sunlit pool. A beautiful summer morning. She listened to bird songs, heard the distant buzz of a power mower. The mild breeze carried a scent of grass and flowers. It felt cool on her bare shoulders. She pulled the sheet higher.

If only she hadn't asked Anthony to come over. The day could've been wonderful. Just her and Jack, lingering in bed, having breakfast by the pool, spending a few hours in the workshop, swimming later and relaxing in the sun.

Damn. That little invitation would end up ruining the day. She'd been an idiot to . . . no, it was the smart thing to do. Give the jerk what he wants, take the wind out of his sails. So far, at least, it seemed to be working; he hadn't bothered them since Thursday night.

He's probably staying home with Ingrid.

The thought made a chill creep up Dani's body. She rolled over. Jack was on his side, facing the other way. She snuggled against him, pressing her thighs to the backs of his legs, molding herself to the warm curves of his buttocks and back, kissing the nape of his neck.

'Mmm,' he said.

'Good morning.'

'Mmm. What time is it?'

'Eight.'

'So we have an hour before Terrible Tony arrives.'

'A whole hour.'

'Good. Just enough time for a swim, a shower, and breakfast.' She slid her hand over his hip. Her fingertips brushed the coils of his pubic hair. 'Swim? I'd rather do something else.'

'Yeah?'

'Yeah.'

Dani lay on her back, arms and legs stretched out, letting the soft breeze cool her sweat. She felt used up and wonderful.

The shower made a quiet whispering sound like a wind in a forest.

She didn't have to move until Jack was through.

She glanced at the alarm clock. Twenty to nine. Just enough time for a quick shower and a cup of coffee before Anthony came.

Terrible Tony.

She smiled. Jack could be so serious sometimes, but his sense of humor was always lurking nearby, ready to spring out and surprise her.

The doorbell rang.

Her stomach tightened. 'Oh shit,' she muttered.

She looked at the clock. Eighteen minutes early. If it's him.

Sitting up, she used the sheet to dry herself. The bell rang again as she climbed off the bed. She stepped into her panties and white shorts, and pulled on her sleeveless sweatshirt as she hurried down the hall.

She opened the door.

'Greetings,' Anthony said. He held out a single, red rose.

'Why, thank you.'

He lowered his head. The ink eye had been washed off.

'Come on in, Anthony.'

He stepped into the foyer and looked both ways.

'Jack'll be along in a minute.'

'I knew he was here. I saw his car.'

'Would you like some coffee?'

'Does he live with you?'

'Yes,' she said without hesitation. It was none of his business, but she didn't want him to know that Jack might only be here on a temporary basis. She hoped it would become permanent, but . . .

'You're not married, are you?'

'No.'

'I didn't think so.'

'I'll put the coffee on.' She shut the door. Anthony followed her toward the kitchen. She felt uneasy walking ahead of him. 'Have you had any breakfast?' she asked, looking back at him.

'I don't eat it.'

'I'll heat up some bagels. You're welcome to join us.'

He sat at the kitchen table while Dani filled the coffee maker.

'Do you live near here?'

'Not far.'

'In an apartment?'

'I'll have a house in another year.'

'That'd be nice. Houses are nice. The prices are outlandish, though.'

'I'll be rich by then.'

'Well, I hope so.' She took bagels out of the freezer, unwrapped them and put them in the toaster oven. 'Do you work?'

'I'm the Chill Master.'

'I mean, how do you make a living?'

'I'm your assistant.'

Before Dani could find a response, Jack grinned at her from behind the bar. 'Been replaced already, have I?'

*Thank God*, she thought. Reinforcements.

Jack entered the kitchen. 'Hi there, Tony. A little early, aren't you?'

'Am I?' he asked, narrowing his eyes.

'I'd say so, yes. I barely had time to put on my face.'

Looking annoyed, Anthony turned to Dani. 'I think we should discuss the terms of my employment.'

'Nobody's mentioned employment,' Dani said.

'Just you, Tony.'

'What we talked about,' Dani explained, 'is showing you a little about how we work, getting you started in the right direction. Just as a favor.'

'You said you'd hire me.'

'No I didn't.'

'She didn't,' Jack said. He smiled at Dani. 'Shall we ask him to leave?'

She shook her head. 'Look, Anthony, I offered to help you. I think you probably have potential, but there are hundreds of people out there more qualified than you, people who've studied, who've worked long hard hours to develop their talents, and I'd be a complete jerk to hire you over one of them. Besides which, I already have an assistant.'

Jack nodded.

'But the offer's still open. If you want, you can spend the morning with us and we'll show you a few things.'

'Won't even charge tuition,' Jack added.

'We'll see how it goes today,' Dani said. 'If it works out all right, we'll discuss doing it again.'

Leaning back, Anthony folded his hands across the front

of his black turtle-neck. 'I guess that's all right,' he said.

Dani poured the coffee. Jack carried two mugs to the table and sat down.

'Cream or sugar?' Dani asked.

Anthony shook his head.

Jack took a sip. 'So, tell me, scared the shit out of anyone lately?'

The boy grinned. 'Oh yes.'

'Want to tell us about it?'

Dani turned away to check on the bagels.

'I can't tell. I'm saving up all my tricks for my first feature.'

'Good idea. Keep 'em close to the vest. We Hollywood types love to steal hot ideas.'

'I know.'

'Should we let him in on our hot project?'

Dani shrugged.

'Oh, why not. The working title is *An American Were-oaf in Sardi's*.'

'Or *The Slobbering*,' Dani said.

'See, there's this guy . . .'

Anthony refused a bagel, but drank two cups of coffee while they ate. When they finished, Dani asked Jack to show him the workshop. She went into the bathroom, glad to be away from Anthony. She undressed and reached for the shower handle. Then she changed her mind. As much as she wanted to postpone returning, she knew it would be unfair to leave Jack alone with him for so long. She cleaned herself with a damp washcloth, brushed her teeth, and brushed the tangles out of her hair. Then she got dressed and headed for the workshop.

Jack and Anthony were at the far end, in front of a shelf lined with white plaster face molds.

'These are negative molds,' Jack said. 'We use them to cast positive molds out of celastic. That's a silicone rubber material. It's fairly rigid, but flexible, and . . .' He stopped and smiled at Dani.

Anthony was smiling, too. He looked eager and happy. 'This stuffs great,' he said.

'Do you recognise any of the faces?'

He turned back to them, and shook his head. 'It's hard to tell.'

Dani stepped up beside him. 'This one's Adrienne Barbeau. Joe Spinell. Jamie Lee Curtis. This is Michael Fisher, who gets his head shot off in *Midnight Screams*, and the last one is me. I've got a small role in *Screams*, too. I also get my head blown off.'

'You're *in* the movie?'

'For about ten minutes,' she said, noticing his surprise. Was it an act? He must've known about her role, already, if he took Ingrid.

'This is Bill Washington,' Jack said, and lifted down both halves of the actor's mold. 'We have to make a prosthetic head of him for Monday.'

'Why don't we do a cast of Anthony's first?' Dani suggested. 'Would you like that?'

'Sure!'

'We'll give you the full treatment, and make a head for you at the same time we do Bill's. That way, you can see the whole process.'

They led Anthony to a straight-backed chair, and had him sit down.

'Would you like to be screaming?'

'That'd be great.'

'Okay. Well do it with your mouth and eyes open.'

Jack turned on a gooseneck lamp and tipped it to shine on Anthony's face.

'You're not wearing contacts?'

'No.'

'You want to get the eyedrops and lenses, Jack?' While he went to the workbench, Dani explained the process. 'We'll be covering your head completely with alginade for the first impression. Any trouble with claustrophobia?'

'No.'

'Well, it only takes about three minutes to dry. It's a bit cold and uncomfortable, but it doesn't last long. We'll put in drops to anesthetize your eyes, and give you a couple of scleral contact lenses to protect them. Okay?'

'Sure,' he said, but his smile faltered.

For just a moment, Dani forgot all the trouble he'd caused. He was a teenaged boy, nervous and vulnerable, trying to be brave. She squeezed his shoulder gently. 'Don't worry, it won't hurt.'

He gazed up at her.

He no longer looked worried.

He looked adoring.

Dani let her hand drop. She wanted to take a step backwards, but Anthony's eyes held her like an embrace.

What have I done? she thought. My God, what have I done?

'Here we go,' Jack said.

His presence surprised her. 'Right,' she said, and felt as if she'd been snapped out of a trance. 'All set, Anthony?'

'I'm ready.'

'You put the eyedrops in, Jack. I'll get the alginade.'

The rest of the morning, she felt the difference in Anthony. The brief, sympathetic touch had changed him. He acted intensely interested in every detail of the work, but he studied Dani's face more often than he watched the procedures. He looked at her as if infatuated. The bitter sharpness was gone from his voice. He stood close to her, sometimes brushing her arm as if by accident.

While they were applying makeup to the finished heads, Anthony asked to use her bathroom. Dani told him where to find it, and he left.

'Want me to go out and keep an eye on him?' Jack asked.

'You can't very well do that.'

'He may do some snooping.'

'He had plenty of chance to do that the other day.'

'The other day, he wasn't so hung up on you.'

'Hung up?'

'Yeah. The kid's obviously fallen for you. I don't particularly blame him; you're easy to fall for.'

'Thanks.'

'But I don't much like the idea.'

'Neither do I.'

'What'll we do?'

'I don't know,' Dani said. 'It's a complication I hadn't counted on. I sure don't want to encourage him, but I don't want to dump on him, either.'

'Let's give him his head and send him home.'

'That won't be the end of it. As far as he's concerned, today's just the start. I think we'd be better off if we play along with him, ask him to come back but not till next Saturday.'

'I don't think he'll be happy about that.'

'We'll just explain that we're too busy during the week, and if he bugs us before Saturday, it's all off.'

'You're willing to have him as a permanent fixture on Saturdays?'

'Look, we can't just tell him to shove off. We'll be right back where we started.'

'When we started, he just wanted to get into special effects. Now, I think he wants you. It's only gonna get worse if we string him along.'

'Next, he'll want you.' Dani grinned, but Jack didn't.

'You've got it all wrong. He wants to *be* me.'

Dani felt a cold tremor in her stomach. 'Did you have to say that?'

'I didn't have to. You already knew it.'

The door from the kitchen opened, and Anthony came in. Dani forced herself to smile at him. 'Well, I think we're about ready to wrap it up for today.'

'It's not even noon,' he said.

'We have some errands to run this afternoon.'

'I'll go with you.'

'No you won't,' Jack said.

Anthony stiffened and glared at him. He turned to Dani, his eyebrows lifting. '*You'll* let me come, won't you?'

'I think we should call it quits for today.'

'I won't be in the way.'

'Jack and I want to be alone.'

'Oh. What about tomorrow?'

'Tomorrow's Sunday.'

'That's all right.'

'We don't work on the Sabbath,' Jack said with a slight smirk.

'We have plans,' Dani said.

'Okay,' he muttered.

Jack picked up the duplicate of Anthony's head, and handed it to him.

'Come on by next Saturday,' Dani said, 'and we'll go over some more techniques.'

His lips peeled back as if he were in pain. *'Next Saturday?'*

'Same time, same station,' Jack said.

'That's *years*!'

'It's a week,' Jack said.

Dani opened the door, and they followed her into the kitchen. 'It'll be here sooner than you think.'

'I was thinking, you know, you'd take me to the studio and stuff.'

'I'd like to,' Dani lied, 'but it's against the rules.'

'You need a union card,' Jack added.

Anthony shook his head.

Dani led the way to the front door and opened it. 'I think it went really well today; You did a great job.'

'Yeah,' Jack said. 'Now you know how to make a decent head.' He tapped the nose of the head Anthony clutched under his arm. 'That's sure a far cry from the one you left on the diving board. Scarier, too.'

'Very funny.'

'If you have any spare time,' Dani said, 'drop by a library and pick up some books on cosmology, anatomy, that kind of thing. They'll help. And we'll see you next Saturday at nine.'

'Okay. Well, thanks.' He stared at Dani's face as if to memorise it.

She smiled nervously. 'Bye, Anthony.'

He nodded, and turned away. He walked slowly toward the driveway, his head low.

Dani shut the door. 'Whew.'

'Alone at last.'

'I'm sweatin' like a huncher. Let's go for a swim.'

'What about those errands?'

'What errands?' she asked, and pulled off her sweatshirt.

# Chapter Sixteen

'No, he's not here just now,' said the woman's voice.

Linda eased the screen door open and peered into the house. A picture window filled the living room with sunlight. The woman wasn't there. Maybe in the kitchen.

'I don't expect him back for quite a while, Helen. He's off playing softball.'

Linda slipped inside. She inched the door shut.

'Certainly. I'll have him call you the minute he gets in. He's already told us all he knows, though. He hasn't seen Joel since Wednesday.'

Linda walked quietly to the staircase.

'He's as concerned as the rest of us . . . I know, I'd be a basket case, too. If I were you, I'd call the police.'

With a hand on the banister to steady herself, she climbed the stairs.

'No, I'm not suggesting anything of the sort, Helen. You're the one who's so sure he didn't just run away . . . I know he's not that kind of boy. That's why I think you should call the police. I wouldn't have waited *this* long, if it was Arnold.'

The woman's voice faded as Linda reached the top of

the stairs. A door stood open to her left, another to her right. The corridor ran back alongside the stairwell with book shelves on the wall opposite the balustrade, and two doors near the end.

She glanced through the doorway on her right. A waist-high platform filled most of the room. An HO setup, complete with green hills, tunnels and bridges, a lake made of tinted glass, a little village with a train station. An assortment of miniature trains stood motionless on the tracks.

Across the hallway was a large bathroom.

Linda moved on. She heard footsteps below. With a glance over the railing, she assured herself that no one was on the stairs. She hurried toward the end of the corridor, and peeked into the room on her right.

A single bed. A cluttered desk and dresser. Plastic ship models on shelves. A poster of Reggie Jackson when he was still a Yankee.

It had to be Arnold's room.

Stepping inside, she quietly pressed the door shut. She went directly to the desk. On top were half a dozen school textbooks, a blue binder, scattered pens and pencils, a ruler, a gooseneck lamp, a pocket calculator, a few loose paper clips, but no envelopes or stationery.

She lifted a straight-backed chair away from the desk and set it down gently. Then she slid open the top drawer. Near the front was a gum eraser, a compass, a sheath knife, a rubber mouse, a Kennedy half-dollar. To the rear, the drawer was heaped with papers, envelopes, and a few picture postcards.

With trembling fingers, she picked a glassy card off the pile. She stared at the grim, greenish face of the Frankenstein monster.

She flipped it over. The back was scrawled with pencil.

Howdy!
Spent today at Universal Studios. Saw the old Bates house from Psycho. Castle Dracula was pretty neat, tho it didn't scare me any. You ought to get out here.

So long.<br>C.M.

C.M.?
Linda would've bet the card came from Tony. Who the hell was C.M.?
Besides, it had no return address.
She dropped it, and picked up an envelope. In the corner was a return address written in shaky letters:

C.M.
8136 La Mar St #210
Hollywood, CA 90038

Spreading open the envelope, she pulled out a folded sheet of paper. Strips hung off one side, like fringe where it had been torn from a spiral notebook. She opened it and read:

Howdy,
How're things in Dullsville? Just got me a place to live and a job all in the same day. Its part time at a Jack-in-the-Box. Where I work, not where I live. Ha ha!
    Been seeing lots of movies. Theirs hundreds of theaters hear and some of them just show oldies all the time. Caught Chainsaw again last night. Its great hear.

Haven't run into Dick Smith or Rick Baker or any of those guys as of yet, but I hope to before to long. I'm going to be big, pal, just you wait and see. You can say you knew me way back when, or even better, you ought to come out here and I'll get you in the movies.

So long from Hollywood.

Your pal,
The Chill Master

It *had* to be Tony.

C.M. Chill Master. What an asshole.

Linda folded the letter, slipped it back inside the envelope, and stuffed the envelope into the rear pocket of her shorts.

She heard voices. She heard footsteps. Arnold came into the room wearing sneakers, and sat on the bed to take them off. He dropped his soiled white socks. Standing, he lowered his jeans and shorts. He hopped out of them. He left them on the floor and walked to his closet. Then he went away.

Linda squirmed out from under the bed, pushing aside his shoes and socks. He'd left the door open. Keeping her eyes on it, she hurried to the closet. She slipped a plaid sports coat off its hanger and put it on backwards so it covered her T-shirt and shorts like a smock. Then she squeezed in behind the sliding doors.

She waited. Her heart pounded so hard it made her feel sick. Her tongue felt huge and rough in the dryness of her mouth. Sweat trickled down her face. She switched Arnold's knife to her other hand and wiped her slippery palm on the jacket.

Finally, he came back. The bedroom door latched shut.

Linda peered out at him.

His hair was wet and tangled. He took off a pale blue bathrobe and tossed it on his bed. He looked very muscular. His skin was tanned dark, his buttocks as white as loaves of unbaked bread. Squatting, he picked up his jeans. He dug into a pocket, came out with a comb, and dropped the jeans.

Linda eased her head out farther and watched him cross to the dresser. He stopped in front of it. Both hands went up, one combing while the other patted his hair in place. This would be a good time to go for him – except for the mirror. She drew her head in.

The comb made a quiet clatter. A few seconds passed. His quiet voice said, 'One . . . two . . . three . . .'

She looked again. Arnold was on the floor, hands clasped behind his head, sitting up. His back curled. He touched his elbows to his knees. 'Four,' he said, and lowered his back to the carpet. His penis, the size of a thumb, was pointed at the ceiling. His rising back blocked Linda's view. 'Five.' Down again.

She took a careful sidestep. Another. Now she was clear of the sliding door. She knelt.

'Eight,' Arnold said, and started down. His back pressed the carpet. He took a breath and gritted his teeth as if to hold it in. His stomach muscles flexed. His penis wobbled. He sat up, hands pulling at his head. Linda scuttled forward. Arnold's elbows brushed his slightly upraised knees. 'Nine.' He dropped back. His damp hair rubbed Linda's thighs, and she smiled down at him. His eyes opened wide. His mouth sprang open.

Linda thrust her open left hand against his mouth and leaned in, putting her weight on it, trapping his folded hands under his head and muffling his outcry as she swung her right arm down. The five-inch blade punched into him just above the navel. His knees flew up. His hands escaped and reached for Linda's wrist but she jerked the knife out and raised it high. He tried to catch the blade. It stabbed his right palm, ripped open his forearm and plunged into his belly. The impact splashed blood high. It sprayed Linda's face. Arnold clutched her wrist. His hand was slippery and trembling, but his grip was strong enough to stop her from pulling out the knife. So she twisted it hard. He screamed into her left hand and his fingers fluttered open. She tugged the knife out.

His body was twisting and bucking, his arms flopping aimlessly, unable to stop her. She pounded the knife in. She found herself counting each time the hilt stopped her thrust. Eight, nine, ten, eleven. At twenty, she plunged the knife into his throat. She left it there, and rubbed off her fingerprints with the jacket.

She was exhausted. She got to her feet and pulled off the blood-soaked jacket. It had done its job well; there was not a drop on her own clothes. Using Arnold's bathrobe, she wiped blood from her thighs and knees, from her hands. It left them with a rusty stain. She turned to the mirror. Her face was speckled and dripping. Her wig, too. She cleaned them as well as she could.

Listening at the door, she heard nothing. She eased it open and checked the corridor. It was deserted. The sounds of a man and woman talking came from below.

She hurried to the bathroom. The air felt warm and moist. The top of the mirror was still fogged from Arnold's shower. She shut the door. Standing at the sink, she used soap and water to wash off the remaining bloodstains. She dried herself with a soft white towel.

Then she crept downstairs. The voices seemed to come from the kitchen. The living room was deserted. She eased open the screen door and stepped outside.

She crossed the lawn with her head down, rubbing her forehead to hide her face from any neighbor or passerby who might chance to see her. Once she reached the sidewalk, she let her hand down.

She noticed a kid across the street. He was hunched over the handlebars of his tricycle, pedaling furiously up his driveway. He didn't look back.

A car approached from the rear. She turned her head away until it passed, then scratched an eyebrow to shield her face from the rearview mirror.

At the end of the block, she walked around the corner to her parent's car. She climbed in. It felt like an oven. She winced as the vinyl upholstery scorched the backs of her legs, but smiled in spite of the pain when she heard the crumble of paper in her rear pocket.

Tony's letter.

With Tony's new address.

# Chapter Seventeen

Sweat and suntan oil streamed down Dani's skin as she sat up. She stretched, enjoying the feel of the late afternoon breeze.

Jack, on the lounger a few feet away, seemed to be asleep. His hands were folded behind his head. His chest rose and fell slowly, skin glistening under his curly layer of hair. A puddle had formed in the depression of his navel. Its gleaming surface shimmered from the motion of his breathing.

Dani was tempted to go to him. He could use a little extra sleep, though, after spending so much of the past few nights awake. Restraining herself, she swung her feet down to the concrete and stood up. She walked silently, taking deep breaths of the breeze, trying to ignore the tickle of droplets skidding down her hot skin.

At the shallow end, she sat on the edge near the Jacuzzi and lowered her legs. She said 'Oooh' as the water closed around her feet and calves. It was 80°F. but felt like the dregs of an ice bucket. After the first chill passed, she scooted forward and dropped into the waist-high water. She took a few steps, gritting her teeth as the bottom slanted down and the water climbed to her shoulders. An agony that she usually avoided by taking the cold shock in one quick dive from the side. But a dive might've disturbed Jack's sleep.

The things I'll do for him, she thought, and smiled.

In a moment, the water felt cool and pleasant. Letting her legs drift up, she did a silent breast-stroke. She neared the far end of the pool, started to make a wide turn, and saw Jack sit up.

'You're awake!'

'Who can sleep through all this splashing?'

'I didn't make a *sound*!'

He laughed softly. 'Actually, I haven't been asleep.'

'Not at all?'

'Not that I know of.'

'Humph!' Flinging up an arm, she caught an edge of the diving board. She raised herself enough to grab it with the other hand, and hung there, half out of the water, facing Jack. 'Come on in, I'll race you.'

'You always win.'

'You wouldn't want me holding back, would you?'

'It'd be the polite thing to do.'

'Want to tie one hand behind my back?'

'How about both?' he asked, and climbed off the lounge. He walked toward the diving board.

'I could drown,' Dani said.

'I'd save you.'

'You'd like that.'

'Likely.' The diving board wobbled as he walked out on it.

Dani swung herself sideways and clutched the end of the board with both hands. She hung on tightly as it shook.

Jack sat down, his legs dangling over the sides. Leaning forward, he looked down at Dani. 'You're beautiful when you're wet.'

'Thanks. What am I dry?'

'Ugly as sin.'

'Aren't you a charmer.'

His toes flicked against Dani's armpits.

With a yelp, she yanked herself up. 'You beast!' she cried.

Jack grinned.

Chin resting on the tip of the board, Dani bared her teeth at him.

He patted her head. 'Eaaasy, girl. Easy.'

'I'm gonna *get* you.'

'Oh, I hope so.'

'Can't tickle *me* and get away with it.'

'I'm not ticklish.'

'You'll be *sor*-ry,' she sang. Drawing her knees up toward the board, she tilted her head away and let go. Her back smashed the water. Blowing air out her nose, she kicked to the surface. 'Get you?'

'You're vicious!' he said, laughing as he raised his wet legs. 'That water's cold!' He got to his hands and knees, and peered down at her.

Lunging up, Dani grabbed the end of the board. She swung up her legs, hooked her feet over the edges, and pressed herself against its warm underside. She wrapped her arms over the top, and smiled at Jack. 'Even?' she asked.

'Even.' He lay down flat and kissed her. 'Something has come between us,' he said.

Dani nodded. 'I don't know about you, but I'm feeling board.'

He kissed her again.

'How about coming in now?' she asked.

He sighed as if frustrated. 'I'd like to, but I've got to get going.'

'*Going?*'

'I'm sorry. I meant to tell you sooner, but . . . hell, I really don't want to go.'

'Then don't.'

'I have to.'

'I've already got two lamb chops defrosted. I thought, you know, we'd barbeque them and . . .'

'It's a dinner engagement.'

'Oh.' She unhooked her feet, dropped into the water, and swam to the pool's edge. She boosted herself up. She walked across the concrete, leaving a wet trail, and sat down on her lounge. Picking up a towel, she began to dry herself.

Jack sat down facing her. 'I'm really sorry about this.'

'It's all right.' The towel was soft and comforting on her face. 'Who's the lucky . . . party?'

'No one you know.'

'Is it a she?'

'It's a she.'

'Your sister, I hope.'

'Methinks the lady's jealous.'

'Is it a date?'

Nodding, Jack leaned forward and braced his elbows on his knees. 'There is this other girl.'

'Oh man,' Dani muttered.

'Her name's Margot. She's a receptionist over at MGM. I met her there about a year ago, and we've been seeing each other on a fairly regular basis.'

'Is it . . . serious?'

'It's damn serious to her.'

'How about you?'

Jack knuckled a drop of sweat off his nose. 'A funny thing happened. I got a job working for this special lady and I wasn't so interested in Margot any more. First thing I knew, I was in love with this lady. She was my boss, though, so I kept it to myself and went on seeing Margot.'

His words warmed away Dani's dread. She moved over to his lounge and sat beside him. He rubbed the back of her neck.

'Anyway, all this with you came up pretty suddenly. The last Margot knew, she and I were still going together.'

'She doesn't know about me?'

'I haven't talked with her since Tuesday. That's when we made plans for tonight.' His hand roamed down Dani's back. 'Then, the next day, bang. Everything changed.'

'I didn't even know you *had* a girlfriend.'

'She's probably going nuts wondering where I've been the past few days.'

'You should've called her.'

'I know. I'm not real handy at unpleasant chores. Besides, I figure it's only fair to let her know in person.'

'You're going to tell her about me tonight?'

'That's the plan.'

'That's awful.'

'Would you rather I didn't?'

'You'd better!'

'I will. I'll wait till after dinner, though. Don't want to ruin her appetite.'

'You'll come over afterwards?'

'It might be late.'

'I'll wait up.'

Dani kissed him good-bye at the door. 'Good luck,' she said.

He made a disgusted face. 'Why don't you come along?'

'Wouldn't *that* be charming.'

'Well, see you later.'

'You won't be too late?'

'I should be back by midnight at the latest. I hope.'

'Okay.'

He left. Dani shut the door. She started to hook the guard chain, but hesitated. If she fastened it, Jack wouldn't be able to let himself in.

I'll let him in, she thought, and pressed the disk into its slide.

Or maybe I won't.

Midnight. Dinner shouldn't take more than a couple of hours. Jack had said the reservations were for eight o'clock. What was he planning between ten and midnight? When *was* he planning to break the news? Right after dinner? Or right after . . . *One last time, for old time's sake.*

She felt disgusted with herself, imagining such a thing. Only

137

a jerk would make love to a woman as a prelude to dumping her. Not Jack. But she could easily see him embracing her, consoling her after breaking the news, one thing leading to another, and maybe in the arms of this Margot he would decide not to give her up, after all.

The thoughts frightened Dani. She was leaning back against the door, breathing hard, her heart hammering, her mouth dry.

To lose Jack so soon . . .

What the hell am I thinking? It's the other girl who's getting dumped tonight, not me.

Poor girl. Christ, the poor damn girl.

Dani took a deep, trembling breath and pushed herself away from the door. She felt weak as she walked into the kitchen.

No good to dwell on that stuff.

Ninety per cent of worry is wasted effort, getting yourself all worked up over matters that never happen.

What about the other ten per cent?

Screw it.

*Please. Once more. For old time's sake.*

She looked at the kitchen clock. Just five. Seven hours till midnight.

I'll go to a movie, she decided. A double feature. Right after dinner.

It seemed like a good idea, and cheered her up. She took a glass from the cupboard, filled it with ice, and made herself a vodka and tonic.

Some women eat to cure their blues. Some buy new clothes. But Dani had found, over the years, that nothing worked better for her than a trip to the movies. It was an adventure. No matter how often she went or how rotten the films, it was always a treat.

Sipping her drink, she stepped around to the other side of the bar. She hopped onto a stool and opened the newspaper to the entertainment section. Her eyes roamed down the ads, seeking out familiar theaters.

She'd already seen most of the films playing nearby. Then she spotted a double bill playing in Culver City; *Zombie Invasion* and *Night Creeper*. She'd never heard of the first, but Larry Holden, a friend from her old job at EFX, had worked on *Night Creeper*.

She phoned the theater. With the next showing of *Zombie Invasion* at seven o'clock, she had two hours to eat, change, and get to the theater.

Setting down her glass, she stared across the kitchen at the two lamb chops she'd taken out for dinner. Her stomach fluttered at the reminder of Jack's absence, of his date with Margot. 'You guys thawed out yet?' she asked. She climbed off the bar stool and went to the counter. She poked one of the chops. Her finger dented the cool meat. 'Guess so.' They would save till tomorrow night, but she was hungry and she'd been looking forward to the lamb.

She put one into the refrigerator, picked up her drink as she passed the bar, and went out back. An hour and a half before time to leave gave her plenty of time to barbeque. She could shower and change while the coals heated.

She rolled her Weber grill away from the wall. Crouching, she opened the vents at the bottom of the drum. Ashes spilled out, dusting her hand. She brushed them off and removed the lid, then lifted out the blackened grill. The grate inside was scattered with powdery charcoal from last time. With tongs, she arranged them into a pile. They would probably be sufficient for broiling one chop, but she didn't want to chance it so she hefted the bag of fresh briquets and dumped in some more. They tumbled and rolled down the heap of gray coals. Putting the bag aside, she used the tongs to set them back on the pile.

A match box was propped against the quart can of charcoal lighter. She picked up both. The can was heavy, almost full. She set the match box on the side tray and flipped open the red plastic cap of the fluid.

She squeezed out a long stream, waving it back and forth over the charcoals. It gave the fresh ones a shiny coat, turned the ashen ones black.

'Dani?'

Her hand jumped.

She tipped the can up and swung around.

He was at the side of the house, leaning in over the gate, a smile on his white, cadaverous face.

'Tony,' she muttered.

# Chapter Eighteen

'What are you doing?' he asked.

At a loss for words, Dani raised the can of charcoal lighter.

'Barbeque?'

She nodded.

'Can I talk to you?' Reaching over the redwood gate, he flicked up the latch. The gate swung open.

Dani licked her dry lips. 'You'd really better leave, Tony.'

He looked hurt. 'I won't get in your way. I promise. I just want to talk to you for a minute.'

He walked toward her. She nodded, trying to smile, well aware that she couldn't force him to go away.

His sunken eyes lowered, studying Dani as he approached.

Her striking bikini was one she never wore in public: a few wisps of filmy orange nylon held in place by knotted cords. She, ached to cover herself, but didn't want Tony to know how vulnerable she felt. She set the fuel can on the tray. With effort, she resisted an urge to fold her arms over her breasts. She picked up her drink and took a sip.

'So, Tony . . .' Her words sounded shaky. She took a deep breath and projected, her voice coming out firm. 'I thought we'd agreed on next Saturday.'

'I know. I'm really sorry to bother you. The thing is, I haven't made many friends since I've been here . . .'

Big surprise, Dani thought.

'And I didn't want to be alone. Not right now.' He looked at her with troubled, pleading eyes.

'Is something wrong?'

'I . . . I just found out my . . . my mother died.'

'Oh no. God, I'm sorry.' She stepped forward and took Tony's hand. She guided him to one of the lounges. 'Here, sit down.'

He lowered himself onto it and stared at the concrete.

'Let me get you something. A beer?'

'Okay.'

She rushed into the house, grabbed a can of Coors from the refrigerator, and hurried outside. Tony didn't look up as she lifted her own drink from the barbeque tray and walked over to him. She gave him the beer. She sat down, facing him. His bony fingers popped the tab, but he didn't take a drink. He turned the can slowly, staring at it.

'Had she been ill?' Dani asked.

He shook his head. 'It was very sudden. A heart attack. Dad said she was just standing there washing up the lunch dishes, and keeled over. She was dead by the time the ambulance arrived.' He shrugged again, and took a sip of beer.

'That's awful, Tony.'

'At least . . . it was over fast. I mean, that's better than a long illness, I guess.'

'Yeah,' Dani muttered. Her own parents were both alive, but she could easily imagine the devastation of losing one. She felt miserable for Tony. 'Were you very close to her?'

'We fought a lot. She didn't want me coming out here.'

'You're from New York?'

'Yeah. Claymore.'

'Will you be going back for the funeral?'

'I don't think so. Dad offered to pay my fare, but . . . what's the point?' He gazed at the top of his beer can, looking forlorn.

'Tell you what. Do you like lamb?'

'Sure.'

'It just so happens that I've got an extra lamb chop. How about staying for supper?'

'I don't think Jack would like that.'

'He won't be joining us.'

'He won't?' Tony frowned as if perplexed. 'Did something happen?'

'He's just got a previous engagement. He'll be back later.'

*By midnight.*

*Please. For old time's sake.*

142

'Why don't you go ahead and start the fire, Tony, while I get cleaned up a bit?'

'Start the fire?'

'Yeah. You know.'

'Maybe *you'd* better do that.'

'It's simple. All you've gotta do . . .'

'No, I can't. I'm sorry. I'll go away if you want, but I can't do that.'

'I'll start it.'

'I'm sorry.'

'That's all right.'

'I caught on fire once. That's why.' He pulled a leg of his black trousers up to his knee. The inner side of his calf was wrinkled and pink with scar tissue 'See?'

'I'll start the fire,' Dani repeated.

He got up and followed her, but stood far back as she squirted more charcoal lighter onto the briquets.

She struck a match.

'Be careful,' Tony said.

'I'm an old hand at this,' she assured him, holding the flame to a coal. When that one caught, she moved the match to another and another until fire ringed the pile. 'That ought to do it.'

She picked up the grill and set it in place. The black grease on its bars hissed and smoked in the flapping blaze.

She turned to Tony. 'All set. Have another beer if you want. They're in the refrigerator. I'll be back in a few minutes.'

'Okay.'

Nodding, she turned away from him. She used the living-room entrance, slid the screen door shut behind her, and left it unlocked so he could come in for beer.

She hoped that was all he would do.

Under the circumstances, she expected him to behave.

She couldn't trust him completely, though. When she shut herself inside the master bedroom, she snapped down the lock button. She closed the sliding glass door and locked it, then pulled the curtains.

Striding toward the bathroom, she saw herself in the full-length mirror – the orange bit of fabric hardly covering her pubic mound, the cord stretching around her bare hips to the brief triangle in back that left the sides of her buttocks exposed. My God, to think that she'd let Tony see her this way! And the top was no better.

The kid got an eyefull.

But at least he'd behaved himself. So far.

Hell, his mother had died. The last thing on his mind should be the state of Dani's undress.

Entering the bathroom, she pulled at the hanging strings of her bikini and slipped it off. She climbed into the tub.

Ten minutes later, dressed in top-siders, white jeans and a silken red aloha shin, Dani left her room. She walked down the corridor, wondering if there would be time to prepare rice. That'd be cutting it close. Only an hour left before it'd be time to leave. Unless she wanted to forget about the movies. No. If she didn't go, how would she ever get rid of . . . Beside her, a door sprang open. She flinched, head snapping toward it.

Tony, just inside the guest bathroom, leaped back.

'Geez, Tony!'

He let out a nervous laugh. 'Startled me.'

'Yeah?' She pressed a hand to her throbbing chest and swallowed hard.

'I hope it was all right,' he said. 'I had to . . . you know.'

'That's what it's for.'

As he stepped out of the bathroom, the corridor seemed to shrink, trapping Dani close to him. She turned away. Her arm swept against the wall as she started forward. Tony stayed beside her. She felt suffocated, but forced herself not to rush. A few more steps. A few more. Then some of the oppression lifted, dispelled by the brightness and open spaces of the living room. She felt as if she could breathe again, but Tony's presence in the house still felt wrong.

He shouldn't be in here.

Not with Jack gone.

'Did you get some more beer?' she asked.

'Yes. Thank you.'

'Well, let's see how the charcoal's doing.'

Tony hurried across the living room and slid open the screen. As Dani stepped through, he moved forward and she brushed against him. She pretended not to notice. She felt relieved to get outside.

At the barbeque, she saw that the edges of the fresh briquets had turned gray. She lowered a hand close to the grill. There was heat, but not quite enough. 'I guess it's about ready,' she said. 'Would you like a salad?'

Tony shook his bald head.

'I'd make rice, but there really isn't enough time. I have to be going pretty soon.'

'Where are you going?'

'There's a couple of films I need to see.'

'You're going to the movies?' he asked, his small eyes opening wide. 'Can I go with you?'

Dani tried not to grimace.

'Please? I'll even buy the tickets.'

'There's no need for that.'

'I'd like to. Really. You've been so nice to me.'

'You've probably already seen the movies, anyway.'

'What are they?'

'*Zombie Invasion* and *Night Creeper*.'

'Wow! When did *they* open?'

'Yesterday, I think.'

'Man, I've really been looking forward to *Night Creeper*!'

Tony was eager to drive.

'No, that's all right,' Dani said as they left the house. 'We'll take my car.'

'Come on. It'll be fun. Have you ever gone in a hearse?'

'No. And it's an experience I plan to avoid as long as possible.' She smiled at her joke. Tony didn't. His mother had just died. Dani suddenly blushed at her tactless remark. 'Anyway,' she said, 'that monster must eat up gas like there's no tomorrow.'

'It is pretty bad,' he admitted.

Dani climbed into her Rabbit, leaned across the seat and unlocked the passenger door. 'What ever possessed you to buy that thing?' she asked, passing it as she backed onto the road.

'It scares people.'

'Doesn't it scare you?'

'That's half the fun.' He turned in his seat to face her. 'It's a fifty-two, you know. It was hauling stiffs more than ten years before I was even born. I figured it all out: if it even carried just two a week, that's more than three thousand in thirty years. It was probably even more. Can you imagine all those bodies?'

'I'd rather not.'

'I've got a coffin in the back. A real nice mahogany one. Silk lining and everything. Sometimes, I sleep in it.'

'Wonderful.'

'Do you believe in ghosts?'

Dani shrugged.

'I do. Sometimes, I hear them when I'm driving.'

'Geez, Tony.'

'Moaning and groaning.'

'You're making that up.'

'No. Honest. And once, around midnight, a hand touched the back of my neck. I almost crashed. When I looked around, though, nobody was there.'

'Stop it, Tony. I'm serious. I don't want to hear this. If you keep it up, I'll turn the car around and that'll be it for the movies.'

'I just thought you'd be interested,' he said, sounding hurt.

'Some other time, all right?'

'Okay.' He sat forward and crossed his arms.

After a while, to break his gloomy silence, Dani asked about his favourite movies.

He immediately cheered up. '*Texas Chainsaw Massacre* is my all-time favorite.'

'Mine too.'

'Really?'

'Yep.'

'How'd you like it when he stuck that girl on the meat hook?'

'I cringed. I could almost feel it going in.'

'Yeah, me too. How about the old guy with the hammer?'

'Yuck.'

Dani found that she was enjoying their talk. As she drove down Crescent Heights toward Pico, they discussed Hooper's other works. The conversation shifted to films by Craven, Romero, Cronenburg, Carpenter. They talked about their favorite scene, Dani sometimes pointing out how certain effects were created.

'How about that shower scene in *Eyes of the Maniac*?'

'Oh, you saw that?'

'Four times,' Tony said. 'How'd you do that with the poker?'

'It actually penetrated a full body appliance we'd made up of Jenny – a dummy.'

'It looked so real.'

'Well, we made it from a cast of her. Basically, the same technique we used on you this morning, except we covered her entire body.'

'Naked?'

'Yeah.' She thought of Ingrid.

'What were the guts?'

'Guts.'

'Real guts?'

'Pig entrails. We get them from a slaughter house.'

He shook his head. 'You do all that stuff, but you don't want to hear about my death buggy.'

'That's right. I still don't.'

'What's the difference?'

'Films aren't real.'

'Pig guts are.'

'I don't enjoy that part. It's just necessary. Besides, I let Jack do most of the real grubby stuff.'

'It wouldn't bother *me*.'

'I'm sure. But anyway, that's the difference. Films are make-believe. Jenny Baylor didn't get skewered with a fireplace poker. After it was over, she went home. Not to a morgue.'

'But it scared the hell out of the audience. It grossed them out.'

'It's just toying with their imaginations. I mean, they let themselves believe the movie's real, but deep down they know it isn't.'

'So they aren't as scared.'

'They're *playing* at being scared.'

'That's why real life is better,' Tony said, and looked at her as if expecting a challenge.

'Skewering people?'

'No, scaring them. I've never hurt anybody. I just like to scare the shit out of them. Have you ever done that?'

'I've jumped out of the dark and yelled "Boo" a few times.'

'Isn't it a kick?'

'It's fun once in a while.'

'Doesn't it make you all shaky and excited. Hiding in the dark, just waiting to pounce?'

She shrugged.

'It turns *me* on.'

'Different strokes,' Dani muttered, and swung the car over to an empty stretch of curb. She glanced at her wristwatch. 'Five minutes to spare.'

Walking toward the ticket window, she opened her purse.

'I'll buy,' Tony said. He sounded determined.

Dani frowned. She doubted he had much money and she didn't want to feel obligated. On the other hand, a refusal might hurt his feelings. Men were usually strange that way. 'All right,' she said, and managed a smile. 'But you've gotta let me buy the popcorn.'

'A deal.'

My God, she thought, this is sounding like a date.

# Chapter Nineteen

Each carrying a tub of popcorn and a Coke, they made their way up a slanted corridor to the entrance of theater three. A sign above the door read 'ZOMBIE'.

For a Saturday night, the auditorium wasn't very crowded. They entered a row near the front, sidestepping past the knees of a teenaged couple.

'Here?' Tony asked.

Dani shook her head, not wanting to block the view of a black family already seated, though she felt a stir of anger at the parents. The baby in the woman's arms was probably too young to notice the violence and gore in these films, but the other two were older. They would notice, all right.

With a quick scan of the audience, she spotted at least fifteen other children. It wasn't unusual, but it never failed to sicken her.

They took seats as the theater lights dimmed. Opening her straw, Dani watched an ad for the *LA Times*. Then a trailer came on, warning the patrons not to flick their Bics 'in the thick of the flick'. It had seemed cute the first few times she'd seen it. She stabbed her straw through the slits of the Coke carton.

Tony's arm eased against her. She leaned sideways slightly to break the contact, and sipped her drink.

During the previews, a teenaged couple stepped into the next row. The boy sat down in front of Dani. For a moment, his head blocked the lower part of the screen. Then he leaned sideways,

150

out of Dani's way, and put his arm around the girl in front of Tony. They whispered a few words. They kissed.

Dani felt a stir of longing. If only Jack were here . . .

*Zombie Invasion* started. The title flashed onto the screen, but there were no opening credits. They'd been edited out. A bad sign.

A young, dark-haired woman was strolling among cemetery monuments at night. She wore a long, white nightgown and carried a sprig of flowers. The scene looked familiar to Dani. As the woman knelt to place her flowers on a grave, a hand burst from the soil and grabbed her throat. It pulled her down. The breaking dirt spilled away, and a ragged, decomposing corpse rose up, its mouth agape to bite her.

*Did you catch that dental work on Stanley the stiff? Bleah! I don't know about you, boys and girls, but I'd rather kiss a toad. This guy is definitely not going to turn into a handsome prince.*

It was Livonia's sultry voice, as vivid as her amazing cleavage in Dani's mind. Livonia, the seductive vampire hostess of *Monster Matinee*. Sunday afternoons. Four o'clock. Channel six.

*Here's a gem you can really sink your teeth into . . . or fangs, as the case may be.*

'I'll be damned,' Dani muttered.

Tony leaned close, his arm once again touching her. 'Huh?'

'I saw this turkey on *television* last month.'

'Television?'

'It was called *Bite of Death*. Livonia showed it.'

'Really?'

'Distributor's shenanigans,' she said. She felt cheated and angry, then just disappointed. To have this happen on top of Jack's surprise date and Tony popping up . . . She sighed.

At least the afternoon had been nice.

Leaning away from Tony, she slumped down in her seat, crossed a foot over one knee and dug into her popcorn. She tried to watch the film. The dubbing was lousy, lips moving out of sync with the words. Even when the characters were outside, their voices reverberated as if recorded in a concrete room.

The story had been a bore the first time she saw it, made bearable only by commercial interruptions and Livonia's sarcastic comments. Watching it now, Dani entertained herself by recalling Livonia's quips and thinking up her own.

She and Jack would be trading remarks in soft whispers if he were here, having a great time, enjoying this dud. She realised, with some astonishment, that they'd seen no movies together since becoming lovers. They'd viewed dailies before, they'd gone to some screenings, but that had been part of the job. So far, they'd never sat in the darkness like kids on a date, holding hands and snuggling.

Maybe tomorrow night.

A drive-in. Fantastic! One of those in the valley. Pick a double feature they didn't really care about, because even if you're not fooling around you can't get that involved with a drive-in movie. And she planned to fool around. Definitely.

They should take a blanket along.

She would wear a skirt.

As her mind lingered on the possibilities, she felt her skin heating, her heart speeding up, her nipples rising turgid against the caress of her shirt. The inseam of her jeans felt like a pressing hand.

Christ!

She sat up quickly to ease the pressure, and glanced at Tony, worried that he might somehow sense her arousal.

He turned toward her, eyebrows rising.

She forced a smile. 'How do you like it so far?'

'It stinks.'

'That's being generous.'

'I don't mind, though. I like being here.'

'Good. I'm glad.'

He stared at her. 'You were awfully nice to let me come along.'

'That's all right.' His gaze made Dani uncomfortable. She turned away. He kept on staring. She scraped up the last of her popcorn and ate it, watching the screen, trying to ignore him. She slipped a napkin from her shirt pocket. She wiped her hands, her mouth. She wadded it and dropped it into the tub. Tony's head was still turned toward her. She sipped the watery remains of her Coke, and finally looked at him. 'You're missing the movie.'

'You're so beautiful.'

His words made a cold place in Dani's stomach. 'Thank you,' she said.

A smile trembled on Tony's lips and he turned away.

Dani took a few slow, deep breaths to calm herself. Then she bent down and placed her empty containers on the floor. She sat up. Her shoulders pressed Tony's outstretched arm. She flinched at its touch, but forced herself not to lurch forward.

'Please, Tony.'

'Did I startle you?' He rubbed her right shoulder, making the silken shirt slide against her skin.

'We're not here for that. Please.'

'Why?'

'I *have* a boyfriend.'

'You mean Jack?' The hand continued to caress her.

'Yes.'

'He's not here.'

'That's not the point. Take your arm away.'

It stayed. 'Don't you like me?'

'Tony!'

It lifted, swung over her head, and settled on the armrest between them.

'Thank you.'

'I didn't mean any harm,' he said, sounding pitiful.

'I know.'

The boy in front of Dani looked back and frowned. 'Sorry,' she whispered. Turning back, he snuggled down again with his girlfriend.

Tony crossed his arms and stared at the screen.

'It's all right,' Dani whispered. 'Don't feel bad.'

He nodded slightly, but didn't look at her. He blinked. Tears spilled from the corners of his eyes, making shiny streaks down his face. He sniffed and wiped them away.

Reaching out, Dani patted his knee.

He gazed down at her hand. She turned it over. Tony's hand pressed against it. She closed her fingers and squeezed gently. 'Friends?' she asked.

'Yeah.'

She held him for a moment. With a final squeeze, she let go and folded her hands on her lap. Bringing him to the movies had been a great mistake. She should've known better. She'd been pushed into it, but she could have refused. A simple no. Instead of that, she'd let her sympathy get in the way and twist her perspective.

She felt a stir of anger. At herself. At Tony. He'd used his mother's death as a lever to force his way deeper into her life. It wasn't fair.

She should've listened to Jack's advice at the outset: don't feed it, maybe it'll go away.

And what does she do? She feeds it. Brilliant move. A little kindness goes a long way. Now this weird kid thinks he's her boyfriend.

And she feels like a jerk for upsetting him.

Just wonderful.

On the screen, a horde of grisly corpses was rampaging through an apartment complex, bashing down doors, dragging their hysterical victims from hiding places in closets and bathrooms, under beds, ripping off arms and legs, devouring flesh.

Not exactly Livonia's version. Most of the gore had been edited out for television.

A cut to the room of Elizabeth, the heroine. She was busy shoving a bureau against her door, not knowing that one of the zombies lurked inside her bathroom.

Almost over. Dani felt a tremor of dread. At intermission, she would have to face Tony in the light. What the hell would she say to him?

Tell him you have to use the restroom, and stay there till the next film starts.

That's a chicken way out.

The zombie swung open the bathroom door. He staggered toward Elizabeth. She was leaning forward against the bureau, unaware of his approach.

Lousy makeup on the zombie. It looked like a Halloween mask. The audience sounded frightened in spite of it.

Only a couple of minutes before intermission. Dani wiped her sweaty hands on her jeans.

Just explain, as gently as possible, that you appreciate his friendship . . .

The zombie reached out, his decomposing fingers only inches from the back of Elizabeth's neck.

You're flattered that he finds you attractive, but . . .

Tony sprang forward, growling, baring his plastic fangs, clutching the neck of the girl in front of him.

# Chapter Twenty

The girl shrieked.

Elizabeth shrieked.

The audience erupted with cries of fright and alarm. The boyfriend whirled around. Dani grabbed one of Tony's arms and tugged it away from the girl. 'Let go!' she snapped. He tried to jerk free, but she held on tight until the boy flung himself over the back of the seat.

The boy fell across Dani, knees digging into her thighs, elbow jabbing her cheek as he clambered over her. He hooked an arm around Tony's head. He twisted it, squirming on Dani, grunting each time he struck. Though she shoved at him, it seemed to have no effect. His fist thudded against Tony. He pounded very fast and very hard, as if he knew he didn't have much time. A horrible, gasping whine came from Tony.

'Stop!' Dani cried.

She dug her fingers into the boy's thick, greasy hair and yanked with all her strength. His head flew back and his body followed, his weight crushing Dani as he swayed, kneeling on her lap. She thrust against him. He fell sideways against his own seat back, crying out as the edge caught his ribs.

The theater lights came on.

The boy tried to untangle his legs from Dani's. She kicked at him until he managed to throw himself over the seat.

A husky, bearded man in a necktie grabbed the boy roughly and jerked him upright. 'Get out of here!'

'But . . .'

'Get! Don't let me catch you in here again!'

Muttering curses and glaring at Tony, the boy followed his girlfriend down the row. At the aisle, he turned around. 'Crazy fuckin' maniac!'

With those two leaving, everyone in the theater seemed to be gaping at Dani and the man.

'You too,' he snapped. 'Out of here!'

For the first time since the assault, she looked at Tony. He was sprawled crooked, half off his seat, arms and legs at strange angles that made Dani think of broken spiders. He was panting hard. His head hung to one side. Blood spilled from his open mouth, his split lips, his nostrils, gashes and a few scratches apparently made by a signet ring. One eye was nearly swollen shut.

Dani gazed at the damage, appalled. A minute ago, Tony's face had been intact. Now it looked worse than some of her makeup effects. But this wasn't makeup; the red stuff wasn't a sweet mix of Karo syrup. This was mauled flesh and real blood.

Looking at him, she felt sick and helpless.

'Come on, sister, move it. You're not outa here in two minutes, I'm calling the cops.'

She grabbed one of Tony's hands and pulled, but only managed to swivel him sideways a bit.

'All right,' the man said, sounding disgusted. 'Move aside. I'll get him.'

'Thank you,' Dani said. As she waited for him to come around the end of the row, someone tapped her shoulder. She turned. A teenaged boy squinted at her through thick glasses.

'You *are* her, aren't you?'

'Huh?'

Shaking his head in disbelief, he reached into a side pocket of a sports jacket too small for his girth and pulled out a Gary Brandner paperback. 'I'm a great admirer of your work, Miss Larson. I wonder if I might trouble you for your autograph.'

'Sure.' She glanced back. The man was pulling Tony out of the seat.

The boy ripped out a page and gave it to her along with the book and a pen.

'Make it to Milton,' he said.

She started to write. Her hand trembled.

'Come on, sister,' the man called from behind.

She continued to write, burning with embarrassment. She'd never been asked for an autograph before. She wished it hadn't happened now.

'I'm really into makeup, myself,' Milton said.

'I'm glad to hear it,' she managed. She gave back the page, the book and pen, then held out her hand. Looking surprised, he shook it. 'Good luck to you, Milton.'

He nodded and blinked and turned red. 'I hope you're not in any trouble,' he said.

'Thanks. I'll survive, I guess.' Then she turned away and hurried up the row.

By the time they reached the lobby, Tony was walking under his own power.

'I'm awfully sorry about this,' she told the man.

'Just keep your boyfriend away from here.'

'He's not . . .' Why bother? 'Yes sir,' she said.

He held the door open, and she hurried outside ahead of Tony. Near the curb, she waited for him to catch up.

'Geez, Tony.'

'You mad at me?' His words were fuzzy and distorted as if he had a bad cold.

'Oh, why should I be mad? I haven't had such fun in ages. It's great sport getting pounded, humiliated, and thrown out.'

Tony frowned and winced. 'Did he hurt you?'

'Not as much as he hurt you, obviously.'

They started walking. Tony moved slowly and stiffly, as if careful not to jostle himself.

'We'd better take you to emergency,' Dani said.

'No. I'm all right.'

'You look all right.'

He touched his face with both hands, exploring the damage. 'He got me pretty good. Think I'll have scars?'

'More than likely.'

'I hope so,' he said, and walked into a parking meter. He bounced off, crying out and staggering sideways. Dani braced herself against his impact. His shoulder bumped her chest and knocked her backwards a few steps. She threw her arms around him, holding him up.

'God, Tony.'

He moaned.

'Come on.' Hugging his arm, she helped him straighten up. They started walking. His upper arm was pressed tight against her breast. She suspected that he was very aware of it, in spite of his condition. She eased away just enough to get his arm off her breast, but continued to grip him with both hands until they reached the car. He leaned against it while she opened the rear door. Then she helped him in. He lay on his back and drew his knees up.

As she drove, Dani considered taking him to an emergency room. He didn't want that, though, and his injuries did seem superficial. Besides, she couldn't just drop him off and leave. He would need transportation back to her house.

Give him the taxi fare.

No, she couldn't do that. She'd have to wait with him, and she hated hospitals.

'Boy,' he said from the back seat. 'Did you hear that gal scream?'

'I heard.'

'She probably wet her pants.'

'Tony.'

'I really got her, huh?'

'I hope it was worth it.'

'It was great.'

'Don't you ever worry about the consequences of your little escapades?'

'Huh?'

'You not only got us both hurt and kicked out, you probably frightened that poor girl half to death.'

'Yeah,' he said, sounding pleased.

'It's nothing to be proud of. Besides, you ruined the end of the movie for everyone in the theater.'

'It was a crummy movie.'

'The people still . . .'

'And even if it wasn't, I mean, I gave everyone there a thrill they'll never forget. You know? I gave 'em more than a movie. Something to tell their friends about. Boy, every time they go to a movie, they'll remember what I did tonight.'

'Hooray for you.'

'I'm sorry *you* got hurt.'

'You should've thought of that before you attacked that poor girl.'

'Yeah. I'm sorry. Honest, I wouldn't have done it if I'd known.'

Dani said nothing.

Tony was silent for a long time. Then he said, 'I'm sorry' again, this time in a shaky voice. She heard him sniff.

He's crying again.

Dani sighed, feeling sorry for him in spite of everything. Christ, he'd lost his mother today, his romantic advances had met a rebuff, he'd been pounded into a bloody mess, even crashed into the damn parking meter. Matters couldn't go much worse for a kid.

He'd brought much of it on himself, but Dani had contributed to his misery.

He lay quiet, sniffing occasionally, until they were on Laurel Canyon. 'Are we . . . almost there?'

'Just about.'

'I guess you don't want to see me again.'

Here's your chance, Dani thought. Say 'That's right,' and it's over. Maybe. But she couldn't do it to him. 'If you think you can behave, you're welcome to come back next Saturday like we planned.'

'Honest?'

'Yeah.'

'Why . . . how come you're so nice to me?'

''Cause you're so sweet.'

He laughed, but it sounded close to a sob.

Approaching her house, Dani saw the hearse parked in front. She hoped to find Jack's Mustang in her driveway, but wasn't surprised when it wasn't there. Only about nine o'clock. He and his Margot were probably right in the middle of their main course.

She parked to the side, leaving room for Jack's car, and climbed out. She opened the rear door for Tony. He stood up, hanging onto it for support.

'Are you all right?'

'I guess.'

'You think you can drive okay?'

He shrugged, grimacing as if the movement hurt. 'I . . . I'm awfully thirsty. Maybe . . . could I use your garden hose?'

'That's not necessary. Come on.' They walked toward the front door, Tony with his arms pressed to his body as if holding himself together. 'You might as well fix yourself up while you're here. Get some disinfectant on those wounds.'

'I don't want to be any trouble.'

'It's no trouble,' she said, opening the door. Remembering her boxed-in feeling earlier, she hurried down the corridor ahead of him. She turned on the bathroom light. Tony entered as she took iodine and a canister of bandages from the medicine cabinet. She set them on the counter. She plucked a cardboard cup from a wall dispenser and gave it to him. His hand was rust-brown with drying blood.

He thanked her.

'You go ahead and patch yourself up.'

'Where are you going?'

'Just in the kitchen.'

'Do you have to go?'

'I think you can handle this by yourself, Tony.'

He made a disappointed sigh, but Dani didn't give in. Already, she felt nervous being in the bathroom with him. If she stayed, he would ask her to help clean him, bandage his wounds.

No way.

'Excuse me,' she said.

He made no attempt to stop her.

The kid's shaping up, she told herself as she stepped into the corridor.

She poured a vodka and tonic, and swung herself onto a stool along the short side to the bar. From there, she could see the length of the corridor. The bathroom door stood open. She heard water running. She assumed he was still in there. But . . .

In her mind, she saw him sneaking out, hurrying to her bedroom while she was busy making her drink, undressing . . . Don't be absurd.

Still, it had probably been a mistake to let him come in. The kid's unpredictable.

The water shut off.

At least he hadn't left the bathroom.

What if he *does* try something?

Dani took a long drink and set her glass down. Her gaze lifted to the counter across the lighted kitchen, lingered on the rack of butcher knives.

Now who's the crazy one?

With a shake of her head, she lifted her glass and drank.

* * *

She was leaning against the bar counter about to sip her second vodka and tonic when Tony stepped out of the bathroom. 'All fixed?' she asked.

He nodded.

Setting down her glass, she pushed herself away from the bar and walked toward him. She felt calm, a bit light-headed. The double shot of vodka in the first drink had worked wonders on her nerves.

She stopped in the foyer.

He walked toward her stiffly, hunched over a bit, his head low, his arms straight at his sides.

'Do you feel like there might be internal injuries?' Dani asked.

'I don't know.'

'There was blood in your mouth.'

'It's cut up inside. I bit my tongue, too.'

'That'll teach you to go around scaring people.'

He raised his head and appeared to smile, though his swollen lips barely moved. His face was a patch-work of bandages, puffy and discoloured. His left eye looked very bad. He seemed to be gazing at Dani through a gash in an oyster.

'Can you see all right?'

'Yeah.'

Reaching for the doorknob, she felt her heart speed up.

Please, she thought.

She pulled open the door. 'Well, be real careful driving home.'

He stared at her. His right eye blinking. 'I'm not sure I can drive.'

'Give it a try.'

He nodded. 'Guess you want to get rid of me, huh?'

'It's been a long day. I'm really tired.'

'Yeah.'

'Goodnight, Tony.'

He stepped into the doorway and turned to face her. 'I'll see you next Saturday?'

'Right. Nine o'clock.'

He took a deep breath, and sighed. 'I'm sorry I messed up. I . . . I like you a lot, Dani. A real lot. I don't want you to hate me.'

'I don't hate you, Tony.' Reaching out, she squeezed his forearm. 'Take it easy, now.'

'Yeah. You too.' He turned away.

Dani stood with a hand on the door until he was gone. Then she swung the door shut, locked it and fastened the chain. She went into the kitchen, turning off its light as she passed. At the window, she watched Tony's dark figure move slowly down the driveway.

She waited. The tail lights came on. Then the hearse pulled forward and vanished. The street was a dead end. She didn't leave the window until the long, black car sped by, heading out.

Then she stepped over to the counter. Lifting the tail of her shirt, she slid the carving knife out of her rear pocket.

# Chapter Twenty-one

He parked in the car port. Climbing out, he crouched by the open door. He reached under the seat and slipped out a towel-wrapped object. He held it against his belly with both hands, and walked carefully to the apartment house entrance.

If he stumbled, if he dropped it . . . The towel would cushion its impact, but probably not enough.

Shouldering open a swinging glass door, he entered the lighted foyer. He made his way up the stairs to the second floor. The hallway stretched before him, dark except for a ceiling light near the far end. Normally, he didn't mind the gloom. Tonight, it worried him. If he tripped over something . . . just be careful, very careful.

At last, he reached his door. He cradled the bundle in one arm, and pushed his key into the lock. The door opened on darkness. He stepped inside, and wished he'd left some windows open. The room was stuffy and hot, almost smothering.

He found the light switch. A lamp came on, throwing its dim glow on the sofa, on movie posters tacked along the wall. The sofa creaked as he sat down under his *Eyes of the Maniac* poster.

He rested the bundle on his lap. With trembling hands, he folded open the towel. He stared at the white, plaster mask. The features looked only vaguely familiar. For a moment, he wondered if, in his rush, he had somehow taken the wrong mask from the workroom. He lifted it toward the lamp, studied it more closely. No, he'd made no mistake. This was Dani, all right.

His fingers caressed the cool, hard contours of her face.

Then he carried the mold to the table in his kitchen nook. He set it down carefully. Stepping around the table, he slid open a window. A slight breeze cooled the sweat on his face. He took off his shirt, stood there feeling the breeze against his skin, then turned away.

In his bedroom, he sat on the edge of the mattress and gazed into the open closet as he pulled off his shoes and socks. All but her legs were hidden behind the hanging clothes.

Stripped down to his shorts, he went to the closet and slid the hangers aside. 'Peekaboo,' he said. Hands under its armpits, he lifted the headless dummy out of the closet.

'Miss me?'

He kissed the smooth latex skin of its belly.

'I brought you a present, honey.'

He kissed a jutting nipple, felt a stir in his groin, and set the dummy down.

'I can't tell you, it's a surprise.

'A hint?

'Let me think. It's something you need very badly if you want to get ahead.'

# Chapter Twenty-two

Ten minutes before midnight, Jack arrived. Dani unchained the door for him. The throat of his sport shirt was unbuttoned, his necktie askew. Gripping the tie, she pulled him close and kissed him. He seemed tense. Dani's stomach tightened.

'Well,' she said. 'How'd it . . .'

'What happened?' Frowning, he brushed a fingertip over her sore cheek.

'Tell you later. Come on, I've got a surprise for you.'

She took his hand and led him toward the bedroom. 'How was dinner?'

'The pits. I didn't have much appetite.'

'You told her?'

'Yeah.'

'How'd she take it?'

'Not good.'

'I'm sorry.'

'She just wouldn't stop crying.'

'Where did you tell her? At the restaurant?'

'At her place. After dinner.' He shook his head. 'God, it was awful. It made me feel like such a bastard.'

'This'll make you feel better,' Dani said, leading him across the bedroom. She slid open the glass door and stepped outside. The overhead lights were off. The pool shimmered pale blue. The Jacuzzi at its near corner bubbled red like a cauldron. Towels were stacked beside it. A pair of wine glasses stood alongside the ice bucket. The neck of a bottle protruded from the ice.

'I don't believe it,' Jack said.

Turning to him, Dani opened her robe and let it fall away. She tugged at his necktie.

He was smiling, shaking his head. 'You're pretty fantastic, you know that?'

'I figure you had a rough night.' She dropped the tie and began to unfasten his shirt, her hands fumbling with the buttons as he stroked her breasts. When the last button was open, she unbuckled his belt. She unhooked the waist, lowered the zipper, and drew down his slacks and shorts. Smiling up at him, she lightly squeezed his scrotum. Her fingers curled around his erect penis, moved up it. 'Did you save yourself for me?' The words seemed to slip out, shocking her.

Jack laughed. 'It weren't easy, babe. I had to fight her off.'

'Really?'

'Yeah, as a matter of fact. She wanted one to remember me by.'

'Did she say that?'

'Not exactly. I don't know. Maybe she thought it'd change my mind.'

'Maybe it would've.'

'I didn't stick around to find out.'

'I'm glad. It would've been lonely in the Jacuzzi.' She leaned into him for a brief kiss, stroking his back, rubbing herself against the soft hair of his chest, feeling his hardness against her belly. 'I feel sorry for her, though.'

'And guilty?'

'A little.'

'Don't. I would've broken up with her anyway. I knew I didn't love her. Even before I met you, I knew that.' He kissed the tip of Dani's nose. 'I *do* love you.'

She hugged him tightly, her eyes suddenly filling with tears. 'I . . . I love you, too.'

For a long time, they held each other and didn't speak. Dani felt very strange: comfortable, lazy, excited, out of focus. Though she'd been sure Jack loved her, his words somehow made it different. She felt close to him as she never had before. 'Guess this calls for a celebration.'

'Well, you've got the right fixin's.'

They climbed down into the spa. Standing in the waist-high swirl of hot water, Dani filled the wine glasses. She handed one to Jack, and sat beside him. 'To us,' she said.

'You and me, babe.'

They clinked their glasses, and drank. Dani scooted down a bit. The seething water wrapped over her shoulders. She felt Jack's hand on her thigh.

'Now,' he said, 'tell me about your face.'

She stared down at the red light near her feet, and took a deep breath. 'A guy . . . he roughed me up a bit at the movies.'

'You went to the movies? Alone?'

'Not alone.'

'Oh?'

'Tony came by.'

The fingers tightened on her leg.

'I didn't know what to do, Jack. He was feeling real down. He'd just found out his mother had died.'

'He came over to cry on your shoulder?'

'Apparently, he doesn't have any other friends.'

'That hardly comes as a surprise.'

'I felt sorry for him. You would've, too, if you'd been here.'

'He must've known I was gone. What time did he show up?'

'A little after five.'

'Just after I left? The bastard was probably watching the house. What ever possessed you to let him in?'

'He sort of let himself in. I was out here. He came through the gate.'

'My God, the nerve of that kid.'

'It's all right, Jack.'

'He didn't try anything funny?'

'He behaved himself fine. At least till we were in the movies.' She told about Tony grabbing the girl, about the boy friend scrambling onto her and pounding Tony, about getting kicked out of the theater.

'At least the jerk got what was coming to him,' Jack said.

'He was really messed up.'

'Good. He deserved it. About time somebody laid into him. I wouldn't mind doing it myself. Christ, he comes sneaking by the first time I'm gone . . .'

'He needed someone, Jack.'

'Yeah. You.'

'He'd just lost his mother.'

'Mighty good timing on the old gal's part.'

Dani turned to Jack. He took a sip of wine and met her gaze. Under the water, his hand stroked her thigh.

'You think I'm pretty callous, huh?'

'I know better. It's just that you've got this thing about Tony.'

'Yeah, this thing. He scares me. He's a sneak and a lunatic and he wants you. What'll he do the next time you're alone? Wait, don't tell me. Let me guess. His father has just passed away, and he's oh so sad . . .'

'Jack!'

'I'm sorry, but from what I've seen of our friend Tony, I'd bet a month's salary that his mother didn't die today. He made it up to get your sympathy.'

'Nobody'd do that.'

'Tony would.'

She stared at Jack, all the evening's events rushing through her mind. She felt dazed at first, then outraged. She knew that he was right. Tony had lied, used her sympathy like a weapon to force his way in. 'How could he *do* that to me?'

'Because, my dear, he's a slimy bastard.'

'He's had it.'

Jack patted her leg. Then his arm lifted out of the water and lowered behind her shoulders. He held her close against him. 'Time to rethink our position on Tony.'

'I don't want to see him again.'

'Next time he shows up, I'll point that out to him.'

'The dirty little shit.'

'On the other hand, maybe his mother *did* die today.'

'Sure,' Dani muttered. 'I'll believe that when I see the death certificate.'

# Chapter Twenty-three

Dear Mom, and Bob,

Please don't worry about me. I'm all right. I can't stand it with these murders, however. I may just be paranoid, but I knew Joel and Arnold and I keep thinking, who knows, maybe I might be next. It's just a feeling I have, but I don't mind telling you I'm scared.

If the murderer wants to kill me, he will have to find me first.

I hope you don't mind, but I borrowed your 'emergency money' in the dresser. I promise I'll pay it back when I can. I also drew out the baby-sitting money from my bank account. It's not a lot, but it will get me by until I find a job.

Don't worry about your car, Dad. I'm the one who took it. I will send a letter, soon, and let you know where to find it. I'll include the parking lot ticket.

I am very sorry about this. I promise to keep in touch, and I will return as soon as the police rid our town of its homicidal maniac.

Love always,
Linda

She placed the note on her parents' dresser, then opened the third drawer from the top. The stack of twenty-dollar bills was hidden between two neatly folded sweaters, just where it had always been. She counted. There were ten bills.

She found her father's Smith and Wesson on his closet

shelf. She stuffed it into her overnight bag and closed the zipper.

It took nearly half an hour to walk to the Big Ten grocery store managed by her father. Along the way, she ran into Ginger Jones. The chubby old lady greeted her like a dear friend. 'Don't you look pretty, now? Where would a girl be going, all dressed up to the hilt that way?'

'I'm meeting Dad at the store. He's taking me in to Buffalo to visit my Aunt Vivian.'

'Well, you give Vi my regards, won't you?'

'I sure will.'

In the store's parking lot, she made a quick scan to look for her father. He wasn't in sight. She climbed into his car, and drove to the bank.

The clerk gave her no trouble. She added $185.63 to her bill fold.

Then she drove out to US 81. An hour and a half later, she took a parking-lot ticket from a machine at Syracuse's Hancock International Airport. She carefully marked the car's location on the ticket before walking to the terminal.

The moment she stepped inside the terminal, panic hit her.

*I don't know what I'm doing!*

She staggered back a step. Still time to get home, tear up the note . . .

No!

She looked at the long counter, the ticket agents.

What's the big deal? All I've gotta do is buy a ticket. People must do it all the time.

How the hell do you do it?

Walk up to the counter. That's all it takes.

She walked up to a counter. A young man in a TWA blazer

smiled at her. 'May I help you?' He raised his eyebrows. He looked cheerful and eager.

Linda relaxed a bit. 'How much is a ticket to Los Angeles?'

'First class or coach?'

'Coach, I guess. That's the cheapest, right?'

'Right. It's $149.00 one way.' He eyed her overnight bag. 'We have a flight out at 1:15 with a change in Pittsburg. That'll get you into LAX at 3:43 Pacific time.'

'That fast?'

He smiled, 'There's a three hour time difference.'

Linda nodded, feeling like an idiot.

'Round trip?'

'One way.'

'Fine. Name?'

'Thelma Jones.'

He started to punch buttons behind the counter. 'Will you be traveling by yourself, Miss Jones?'

'Just me.'

'Smoking or non-smoking?'

'Non.'

He pressed a few more buttons, then asked, 'Any baggage to check?'

'Is it okay if I just carry this?' Linda asked, lifting her satchel.

'No problem.'

She opened her billfold. 'How much was that?'

'One forty-nine.'

She took out eight twenty-dollar bills.

'Now, you'll have to change planes in Pittsburg. Our flight's on schedule, so you shouldn't have any trouble making the connection.'

With a nod, she handed over the money.

Finally, she had her ticket, her boarding pass, and she could hardly believe it was all so easy. She felt relieved, almost carefree, as she walked in the direction pointed out by the man.

That ended when she saw the people ahead stopping at a gate-like affair and turning over their bags to a uniformed woman. The woman set the bags on a conveyor belt. They vanished inside a metal machine and reappeared on its other side, where the people picked them up after passing through the gate.

'Oh shit,' she muttered.

She turned away. Near the other end of the terminal, she found a restroom. She stood at a sink, washing her hands and brushing the short hair of her wig until she was alone. Then she dumped her pistol into a waste bin. She passed through security without any trouble.

The taxi crept up the San Diego Freeway in rush-hour traffic. 'Where are they all going?' Linda asked, half to herself.

'Home from work,' the driver said, smiling back at her. 'Home from shopping, home from the airport, Disneyland, the beach. You name it.'

'I've never seen so many cars.'

'Then you've never been to LA. I tell you, one of these days there's gonna be one single car too many coming on, and that'll be it. Nobody'll move. I've got ten days rations in the trunk for the day it happens.'

'Really?'

'Would I kid you?' He swung abruptly into a right-hand lane, slipping into a space barely long enough for the taxi. The car in front slowed down. Linda braced her feet on the floor as the taxi braked. She waited for an impact from the rear. It didn't come.

Her left leg ached as she let her muscles loosen. She rubbed it through her dress.

The driver seemed unconcerned about the close call. 'Make sure you take in Grauman's Chinese,' he said. 'They don't call it that anymore, but it's still got the stars' footprints. That's just a few blocks from where I'm dropping you.'

'Okay.'

They moved slowly down a ramp leading onto another freeway. This one looked just as crowded as the other.

Linda glanced at the meter. Seven-fifty. She still had more than two hundred dollars, so . . .

'The Walk of Fame's there, too. You know, the stars in the sidewalk?'

'Yeah, I've heard of it.'

'Some good bookstores along there, too. You into books?'

'A little.'

'Me, I do screenplays. I've picked up some option money, here and there, but I haven't been produced yet.'

'Maybe you should write a book.'

'I've tried. I can't do prose.'

'You write your screenplays in verse?'

He laughed. He didn't explain what was funny, but continued to talk about his writing as he left the freeway and drove up a crowded street named La Brea. Linda felt smothered by the traffic. Often, they had to wait through three cycles of a stop light before getting across an intersection. The amount on the meter continued to rise.

'Hollywood Boulevard,' he finally announced, making a right-hand turn. 'Grauman's, all that, is just up ahead. We'll be turning off, though.'

A few blocks later, he made a left. Then a right onto La Mar

Street. He stopped in front of a shabby apartment house, and turned in his seat. Linda gave him thirty dollars. She told him to keep the change.

'Good luck with your poetry,' she said, and left him smiling.

Alone on the sidewalk, she took Tony's letter from her purse. She checked the return address against the numbers beside the building's double glass doors. They matched.

Taking a deep breath, she walked toward the doors. She pulled one open. The lobby seemed dark after the glare outside, and felt slightly cool.

Near the foot of the staircase, she found rows of mail boxes. Each was labeled with two strips of red plastic tape. Her eyes moved swiftly to the strip marked 210, and lowered to the name: A. Johnson.

She'd found him!

She climbed the stairs slowly. At the top, she leaned against the wall. Her breath was coming fast, her heart racing, but not from the exertion.

Shutting her eyes, she saw the naked, cadaverous specter leering down at her through the darkness. The severed head tumbled down the stairs. It bumped her. Its vacant eye peered at her through the gap of her upraised legs. She felt the warm spread of urine. He was coming down, lifting the ax. She felt her terror, her certainty that she would be killed, at last the welcome taste of fresh night air when she made her escape. Then the explosion of pain as the car tore into her.

She gasped and her eyes jerked open as if she'd been startled from sleep.

Her legs were dripping. The insides of her shoes felt slippery. The faded green rug was dark between her feet.

Stunned, she looked down the corridor. At least nobody was around.

She peeled off her sopping panties. With Kleenex from her handbag, she wiped, herself dry. She left the panties and tissues in a wet heap, and hurried toward room 210.

All his fucking fault! Everything!

Don't blow it, she warned herself as she raised a fist to strike the door.

She knocked gently.

She waited, hands folded to conceal the blotch on her dress.

The door stayed shut.

She knocked again.

Finally, she gave up. She took the back stairway to the first floor. Stepping out a rear exit, she found herself in an alley. She walked down it, holding the wet part of her dress away from her skin.

In her overnight bag, she carried a change of clothes. She considered ducking between trash bins and ridding herself of the fouled dress.

No. The sun would dry it, soon enough.

She wanted to save the clean clothes for her trip home. Whatever she wore tonight would very likely get messed up with blood.

If she was lucky.

She walked for a long time, sticking mostly to alleys. Finally, she returned to Tony's apartment. She knocked on his door and waited.

Then she went out the front. She crossed the street. Near the end of the block, she sat down on a curb and watched the front of the building and waited.

# Chapter Twenty-four

'Okay okay,' Roger said. 'Ready for the splash shot. It's been a long day. Let's get it right and we'll wrap.'

Jack, crouched on the low roof of the shack facade, gave a nod and pulled the ski mask down over his face. He picked up the ax with both hands.

'Be careful,' Dani called.

'Just get it right,' Roger said, apparently still miffed about last week's foul-up with the shotgun.

Jack's hesitation to blast Ingrid's head. The thought of it made Dani smile. Thank God for such foul-ups. But her good feelings vanished in an instant when she remembered Ingrid's disappearance.

Ingrid, her double.

Tony fondling the dummy, handling its breasts, its buttocks and groin, calling it by her name.

He's just sick enough . . .

'Action.'

Jack leaped from the roof. He landed on his feet in front of the chair where the mannequin of Bill sat with a beer bottle raised to its lips. He swung the ax sideways. It caught Bill across the left eyebrow. The top of the head flew off with a burst of red gore, tumbled and thudded on the porch floor. 'Cut!' Roger called. 'Beautiful. That's a print.'

'Do you want me to go in with you?' Jack asked.

Dani shook her head. 'I'm sure it's all right. He's probably still home licking his wounds.'

'I'd better.'

'If you insist.'

They climbed out of Jack's Mustang and walked toward the front door.

'He didn't pull anything yesterday,' Dani said.

'He didn't dare. I was with you all day.'

She unlocked the door. They stepped inside. The house was silent. They walked through it as quietly as intruders, checking all the windows and doors.

'I guess it's all right,' Jack whispered when they reached the kitchen.

'Then why,' she whispered, 'are we whispering?'

He grinned. 'Beats me,' he said in his normal voice.

Dani glanced at the workroom door. The lock button protruded from its handle. 'Did we leave that unlocked this morning?'

'Might've.'

With a shrug, she stepped around the kitchen table and opened the door. She flicked the light switch. 'Anybody home?' she asked.

'Let's make sure.'

They entered the workroom. It felt hot and stuffy.

'I'll check the back door,' Dani said.

Jack nodded and stepped around the lathe, making his way toward the side window.

As she passed the workbench, Dani picked up the rusted machete. 'Maybe I should keep this with me,' she said. Smiling across at Jack, she waved it overhead.

'Give him forty whacks.'

'Yuck.' She set it down and continued toward the rear door.

'Window's all . . .'

'Jack!' She staggered backwards a step, her gaze fixed on the empty space of wall.

He rushed to her side.

She pointed. 'My life mask. It's gone.'

He was silent for a moment. 'Let's look around. Maybe it's just misplaced.'

She shook her head. She felt weak and dizzy. Jack's hand pressed gently against her back.

'It was here Saturday morning,' he said.

'We showed Tony how. He . . . he wants my head on Ingrid.'

Jack mussed her hair. 'As long as he doesn't get the real one.'

She tried to smile.

'Honey, it's only a hunk of plaster.'

'It's my *face*. And Ingrid's my *body*. God, I can almost feel him touching it.'

'That's me,' Jack said, pulling her close. He stroked her back. His lips pressed her mouth. She held him tightly. 'We'll get Ingrid,' he finally said.

'How?'

'Tony's bound to show up.'

Jack checked the rear door. Then they left the stifling workroom.

'I'll only be gone an hour,' he said.

'You sure I can't help?'

'You'd be grossed out.'

'Your place can't be *that* messy.'

'If you're afraid to stay here . . .'

'No.'

'I'll just grab enough for one suitcase, and scurry right back.'

When he was gone, Dani chained the front door. She went into the bedroom. Through the glass door, the swimming pool looked shiny and inviting. She could almost feel the cold shock of water. But she was afraid.

Afraid to use her own pool because she was alone and Tony might come through the gate.

'Damn him,' she muttered.

Might as well play it safe, though. Why take chances? Just stay locked up in your cage so the bastard can't get at you . . .

Some cage. A glass house. If Tony wanted, he could get to her in seconds.

With that thought, she convinced herself: she was no safer in the house than outside.

'Clever me,' she muttered.

Laughing softly, she stripped off her sweaty clothes. She went into the bathroom and reached for the bikini hanging over the shower door. It was the skimpy orange one she'd been wearing Saturday. When Tony dropped in.

'No way,' she said.

She went to her dresser and took out a green, one-piece suit. Though low cut and backless, it was a vast improvement over the bikini. She stepped into it, pulled it up her legs and lifted the front over her breasts. As she slipped her arms into the straps, she suddenly realised why she was putting it on.

So Tony wouldn't see her in the bikini.

Did she *expect* him to show up?

Yeah. Or why the modest suit?

'Let him,' she said. Picking up a towel, she walked to the door, slid it open and stepped outside. The sun felt warm. A mild breeze blew against her.

'Where'd Jack go?' Tony asked.

Dani's head jerked to the right.

Tony was sitting shirtless on a lounger, hands folded behind his glossy head. The bandages were gone. His face was bruised, blotched and streaked with brown scabs. His left eye was nearly hidden under bulbs of swollen flesh.

Dani stared at him, more confused than alarmed, feeling as if she'd somehow conjured him up. 'How long have you been here?' she asked. The sound of her voice brought back a sense of reality.

'Just a few minutes. I hope you don't mind.'

'You saw Jack leave?'

'No. I just noticed his car wasn't out front.'

'You were coming by anyway?'

He nodded.

'Quite a coincidence.'

'Huh?'

'Jack happens to be gone every time you show up.'

'Yeah. I keep missing him.'

'You're watching the house.' It was not a question.

He looked at Dani as if she were mad.

'And your mother didn't die on Saturday.'

He unlocked his hands from behind his head and leaned forward, frowning. 'She died. Just like I said. Why should I lie?'

'Worked out pretty well, didn't it? I let you stay, I fed you, I took you to the movies. You got your chance to put some moves on me . . .'

'You're crazy!'

'I was crazy to believe you. But, oh, I fell for it, didn't I? You must figure I'm a real push-over. Give me a sob story, I'm putty in your hands. What'll it be today, Tony? Father die? Dog hit by a car? Come on, let's hear it. You wouldn't come without a story for the old softie here.'

He stood up.

Dani backed away as he slowly approached.

'I just can't stay away from you.'

'You do a good job of it when Jack's around.'

'He hates me.'

Reaching behind her, Dani gripped the door handle. 'I want you to leave. Right now.'

He shook his head. 'I can't. I love you. I love you so much.'

'Then do what I want. Go away. Please.'

'I've never loved a woman before. I've never *made* love before.'

'I don't want you, Tony,' she said in a shaky voice.

'Yes you do.'

She suddenly tugged the handle. As the door skidded open, she whirled around and lunged into the bedroom. She tried to jerk the door shut. Tony's body stopped it. He shoved it aside and entered.

Dani staggered backwards. 'Get away,' she gasped.

'I love you. I won't hurt you.'

'Tony!'

'We'll make love. You like that. You do it all the time with Jack.'

'You're not Jack!'

'I'll make you happier than he ever could. You'll see.' He walked toward her.

Dani glanced back. She could try for the bathroom, but its lock wouldn't keep him out for five seconds and she would be trapped. Her only chance was to run for the corridor.

'Don't,' Tony said. 'Don't try to get away. I love you.'

'I hate you!' she shouted, still backing away.

'Oh, don't say that. You know it's not true.'

'Leave me alone!'

'Take off your swimming suit. I want to see you naked. I want to touch you. I want to kiss you all over and . . .' His body went rigid. He took a quick step back.

Dani spun around and gasped.

In the bedroom doorway stood a big man. He wore jeans, a parka. A blue ski mask covered his head. His gloved hand clutched a machete.

He raised the machete overhead and charged.

Tony darted through the sliding door.

The man rushed past Dani. In silence, he pursued Tony along the side of the pool. Tony reached the redwood fence well ahead of him, leaped, and clambered over the top.

The man came back. He tossed the machete onto one of the lounge chairs, and pulled off his ski mask.

Dani threw herself into his arms.

# Chapter Twenty-five

'Are you all right?' Jack asked.

Dani hugged him tightly. 'He was going to . . .'

'I know.'

'I was so scared. I couldn't have stopped him. Oh God, Jack.'

'It's all right.'

'I couldn't have stopped him,' she sobbed, pressing her face to Jack's shoulder. 'If you hadn't come . . .'

'I was pretty sure he'd take the bait.'

She looked up at Jack. His face was blurry through her tears. 'I don't understand.'

'I expected something like this. I found his hearse on the next street up, so I left my car there and ran back.'

'In costume?' she asked, wiping her eyes.

'I figured I'd give him a dose of his own medicine. When I got here, I saw you outside with him. I went in the workroom for the machete, and by the time I came you were in the bedroom.'

'You mean you never really planned to go to your apartment? You just left me alone to lure him in?'

'That's about it.'

She smiled up at him. 'You're a pretty sneaky fellow, Jack Somers.'

'Takes a sneak to catch a sneak.'

'You could've let me in on your plan, you know.'

'And ruin the surprise?'

'I wouldn't have minded.'

With a smile, he stroked the back of her head. 'Actually, I do have to go to my apartment.'

'What's this, another test to see if Tony shows up?'

'I think he's learned his lesson. But just in case I'm wrong, you're coming with me.'

'What about the mess?'

'If you're grossed out, you can shut your eyes.'

He stared at a gray Mercedes parked in front of the apartment building. 'Uh-oh.'

'What?' Dani asked.

'Margot's car.'

'Oh no.'

He swung his Mustang to the curb. 'I guess she didn't take no for an answer.'

'Maybe I'd better wait here.'

Jack grinned at her. 'Scared?'

'I'm not sure I'm up to any more confrontations.'

'Come on.'

'I don't know, Jack.'

'I'm warning you, she might have designs on my body. You'd better come up to protect your interests.'

'Well . . .' Dani shrugged and climbed from the car.

Jack took her hand. 'Don't be nervous.'

'Sure.'

As they climbed the stairs to the second floor, Dani's reluctance grew. Her stomach hurt. Her heart pounded hard. Her hand was sweaty in Jack's grip. 'I don't know about this,' she whispered.

'I haven't seen a good cat fight in ages.'

'Oh wonderful.'

'Don't worry, I won't let her hurt you.'

'You may think this is amusing, but I bet Margot won't.'

'I really should've taken my key away from her. Hope she's not in there wrecking the place.' He slid a key into the lock, turned it, and eased open the door. He leaned into the gap. 'Oh my God,' he muttered. 'Margot!'

Then he shoved the door open wide.

Dani glimpsed a naked woman and quickly turned away. 'I'll meet you in the car,' she said.

Jack grabbed her arm. 'Oh no you don't.'

'You despicable cad.'

'I know,' he said. Grinning, Jack sipped his margarita.

Dani raised herself off the lounge chair and turned it away from the pool's glare. She sat down again, facing Jack.

'Do you still love me?' he asked.

'You're so damned pleased with yourself.'

'I have to admit it, I am.'

She licked the salty rim of her glass, and took a drink. 'You really put me through it.'

'I am rather sorry about that.'

'*Rather* sorry?'

'Will you forgive me?'

'I'll give it some thought.'

Setting his glass aside, he dropped from his chair and knelt in front of Dani. 'Oh please. I humble myself before you.'

'I don't know.'

He pressed his forehead against her knees. His hands moved up her thighs.

'What are you doing?'

'Humbling myself.'

'That's not what it feels like.'

'This is how a cad does it,' he said, and plucked open the bikini strings at her hips.

Dani dumped her margarita on his head. He flinched and cringed, raised his dripping face and grinned. 'Does this mean we're even?'

She smoothed his wet hair. 'Actually, you're a very thoughtful guy in your own perverted way.'

'I know.'

'Have I thanked you?'

'Not yet.'

'Remind me. I'll thank you after dinner.'

They ate pork chops and rice by candle-light in the dining

room. When they were done, Jack reminded Dani to thank him.

They each carried a candle down the dark corridor to the bedroom and placed them side by side on the dresser. The mirror caught the flames, made twins of them.

Dani turned to Jack. She caressed his chest, hands roaming over his soft hair, feeling the firm smoothness beneath, thumbs stroking his nipples while he untied the strings behind her neck and back. Her bikini top fell away. She trembled as he touched her breasts, as his fingers slid down her body and plucked the strings at her hips. Then she was naked. A hand was big and warm, moving over her buttocks. Another hand curved over her thigh. Like a breeze, it stirred the hair between her legs. It pressed in. It rubbed. Squirming against it, Dani tugged at Jack's trunks. The hand slid upward, making a wet trail on her belly as she crouched and lowered the trunks to his ankles. She kissed the tip of his rigid penis. Her lips spread over it and she sucked it deep into her mouth.

Then she was on the bed beside Jack, breathless as his tongue thrust into her mouth. He was long and smooth against her. His mouth went away. Kneeling over her, he licked a nipple, squeezed it with his lips, slid a hand down between her legs. A finger dipped into her and stroked.

The doorbell rang.

Jack groaned.

'Wonderful,' Dani muttered.

It rang again.

His mouth lifted off her breast. Dani took hold of his hand to stop it from leaving. 'Never mind the door,' she said.

Neither of them moved as they waited for the doorbell to stop.

It kept ringing.

'Persistent bastard,' Dani said.

'I'll see who it is.'

'No, he'll go away.'

There were moments of silence, but each time that Dani thought the intruder had left, the bell rang again.

'Shit.'

'I wonder if it's our friend,' Jack said.

'He wouldn't show up with you here.'

'I'll be right back. Don't go away.'

Propped up on an elbow, she watched Jack step into his trunks and hurry from the room. When he was gone, she sat up. Sweat trickled down her body. She wiped it off with a sheet.

The doorbell stopped.

She gazed through the fluttering candle light at Jack's gift, and smiled. If not for the interruption, her little 'thank you' might be over by now.

This gave them both a chance to cool off.

When Jack returned, they would start fresh.

She stared at the dark corridor beyond the doorway. She heard no voices, no footsteps.

It shouldn't take him this long.

'Jack?' she called.

No answer came.

Suddenly concerned, she scurried off the bed. She grabbed her robe off a closet hook and rushed to the doorway. Leaning out, she peered down the long corridor. Nothing seemed to move in the darkness.

'Jack?' she asked in a hushed voice.

There was only silence.

She stepped out of the room. Clawing the wall near the door

frame, she found the switch panel. Three overhead lamps came on, filling the corridor with light.

No one was there.

She ran to the front door.

Shut.

Racing past it, she scanned the dark living room. The dining room. She rushed around the bar, into the kitchen. Turned on a light. The kitchen was empty. Her bare feet slapped the linoleum floor as she ran to the workroom. It was dark. Reaching in, she flicked a light switch. She stepped through the doorway. Nobody there.

She ran back to the front door and flung it open. She gazed into the darkness.

Nothing moved.

'Jack!' she yelled. 'Jack, where are you?'

When no answer came, she walked over the cool wet grass to the middle of the lawn.

His Mustang was still in the driveway beside her Rabbit. She crossed over to it and peered inside. The car was empty.

She walked down the driveway to the street. Standing by the curb, she looked both ways. There were parked cars, lights shining in the windows of a few houses, but she saw nobody.

Shivering, she drew the robe more tightly around her body and hurried back to the door.

In the kitchen, she took her largest butcher knife from the rack.

*The machete . . .*

But it was out by the pool. She wouldn't go out again.

She turned off the light. Clutching the knife so hard her hand ached, she sat down on the floor. She leaned back against the bar, drew her knees up close, and waited.

# Chapter Twenty-six

Opening his eyes, Jack saw blackness. He blinked to be sure they were actually open. A wave of pain crashed inside his head.

He raised a hand to his face, vaguely aware of his elbow sliding on a smooth surface at his side. He thought little of it as he rubbed his temples.

What the hell was wrong with his head?'

He remembered being with Dani. Oh. Right. The doorbell. He'd left her to answer the door. Then he must've gone back.

Christ, his head felt like it might explode.

How the hell many margaritas did he have? Two? And wine with dinner.

Why is Dani's room so dark?

She must have aspirin in the bathroom. He hoped he could get there without tripping over the furniture.

He started to sit up. Something slammed against his forehead. He fell back, dizzy with pain, and grabbed his head with both hands. Cushions of some sort held his elbows in.

As the pain subsided, he poked his right elbow against the obstruction. It sank into padding and struck a hard surface. His left elbow did the same. He raised a fist. Not more than a foot above his face, his knuckles hit wood.

Feeling with both hands, he found that he was boxed in. He braced himself and shoved with all his strength against the lid. The effort sent a tide of pain into his head. He kept on pushing.

His muscles quivered with the strain, but the lid didn't give at all. Gasping for breath, he lowered his arms.

This is not good, he thought.

There was a whisper of panic in his mind. He knew he was sealed inside a coffin, the coffin Tony kept in his hearse. When he opened the front door, Tony must have bashed him, knocked him out . . .

*Dani!*

Oh my God, he's going for Dani!

Suddenly, Jack felt motion. Not of the coffin itself, but of the surface on which it rested. Tony, he realised, must be driving him somewhere. Away from Dani's house? So she was safe for now.

Unless Tony had already finished with her.

Christ, why did he have to open the door? Dani had told him not to bother. He should've stayed with her, protected her. Now he was powerless to help. Maybe it was already too late. He saw her sprawled on the floor of her bedroom, naked and bleeding. Dead.

'*No!*' he yelled.

I've got to calm down, he warned himself. There can't be much air in here. Can't waste it. Breathe easily.

The hearse turned, pressing his shoulder to the coffin wall.

You've got to believe he hasn't hurt Dani. He's just taking me out of the picture.

*Just?*

And then he'll go for her, and I won't be around to stop him *unless I get out of this fucking coffin!*

He forced his knees against the lid and shoved it while he pushed with both hands. It didn't yield.

Maybe the side panels aren't so strong. He rolled. There

was just enough space for his shoulders. With his back pressed to one padded wall, he thrust against the other side. No good.

As he relaxed his muscles, the coffin jostled him. He pressed himself against the sides again to steady himself.

The car must have gone off the street. From the bouncing, he imagined it traveling over a rutted dirt road or a field.

Where is he taking me?

A cemetery? The thought made a cold, tight place in Jack's stomach.

No. Cemeteries have gates, watchmen. Don't they?

Besides, there isn't one around here. Not that Jack knew of.

Tony wouldn't need a cemetery. Just an isolated spot where nobody would see him dig a grave.

A grave.

Jesus Christ!

He tried again to force the sides, and then the bouncing stopped. All movements stopped, even the barely perceptible vibration from the car's engine.

For a few moments, nothing happened.

The coffin jerked and rolled with a muffled rumbling sound. The end started down. Jack stretched out his legs to catch himself as he slid on the smooth upholstery. Realising what would happen next, he braced himself up with his elbows. The coffin suddenly dropped out from under him. His head bumped the lid. Then he was slammed down hard. The impact knocked his elbows up, sledged his back, drove his wind out. As he gasped for air, he heard a rapping on the lid.

'Hello in there.'

Tony's voice. It didn't sound distant and muffled. It seemed, somehow, to creep inside the coffin with Jack.

'Cozy?'

Jack lay motionless and said nothing.

'Ever see *Premature Burial*? American International, 1962? One of Corman's best, I think. A real chiller. Me, I can't think of anything much worse than getting buried alive. Drowning, maybe, but that's over a lot quicker. Bury a guy alive and he suffocates real slowly. Has lots of time to think about it. Lots of time. I bet you're already thinking about it. Are you, Jack?'

Jack didn't answer.

'Are you awake in there?' Tony knocked on the lid. 'Hey, are you awake? I don't want you missing this.'

There was a brief silence.

'If you ask me real nice, maybe I'll let you out. Why don't you beg me? Say, "Please, oh Chill Master, please let me out. I'm too young to die." No? Well, any last words for Dani? I'll be seeing her later on. I'd be glad to give her a message.'

Jack ached to shout out his rage, to slam his fists through the coffin lid and grab Tony's throat. But he remained silent and didn't move.

Let Tony think he was still unconscious.

The bastard thrived on terrifying people. Let him think he failed, at least this once.

The coffin shook, and the foot of it lifted. It was being dragged.

It dropped with a sudden shock.

Something hit the wood above Jack with a soft thud. He felt a trickle on his chest and touched it, rolled it against his skin. Tiny granules. Soil.

More spilled onto him. Jack reached up to the lid. His trembling fingers found a smoothly bored hole.

An air hole.

For a while, he counted the heavy slaps of dirt on the coffin. Even after he lost count, he held his finger to the hole.

Finally there was silence, a heavy, dull silence as black as death.

# Chapter Twenty-seven

There were no empty spaces in front of Tony's apartment house, so he double-parked. He rushed upstairs.

In his room, he propped the shovel against a wall. He tugged off his shoes and socks, pulled off his soiled pants and climbed into the tub. He turned on the shower. The hot water smacked his skin. Gray streams rolled down his arms, his chest and belly. He let the water hit his face. It felt like fire on his wounds. Quickly, he soaped himself down and rinsed. Then he climbed from the tub.

As he dried himself, he thought about shaving. The two days growth of whiskers made him look grubby. But shaving would be too painful, so he decided against it.

He dumped a pool of cologne into his hand. He splashed it on his cheeks and neck, enjoying the musky fragrance. Then he dabbed some on his penis.

He brushed his teeth.

From his closet, he took a pair of blue slacks and his sport shirt. Not bothering with underwear, he put them on.

He put on clean socks.

He dumped loose soil from his sneakers. Wishing he had a better pair of shoes for the occasion, he slipped them on.

Then he hurried down to his hearse.

Everything was going his way.

Almost everything. Climbing in behind the wheel, he again felt a stir of disappointment about the business with Jack. He must've beaned the jerk too hard. It would've been nice to hear him blubber and beg and scream, but at least he was out of the way. He wouldn't be popping up to ruin the night.

Not this time.

Tony grinned. It made his lips hurt. He licked them and tasted blood, and laughed.

# Chapter Twenty-eight

The sudden ring of the doorbell sent a shock through Dani. Her head jerked back, striking a cupboard door. She shoved away from it, and got to her knees.

She was puzzled. She'd expected Tony to break in through the rear of the house, not simply step up to the front door and ring the bell like a casual visitor.

Maybe it's Jack.

But where had he been all this time?

The bell rang again.

If it were Jack, he would call out.

Tony, all right.

Getting to her feet, she walked around the bar. The knife hilt was slippery. She wiped it with the front of her robe, rubbed her hand dry and gripped it again.

She stopped at the front door. Leaning a shoulder against the frame to steady herself, she took a few deep breaths. They didn't help much; her heart seemed to be knocking the air from her lungs.

'Who is it?' she asked.

'It's just me.'

The strength drained from Dani. She sank to a crouch. 'What do you want?'

'I thought, you know, I'd just drop by and see if you're in.'

'Where's Jack?'

'Oh, isn't he here? His car's outside.'

'Please, what'd you do to him?' Dani didn't like the pleading sound of her voice.

'If he's not here, I don't know where he could be.'

'Tony!'

'Maybe he went for a walk. Why don't you let me in, and I'll keep you company till he gets back.'

'Stop *playing* with me!' she shouted. 'I know you've got him!'

There was a long silence.

'Don't be mad, Dani. I didn't hurt him. I just made sure he wouldn't be around. He kept getting in the way, coming between us. I mean, he wouldn't leave us alone. I *had* to get rid of him.'

'What did you do to him?' she whispered.

'Huh?'

'Where is he?' she asked, forcing herself to speak louder.

'He won't bother us. Let me in.'

'No.'

'Don't be this way, Dani. I love you. I won't even try to scare you, I promise. I don't care about that when I'm with you. I just want to hold you in my arms.'

'If I let you in, will you tell me where Jack is?'

'All right.'

Dani straightened up. Holding the knife behind her back, she slipped the guard chain free. She stepped back. She reached out with her left hand, and turned the knob. She swung the door open wide.

Tony, standing on the dark stoop, gazed in at her. He looked strange, almost normal, in slacks and a short-sleeved shirt.

All dressed up.

He thinks this is a date.

'Come in,' Dani said.

With a slight nod, he stepped forward. He entered. As he shut the door, Dani's chest constricted. She felt trapped and suffocating. She gasped for air.

'Don't be afraid,' Tony said.

'Where's Jack?'

'We haven't even kissed yet.'

'Tell me.'

Tony shook his head, and took a step toward Dani. She swung the knife from behind her back. She shook its blade at him. 'Tell me where Jack is,' she demanded.

Tony sighed. 'Why don't you forget about him? You have me, now. Forget about Jack. He's nothing.'

She jabbed at his belly. He lurched backwards against the door and flung out his open hands to shield himself. Dani slashed. The blade sliced his left palm.

'*Ow!* Dani! For Godsake, you *cut* me!'

'Tell me where Jack is.'

'All right, all right. God!' He stared at his cupped hand, a horrified look on his face as blood welled up and spilled over the sides. 'God, you really cut me.'

'I'll do it again. Talk.'

His hand jumped, flinging the pooled blood at Dani's face. It flew at her like a tattered red cloth. It splashed her cheeks and eyes. Blinded for a moment, she lashed out wildly with the knife. A fist clubbed her left cheek. The impact snapped her head sideways, turned her whole body, and sent her to the floor. She landed on her side. The knife was still in her hand. Hanging onto it, she pushed herself to her knees.

Tony kicked her arm out from under her. As she collapsed, the knife flew from her numb hand.

He grabbed her ankles. He lifted her legs and swung them across each other. Dani tried to clutch the carpet. No use. In an instant, she was forced onto her back. She tried to kick free, but Tony held her feet tightly, bracing each against one hip. She bucked and twisted and squirmed. Her efforts did no good. Exhausted, she gave up and tried to catch her breath.

Tony didn't move. He stared down at Dani.

The struggle had loosened her cloth belt. Her robe had fallen open. She lifted it from the sides and started to close it over her breasts.

'Don't,' Tony murmured.

She wrapped it tightly across her. Glaring up in defiance, she pressed a hand between her legs.

'You're not being nice.'

'Fuck you,' she gasped.

'This isn't the way it was supposed to be. You were supposed to be sweet and gentle. You weren't supposed to fight me.'

'You wouldn't tell.'

'Huh?' He frowned as if confused.

'I would've been sweet and gentle . . . but you didn't tell.'

'Really?'

'Really. Tell me now. That's all I want. Then I . . . I won't fight you anymore.'

'You'll be nice?'

'I'll be wonderful.' She slid her hand away, uncovering her vagina. She spread the robe away from her breasts. 'Tell me.'

'He's in my coffin. Buried someplace.'

'Oh my God,' Dani muttered.

Tony grinned, and blood trickled from his scabbed lips.

'Where?'

He shook his head. 'I'll save that for later.'

'All right.'

'I want you to undress me. Do it the way you undressed Jack by the pool Saturday night.'

'You watched?'

'Oh yes. You were so beautiful. You were far away, though. I couldn't see as well as I wanted. But the way you slowly undressed him and touched him . . .' Tony lowered her feet to the floor. 'And then later, when he made love to you in the whirlpool . . .'

'Did it excite you?' Dani asked, standing up.

'Oh yes. But it made me mad. It should've been me.'

'Tonight, it will be you.' Stepping close to him, Dani shrugged the robe from her shoulders. She stood motionless while his eyes wandered over her body. He licked a speck of blood from his cracked lips. Then he raised his hands. They felt like ice on her shoulders. The cut hand was slippery. His fingers trembled as he caressed her. He was breathing hard.

Slowly, Dani unfastened the buttons of his shirt. She untucked it and spread it open. His chest was white and hairless, bony as if the skin had been stretched taut over a skeleton. Reaching up, she slipped the shirt off his shoulders. He lowered his arms to let it fall away.

As she pulled at his belt buckle, his hands slid down to her breasts. She went rigid and shut her eyes.

It's all right, she told herself. Don't try to stop him.

The fingers curled around her breasts, squeezing and writhing like snakes.

She jerked his buckle open. It pulled from her hands as Tony crouched. Caressing her buttocks, he kissed her left breast. She looked down at him. He licked her nipple, sucked it into his mouth, opened wide as if trying to draw in her entire breast. She felt the painful pulling, the scrape of his teeth, the push of his probing tongue.

'You're hurting me,' she said.

Obediently, he slipped his mouth off the breast. 'I'm sorry,' he said. He gave her an apologetic glance, then moved his face to the other breast. It was smeared with blood from his hand. His tongue circled it, lapping the blood away. Clutching her buttocks, he rubbed it with his face. She felt his whiskers, the stiff touch of his scabs. He pushed an eye against her nipple, and she felt its quivering lid. His head turned slightly, and he slid the nipple across his other eye. Then he took it into his mouth.

Dani stroked his head. 'Now,' she whispered. 'I want you now.'

He stood up. He held her breasts as she unbuttoned his waist band.

'This is . . .' He swallowed. 'Better than I ever imagined.'

'Me too.' Dani slid his zipper down. His erection sprang out. Crouching down, Dani lowered his pants. She held them at his knees. Her right hand eased up his thigh.

Tony moaned.

He bellowed when her fist smashed into his scrotum. He staggered backwards. The pants tripped him. He dropped to his rump and fell sideways, curling up and clutching himself.

Dani scrambled for the knife. She spotted it under the coffee table. Dropping to her knees, she reached under and grabbed it. Then she hurried back to Tony.

He was still curled up, writhing and groaning.

She knew she could get away while Tony was helpless. In another couple of minutes, though . . .

She raced into the kitchen, threw open the workroom door and slapped the light switch. On a hook near the window hung a coil of rope, the remains from what they'd used to tie up the Sandra Blaine mannequin for *Carrion*. She ran for it. The edge of the workbench gouged her hip. She winced and gritted her teeth against the pain, but didn't stop, Stretching up, she grabbed the rope and yanked it free.

She dashed into the kitchen. Her sweaty feet slipped on the linoleum, but the dining-room carpet gave good traction and she sprinted for the living room.

Tony was gone.

# Chapter Twenty-nine

Dani stood on the carpet where, less than a minute ago, the boy had been squirming in agony. Now, only his trousers and a few smears of blood remained to mark the place.

She looped the rope over her head to free her left hand. She scanned the living room, turning slowly. The only light came from the foyer. It reached the area where she stood, casting her shadow over the pale carpet, dimming a short distance beyond and leaving much of the room murky.

Tony would be there. Maybe hiding behind the curtains that stretched across the sliding door and picture windows. Maybe crouched by the sofa or easy chair. Maybe hunched down next to the stereo console. Waiting. Ready to spring at her.

She backed away. Standing under the light, she glanced down the long corridor.

He might even be down there. Waiting inside the guest bathroom or her bedroom.

The knob of the front door pressed cool against her rump. In seconds, she could be outside, racing to a neighbor's house. But that wouldn't help Jack.

Buried alive.

My God, *buried alive*!

How long could he last?

Dani shoved away from the door and walked straight forward. Her shadow moved ahead of her, faded as she left the light behind. She went up the middle of the room, turning, sidestepping, walking backwards, never pausing as she checked the dark places where Tony might be hiding. In the corner, she kicked an armchair against the wall. She ducked to peer under a lamp table. She climbed onto the sofa and walked the length of it, her feet sinking into the soft cushions, her hand trailing through the curtains behind it. At the end, she stepped onto the coffee table. A long stride took her to an overstuffed chair. She leaned over its back. Nobody there. She jumped down. With her back pressed to the wall, she used one hand to pull the draw cord. The curtains slowly skidded open, revealing an expanse of window and the shimmering blue surface of the lighted pool.

Her gaze swept through the room.

'Tony!'

No answer.

She made her way back, pivoting, ducking, peering into shadows behind furniture. In the dining area, she squatted low and scanned the space under the table. There was darkness and a forest of oak legs. She straightened up. She turned around. She stepped to the long side of the bar, planted a knee on a stool cushion and crawled onto the counter top. Inching forward, she looked over the edge and found him.

The coil of rope around her neck stopped swaying.

Tony jerked it hard.

Crying out, Dani braced herself on stiff arms as pain hit the back of her neck like a club. Her head snapped down. The rope scorched her ears, burnt a swath up the back of her head and was gone. Before she could move, Tony whipped it across her face. She threw herself backwards, eyes squeezed shut with pain, and felt another vicious lash. Her right knee left the counter. The oak edge hammered her hip, scraped along her ribs, tore at her breast, caught her under the arm and seemed to shove her away. Her knee knocked a stool over. The side of her ribcage hit another, flipping the stool sideways. She fell on it, her body slamming against the seat edge, the legs and rungs. In a daze, she rolled off it.

She pushed herself to her hands and knees. The knife was gone. She lurched forward, scuttling over the carpet, digging in her toes, shoving away with her fists, trying to stand. With a *whish* and smack, the rope seared her rump. Then she was on her feet. She dodged around the corner of the bar, and ran.

Footfalls and harsh breathing close behind. *Whish!* The rope cut across her back.

She raced past the front door, into the corridor. Then a hand rammed against her back. She flew forward, legs flinging out wildly to stay under her. But it was no use. She hit the carpet chest-first and skidded to a halt.

'You're mine now,' Tony gasped. 'You should've been nice.'

He stepped on her.

He stood on her buttocks with both feet.

'I loved you, Dani.' He bounced, grinding her pelvis against the carpet. 'I never loved anyone else. I think I'll skin you. I'll tie you up and cut your skin off a piece at a time. No. No, I'll use my teeth. Would you like that?' He bounced again.

Dani thrust herself up. The feet shot off her rump. Glancing back as she scurried over the carpet, she saw Tony hit the wall with his shoulder and sprawl backwards, arms flailing.

She dashed down the corridor. Grabbing the door frame, she hurled herself into her bedroom. She slammed the door. Her thumb jabbed the lock button down.

'You can't get away from me!' Tony kicked the door, but it held. 'I'm gonna get you! I'm gonna rip your skin off!'

He stepped back, ran at the door and smashed his shoulder against it. The impact hurled him back.

'I'll *get* you!' he yelled.

Then he raced to the guest bathroom. He flicked on the light, tugged open a drawer under the sink. A fingernail file. It was metal and pointed. He ran to the bedroom door. His hand trembled badly. Then the point scraped into the key hole. He twisted the file and heard a soft, ringing *pop*.

He threw the door open, stepped inside, and shut it.

Except for the flames of two candle stubs on the dresser, the room was dark.

'Where *are* you?' he sang. 'I'm gonna *get* you.'

He stared at the bed: the coverlet heaped at its foot, the top sheet thrown back, the pillows crooked. She must've been on it earlier with Jack. Making love. By candlelight.

Rushing forward, he dropped to his knees and peered into the darkness under the bed.

Not there.

He stood up, turned around. The door to the master bathroom was shut.

'Well, well, Dani.' As he took a step toward it, he heard the sound of a heavy splash.

He whirled. He charged past the end of the bed and batted the curtains aside. The glass door was open. The water in the lighted pool still trembled from the impact.

He ran to the pool's edge.

He stared.

The body was face-up in the deep water near the diving board, rigid as a corpse, sinking slowly toward the bottom.

'Dani!'

Her eyes gazed up at the surface as if entranced by the view. Her mouth was wide open.

Tony sidestepped along the rim of the pool.

God, she looked beautiful, the lights shimmering on her naked body, her hair drifting as if stirred by a strange wind.

Tony wanted her so badly.

But he couldn't go into the water, not even for Dani. Suppose it was a trick, and she grabbed him and held him under . . .

If it's a trick, she'll come up for air.

But she didn't.

She sank to the bottom.

She blurred and streaked as tears filled Tony's eyes. 'Oh Dani,' he whispered.

Then pain split his head.

Tony winced. His head throbbed. He wanted to hold it, but when he tried to raise his hands, they wouldn't move. He opened his eyes.

He was outside, facing Dani's house, lashed to the aluminum frame of a patio chair.

His head pulsed as he looked from side to side. At first, he saw no one in the darkness. Then a pale figure stepped out from behind the distant barbeque.

It walked slowly toward him.

It was a naked woman, her skin pale in the moonlight.

She held a machete in one hand, a canister in the other.

'Who are you?' Tony gasped.

'You know me.'

She was near enough for the pool lights to flutter dimly on her face.

'Get away!'

She shook her head. She tossed the machete aside, its blade clattering on the concrete. 'I almost used the blade,' she said. 'I would've, but I need some information.'

She shook the canister in her left hand. Tony heard sloshing liquid.

Charcoal lighter!

She flicked up the plastic cap. Without another word, she squirted the fluid onto him. It came out in a thin stream, splashing over his shaven head, running down his face. It felt cold except when it touched his wounds, and then it burned.

'You can't do this!'

She said nothing. The stream stopped for a moment. The can made a hollow, buckling sound, and squirted again. She moved it back and forth, criss-crossing his chest, his belly.

'What do you want?'

The can made another popping sound. She aimed the fluid between his legs. It matted his pubic hair, splattered his limp penis, trickled down his scrotum.

She walked away.

'Where're you going!'

'To get the matches.'

'No! Please! Oh my God, don't! I'm sorry! I was just kidding about skinning you! Honest! I'm sorry! I'll leave you alone, I promise! I'll do anything! PLEASE!'

She stopped and turned.

'Tell me where to find Jack.'

# Chapter Thirty

She left Tony tied to the chair. Rushing across her bedroom, she tossed the machete to the floor. She grabbed her handbag from the dresser and blew out the candle flames.

In the living room, she scooped her robe off the floor. She shoved her arms into it as she raced for the workroom. Propped against the side wall beside the rake was a spade. She grabbed it.

Then she was outside, sprinting across the cool wet grass, the robe fluttering behind her like a cape. At her car, she jerked open the handbag. She felt inside for the key case, couldn't find it, crouched and dumped the contents on the driveway. She snatched her keys and billfold from the heap. Clamping the billfold under her arm, she snapped open the key case. She found the car key. It kept missing the lock hole. She held her hand steady with her other hand, and the key slipped in.

She twisted it, tugged open the door and threw the shovel across the back seat. She flung herself behind the wheel and managed to fit the key into the ignition. The engine sputtered to life. She rammed the shift into reverse, remembered to shut the door but forgot to release the emergency brake. When she popped the clutch, the car lurched and died.

Dani whimpered.

She took the brake off. The car started rolling backwards. She turned the key and gunned the engine and sped down the driveway.

\* \* \*

Tony, still sobbing from the ordeal, squirmed on the chair. The ropes burnt into his arms and feet as he struggled. Though his arms seemed bound securely, he felt some give around his feet. He strained against the ropes. He kicked. The bindings seemed to loosen. Pressing his right ankle against the aluminum tubing of the chair leg, he drew his foot up. His heel squeezed out! He drew his knee up, and his foot slipped free.

Using it to shove at the rope wrapped around his left foot, he had little trouble pulling loose.

He thrust himself forward. The chair tipped onto its front legs. He stood, hunched over the chair pressed to his back and rump, and took a waddling step.

If he could just get inside, get to the knife or machete . . . If he just had enough time, he knew he could cut himself free.

Sweat and charcoal lighter streamed down his body as he took another step toward the house.

Dani waited at the intersection with Laurel Canyon Boulevard. She moaned in frustration as the cars sped by. 'Come *on*,' she muttered, pounding the steering wheel with her palm.

Finally, there was a break in the traffic. She shot out, tires whining as she swung to the left. Her foot shoved the accelerator to the floor.

Thank God, the field where Tony left Jack wasn't far away. Maybe a five-minute drive.

Five minutes.

Each second must seem like forever, trapped in a coffin.

How long could the air last? Not very long. Jack might already be . . .

'Hang on,' she said. 'Please.'

The traffic light on Mulholland turned red. The cars in front

of Dani slowed down, stopped. She crept up close to the tail of
the Rolls in front of her, pushed the brake pedal down, pressed
her forehead to the steering wheel and wept.

Tony had only taken a few short steps toward the sliding door of
Dani's bedroom when a voice said, 'Hello.' His head jerked
sideways.

A girl stepped away from the gate at the far side of the house.
She wore a pale dress.

'Help me,' Tony called.

'Sure,' she said. 'I'll help you.'

Something about the voice sent a chill through Tony. He
tried to straighten up. The chair hit the backs of his knees.
They buckled and he fell. The chair caught him, scooted back,
tipped, but not enough to throw him over.

Just this side of the barbeque, the girl paused. She squatted
and stood up again. 'I've been watching you,' she said, slowly
walking closer. 'You had a very close call.'

'The woman's nuts. She was gonna kill me.'

'I'm glad she didn't.'

'Untie me?'

'I don't think so.'

'Please?'

She shook her head. In the wavering light from the pool, her
face looked familiar. 'Who are you?'

'Don't you remember? The old Freeman house?'

His heart thundered. He could barely breathe, but managed
to gasp out, 'Linda?'

'You do remember.'

'Wha . . . what are you doing here?'

She didn't answer.

'Where'd you come from?'

'Your hearse.'

Twisting his head as far as he could, he saw her stoop down and pick up the tin of charcoal lighter.

'Linda!'

She stepped in front of him. She shook the container. In her left hand was a box of matches

'Oh Jesus, don't.'

He kicked at her, but she simply stepped to the side of the chair, out of reach.

Fuel squirted onto his head.

'No! I never hurt you! Please! God, Linda, don't! I never hurt you! I never hurt *anyone*!'


The car bounced under Dani as she sped over the grassy field. She steered between two trees, turned sharply right to avoid another, and her headlights swept across the coffin.

It was resting on the ground, no more than twenty feet ahead.

Not buried at all!

She leapt from the car and ran. Undergrowth stabbed her bare feet, bushes lashed her legs. A root tripped her. She fell sprawling and scurried up and ran and dropped to her knees beside the coffin. Her hands thrust into the piles of dirt on top. She flung her arms back and forth, smashing through the loose soil. It rained against her. She spit to clear her mouth. Then the lid was clear.

She pounded on it. 'Jack! Jack!'

No answer.

Along the rim of the lid were half a dozen metal wing-bolts. She grabbed one and began to unscrew it.

* * *

A match flared, casting grotesque shadows over Linda's face.

'No! Come on!' Tony rammed his feet against the concrete, shoving his chair backwards a few inches.

Linda puffed out the match.

'Please! I never meant any harm!'

She struck another match. She took a step toward him. Whimpering, Tony thrust his chair further back. Linda flicked the match. Its flame drew a bright, curving mark through the air, went dark, and landed near his feet.

He scooted back.

Another match burst to life.

'*Please!*'

'Scared?' Linda asked, holding out the match.

'I'll do anything!'

'You've already done too much.' The flame burned close to her fingers. 'Tell me you're scared.'

'I'm *scared*!'

She shook the match out, and lit another. 'I was so scared I pissed myself.'

'Okay!' His muscles seemed too tight.

Linda struck another match.

'I'm trying!' Then a hot stream was shooting out, splashing his legs. 'There! See?'

'Isn't it fun?' Linda asked, and tossed the match. The brilliant tear of flame arced toward him.

Tony rammed his heels into the concrete. The chair jumped backwards. The match fell on his lap and he almost laughed in spite of the searing sting because it had gone out an instant before it touched him.

But he didn't laugh.

He shrieked.

He seemed to fall forever, screaming and kicking at the sky. Then the water silenced him.

Dani tossed aside the final bolt and tugged at the coffin lid. She raised it a bit. Her fingers slipped and it thudded down. She grabbed it again and lifted. This time, it felt strangely light. It slid off, and she saw why it had moved so easily.

Jack had helped.

He sat up.

Dani threw her arms around his head, hugging it to her breasts and sobbing.

'I can't breathe,' said his muffled voice.

Dani released him. Taking his arm, she helped him climb from the coffin. 'Why didn't you answer me?' she asked.

He shrugged. 'Thought I was dreaming. I was having a fine dream till you dropped the lid.'

'Sorry.'

'I'll forgive you.' Jack pulled her against him. His powerful body began to shake, and she heard him sobbing, too.

For a long time, they held each other.

# Chapter Thirty-one

'I guess he never really intended to kill me,' Jack said. 'Otherwise, he wouldn't have drilled the air hole in the top. He must've cleaned it off after he piled the dirt on.'

'Thoughtful of him,' Dani muttered. She slowed down, and turned onto Asher Lane. 'What'll we do with him?'

'Let the cops take care of it. Assault and battery, attempted rape, that oughta be enough to put him away for . . .'

'Oh my God!'

She stared ahead at the empty length of curb in front of her house.

The hearse was gone.

Jack squeezed her thigh. 'Don't worry. They'll get him.'

'I . . . it's just that . . . I hoped it was over.'

'It's all right.'

She pulled onto the driveway beside Jack's Mustang. Climbing out, her foot came down on lipstick and a compact. She squatted down and started to load her handbag. Jack knelt beside her and helped. Then he put an arm around her. They walked to the front door.

The house was silent, and dark except for the corridor lights.

Dani frowned. She pointed.

Tony's blue slacks were draped over the back of a nearby chair, the pocket linings hanging out like pale tongues.

'He must've been in quite a hurry,' Jack said.

They stepped over to the bar. As Jack phoned the police,

Dani picked up the two bar stools she'd knocked over. She started to make drinks.

Jack finished.

Dani placed a vodka and tonic in his hand.

'I want to propose a toast,' he said, staring at her with solemn eyes. 'To Ingrid.'

'To Ingrid. The nicest gift anyone ever gave me. And certainly the most useful.'

They clinked their glasses and sipped.

'You never finished thanking me,' Jack said.

'I'll have to thank Bruce, too. I feel so awful, giving him a hard time like that. I as much as called him incompetent for misplacing her that way.'

'He was a good sport. Kept his cool. Didn't give me away.'

Dani nodded. 'Well, why don't we go ahead and fish her out?'

They went outside. They walked to the edge of the pool, and Dani clutched Jack's arm.

Neither spoke.

They stared down into the water.

Tony was there, hands still lashed to the patio chair, staring up at them from the bottom of the pool. Ingrid was there beside him, face down. One of her arms was stretched out, though Dani was sure they'd been at her sides when she threw the mannequin into the pool.

The hand of the reaching arm, probably urged by the currents of the filtering system, had found its way to Tony's throat.

'Let's go back inside,' Jack whispered.

They turned away, holding hands tightly, and walked toward the house.

# Chapter Thirty-two

'Hi, Mom? . . . Yes, it's me . . . Sure, I'm fine . . . I flew to Chicago . . . Yes, I'm coming home. I realised I was just being silly, running off like that. I mean, what are the chances the killer'd come after me? Yes, I love you, too. Give my love to Dad and Bob . . . I'll see you tomorrow.'

# Allhallow's Eve

# Chapter One

Clara Hayes had lived alone in the last house on Oakhurst Road ever since a heart attack struck her husband at the top of the stairs and he tumbled down to land at her feet. Dr Harris said the broken neck killed him before cardiac arrest got the chance. That was eleven years ago.

He'd been a cranky old bastard, and she was well rid of him.

Alfred was a far better companion than her husband had been, even though Alfred spent most of the day stalking through the cemetery behind the house.

The ten o'clock news came on, so Clara knew it was time for Alfred to come in. She used her remote to turn off the television, then picked up her cane and hobbled out to the kitchen. She opened the back door.

A chilly wind blew against her. She took a deep breath of the fresh October air, and peered across her yard.

'Al-l-l-fred!' she called.

Generally, she would hear the clink of his collar tags before ever seeing him. She listened, but heard only the dry shuffling of leaves on the graveyard trees.

'Al-l-l-fred?'

Careful not to fall – her broken hip last year had laid her up good and proper for five months – she stepped down the three wooden stairs to the yard. She made her way across the moonlit lawn, and stopped at the edge of her flower bed. From there, she peered through the bars of the cemetery fence. So dark over there, the trees shading the moon.

'Al-l-l-l-fred!' she called. Much too loudly. She imagined heads rising in their coffins, turning – corpses listening to her voice. Softly, she called, 'Here, kitty-kitty-kitty.'

Her eyes searched the darkness.

Saw a solitary figure near the cemetery fence.

Gasping, she took a quick step backwards. Her foot slipped on the dewy grass. She jabbed down her cane, and caught her balance.

'Dear me,' she muttered.

She looked again at the dark figure – the stone angel of a monument she'd seen thousands of times before, in daylight. The graveyard looked so different at night. She didn't like it, not one bit. She should've stayed in the doorway to call Alfred, the way she always did after dark.

'You just stay out,' she muttered, 'if that's your drother.'

She turned away from the cemetery, and started her journey back to the open kitchen door. She hurried. The back of her neck tingled with gooseflesh, and she knew it wasn't the wind's doing.

I'm just being silly, she thought. That graveyard's safe as apple pie. I'm just letting my jitters get the best of me.

Never yet been a corpse crawl out of its hole and go chasing after live folks. It's not hardly about to start happening tonight.

Fur brushed her leg, and she yelped.

Alfred scampered up the porch steps, stopped abruptly in the doorway, and looked over his shoulder at Clara.

'You rascal,' she said,

She took a deep, shaky breath, and pressed a hand to her chest.

'Scared my wits out,' she told him.

She started to climb the steps.

That's when she heard a quiet, muffled clank rather like a crowbar dropping onto a wooden floor. Staring at Alfred, she hardly breathed.

The cat turned away, as if bored. He disappeared into the kitchen. Clara hurried in after him. She swung the kitchen door shut, and locked it.

Alfred sat down in front of the refrigerator. He looked back at Clara.

'Not just now,' Clara whispered.

Turning off the kitchen light, she limped into the dining room. She made her way past her highboy. The room was dark, but she saw no use in planting herself smack in front of the window where she just might be seen – so she approached the window from its side.

If she just had one of those cardboard periscopes like Willy used to play with ... Well, you couldn't ever see much with that contraption, anyhow.

Bracing herself on the cane, she leaned toward the window. She eased aside the soft, priscilla curtains and peered out.

The Sherwood house, next door, looked no different from usual. The old colonial was just as dreary and forlorn as could be: its driveway and lawn overgrown, its siding sadly in need of paint, its windows boarded over.

Though she couldn't see its front door from here, she knew it was padlocked shut. So was the back door. Glendon Morley, the real estate man, had the only keys.

Maybe he'd gone in, for some reason. Didn't seem likely, though. He hadn't come by with house-hunters since July, and Clara suspected he'd given up on trying to foist off the place. Who'd want to live there, after what happened?

If it wasn't Glendon in the house, though, who could it be?

Maybe some kids broke in. They'd done that once, a couple years back, and run around hooting and howling like a bunch of banshees.

She'd rung up Dexter, that night, and he'd gone in and rounded them up and brought them out in cuffs.

Clara frowned. She hated to bother him at this hour, just to send him on a wild-goose chase. Could be the noise she'd heard didn't come from the Sherwood house at all.

She'd swear it did, though.

And she knew she wouldn't get a wink of sleep, knowing someone was inside that grim old house, wandering its dark rooms, and probably up to no good.

Might even be the killer, himself. They never did find out who did away with all those Sherwoods. Maybe he came back, after all these years . . .

She got the shivers, just thinking about it.

'Well,' she sighed.

Letting the curtain fall, she stepped away from the window. She hobbled out of the darkness and into the comforting lights of her living room. Lowering herself to the couch, she picked up the telephone. She placed it on her lap and dialed 0. As she listened to the ringing, Alfred sprang onto the couch and nuzzled her arm.

'Directory assistance,' said a flat voice.

'Put me through to Dexter Boyanski, on Jefferson Street.'

'What city, please?'

'Ashburg.'

She scratched Alfred's neck. He purred loudly.

'That's 432–6891.'

'I'm blind,' she lied. 'Would you dial that for me?'

'Certainly.'

Moments later, she heard quiet ringing. Then Dexter's voice. 'Yes?' he asked.

'Dexter, this is Clara Hayes.'

'How *are* you?'

She laughed softly. 'I'm still in working order, thank you.'

'Well, that's mighty good to hear. Betty says you haven't been to bingo lately.'

'Nor will I, long as Winky Simms is calling. He calls so slow, I grow moss in my ears just waiting on him. Why they let him keep on is more than I can fathom – the poor man stutters like a scratched record.'

'Well . . .'

'Anyway, that's not why I called. I was out back calling in my cat, a while ago, and I heard some noise in the old Sherwood house. Now, I had a long look at the place. It appears just as dead as always – but then, you can't tell much from looking 'cause it's all boarded up. I'm not up to snooping around to see if it's still locked, but I'll wager it's not. Dexter, there's somebody in that house.'

'I'll come out and have a look.'

'I think you'd best.'

Dexter, having just finished a shower when Clara phoned, was wearing his bathrobe. Since he had to get dressed, anyway, he decided he might as well put on his uniform.

Too chancy, doing police work in civvies.

As he dressed, he thought about calling the station. Either of the men on night shift could handle this as well as him. Clara was an old friend, though. If she wanted Chet or Berney, she would've called the station. She was probably hoping he'd drop in, afterwards, and chat a spell.

Dexter got into his Dingo boots. He hurried out the front door, strapping on his gunbelt, and ran to his car.

When Clara heard an engine, she went to the side window of her living room and looked out. A car turned into the driveway of the Sherwood house. It wasn't a white police car with a rack of lights on top, like she expected, but a big man in uniform and a Stetson climbed out. He turned toward her and raised a hand in greeting. So it was Dexter, all right. She waved back, and he turned away.

She watched him stride through the knee-deep weeds. He climbed the porch steps, vanished briefly behind the pillars of the veranda, and reappeared for a moment before entering the recess that hid the front door from her view.

He wasn't out of sight for more than a moment before he stepped back and trotted down the stairs again.

He walked toward her, shaking his head. At the corner, he turned and walked along the side of the house.

Face close to the glass, Clara watched Dexter until he turned the corner.

It'll take him a bit to check the back door, she thought. If it's locked proper, he'll probably go around the other side of the house to the front, and then come over and say, 'She's locked up tight as a drum, Clara.'

'I know I heard something.'

'Well, maybe it came from the Horners' place.'

Gazing out the window, she suddenly hoped the noise *had* come from the Horner house. She hated to think of Dexter finding the back door broken open, and walking into that dark house where such awful things had happened.

She wished, now, that she hadn't called him.

Could've phoned the station house instead, and they'd have sent out one of those other cops. Wouldn't matter so much, a different cop going in that dark old house.

They weren't her friends.

Wouldn't matter, so much, if they never came out.


The padlock was fastened in place, but four screws were missing from the latch plate on the back door. Dexter turned the knob. He pushed the door open.

Unholstering his revolver, he looked into the kitchen. He shined his flashlight in. It lit the linoleum floor, the closed door to the hallway, the gap where the refrigerator used to be.

And he remembered that other night, so long ago. The refrigerator's white door smudged with bloody handprints. Hester Sherwood's handprints. She must've staggered into the kitchen hoping to get a weapon. Half-dead already. Bracing herself against the refrigerator, leaving those grotesque, three-fingered prints with her right hand. They'd found her severed fingers upstairs, on the bedroom carpet. Somehow, she got this far before the killer caught up to her. Just far enough to leave those deformed prints on the refrigerator, before he threw her down and did the rest.

Suddenly, Dexter didn't want to enter the house. He didn't want to take those two or three steps, and look at the place on the floor where they'd found Hester.

Found her naked.

He'd danced with her once, at the prom they'd both chap-eroned a year before the killings. Held her in his arms. Felt the push of her stiffly brassièred breasts against his chest. All of her encased under the soft gown, armored to protect her skin from touch. She even wore white gloves to her elbows.

There on the floor, armor gone. Flesh laid open, breasts . . .

Quickly, to stop remembering, he stepped into the kitchen. He swept the flashlight past the cupboards, stove, sink. Refused to look at the floor. Hurried into the hall.

It used to be carpeted with a plush, red runner. Now the hardwood floor was bare. He opened a door to his left, and entered the dining room. He shined his light on the wall where kids had painted their names, a couple of years ago. The names remained, 'John + Kitty', circled by a heart. Innocent, out of place in this crypt of a house.

Dexter suddenly noticed splashes of red on top of the painted heart.

He raised his flashlight up the wall, and groaned.

*Who the hell?*

Someone had painted a large hand above the heart – a hand dripping blood from the stubs of two severed fingers. The paint glistened in Dexter's light. He stepped close to the wall. Clamping the flashlight between his thighs, he raised a hand and touched the paint.

Still wet.

He grabbed the flashlight and spun around, shining it on the other walls, the ceiling. No more murals, thank God.

The guy who did this, though – the sick bastard who painted the hand – he might still be inside the house.

Dexter rushed across the empty room. The double doors to the foyer stood open. He stepped through them, sweeping his light from the front door to the living room entrance, and up the stairway on his right.

He'd leave upstairs till last, he decided.

Silently, he stepped past the banister. He looked down the narrow hallway that led back toward the kitchen. Then he crossed it and entered the living room.

His light cut through the darkness in a quick circle as he pivoted. Nobody in the room but him.

Something didn't belong, though.

Propped against the wall.

He walked toward it, uncertain what he was seeing. It looked like a cage, or . . .

*I'll be damned*, he thought.

Window grates. Half a dozen of them leaning against the wall.

Somebody – maybe Glendon Morley – must be planning to fix the place up. Take the boards off the windows. Put up the wrought-iron bars, instead, to keep the vandals out.

Raising his light, he saw that grates were already in place on the living room's three side windows.

On the inside though.

*What kind of fool . . .?*

Behind Dexter, a floorboard creaked.

He spun around, gasped, and raised his pistol.

Clara, still bent and peering out her window, was so worried she could hardly bear it.

Dexter must've found the house open, just as she'd feared. Otherwise, he would've shown up long ago.

He's in there, this very second. Even with her eyes wide open, Clara could imagine him climbing those long, dark stairs, going into the very bedroom where they'd found James Sherwood with his eyes carved out – so they say. The real story never did come out, but she guessed that most of what she heard was true. Poor Dexter. Why, she wouldn't set foot in that house for a million dollars.

Bad enough, just living next door. She'd have moved away, long ago, if she'd had the money to spare.

How could he go in there? Well, it was her fault. She'd asked him to.

Damnation, she wished she'd rung up the station house instead of Dexter.

*Oh, thank goodness!*

She breathed a deep, shaky sigh of relief as she saw him walk around the far end of the veranda.

Nobody in tow.

Must've been a false alarm, after all. What took him so long, though? He must've found the back door open, and gone in to search the place. Whoever made that noise probably ran off before Dexter got there. Either that, or hid real good. She didn't much like the idea of *that*.

He waved to her.

Clara gestured for him to come on over.

He nodded, his Stetson tipping forward, and Clara left the window. She hobbled across the living room, opened the front door, and stepped halfway out to hold open the screen for him.

Dexter walked slowly through the darkness, his head down.

'Didn't find him, huh?' she asked.

Dexter didn't answer. He didn't look up.

'Dexter, what's wrong?'

He shook his head.

As he climbed the porch stairs, Clara reached to the wall and flicked on the overhead light.

Blood! All over his uniform shirt and trousers as if a bucketful had been dumped on his head.

'Oh my Lord!' Clara gasped. She covered her mouth.

Dexter took off his Stetson and grinned at her. For an instant, she thought he'd put on a Halloween mask to scare the daylights out of her. Then she knew it wasn't a mask. It wasn't Dexter at all, inside that blood-soaked uniform.

A bare foot kicked her cane away.

With a tiny gasp, she fell against the man. He flung her inside the house.

Her head smacked the floor.

Whimpering, she opened her eyes.

The front door swung shut, and the man stood above her.

# Chapter Two

Eric Prince woke up, that night, with a straining bladder. He climbed from bed, and made his way to the shut door.

A straight-backed chair was propped under its knob, a precaution he always took when he went to bed in the deserted house. Though fifteen, and too old to be afraid of staying alone, he liked the secure feeling that came from having his door barred.

As he removed it, he wondered vaguely if his mother was home yet. He had no idea what time it might be. When he opened his door, though, he saw that the hall light was still on.

Mom would've turned it off.

She must still be out. Eric's worry came back, the same worry that fluttered in his stomach every time Mom went out on a date – that he would wake up, in the morning, and she would still be gone. He'd wait and wait, but she would never come back.

Maybe she had run away with a handsome stranger she met in a bar. Eric would get a postcard, a week later, from a distant city.

Or she'd been killed in a car accident.

Or the worst of all – a worry that started after he read an old paperback called *Looking for Mr Goodbar* – she'd met a terrible man on one of her dates, and he had slaughtered her.

Chief Boyanski would come to the house. 'Son, I'm afraid I've got some bad news for you.'

Then Eric would be alone. An orphan. Nobody, in all the world, to take care of him. Maybe he could be like *The Little Girl Who Lived Down The Lane*, and stay alone in the house . . .

These thoughts upset him, driving his grogginess away so that he was completely awake when he pulled open the bathroom door and saw a naked man urinating. Eric jumped back, yelling. The startled man flinched.

Eric ran for his room, clenching his muscles to keep his own pee inside. He was almost to the door when his mother stepped into the hall.

She blinked in the brightness, and tied the belt of her threadbare flannel robe. Her hair was mussed. She looked confused. 'Eric, what're you doing up?'

'There's a *man* in the John!'

'Oh. That's only Sam.' She smiled sadly. 'He must've given you quite a scare, huh?'

Eric nodded.

Down the hall, the toilet flushed. 'Sounds like he'll be right out,' Mom said.

'Who is he?'

'A friend.'

*She's naked under that robe.*

Eric looked away from her. 'Night,' he said, and went into his room. He shut the door and stood in the darkness.

'Damn,' he heard a man say. 'I'm sorry about that.'

'It's okay,' said Mom. She sounded depressed. 'Something like this was bound to happen, sooner or later.'

He heard them walking away.

'Maybe I'd better leave,' the man said.

'No, don't. Please.'

'Shouldn't you have a talk with him?'

'It'll wait. This wouldn't be a good time, anyway.'

He heard the soft bump of a shutting door. If they were still talking, Eric couldn't hear them.

He opened his door. The hallway was deserted and dark. He walked silently to the bathroom, and locked it in case the man came back. Standing over the toilet, he freed himself and started to urinate.

The man had stood right here, naked, just like he owned the place. And he had such a big *thing*. Had he really been putting it into . . . Sure he had. The thought of it made Eric feel sick, as if he'd swallowed a milkshake too fast.

He flushed the toilet.

He walked back to his bedroom, and opened the door. Without stepping inside, he shut it. The noise sounded loud in the stillness.

As silently as he could, he left the house by the back door. He hurried through the chilly, wet grass alongside the house. Mom's VW in the driveway. A bigger car was parked at the curb.

Eric stared at that car for a long time, wondering about the man who owned it, the man in bed with Mom even at this moment. Fucking her. It sounded so dirty and exciting, like jacking off only a hundred times better. He'd day-dreamed a lot about doing it, and imagined it was the neatest thing in the world especially if the girl was someone beautiful like Miss Bennett, or Aleshia Barnes. Even if the girl wasn't beautiful, it'd be great just getting to see her naked, getting to touch her breasts. He could hardly imagine what it would feel like to touch someone's breasts. They must be *so smooth* . . .

He looked down. His penis was poking erect through his pajama fly. He slid his fingers down it, trembling. Then he quickly covered it. This was no time to get all horny.

He rushed to the VW, and ducked beside it. Peering over the hood, he saw that the windows of Mom's bedroom were dark. He crept to the rear of the VW. Squatting beside it, he looked both ways. The road was clear, and he saw no activity at any of the nearby houses.

No excuse to wait.

He dashed down the driveway to the rear of the other car and ducked behind its trunk. On hands and knees, he dug into the curbside debris. His fingers pushed through soggy leaves, twigs, something slippery that writhed away. And then he found a triangle of glass from a broken bottle.

Just the thing.

Gripping it firmly, he pressed the shard against the shiny surface of the trunk, and dragged it down. The sound, like fingernails scraping a blackboard, made him cringe. But it didn't make him stop.

He cut a huge X into the top of the trunk. When he finished, he ran a finger along one of the furrows, and smiled.

# Chapter Three

Sam Wyatt woke up. The bedroom was gray and chilly, but under the covers he was warm. Rolling onto his side, he looked at Cynthia. Her eyes were open. She turned her head toward him, and smiled sadly.

'Didn't you sleep?' he asked.

'A little, I guess.'

'Worried about Eric?'

She nodded. 'I feel so damned rotten.' Her voice trembled on the last word, and she pressed her lips tightly together as if fighting not to cry.

Sam put a hand on the hot skin of her belly. Cynthia stroked the back of it.

'You're anything but rotten,' he said. 'You did all you could to keep him . . .'

'In the dark?'

'Protected.'

'I feel like such a slut.'

Sam started to take his hand away, but she held it.

'No, I don't mean *that*,' she said. 'With you . . . I've never felt so happy and alive. And clean. But Eric . . . he doesn't know. You're a stranger to him, and he must think his mom's sleeping with a stranger.'

'You can tell him different.'

'I will. I just wish it hadn't happened this way. I mean, what a way for him to meet you.' She shook her head. 'It was supposed to be for his own good, you know? I didn't want him knowing the men I dated – getting attached to them. That happened a couple of times, where he started looking on them as – like father figures. He was just devastated when these men suddenly disappeared from his life. I mean, it's bad enough for an adult when a relationship ends. But for a kid who's never had a father . . . I just couldn't put him through that, anymore. It wasn't fair to him. Maybe that was a mistake, I don't know. But I think it saved him from a lot of heartache.'

'Maybe so.'

'Do you think I was wrong?'

'You didn't have to protect him from me. I'm not going to disappear.'

Her eyes went cold. 'No?'

'No.'

'I've heard that before.'

He looked into her accusing eyes. 'Don't blame me for what the others did.'

'I'm not.'

'Because I'm not them, I'm me. It's bothered me for a long time that you didn't want me to meet Eric. I just let it go, but it didn't make me feel good to be kept hidden from him as if you're afraid I'll contaminate him.'

'He would like you, Sam. He'd . . .' Cynthia's eyes brimmed with tears. 'He'd fall in love with you, just like I did.'

'Would that be so awful?' he asked. He tried to smile, but his mouth trembled.

'Yes,' she said. 'If you ever left him. He's been left so many times before.' She rolled onto her side, crying softly, and Sam took her in his arms.

'I think I'd better stay home with Eric, tonight,' Cynthia said as they walked down the driveway.

A chilly wind was blowing. Sam liked the way it tossed her brown hair.

'I'll tell him about you,' she said.

'Why don't I take you both out to dinner, one of these nights?'

'We'll see.'

Frowning, he stepped to the rear of his car and looked down at a big X scratched into the paint of his trunk. 'For Christsake,' he muttered. He ran a finger down one of the deep grooves.

'That's *terrible*. Did it just happen?'

'I don't know. I haven't seen it before. Somebody must've done it last night.'

'Kids, probably.'

He stepped over to Cynthia's VW, and looked it over. 'At least yours is okay.'

'What kind of creep would do a thing like that?'

Sam shrugged. 'Somebody who recognized my car, probably. I'm not too popular with some of the people in town. I always keep it garaged at home. My tires got slashed a couple of times when I was leaving it out.'

She stared at the scratches. 'I'm awfully sorry.'

'Well, these things happen. We've got a saying, "If you want to be loved, be a fireman." '

'You think it's because you're a policeman?'

'More than likely. Well, I'd better be on my way.'

'Yeah. It's time for me to wake up Eric.' She stepped into his arms.

He felt her shivering through the frail robe.

'Call me tonight?' she asked.

'Sure.' He kissed her. 'You'd better get inside before you catch pneumonia.'

He stopped at his duplex for a quick shower and shave, then drove to the station. The office was deserted except for Betty on the switchboard. She swiveled around to face him. 'All quiet on the western front,' she announced, smiling.

'*Das ist gut,*' Sam said. He poured himself a cup of coffee, and wished he'd grabbed something from the refrigerator before leaving home: a hunk of cheese, a hot dog. The coffee tasted wonderful. 'Where's Dex?' he asked.

'I would hazard a guess that he's on the way.'

Sam glanced at the clock. 'He's never late.'

'Rarely.' She took a sip from her own coffee mug, and rubbed the lipstick print with her thumb. 'In the twelve years I've spent laboring under his yoke, he's been late only four times. Five, including today.'

'Absent?'

'Six days, four of them the week Thelma left.'

'Hangovers from celebrating?'

'That should've been the case, but it wasn't. To look at him, you'd think the world had ended. Men can be so foolish when it comes to pretty women.'

240

'You should know.'

'Indeed I do.' At fifty-two, Betty was still a slim, good-looking woman. 'And I'll admit, I've occasionally taken advantage of starry-eyed men. My husband is a perfect example.' She laughed softly. 'But there's absolutely no excuse for a woman to behave like Thelma. Beauty doesn't give one license to abandon common decency. It's a crime the way she treated that man.'

'Speaking of crime . . .' Sam finished his coffee, and rinsed out the mug. 'I'd better hit the road.'

'Let me just ring up Dexter.'

While she dialed, Sam unlocked the gun cabinet and took out a sawed-off Browning.

'He doesn't answer,' she said.

'I'll head over to his place.'

'Why don't you? I know he's only ten minutes late, but it's so unlike him.'

'I'll check, and let you know.'

'Thanks, Sam.'

As he got into his patrol car, he half expected Dexter's Firebird to swing into the parking lot. It didn't, though, and he found his muscles tightening with worry as he drove out. He couldn't imagine the chief over-sleeping. The big man had been raised on a farm, and often spoke of the built-in alarm clock that woke him at dawn, no matter what.

Car trouble, maybe.

*Heart attack*, whispered a corner of Sam's mind.

He kept an eye on all the cars he passed, on those parked along the curbs. At a stop sign, he glanced at Ed's Chevron. No Firebird.

For a moment, he wondered if the vandal who scratched the back of his own car had gone to Dexter's house – maybe slashed

Dex's tires, or sugared the gas . . . That didn't seem likely, but it was possible. A minor-league vendetta against the Ashburg PD?

Finally, easing around a corner, he came into sight of Dexter's house and saw the chief's red Firebird parked in the driveway.

He picked up the radio mike. 'Car Five.'

'Go ahead, Car Five.'

'Chief's car's parked in his driveway. I'll see if he's home, Betty.'

Sam walked up the driveway, giving the Firebird a quick inspection as he passed it. No flat tires, at least. Nothing unusual about its appearance.

He hurried to the front door and rang the bell. Dexter didn't answer. Sam took a deep breath, and realized he was trembling. He jabbed the doorbell button again and again, then swung open the screen door and banged the wood with his knuckles.

What's the use? He's not home.

Or if he is, he's on the floor dead of cardiac arrest. Or he ate his gun. No, Dex wouldn't do that. Or would he? Or did someone break into the house last night, someone with a major-league vendetta?

None of the above, probably.

Sam tried the door knob. It turned.

Thank God. Dex'd blow his stack if I had to break in.

He stepped inside, automatically wiping his feet on the entry rug as he looked around.

'Dexter?' he called. 'Dexter, you here?'

Beside the easy chair, a lamp was on.

Sam rushed through the living room and up a short hallway to the bedroom. The shades were drawn, the lamp on. It seemed so wrong, in daylight – like the shunned room of an invalid.

The bed was made.

Okay. Whatever happened, it was probably last night before Dex went to bed. Whatever . . .

'Dexter?' Sam called again.

The house was silent.

He stepped around the end of the bed. He dropped to his knees, and glanced under it. Nothing there except the electric blanket control. He got up, and looked inside the closet. A few pairs of shoes were scattered on the floor, but the old Dingos weren't among them.

*He's in uniform, then.*

Sam shut the closet door. He wiped his sweaty hands on his pants, took a deep breath, and felt a tightness in his bladder.

Damn, why hadn't he locked the bathroom door, last night? Must've scared the hell out of that poor kid . . . He left the bedroom.

He walked down the hall, past the open bathroom door.

Might as well take care of it now.

Stepping into the bathroom, he glimpsed himself in the medicine cabinet mirror. Looked damn edgy. He rubbed his face. He bent down, and lifted the toilet seat, and saw an eyeless face look up at him through the pink water, gray hair floating as if tugged by a strange wind, tongue lolling.

The lid banged down.

Sam backed against a wall, gasping. Hot fluid gushed up his throat. He covered his month. The sink was too far. He jerked open the shower curtain and bent over the tub and his teary eyes looked down on the blur of a split torso, detached arms and legs.

# Chapter Four

The rear doors of the coroner's van were slammed shut. Sam and the other four officers of the Ashburg Police Department stood on the front lawn of Dexter Boyanski's house, silent until the van was out of sight.

Berney Weissman, the assistant chief, took off his silver-rimmed glasses and squeezed the bridge of his nose. 'All right,' he said in a weary voice. 'Let's take a look at what we've got so far.'

'We've got zilch,' said Chet Summers.

During the past two hours, they'd sketched and photographed the crime scene, searched the house, vacuumed the bathroom floor, and lifted two dozen latent prints. Most of the prints on the labeled cards could probably be weeded out later, as belonging to either Dexter or Sam.

'We know it happened last night,' Sam said.

'Between nine and twelve,' Berney added, quoting the coroner's estimate. 'Chet, you go back to the station and check the log book. See if any calls came in that might have a bearing. Go through the whole day, everything till now. Then get in touch with Ethel and George, find out if anything happened that they maybe didn't bother logging.'

Chet nodded, and walked to his car.

'I'll take this side of the street. Sam, you take the other side. Buck, I want you over on Jackson Street – maybe someone behind Dexter's place heard something.'

'A lot of folks'll be at work,' Buck said.

'So we'll come back again tonight. Let's go.'

* * *

Sam crossed the street, heading for the corner house. Damn it, he'd spent last night only three blocks from here. After dancing at the Sunset Lounge, they'd driven up Jackson Street to Cynthia's house. At about eleven o'clock. They might just as easily have taken Jefferson instead, and gone right past Dexter's place, maybe seen a strange car parked in front, or heard a noise . . .

Well, it hadn't happened that way. No use spending brain power on a pile of ifs.

He pressed the doorbell of the corner house, and heard ringing chimes inside. A dog started yipping. From its high-pitched frenzy, he guessed it was a small dog. Probably one of those miniature poodles. He waited a few seconds, then rang the bell again. The dog *yip-yapped* frantically.

Sam wrote the address on his clipboard. Beside the address, he wrote, 'No response – (dog).'

Then he cut across the yard to the front stoop of the next house. He pushed the doorbell. This one buzzed.

A gaunt man in a green jumpsuit opened the door and looked up at Sam like a weasel peering from its hole. The friendly, curious tone of his voice surprised Sam. 'What can I do for you, officer?'

'A crime was committed across the street last night. I'm interviewing everyone on the block. Did you see or hear anything . . .?'

'At whose place?'

'The Boyanski . . .'

'Dex? Shitfire! What'd they do to 'im?'

'He was murdered.'

'Dex?' Sorrow and disbelief filled the man's eyes. 'Goddamn.'

'Did you notice anything?'

'What time you say it happened?'

'Between nine and midnight, probably.'

He ran a hand over his thin, gray hair. 'Damn, I wish I had. I was reading in the back room, most of that time. We'd get together over a six-pack, you know. Goddamn.' He rubbed his chin. 'If I was you, I'd take a mighty hard look at what Thelma was doing last night. You know Thelma?'

Sam shook his head. 'Never met her.'

'Just have a look at what she was up to last night. That's all.'

'You think she killed him?'

'Well, you know she ran off with that bartender, Babe Rawls, from over at the country club. That was five-six years ago. Nearly busted Dex's heart. I told him, though. "Dex," I said, "you can thank your lucky stars you're rid of that gal." Took him a long spell to get over her, but he finally did.'

'I thought she'd moved to Milwaukee.'

'That's what I heard, too. Saw her over at the Food King yesterday afternoon, though.'

'We'll look into it,' Sam said. 'Could I have your name?'

'Charley Dobbs.'

He wrote it on his clipboard. 'Thank you for the help, Mr Dobbs.'

'He was a good man, Dex.'

'Yes.'

'Goddamn.'

The door shut. Next to Charley Dobbs's name, Sam wrote, 'Saw nothing. Thelma in town?' Then he crossed the lawn to the next house. Nobody answered the door. He wrote 'No response' beside the address, and moved on.

This house was directly across the street from Dexter's place. The door opened as he reached toward its bell.

'Officer?' The sleek blonde wore tweed slacks and a white blouse as if dressed for a luncheon – or a visitor.

'My name's Sam Wyatt.'

'I'm Ticia Barnes.' She offered her hand, and he shook it.

'Do you have a couple of minutes, Mrs Barnes?'

'Certainly. Please come in.'

He thanked her, and stepped into the house.

'Would you care for some coffee?'

'No thanks, I just had some.' He followed her into the living room. He could smell the warm odor of coffee, and wanted a cupful. But he preferred to avoid bathrooms. God, he'd never be able to raise a toilet lid without seeing Dexter's head . . .

'Are you all right?' asked the woman.

He nodded. 'It's been a rough morning.'

'I should imagine.' She sat near the end of the couch, and nodded toward a chair. 'I noticed all the . . . activity at Mr Boyanski's house. The coroner was there?'

'Mr Boyanski was killed last night.'

Her lips pursed. She said, 'Ooooh.'

'Did you see or hear anything?'

'No, I'm afraid not. I always draw the curtains at night, and of course it's been too chilly, lately, to leave the windows open. Was Mr Boyanski *murdered*?'

'Yes.'

'How horrid! Right across the street?'

'We're not sure that's where he was killed, but we . . . found him there.'

'Dreadful.'

'Was anybody else in the house who might've seen something?'

'My husband's away on business. He's *forever* away. My daughter may have noticed something, though. Her bedroom windows face the street. What time . . .? Do you know when it happened?'

'Probably between nine and midnight.'

'Aleshia was in her room, then,' the woman said. 'I hardly ever see her, since we gave her that telephone. So she may very well have noticed something. Of course, she's in school right now. A junior at Hi. She won't get home until – oh – around five, I imagine. Cheerleader practice.'

Sam noted it on his clipboard, and got up. 'I'll drop by this evening, then.'

'Fine. Any time after seven.' She rose. 'Are you certain I can't get you some coffee?'

'I'm certain. Thanks, though.'

They walked toward the door.

'You don't suppose . . .?' She hesitated. 'I do get nervous, sometimes, being alone so much. Is there any chance . . . You don't suppose he'll strike again, do you?'

'It's possible. I'd keep my door locked, just in case.'

'We've never had a murder across the street.'

'We don't get many in this town.'

'The fewer the better, as far as I'm concerned.'

'Me, too.' He thanked her.

'We'll be expecting you later, then.'

'Right,' he said, stepping outside.

'Good luck.' With a quick smile, she shut the door.

Sam made notes on his clipboard, then crossed the yard to the next house. He pushed the doorbell button, but didn't hear it ring inside. So he knocked on the aluminum frame of the screen door. A few moments later, the inner door opened.

'Hi, Ruthie.'

'Sam?' The hefty woman rubbed an eye with the palm of her hand. She wore a quilted pink robe and her feet were bare. 'What's up? Some kind of trouble?' She swayed to one side and craned her neck as if to see what might be going on behind him.

'Dexter's been killed. Murdered.'

Her mouth dropped open. 'Oh my *God.*'

'It happened last night, between about nine and twelve. We're going door-to-door to see if anyone noticed anything unusual.'

'Anything unusual,' she muttered. 'I better call Mike. Maybe he . . .'

Sam shook his head. 'No need to bother him just now. I'll stop by the store later on today.'

'I'm going in, soon as I get myself together. I'll tell him to give it some thought. You know, I *did* see something struck me a little strange.'

Sam's pulse quickened.

'I ran out of cigarettes, last night, and remembered I had a pack in the glove compartment. I was right, too. Found half a pack. Anyway, I was heading back to the house and I heard a car start up. It was Dexter's car. He pulled out of his driveway and headed up the road real fast. I remember thinking he must've got some kind of emergency call.'

'What time was that?'

She frowned. Her tongue pushed against her cheek, bulging out the pale skin as if a nervous animal were trapped in her mouth and trying to burst out. 'During the news,' she finally said. 'The ten o'clock news. I was waiting around for that silly sports announcer to come on – the one that looks like a chipmunk? He didn't come on till almost the end, and that's when I made a beeline outside to fetch my cigarettes. So I guess it must've been around ten twenty-five.'

Sam wrote it down. 'Which way did Dexter go?' he asked.

Ruthie nodded to her left. 'He went speeding up that way, and turned left on Third Street. His tires squealed, he took the corner so fast.' Her tongue made a knob in her cheek again, and she shook her head. 'Wherever he went, he was in a big rush.'

# Chapter Five

'You rat on me, I'll cut your dick off. You understand?' Nate pushed his face close to Eric's. Though only sixteen, the boy had dark whiskers like someone much older. He also had breath that made Eric think of dead snakes baking in the sun. 'You understand, fag?'

'I'm not a fag.'

'Oh yeah? Coulda fooled me.'

'You've got my money. Why don't you just leave me alone?'

''Cause you're a wimpy little fag, shitface.'

He spat on Eric's face, and grinned. Eric gagged at the sweet smell of the dripping saliva. With a laugh, Nate shoved him against a urinal.

'Thanks for the loan, fag.' Nate left.

Still gagging, Eric hurried to a sink. He splashed water on his face, then scrubbed it with the grainy pink soap powder. After rinsing, he thought he could still smell Nate's spit. He gagged again, and once more scoured his face.

The bathroom door swung open.

'Prince!'

He recognized the voice of Mr Doons, the vice principal. Quickly, he splashed water onto his face.

'Prince, what're you doing in here? Have you got a pass?'

'No, sir.'

'What're you doing out of class?'

He reached for the paper towel dispenser. 'I came in between periods, Mr Doons.'

'What are you, deaf? The bell rang five minutes ago.'

'I'm sorry.'

'Sorry doesn't cut it, Prince. When're you gonna shape up?'

Eric rubbed his face with the rough, brown paper.

'Answer me.'

'What do you want me to say?' he asked, his voice trembling. He swallowed. He didn't want to cry, especially not in front of Mr Doons.

'You've got a crappy attitude, Prince.'

'What'd I *do*?'

The v.p. stabbed a blunt finger at the floor. 'Give me thirty push-ups, Prince.'

'That isn't fair.'

'*Now*.'

Eric lowered his eyes. The tile was spattered with water – or worse. 'The floor's wet.'

'Do it!'

'There's piss on the floor!' His voice cracked, and tears flooded his eyes.

Doons smiled. 'It'll do you good, Prince.'

Eric crouched, and placed his hands on the gritty floor. The tile under his left hand was wet. Crying silently, he started doing push-ups.

'Let's hear it.'

'Three, four, five . . .'

'All the way down, Prince.'

'Six, seven . . .'

'Louder.'

'Eight.'

'I can't hear you.'

'*Nine, ten, eleven . . .*'

'Think you're real smart, don't you?'

'No.'

'Gonna cut class again?'

'No.'

'Gonna wise off?'

'No.'

'Gonna put another dead rat in Miss Major's desk?'

'No.' So *that was it!* 'Twenty-three.'

'Thought that was smart, didn't you?'

'No.'

'Made her puke.'

'Twenty-eight,' he said, no longer crying as he remembered the way she barfed. It had served the bitch right.

'Twenty-nine, thirty.' He quickly dried his eyes as he stood up.

'That was a sick, perverted thing you did to her, Prince.'

Eric lowered his eyes. He'd thought, at the time, that he'd been let off too easily. He decided that Miss Major was too embarrassed by the incident to tell the administration. She wouldn't want her own part to come out.

Apparently, he'd been wrong.

She'd told some of it, at least. To Doons. Not all of it, though.

She certainly couldn't tell the reason Eric put the rat in her desk. She wouldn't dare.

'Do you want to know why I did it?'

''Cause you're a sick little wise-ass. Now get to class.'

Eric turned to the sink.

'No time for that. Get going. And next time you step out of line, Prince, you're gonna wish you hadn't.'

'Yes, sir.'

Eric left the bathroom. Doons followed him, a few steps behind, as he walked up the hallway. He opened the door to his English class, and entered.

Miss Bennett glanced at him. There was no malice in her eyes. She continued talking about Huck Finn.

Eric hurried to his seat. The rat had been worthwhile, if only because it got him transferred to Miss Bennett's class. He liked her a lot. She was pretty – so pretty that he often got horny just looking at her – and she never put him down.

He watched her talk. Her blue eyes were shiny and intense. She held a paperback copy of *Huckleberry Finn* in one hand. Her other hand gestured, pointed to students for answers, and sometimes brushed aside the blond hair over her forehead.

Eric's own hair hung down, tickling his right eyebrow. He wanted to push it into place, but Doons hadn't let him wash his hands. He didn't dare touch himself.

God, what a crud.

Doons and Nate both.

They're probably pals.

Eric used the back of his wrist to shove the hair away. He rubbed his eyebrow.

'Eric?' asked Miss Bennett.

'What?'

'Do you have something to contribute?'

'Uh, no.' He blushed. 'I was just scratching.'

The class laughed.

God, what a day!

When the period finally ended, he rushed to the bathroom and washed his hands. No matter how much he scrubbed, he still felt they were dirty.

He went without lunch because he had no money to buy it.

The rest of the day, his stomach felt empty and he was careful to keep his hands away from his face.

Finally, the last period ended. He walked home alone, and opened the mailbox. Quickly, he flipped through the envelopes. One neatly typed envelope was addressed to him.

Unlocking the door, he hurried into the house. He tossed the other mail onto a lamp table. With a trembling hand, he tore open his letter.

He pulled out the single sheet of paper and unfolded it.

JOIN THE FUN
SPOOK-HOUSE HALLOWEEN PARTY!!!
THRILLS, GAMES, PRIZES, REFRESHMENTS!!!
COME IN COSTUME – BRING A FRIEND
TO THE BIGGEST, BEST
SCARIEST!!
HALLOWEEN PARTY EVER
WHEN? OCTOBER 31, 9 PM
WHERE? THE OLD SHERWOOD HOUSE
823 OAKHURST ROAD
*DON'T MISS OUT!!!*

# Chapter Six

Martin Bodine, proprietor of Marty's Motor Lodge, scowled at the photo. 'Not here,' he said.

'The picture's six or seven years old,' Sam told him.

'Still not here.' He pushed the photo back across the registration desk. 'Sorry,' he said. He didn't look sorry.

'*Has* she been here?'

'When?'

'Within the past week.'

'No.'

'She could look different now. A different hair style or color . . .'

Martin sighed. 'I've got twenty rooms, *Mister* Wyatt. As of right now, fourteen of 'em are vacant. That means I've got six parties under my roof. You think I wouldn't know it, if this gal was one of them? Let me tell you, I'd know it. She's not here. She wasn't here last night, or the night before. As far as I know, I've never seen the gal my whole life. All right?'

'All right,' Sam said. 'Thanks for your help.'

'Any time.'

Sam walked to the door, clamping the photo of Thelma to his clipboard. Marty's Motor Lodge was the second motel he'd checked after searching Dexter's house and finding a picture of the ex-wife. He'd struck out at both. There were no more motels to try – not in Ashburg. Maybe she'd taken up lodgings in one of the neighboring towns, but Sam doubted it. More likely, she was staying with a friend.

He climbed into his patrol car and drove to the Food King, where Charlie Dobbs had spotted Thelma yesterday. Outside its doors was a pile of pumpkins. Sam remembered buying one only a few days ago. He'd planned to carve a jack-o'-lantern this evening. Now, he doubted he would get to it. He wondered if Cynthia had a pumpkin. It would be fun, getting together with her and Eric to make jack-o'-lanterns. Maybe next year, he thought, hurting with regret.

Inside the store, he found the crew-cut manager behind a booth, okaying a woman's check. He waited until the woman left.

The manager beamed at him. 'Yes?'

'I'm looking for information about a customer who was in here yesterday,' he said, and handed over the photo. 'Do you recall seeing her?'

'Mmm. Say, isn't this Thelma Boyanski?'

Sam nodded.

'You say she was here?'

'That's what I heard.'

'Golly, I haven't seen her for years. Back in town, is she?'

'Apparently.'

'What a gal. I always wondered what happened to her. She used to be in here two-three times a week. Ran off with Babe Rawls, last I heard. Come back, has she? Well, doesn't surprise me. She was a dope to step out on a guy like Dex. Must've finally come to her senses.'

'You didn't see her yesterday, though?'

'Nope. But I keep pretty busy. Could've missed her in all the rush.'

'Okay if I talk to your clerks?'

'Help yourself.' He gestured for Sam to follow. They went through a closed checkout aisle. Near the back of the store, a young man was stamping new prices onto coffee cans. 'Paul, Officer Wyatt wants to ask you a few questions.'

Paul blushed. His chin was pitted and raw with acne.

Sam showed him the picture, and asked the question.

Paul looked as if he wanted to faint with relief. Sam wondered, briefly, what the clerk had done to cause such guilty responses. Probably nothing more than an illegal U-turn a week ago.

'I don't think I've ever seen her in here,' Paul said.

'Have you seen her someplace else?'

'I don't think so.'

'Okay, thanks.'

The manager squinted at Paul, and turned away. They walked down the aisle. 'Wonder what that boy's got on his conscience?'

'Hard to say,' Sam said.

'You see how he looked? He looked as guilty as Judas. Like he thought you'd put him under arrest. I wonder if maybe he hasn't been taking home some merchandise in his pockets.'

'Could be. Plenty of folks do. I wouldn't suspect him, though, just because he got flustered. We've all done things we're ashamed of, and wouldn't want the police to know about.'

'Think I'll keep on eye on him, just in case.'

Half a dozen people waited in the 'Express Line.' Sam smiled at two of the women he recognized. Then he turned his eyes to the manager, who was speaking quietly to the checkout girl. The 'girl' was pushing fifty. She had a lean, tough look. She glanced at Sam, one eye squinting, and nodded. She mouthed a silent, 'Over here.'

They left the manager at the cash register, and stepped over to his deserted booth.

'What's your pleasure?' she asked. Her voice wasn't low and harsh, as Sam expected. It was a high-pitched, musical voice.

'I'm looking for this woman.' He gave her the photo.

'Oh?'

'I heard she was in here yesterday.'

'She most surely was,' lilted the clerk. Her plastic nametag read, 'Louanne.'

'You saw her?'

'With my own eyes. She didn't look exactly this way. Wears her hair up, now, and it's more a dishwater color. Thinner, too. But I saw her, no mistake about that.'

'Did she go through your line?'

'Oh yes.'

'Did she pay with a check?'

Louanne fingered her upper lip. 'No, not with a check.'

'She paid cash?'

The clerk grinned. 'Didn't do that, either. You'll never guess.'

'I give up.'

Her eyes sparkled. 'This lady didn't pay for her groceries at all. I saw a man slip the money into her hand while they stood in line. He did it just as slippery as you please, sneaking it to her 'cause he didn't want nobody spying. I just happened to see him, though. I like to keep my eyes open.'

'Do you know who the man was?'

'I surely do. And it seems mighty strange for a good-looker like this gal to run around with a toad like him.'

'A toad?'

'It was Elmer Cantwell.'

'Elmer Cantwell?' An odd match, all right. 'That's hard to believe.'

'I had to pinch myself, but it was him all right.'

# Chapter Seven

'Come *on*,' Nate said.

'Where to?'

'You coming, or you just gonna stand there with your fist up your ass?'

'Sure.' Bill Kearny slammed his locker shut. 'Where we going?'

'You'll see.'

They walked together up the deserted hallway, their sneakers squeaking loudly on the linoleum. Ahead of them, a classroom door opened. Miss Bennett stepped out. Setting down a stack of books and file folders, she glanced at Nate and Bill. She smiled a quick greeting, then turned away to lock her door.

Bill grinned at Nate.

Nate wiggled his heavy eyebrows, and rubbed his hands together.

They passed Miss Bennett, and turned a corner.

'*There's* one teacher I wouldn't kick out of bed,' Bill said.

'Yeah? I'll take Nelson any time. You seen the tits on Nelson?'

'Nelson's a cow.'

'Yeah,' Nate said. 'Great udders. Let me at 'em! Wouldn't mind Bennett, either, though. Get her alone sometime, you know, and slip her the ol' dick.'

'Do you think she does it?'

'Fucks? Bennett? Are you kidding? A gal that looks like her?

She probably bangs her brains out every night and twice on weekends.'.

'She wouldn't do it with a kid, though.'

'Who's a kid?'

'Us.'

'Hey, maybe I'm just sixteen, but I've got a major league bat. A regular Louisville Slugger, man, and I hit a homer every time I get up.'

They trotted down a staircase to the first floor, and nearly collided with Mr Doons. They dodged away from him, and kept on walking.

'Whoa there. Houlder, Kearny, back up.'

They came toward him, shrugging and grinning.

'What're you two doing in the halls?'

'We're on our way out,' Nate said.

'Sixth period ended twenty minutes ago. What've you been up to?'

Bill lowered his eyes, as if ashamed. 'I had to stay after for Mr Fredricks.'

'What about you, Houlder?'

'I was helping Miss Bennett.'

'Helping her how?'

'Washing desks.'

'I'll just bet.'

'Yeah. You should've seen what they wrote on those desks.' Nate grinned. 'Lots about you, you better believe.'

'That so?' He glared at Nate.

'Very complimentary.'

'I'll just bet.'

'Wanta hear one?'

'Wanta tell me one?'

'Sure, but you gotta promise not to bust me. I mean, I'm not the guy saying it. I'm just reporting what some other kid wrote on a desk.'

'I understand that.'

'And you promise you won't bust me?'

Doons nodded. Bill didn't like the man's narrow, challenging eyes. 'Go ahead.'

'Don't,' Bill said. 'Come on, let's go.'

'I want to hear it,' Doons insisted.

'Okay. Here goes. One said, "Doons eats poons." '

His lips curled up. 'How clever.'

'And one said . . .'

'Come on, Nate.'

' "Doons sucks Miss Major." '

The man's face burned red. His nostrils quivered. 'Cute,' he muttered. His arms were stiff at his sides, his fists tight. 'One of these days, Houlder, somebody's gonna take you apart.'

Nate grinned as Doons took a step toward him. 'I was only reporting . . .'

Doons's straight arm barely moved from his side, but his fist knocked into Nate's groin. Nate grunted. He doubled over, clutching himself.

'What's wrong with Houlder?' Doons frowned at Bill as if perplexed. 'Looks like your buddy hurt himself, Kearny.' Laughing softly, he stepped into his office and shut the door.

Nate grabbed the edge of the drinking fountain to hold himself up. Words squeezed through his clenched teeth. 'Stinkin' rotten no-good mother-fuckin' . . .'

'Can you walk?' Bill asked.

Nate groaned as he unbent himself. He scowled at the closed door of Doons's office. 'Cocksuckin' fag!'

'Shhh.'

'Let him hear.'

'Come on, Nate.'

He took a step, and grimaced. 'The bastard,' he muttered. 'You don't fuck around with a guy's tool.'

'Let's just get out of here.'

They took a few steps up the hallway. Then Nate turned around. Walking backwards, he yelled, 'Doons eats shit!'

Doons's door swung open.

Nate and Bill dashed up the hallway, the slap of their sneakers echoing. They dodged to the left. Picking up speed, they crashed open the main doors, burst outside, and hurried down the concrete stairs.

They ran along the faculty parking lot.

Miss Bennett, arms loaded, was walking toward them. Apparently, she'd left school by the north wing exit.

Instead of stepping aside to let them pass, she blocked the walkway. 'Slow down, boys,' she said. 'No ru . . .' Quickly, she sidestepped.

Nate adjusted his course, and plowed into her. She flew backwards, books exploding from her arms. A hedge caught her behind the legs. She tumbled over it. Nate kept running.

Bill stopped.

Miss Bennett lay on her back behind the hedge; trying to free her upraised legs from the bushes. One of her loafers had come off. She was wearing green knee socks. Bill glanced at her bare thighs, and her pink panties. She quickly flipped her skirt down. Her eyes met Bill's, and he saw they were awash with tears.

'Gee, I'm sorry. Are you okay?'

'No.' She tucked the skirt between her thighs. 'Leave me alone.'

'Here.' He lifted her left foot out of the bushes. Holding it up, he saw that the underside of her leg was scratched and bleeding. He picked up her other foot, and pushed them both sideways. Miss Bennett twisted on her back, and brought her legs down.

'Thank you,' she said in a small voice.

'I'm awfully sorry.'

She stood up. Lifting the rear of her skirt, she looked back at the damage. 'That's a nice friend you've got.'

'He was mad.'

She sniffed, and wiped her eyes dry with the back of her hand. 'Mad, huh?'

'Doons punched him in the nuts.'

Her blue eyes locked into Bill's. 'He what?'

'Doons smashed him right in the balls. With his fist.'

'You're kidding,' she said.

'Honest. That's why Nate was so mad.'

'He was running at a pretty good clip for a guy who'd just been socked in the groin.'

Bill shrugged.

Miss Bennett squatted down, and began to gather the spilled contents of her handbag.

'Here's your shoe,' Bill said, and dropped the loafer over the hedge.

'Thanks.'

While she picked up what had fallen on her side of the bushes, Bill went after the books and file folders along the walkway. He stacked them neatly. Miss Bennett walked around the far end of the hedge, and came up the sidewalk toward him.

She *was* beautiful. Not very old, either – not for a teacher. Maybe twenty-four, twenty-five. As she walked forward, Bill remembered the look of her bare legs. And her pink, nearly transparent panties.

*. . . slip her the ol' dick.*

He felt a warm swelling, and held the books in front of himself to hide the bulge in his jeans.

'I'll take your stuff to your car, if you want,' he said.

'All right. Thank you.'

'You want me to take those?' He nodded toward the four books in her arms, clutched just below her breasts.

'No, I've got 'em.'

They walked, side by side, across the nearly deserted parking lot.

'What's your name?' she asked.

'Bill.'

'Bill what?'

*Is she gonna report me?* 'Kearny.'

'I'm Miss Bennett.'

'Yeah, I know.'

'Bill, you seem like a pretty nice guy.'

He smiled uncertainly.

*. . . a pretty nice guy, and I'd like to know you better. Why don't you come on home with me . . .?*

Unreal, like one of those dreams. Couldn't happen.

He was right.

'The thing is,' she said, 'you could get messed up if you keep running around with a guy like Nate Houlder. I've heard a lot about him, and none of it's good.'

'He's not so bad.'

Miss Bennett gave him a direct look, then set her books on the roof of a white Omni. He expected her to keep at him, keep hammering the way adults always do. But she said nothing more. She took the keys from her handbag, and opened the car door.

'Well,' Bill said, 'I'll think about it.'

She smiled. 'You get going, now. And thanks for helping me.'

'Oh, you're welcome. I'm just sorry you got hurt.'

He stepped backwards, smiling and nodding. Then he turned away. He crossed the parking lot. At the walkway, he looked around. Miss Bennett, still standing beside her car, was folding a ragged, red towel. She bent into the car, and spread her towel on the seat.

Doesn't want blood on the upholstery, Bill thought.

She looked at him.

Bill nodded, and started walking. He took three steps, glanced back, and saw Miss Bennett quickly lift the rear of her dress before sitting in the car.

That bastard, Nate.

Angry, Bill turned away. He walked toward the end of the building, and Nate stepped out from behind a telephone company van, clapping. 'Hey hey hey, lover boy.'

'She got all scratched up in the bushes.'

'Aww.'

'It's not funny, Nate. You hurt her.'

'Big fuckin' deal. She's a teacher.' He suddenly scowled. 'Hey, you better not've told her my name.'

'I didn't have to.'

'It's tough being a celebrity.' Grinning, he pressed a fist to his forehead and flexed his biceps. 'My reputation doth proceed me. So, Romeo, hows about heading over to my place?'

'I don't know.'

'Got something better to do?'

'No. I'm just a little pissed at you.'

'Yeah? That shows how dumb you are.'

'Oh yeah?'

'Yeah, man, if you had any brains, you'd see what a big favor I did for you, blasting Bennett on her ass. I *saw* you looking down at her, her feet in the air. Bet you saw enough to give you wet dreams for a month. You felt up her legs, too.'

'I was helping her.'

'Sure. Helping yourself, too. And kissing up to her like that, you probably impressed the shit out of her. Next thing you know, you'll be slippin' her dick.'

'Shut up, okay?'

'Is that gratitude?'

'You hurt her.'

'But I sure helped you. Now come on, let's head over to my place and grab some suds.'

'Yeah, all right.'

They started walking across the field. Far to their left, the football team was exercising: running in place, suddenly dropping facedown, scrambling to their feet again and pumping their knees until another signal came to drop.

'Assholes,' Nate muttered. 'I could take down any two of those pricks. Blindfolded.'

'Like you did Miss Bennett?'

'You really got a hard-on for her.'

Bill shrugged.

'Tell you what, Billy-my-lad. I'll hold her down, you fuck her.' With a laugh, he shoved Bill sideways and ran. Bill chased him until he was close enough to kick Nate's trailing foot. It tangled with the other foot, and Nate plunged to the ground.

'Aw jeez! Jeez, you've broke me!' Nate grinned, and scurried to his feet.

* * *

A magazine in a brown paper cover propped open the lid of the mailbox on Nate's front porch.

'Hey *hey*, it's Dad's *Playboy*.'

He pulled out the magazine, and the rest of the mail. The lid banged shut.

'Here, hang onto this stuff.'

He handed the mail to Bill, then dug into a pocket of his Levis and came up with a key. As he shoved it into the lock, Bill tried to slip the wrapper off the *Playboy*. The magazine bent, the wrapper came free, and Bill dropped half a dozen envelopes.

He bent to pick them up.

'A letter for you,' he announced.

'Yeah? Who's it from?'

Bill checked both sides. He found no return address. 'Doesn't say.' He followed Nate into the house, and handed him the letter.

'Can't be nothin' bad,' Nate said. 'Bad shit's always got a fuckin' letterhead in the corner.'

He tore an end off the envelope, and pulled out a sheet of triple-folded paper. He flipped it open and grinned. 'Well well well, somebody in this armpit of a town has good taste.'

'What is it?'

'An invitation, my man. "Join the fun. Spook-house Halloween Party." Sounds right up my alley.' He scanned the sheet. ' "Come in costume." Maybe I'll come as myself, give 'em a treat.'

In Nate's bedroom, they drank two beers each, and looked at the *Playboy*. Nate commented on each picture.

'How'd you like to sink your teeth into one of those?'

267

'Mmmm, look at that hairy mazoo.'

'Oh hon, suck me off.'

Staring at the photos, listening to Nate, Bill often found himself thinking about Miss Bennett – the way she'd looked on her back, her legs up, her eyes full of tears. He imagined her naked, then felt guilty as if such thoughts were an insult to her.

When he finally got home, late that afternoon, his mother handed him an envelope. 'This came for you today,' she said.

He looked at the envelope, its neatly typed address. He knew, before opening it, what he would find.

'Aren't you going to open it?' asked his mother. She seemed very curious.

'Sure.' He tore the envelope, and pulled out the invitation. The paper was slick and shadowy – the paper of a cheap photocopy machine. He unfolded it. ' "Join the fun," ' he read.

'Let me see.'

He gave it to her, and she read it, silently mouthing the words. When she finished, she shook her head. 'Says it's at the old Sherwood house.'

'Yeah. That'll be neat.'

'I don't know, Billy. Don't know if you oughtta be going there. It's a bad place, been deserted fifteen years.'

'You don't believe in ghosts, do you, Mom?'

'It's a bad place, honey.'

# Chapter Eight

The Ashburg Public Library was silent, and smelled like furniture polish. Sam walked softly over its carpet.

Behind the circulation desk slouched Elmer Cantwell. More like a bullfrog than a toad. His bulging eyes blinked at Sam.

'May I be of assistance?' Elmer asked in a low voice.

'Is there somewhere private?'

The big head didn't move, but the eyes slid from side to side. 'We seem to be alone. As you may notice, I am presently manning the desk. I can hardly leave my post, can I?'

'Fine.'

'Never fear, I *am* wearing pants and they are zipped. Would you care to see?'

'No thanks.'

'I take it there have been no complaints?'

'Not recently,' Sam told him.

'I shouldn't think so. I have conducted myself with extreme decorum during the past eight months.'

'I'm not here about that.'

'Ah,' Elmer grinned with mild surprise. 'Then what brings you into my presence? Certainly you're not here for a book?'

'That's right. I'm here looking for Thelma.'

'Who?'

Sam held up the photo. 'Thelma Rawls, formerly Boyanski, formerly Connors.'

'Oh, *that* Thelma. I believe she moved to Milwaukee.'

'I believe she's back. Where's she staying, Elmer?'

'I wouldn't have the vaguest notion.'

'Think again. Obstructing a criminal investigation is a lot more serious than jogging around town with your jollies hanging out.'

His slick lips drew back. 'No call to be crude, Officer.'

'You were seen with her. Where's she staying?'

'You might try the Sunset Lounge. That's where I found her.'

'When?'

'Shall we say Tuesday night?'

'Did you leave with her?'

'Yes, I believe so.'

'Where did you go?'

'For a drive.'

'Where?'

'To a quiet, secluded place.' His eyes rolled upward and he smiled. 'Oh, she was just luscious. Would you care for me to recount our exploits?'

'That won't be necessary. Just tell me where you left her.'

'Back at the Sunset Lounge. Her car was there, I believe.'

'Okay. Wednesday. You went to Food King with her. You paid for her groceries. Where did you meet her, where did you take her?'

'We met for lunch at the Oakwood Inn. After shopping, I let her off at the inn's parking lot.'

'Why did you pay for her groceries?'

'Because, Officer, I am a gentleman.'

'Okay. Last night.'

'Yes?'

'Where did you take her?'

'No place at all. I spent the evening at home with Mother. I'm certain she'll be pleased to verify that.'

'I'll check.'

'I know you will. Persistence is such an admirable trait.'

'When did you see Thelma last?'

'Yesterday afternoon, when I dropped her off at the Oakwood Inn.'

'You're sure?'

'Would I lie to you?'

'If I find out you have lied, Elmer, I'll put you in jail.'

'Meany.'

In his patrol car, Sam called the station. Ethel's voice came over the radio. Betty, he realized, had already gone home; the day shift was over.

'Would you look up Elmer Cantwell's home address for me?' he asked.

'Hold on,' said Ethel. Moments later, she gave him the address.

As he drove there, he thought about what he'd learned from Elmer. Thelma had been in town as of Tuesday night, at least. She'd spent some time with Elmer, and made it with him – hard to believe.

According to Elmer, they'd been together yesterday afternoon, but not last night. So she didn't have him as an alibi for the time Dexter was murdered.

She still looked good as a suspect.

Looking better all the time.

Sam stopped at Elmer's house. He rang the doorbell a dozen times. Though he felt sure that the mother was home, she didn't answer the door.

Elmer probably phoned, gave her advance warning.

Could Thelma be inside, too? Possible, but not likely. If the rumors were true, Elmer wouldn't want his mother knowing he was involved with another woman.

He rang a few more times, then left and returned to the station.

# Chapter Nine

She spooned thick tomato sauce onto Eric's spaghetti. He counted the chunks of Italian sausage, and saw that she was giving him more than usual. Too many chunks to count. He smiled up at her.

'Did you have a good day at school?' she asked.

He thought about his troubles with Nate and Mr Doons. He sure wouldn't tell Mom about that. 'I got invited to a Halloween party,' he said.

'Oh? That sounds, nice. When is it?'

'Halloween night.'

She stepped to her side of the kitchen table, and began serving herself. 'Who's having it?'

'Somebody from school.'

'Anyone I know?'

He shook his head. 'It's a costume party.'

'What'll you wear?'

'Haven't decided.'

She sat down. 'Would you like to say grace?'

He lowered his head, and rattled off his memorized prayer. 'Dear God, who giveth us food for the body and truth for the mind, so enlighten and nourish us that we may grow wise and strong to do thy will, Amen.'

'Amen,' she mumbled.

Eric started to stir his spaghetti. 'Are you going out?'

'Tonight? No, I don't think . . .'

'I mean on Halloween.'

She shook her head. 'I'll stay here for the trick-or-treaters, I guess.'

'Will Sam come over?'

He watched her face turn red. 'Sam has to work. He's a policeman.'

'He *is*?'

'He's an awfully nice man, Eric. We've been . . . I've been seeing him for a long time, now. We're very good friends.'

'Oh.'

'He'd like to meet you.'

'I don't want to meet *him*.'

'*Eric*.' She sounded sad. 'He's my *friend*.'

'Must be.' Eric took a bite of sausage, and slowly chewed. It was his favorite meat, but he felt tight inside and he didn't want to swallow.

'I'm sorry you ran into him, that way.'

'Does he come here every night?'

'No. He's only been here a few times.'

'Sneaking around.'

'He does not sneak around. I just didn't want you to meet him, yet, because . . . things don't always turn out and I didn't want you getting attached to him, like you did with John and Raymond.'

He managed to swallow. He pushed at his spaghetti, but

didn't take another bite. 'You shouldn't go messing around with men if you aren't married.'

'You don't have to be married to love someone.'

'Then you get kids without fathers.'

'You have a father.'

'Oh yeah? Where is he?'

'He went away.'

'Because he got you pregnant and you weren't married.'

'That isn't why.'

'Then why?'

'He asked me to marry him, but I wouldn't.'

'Why not?'

'Your father wasn't a nice man.'

'Then why did you . . . go with him?'

'I didn't.' She stared at her spaghetti. So far, she hadn't taken a single bite. 'He was just a guy in school. We hardly knew each other. He followed me home, one day, and nobody was there but me, and – well, things happened. We were both only sixteen, and . . . He got kicked out of school, and got a job at a gas station. He wanted me to marry him, but I just told him no. And then he left town, about a month before you were born, and he never came back.'

'You should've married him.'

'How can you say that? You don't even *know* him.'

'You should've. You should've let me have a dad. It's not fair.'

Her eyes got shiny and her mouth started to tremble. She pushed herself away from the table.

Eric started to cry. She'd made his favorite meal, and now everything was ruined. 'Mom, I'm sorry.'

'Never mind,' she sobbed. 'Just never mind.' She rushed out of the room.

# Chapter Ten

Sitting in his car, Sam watched the house. He was across the street, and half a block away. As he watched, he ate a cheeseburger he'd bought at Jack-in-the-Box.

He had arrived at five o'clock, dressed in civvies and driving his own Chrysler. Darkness closed quickly over the street. Lights appeared in the windows of nearby homes. The home of Elmer Cantwell, however, remained dark, and Sam wondered if he'd been wrong about the mother.

At 5:52, light appeared in an upstairs window. It soon went off. A few minutes later, the picture window lit up, and he could see into the living room. Then the draperies slid shut.

He hadn't been wrong about the mother.

At 6:10, a Volvo entered the driveway and stopped. A man climbed out. From his bulging shape and the slouch of his walk, Sam knew it had to be Elmer.

Elmer entered the house, leaving his car in the driveway.

Going out later?

Sam finished his cheeseburger. He turned on the radio, and listened to quiet music. As he waited, a chill seeped through his trouser legs. He had a blanket in the trunk, but didn't want to bother with it. He turned on the car engine. Soon, the heater was blowing warm air on him, and the car began to feel cozy.

Not as cozy as home, though. Nice to be back at his duplex, sitting on the couch, staring at the TV news and sipping a vodka gimlet. Nicer to be with Cynthia. He wouldn't be with her tonight, though, even if this hadn't come up. Maybe she would straighten things out with Eric. It'd be good to know the kid. The three of them could get together, go to movies, go fishing. Not right for a kid to grow up without a father.

Better no father, though, than the guy Eric would've been stuck with if Cynthia'd married that bastard who raped her. Harlan. Scotty Harlan. Damn good thing he'd left town. If Sam ever got his hands on the guy . . . Christ, to do a thing like that to Cynthia! She'd cried the night she told Sam about it, cried so hard she could barely talk as she described how he stood with a knife and made her strip, how he pressed the blade to her throat as he took her, and threatened to slice off her nipples if she ever told.

People saw Scotty leave the house, and knew he was the one when she got pregnant, but she never told anyone how it happened. No one but Sam, on a night fifteen years later when he asked about Eric's father and she spoke in a voice so broken by sobs that he cried, himself, and held her tightly.

A guy like Scotty Harlan shouldn't be allowed to live.

Sam had never killed anyone, but he'd like a chance at Harlan.

Maybe not kill him, Sam thought. Maybe just blast apart his knees. And his elbows. And shove the muzzle against his cock and blow that off.

He realized that he was trembling with rage. He took a deep breath. He wiped his sweaty hands on his trousers.

Keep your mind on the job, he warned himself. No point dwelling on Scotty. You'll never get a chance to do anything about him, never get a chance to stick your gun up his ass . . .

*Stop it!*

Think about Dexter.

Somebody hated Dex awfully bad to cut him up that way, hated him the way I hate Scotty. So who did Dex rape?

He wouldn't.

Berney had Chet and Buck looking through the station files for suspects – guys Dexter had stepped on, over the years. Guys who might want to return the favor. Even in a town the size of Ashburg, a cop could accumulate plenty of enemies.

Sam put his money on Thelma, though. Former spouse. Showed up in town the day before he was killed. Has to be a connection of some kind. If she didn't handle it herself, she might've put somebody else up to it.

Maybe Elmer.

Even as he thought about the man, he saw Elmer Cantwell leave the house. The hunched figure crossed the lawn and ducked into the Volvo. The car backed out of the driveway.

Sam swung away from the curb, and followed. He stayed a full block behind Elmer's car as it moved up the deserted street. At an intersection ahead, another car pulled in front of him. With this one as a shield, he narrowed the gap. It soon turned onto a driveway. By this time, Elmer was passing the Baptist church. The business district was only a block away. With traffic picking up, Sam didn't bother to drop back. He stayed several car-lengths behind Elmer, and kept moving when the Volvo swung into the parking area of Harney's Liquor.

Near the end of the block, he pulled up to a vacant stretch of curb. He waited, wondering if he was crazy to be tailing Elmer. Tailing him on an *errand*, for Christsake! His old lady probably ran short of apricot brandy . . . On the other hand, maybe Elmer planned to do some entertaining.

This could pan out, after all.

Sam chewed on his lower lip, and watched the rearview mirror.

Soon, a car backed onto the road. Sam looked away as it approached. When it passed him, he looked. A Volvo. He let it get a good headstart, then pulled onto the road behind it.

The Volvo approached an intersection.

If he's heading back home, Sam thought, he'll turn here.

He didn't turn.

Sam grinned, and followed. The Volvo led him away from the business district, down tree-shrouded streets. Not far ahead was the entrance to the Ashburg Golf and Tennis Club.

Where Babe Rawls once tended bar.

Where Thelma used to hang out.

But Elmer drove past it.

The open fields of the golf course began. On the other side of the street, the last few houses were left behind, and the cemetery took over.

Sam's headlights lit a wooden sign. 'You are now leaving Ashburg,' it read. 'Come back soon.'

Where the hell's he taking me? Sam wondered.

Better be to Thelma.

# Chapter Eleven

Eddie Ryker was drying the supper dishes when the telephone rang. His mother lifted a plate out of the sudsy water. 'Would you get that, honey?'

'Sure.' He balled up the dishrag. As he backed away, he shot it toward the sink. It flared out, and dropped like a sheet over the rack of dishes waiting to be dried.

In two long strides, he was at the kitchen door. He picked up the wall phone.

'Hello?'

'Eddie?' asked a soft, breathy voice.

He smiled. 'Oh, hi Aleshia. How are you?'

'I miss you.'

'Me too,' he said, and wished he'd picked up the phone in a different room. He never expected the caller would be Aleshia. She usually phoned much later, talking quietly from her dark bedroom.

'How was football practice?'

'Just fine,' he said. He remembered her waving as she ran by with the other cheerleaders, her legs quick under the pleated skirt. 'How did your practice go?'

'Oh, just fine. Except for Sue. She's such a know-it-all. I just wish she'd fall off her pedestal and break a leg. Or something higher up, if you get my meaning.'

Eddie smiled.

'I suppose you heard about Chief Boyanski?'

'Yeah. It was on the news.'

'Isn't it just ghastly? To think there's a *murderer* running around town! Yick!'

'Well, they'll probably catch him.'

'I hope *so*! It's *disturbing* to have a thing like that, especially the day before Halloween.'

'Well . . .'

'Anyhow, that's not what I called about. I came into a very rude surprise, when I got home from practice.'

'Oh?'

'An invitation came for me in the mail.'

'For that Spook-House Halloween Party?'

'You got one, too?'

'Yeah.'

'Well, do you realize what night that party's scheduled for?'

'Tomorrow night.'

'Precisely.'

'And what else is that night?'

'Your party, of course.'

'Precisely.'

'Well, I wouldn't worry about it. I'm still planning on yours.'

'I should certainly hope so. But what about everyone else?'

'I don't know.'

'I invited a dozen friends to my party. Now suppose half of them decide they would rather go over to the creepy old Sherwood place? What kind of party'll we have, then?'

'A small one.'

'You may be amused, Edward Ryker, but I most certainly am not.'

'I just don't think it'll happen. Some of the kids you asked might've gotten invitations to the other party, but I'll bet every one of them will decide on yours.'

'Do you think so?' she asked, sounding relieved.

'I'm positive.'

There were a few moments of silence, rare during conversations with Aleshia. 'You don't suppose,' she finally said, 'that somebody concocted this other party just to spite me, do you?'

Eddie laughed. 'Who'd do that?'

'Just about anyone I didn't invite to *my* party, of course.'

'Well, maybe, but I doubt it. I think it's just a coincidence.'

'Maybe yes and maybe no. Anyhow, I have a jillion calls to make. I'll give you a buzz later.'

'Okay.'

'Around ten.'

'Fine.'

'From my bed.'

He grinned. 'Okay, great. Talk to you then.'

'Bye-bye.' She hung up.

'Beth, telephone. It's Aleshia.'

'Right there,' she called to her father. She flipped through the pages of her physiology book, counting. Six to go in the chapter, but two were mostly diagrams. Not so bad. She could handle that.

She dropped a pencil into the crack of the open book, and got up from her desk. As she stood, she watched herself in the window reflection. The image on the dark glass, transparent as a ghost, hinted of beauty and mystery. It looked good to Beth.

In the reflection, her freckles and braces didn't show.

With a shrug, she turned away. Her eyes avoided the full-length mirror on the closet door: it would show details she didn't want to see.

She hurried down the upstairs hallway, entered her parents' room, and picked up the telephone extension.

'. . . absolutely marvelous pyramid, and then we all collapse into a pile . . .'

'I've got it,' Beth said.

'Okie-doke,' said her father. 'Bye now, Aleshia.'

'Bye-bye, Mr Green.'

Beth heard the phone go down. 'Hi-ho,' she said.

'I just adore your father.'

'He's not bad,' Beth said, smiling.

'I only wish *my* father was as cute and charming.'

Beth shrugged. She had never seen Aleshia's father. He seemed to be out of town constantly.

'Anyhow, I just gave you a buzz to find out if you're coming to my Halloween party.'

'Yeah,' she said, confused. She'd already told Aleshia she would be there. 'Is something the matter?'

'It appears that someone has decided to go into competition.'

'Oh, you mean the other Halloween party?'

'Precisely.'

'You think it's for real?' Beth asked.

'Why wouldn't it be?'

'It looks awfully queer.'

'Queer?'

'First off, my invitation wasn't signed. It doesn't give the first hint about who's throwing the party, or even ask for an RSVP.' She sat on the edge of the bed, and lay back. 'Second, it's supposed to be at the old Sherwood house. That place has been boarded up for as long as I can remember. How'd they even get in to *have* a party? I just think the whole thing's queer. I bet somebody sent out those invitations for a gag.'

'Or to ruin *my* party.'

'If it is for real, nobody's gonna go. Nobody with sense, anyway. I wouldn't be caught dead in the old Sherwood house myself.'

'Oh, I imagine half the kids in town would love to get in there, especially on Halloween night. It is the creepiest place in the whole world. Wouldn't you like to see where it all happened?'

'No. Thanks anyway.'

'I certainly would, but not when I'm having my own party. I'll just die if nobody shows up 'cause they're all over at the Sherwood house traipsing through gore.'

Beth laughed softly. 'I don't think the gore's still there. Someone must've cleaned it up. I mean, it's been about fifteen years or something.' The hand resting on her flat belly bounced as she laughed. 'And even if it didn't get cleaned up, it'd be all dry, by now. It'd take a putty knife to pry it off the floor.

'Beth! You're awful!'

Beth couldn't stop laughing. Her eyes teared. 'Oh,' she gasped. 'Oh, wouldn't that be a sight . . .! Some old janitor crawling around with a putty knife . . . trying . . . trying to jimmy the guts off the floor!'

'Beth, you're sick,' Aleshia said through her own laughter.

'Ohhh. Oh wow.' She wiped her eyes, and tried to catch her breath. 'Oh. Don't know . . . what got into me.'

'While you're on that subject, who's your date for the party?'

Beth took a deep, shaky breath. 'I . . . I don't know.'

'You *what*?'

'I don't know.'

'Beth, the party's tomorrow night!'

'Oh, I'll find someone to take me.'

'I certainly do hope so. Well, I'd better leave you, now. I've got a jillion more calls to make.'

'Are you phoning everyone you invited?'

'I just might, Beth.'

Karen Bennett sat at the kitchen table of her rented house, correcting a stack of papers turned in yesterday by her fourth period class. She finished Dave Sanderson's Halloween theme. At the bottom, in red ink, she scribbled, 'Cats are people, too.' She flipped to the front page and marked the top B-.

She took a sip of Chablis.

She scooted a bit farther forward, and gently rubbed the underside of her right leg. Earlier, she'd bandaged the worst of the scratches. For the past hour or so, they'd been feeling itchy. If she used her fingernails, though, they hurt.

That creep, Houlder. She really ought to report him. She couldn't write him up, though, without implicating Bill. She hated to do that.

Hell with it.

She lowered her eyes to the next theme, and moaned. Jim Miller had used a pencil. After all the times she'd told them only to use ink. Doesn't anybody listen, for Christsake? She picked up her red pen.

'Use ink only!' she wrote at the top.

Then she began to read. 'Halloween is the time for tricks and treats. Little kids get dressed up like pirates and hobos and wiches and nurses, and docters and bums . . .'

The telephone rang.

Thank God.

She put down her pen, picked up her wine glass, and went to the phone. 'Hello?'

'Hello, Miss Bennett. This is Aleshia.'

'Oh, hi, Aleshia.'

'I hope I'm not disturbing you.'

'No, not at all. What's up?' Reaching down, she scratched the back of her leg, and winced.

'I'm calling about my Halloween party?'

'Yes. I'm looking forward to it.'

'Oh good. I was a little bit worried that you might change your mind, or something.'

'I've already got my costume ready.'

'Oh, super. I was just wondering, because it turns out there's this other party tomorrow night and I'm afraid some people might decide to go to it instead of mine.'

'Not me.'

'Did you get an invitation to it?'

'No. Yours is the only one I got.'

'Maybe they're not asking teachers.'

'Maybe not.'

'I mean, I didn't invite any, either. Just you. But that's because you're really special, and not like a real teacher.'

'I'm not?' She grinned. 'I hope the Board of Education doesn't find out.'

'I mean, you're a real teacher. You're the best. But you're not like the others. You listen to us, and stuff.'

'Well . . .' She realized she was blushing. 'Thank you, Aleshia.'

'Do you have a date?'

'He's all lined up.'

'Oh good. Who is it?'

'That'll be my secret.'

'*Oh*, Miss Bennett.'

'You'll find out, tomorrow night.'

'Is it someone I know?'

'That'd be telling.'

'You're awful!'

'An ogre.'

'Well, I'm just dying to see who it is. I'd better hang up, now. You must have a jillion things to do.'

'Nice talking to you.'

'Okay. Goodnight.'

'Night, Aleshia. See you tomorrow.'

She hung up, and stared across the kitchen at the pile of Halloween themes. A *jillion things to do*. Seemed like a jillion, all right, when she had to struggle through pencil-written messes like that turkey Jim Miller turned in.

She took a sip of wine.

With a sigh, she returned to the table.

# Chapter Twelve

Just outside the city limits of Dendron, a town fifteen miles east of Ashburg, the Volvo slowed and swung into the driveway of the Sleepy Hollow Inn.

Sam eased off the gas. He watched Elmer drive up the L-shaped lane where half a dozen cars were already parked. The Volvo pulled into a space. Sam wanted to stop. He needed to see which room Elmer entered. The risk of being spotted was too great, though, so he drove past the motel.

He made a U-turn. He sped back to the entrance and pulled in, but Elmer was nowhere in sight. Slowly, Sam drove down the parking area. He counted twelve rooms, each with a bright orange door. Every room had two parking spaces. Elmer's Volvo was in front of Four, beside a white Datsun.

Probably, he'd gone into Four.

Light came through the room's pale curtains.

The spaces in front of Six were empty. Sam pulled in, and climbed from his car. A cold wind blew against him. He zipped his jacket, stuffed his hands into its pockets, and strolled up the walkway.

Slowing to listen at Four, he heard voices and laughter from a television. The sliding windows were shut. Nothing showed through the curtains. He kept walking.

He went to the motel office. It was well-lighted and warm. A young woman behind the registration desk looked up at him from a magazine. She took off her glasses and smiled. 'Hi. How are you tonight?'

'Just fine,' Sam said. Stepping close to the desk, he caught the odor of her perfume. The same perfume Cynthia wore. Suddenly, he was struck by her beauty: her wide eyes, her full lips and soft chin, the way her hair hung softly to her shoulders. She wore a white pullover that hugged her breasts.

'What can I do for you?' she asked.

Sam raised his eyes to her face. She looked amused, one eyebrow high. Was he *that* obvious about studying her? He blushed.

'I don't come with the rooms,' she said.

Sam laughed. 'You're a mind reader.'

'I know a randy man when I see one.'

'I'm randy, but I'm engaged.' It was a minor lie; he *felt* engaged, but so far hadn't asked Cynthia.

'Is the lucky girl with you?'

'Not tonight.'

'Then you'll probably want a single.'

He shook his head. 'I'm not here for a room.' Reaching into his rear pocket, he took out his billfold. He held it open on the desk. 'My name's Sam Wyatt.'

'Is that real gold?' the woman asked, staring at his shield.

'Gold-plated.'

'Okay if I touch?'

'Sure.'

Her fingertips stroked the badge. 'Say, that's nice.' She grinned up at him. 'Are you here to arrest someone?'

'Maybe.'

'Not me, I hope.'

'Not you.'

'That's good.' She slipped the badge out of the wallet. 'It's a heavy thing.'

'I need to know who's in number Four.'

'Sure.' She pinned the badge on her sweater. It dragged down the soft fabric, and settled on her left breast. 'How do I look?'

'Terrific.'

'Melodie Caine, homicide.' Folding her hands on the desk, she leaned forward. 'Are you a homicide cop?'

'Yeah,' he said, losing his smile. 'Afraid I am, tonight.'

Melodie's smile dissolved. 'I guess this is serious, then.'

'Yeah.'

'Hold on.' She opened a file box, flipped through a few cards, and pulled one out. 'This is the registration card for unit four.'

'Thanks.' Sam looked at the neatly printed name. 'Ms Mary Jones.' The home address was in Greendale, a suburb of Milwaukee.

'Is she your suspect?'

'Maybe.' Sam wished he'd thought to bring the photo along. 'What'd she look like?'

Melodie's heavy lips pressed together. Her eyebrows drew downward. 'She's about thirty-five or forty. She's a couple of inches taller than me, and thin. Too much make-up, especially around the eyes. I couldn't see what she was wearing, except for a gray trench-coat. I think she wore heels, though. And nylons, of course.'

'What color was her hair?'

'Blond. Dishwater blond.'

'When did she arrive?'

'Tonight. Half an hour ago, I guess. Think she's the one?'

'I don't know. Could be.'

'Want to find out?'

Sam nodded.

Melodie bent down, the badge swinging as it tugged her sweater out. She straightened, and dangled a key in front of Sam. 'Okay if I come along?'

'Better not. I don't expect trouble, but you never know.'

She gave him the key. 'Hurry back.'

Sam left the office. He was halfway to the room when he realized Melodie still had his badge. He didn't want to bother going back for it.

'Sam?'

He looked around. Melodie was standing in the office door-way, the wind blowing her hair.

'Want your badge?' she asked.

'Later.'

She stayed in the doorway, and folded her arms across her breasts. Sam turned away. He walked to the door of Four. Standing aside, he knocked. Seconds passed. He knocked again.

Over the sound of the television, a woman's voice called, 'Who is it?'

'Ms Jones?' he asked.

'Just a minute.'

He lowered his hand, and popped open the safety strap of his holster. His stomach felt tight. He took a deep breath, trembling as he exhaled.

The door opened several inches until its guard chain rattled taut. A woman's face appeared in the gap. Her eyes met Sam's. She blinked, and her mouth dropped open. 'Mr *Wyatt*?'

He stared, confused, trying to recall where he'd seen her. Then he remembered. This morning. Across the street from Dexter's house. 'Mrs Barnes?'

'What . . . what are you doing here?'

'Is Elmer Cantwell inside?'

'No.'

'His car's parked in front.'

'So? I don't know any Elmer Cantwell.'

'Who's with you?'

'My husband.'

'You came all the way out here to a motel with your husband?'

'Yes. We . . . like the privacy. Away from home.'

'I'd like to speak to him.'

'He's in the bathroom.'

'I can't leave until I've seen him.'

'Goddamn it,' she muttered. Tears glistened in her eyes.

'Mrs Barnes, I'm not interested in your personal life. I

certainly have no intention of telling anyone you were out here. But I'm investigating a homicide, and I have to know if Elmer's in there with you.'

Holding her blouse shut with one hand, she wiped tears from her eyes and smeared her mascara.

'Tell him to come to the door.'

'He's not *here*.'

'Do you read the "Crime call" in the *Clarion*?'

Her chin started to tremble.

'If I have to arrest you, Mrs Barnes, you'll be reading about yourself. So will everyone else in town, including your husband and daughter.'

'You can't arrest me,' she muttered.

'Of course I can. Tell Elmer to come to the door. Right now.'

The door shut.

Looking to the side, Sam saw Melodie standing in the office doorway, still watching. She raised an open hand in greeting. Sam nodded.

He heard the guard chain rattle and skid. Then the door swung open. Elmer, fully dressed, smiled out at him. 'May I help you, *Mister* Wyatt?'

'I'm looking for Thelma.'

'Do you think she's here?'

'Mind if I look?'

Elmer blinked his bulging eyes. 'You've seen who's with me.'

'I'd like to look around.'

'You are a persistent devil.'

Elmer stepped aside, and Sam entered the room. The Barnes woman was nowhere in sight. One of the double beds was messed, its blankets still in place but rumpled. A bottle of Scotch stood on the night table, two drinking glasses beside it. Green slacks were folded neatly over the back of a chair.

Dropping to his knees, Sam glanced under the bed.

Elmer chuckled.

Sam pulled open the closet door. Then he said, 'Ask Mrs Barnes to come out of the bathroom, please.'

'Do you really think that's necessary?'

'Yes.'

'Thelma is *not* hiding in the tub, if that's what's on your suspicious little mind.'

'I'd like to make sure.'

'With a loud sigh, Elmer stepped to the bathroom door.

'Ticia? *Mister* Wyatt wants you to come out.'

'No!'

'Do as he says, darling.' Elmer scowled at Sam. 'You've upset her terribly, you realize.'

The door opened. Ticia Barnes came out, her blouse now buttoned, a bathtowel wrapped around her waist. She glared at Sam. Her eyes looked red from crying, but the dark smudges of mascara were gone.

'Excuse me,' Sam said. He stepped past her, and entered the bathroom. He slid open the shower door. Nobody in the tub. He shut it. Turning away, he looked at the toilet. Its lid was down.

He glanced at the empty sink, then back to the toilet.

Crazy, he thought. But he couldn't stop himself.

Bending, he raised the lid.

A face looked up at him and he leaped back, gasping, before he realized he'd seen only his own reflection on the water. The lid crashed down.

'What *are* you doing?' Elmer asked.

Sam didn't answer. He stepped out of the bathroom.

'Did you find her?' Elmer asked, grinning. 'Was she hiding in the toidy?'

'Thanks for your cooperation,' Sam muttered. He walked toward the door.

Elmer stayed beside him. 'I am a trifle curious, *Mister* Wyatt. Did you follow me out here?'

'That's right.'

'You thought I'd lead you to Thelma? So sorry to disappoint you.' Elmer pulled open the door for him. 'Do have a pleasant evening.'

'If you know where Thelma is . . .'

'I haven't the vaguest. Nighty-night.'

Sam left. Walking toward Melodie, he heard the door shut.

'No luck?' she asked.

'A disaster.' He gave her the key, and followed her into the office.

'Let me get you some coffee. It'll make you feel better.'

'Sounds good,' he said.

'Come on through here.' Behind the registration desk, Melodie opened a door. 'Home sweet home.'

'This is where you live?' Sam asked. The softly lighted room looked cozy.

'This is it. I've also got two bedrooms and a kitchen. Have a seat.'

He lowered himself onto the couch, and leaned back.

'Cream or sugar?'

'Just black.'

'Right.' She hurried across the room, her kilt flipping against her legs.

Sam shut his eyes. Let's not complicate the disaster, he warned himself, by getting involved with this gal. A cup of coffee, and that's it.

She came back with a ceramic mug in each hand. She gave one to Sam, and sat down beside him. He took a deep breath of her perfume.

'Must be a strange life,' he said.

'What?'

'Living in a motel.'

'I love it.'

'Meet lots of interesting people?'

She smirked. 'A few. You, for instance. You're very interesting.'

'I'm engaged, remember?'

'Engagements get broken.'

He looked at her hands. Both were wrapped around the mug, as if savoring its heat. She wore no ring on her left hand. 'You sound like you know.'

'First-hand.' She searched his eyes for a long time. 'You're not the kind of guy who dumps people,' she said, still staring.

'I try not to.'

'You've got such gentle eyes.'

'Well . . .' Blushing, Sam shrugged.

'Whoever you're engaged to, she's a lucky woman.'

'I keep telling her that.'

'She'd better know it.'

Sam took a sip of coffee. 'I have to get going.'

'Worried?'

'A little.'

'Don't be. I'm harmless.'

'Are you?'

'You're engaged, remember?' She sipped her coffee, and

set the mug down on the table. 'I'd better give this back,' she said. Smiling, she lifted the badge. 'We're not pinned, after all.'

He watched her hands work at the clasp, and slide the badge off her sweater. It left two tiny holes over her breast.

She placed the shield on his palm, and folded his fingers over it. 'You're the first guy,' she said, 'who ever let me wear his badge.'

'Maybe we can do it again sometime.'

Her eyes turned sad. She gave his closed hand a quick squeeze. Then she let go, and stood up. She backed away, rubbing her hands on her kilt. 'Should I keep an eye on that room for you?'

'Not much point, I guess.' Sam finished his coffee, and stood. 'Of course, if another woman shows up . . . I don't think that's likely to happen, though.'

He followed Melodie through the door to the office.

'I'll keep an eye out,' she said.

'I appreciate all your help. And your coffee.' Reaching for the doorknob, his back to Melodie, he felt uneasy – as if he'd forgotten something important. He turned to her, wondering what it could be. 'Thanks again,' he said.

'It's been nice knowing you, Sam Wyatt. However briefly.'

He pulled her against him, felt her softness and warmth, her lips and the wetness of her mouth. Then her cheek was damp against his face, and he saw that she was crying.

'I'm sorry,' he whispered.

She pressed her wet eyes to the side of his neck. 'That's okay,' she said. 'I was afraid you'd leave . . .'

'I have to.'

'. . . without kissing good-bye.'

# Chapter Thirteen

Lynn Horner was watching television with her two boys when the lights went out.

'Oh no,' said the older boy, Joe.

'Hank?' Lynn asked. She saw the vague figure of her husband sit upright in his chair.

'Probably a fuse,' he grumbled. He sounded only half awake.

'Well, go see.'

'Yeah,' Joe said. 'We're gonna miss the best part.'

'That'd be a pity,' Hank said, getting to his feet.

'Just 'cause *you* fell asleep.'

'I'll go with you,' said Mike.

'Sure, come on.'

The younger boy sprang to his feet. In the dark, he collided with his brother.

'Hey, watch who you're stepping on,' Joe complained. 'Klutz.'

'Oh, go soak your head.'

'*Boys*,' Lynn said.

Mike hurried after his father. 'Hey, wait up, Dad.'

'Get a move on, then,' his voice called from the hall. 'God forbid anyone should miss the end of the show.'

'Boy,' Joe muttered. 'What a crummy thing to happen.'

'It's not the end of the world,' Lynn said. Turning around on the couch, she pulled aside the curtain and looked outside. The nearby streetlight was shining brightly. There were no houses across the street, though, to check for lights. The trees on the golf course were blowing fiercely. 'The wind might've knocked down a power line,' she said.

'Wouldn't *that* be great.'

'You can always catch the rerun.'

'Sure. Six months from now. If we're home. If the television doesn't bust again.'

'You're probably just missing a commercial, anyway.'

'Yeah, sure.'

'I always thought it was fun to lose the power. It used to happen all the time, during thunderstorms. We'd get out candles, and tell scary stories . . .'

'Sounds like a ball.'

'My son, the cynic.'

'What's taking them so long?'

'Maybe a goblin got 'em.'

'Sure.'

'Ate 'em up.'

Joe laughed. 'You're nuts.'

'Ghoulies,' she moaned. 'And ghosties, and long-leggity beasties . . .'

'Oh, cut it out.'

'Tomorrow's Halloween. Maybe they're out early, this year, and came creeping and crawling out of their graves, looking for little boys.'

'*Mom.*'

'They get lonesome in their graves and crypts. On Halloween, they like to crawl out and creep around, and grab little boys to take back with them – to keep them company.'

'That's disgusting.'

'They like cynical little boys the best.'

'Yeah?'

297

''Cause they make such good conversation.'

'Sometimes I think you're cracked.'

'*Woooooo.*'

'Cut it out, would you?'

'*Wooooooooo!*' Slowly, arms out, she stood up and stepped toward Joe. '*Woooooooooo.* Time to come with me to the grave. It's so cold and lonely down there.'

'Mom!'

She grinned at the tremor in his voice. 'And I get so *hungry*, down there.' She lunged at him.

Joe squealed and rolled out of her reach. 'Stop that!' he snapped, crawling across the carpet.

'You can't get away from me.' She lumbered toward him.

'Would you *stop*! I'm not amused.'

Lynn dropped her arms. 'Party pooper.' She returned to the couch, and flopped down. 'Must not've been a fuse,' she said. 'They'd have things fixed, by now.'

'Great.'

If the power isn't on by bedtime, she thought, she'd have to dig out the travel clock. Where had she stored it? She concentrated, and remembered leaving it in her suitcase so she wouldn't have trouble finding it, next time they took a trip. The suitcase was in the garage. Lovely.

'Jeez,' Joe said. 'The show's probably over, by now.'

'Well, those are the . . .'

The lights and television blinked on.

'There!'

'See what I told you?' Joe asked. The show's theme was playing as its credits rolled up the screen.

'Well, it's too bad. Could be worse, though.'

'I doubt it.'

'Why don't you go upstairs and get your p.j.'s on.'

'Mom!'

'It's nine o'clock.'

'It isn't fair.'

'You scoot upstairs and get ready for bed, then you can come down and watch TV until Mike's ready.'

'All *right*!' He scurried to his feet, and ran from the room. Lynn heard his footsteps pounding on the stairs.

The air in the den felt chilly. She pressed her legs together, and wrapped her red robe more tightly around herself.

Hank must've opened the back door, for some reason.

She folded her arms. Their warm pressure felt good on her taut nipples. She rubbed her legs against each other. Their skin was pebbled and achy with goose-bumps.

Had he *left* the door open?

She got up from the couch, and stepped out of the den. She walked down a dark hallway toward the kitchen. The swinging door was shut. A band of light showed beneath it.

Hank and Mike were sure taking their time. Maybe they'd decided to polish off the angel food cake.

Pushing open the door, she stepped into the kitchen. Her bare foot splashed into blood. It slipped and shot forward. She fell back, grabbing the waste basket. It tumbled onto her, throwing coffee grounds and chicken bones on her robe. The door swung against her shoulder. Shoving it away, gasping, she sat up. The floor was puddled with blood, the oven door dripping.

'Hank!' she cried.

She struggled to her feet. She stepped past the refrigerator. Looking toward the alcove at the far end of the kitchen, she saw Hank sitting upright at the breakfast table. Mike lay on the table, shirt open, a knife and fork protruding from his belly.

'*Hank?*' she gasped.

She saw Hank's arm on the floor near his feet. Her mouth jerked open to scream. A hand covered it – a slippery hand that stank of blood. It yanked her backwards against a panting body. Another hand swung around from the side, plunging a carving fork toward her belly. She brought up her arms. The long tines jabbed into her forearm. Pain blasted through her.

Twisting, she kicked up her legs. The man lost his grip, and she fell to her rump. She flung herself sideways, rolling, and got to her hands and knees before the man grabbed the back of her robe collar and threw her down. Her back hit the floor.

He stomped on her belly, driving the wind from her. She doubled and clutched her knees until the man took her ankles. Her robe and nightgown flopped down, covering her face as he lifted, her off the floor.

He swung her by the feet.

Swung her in a circle like a father playing with his child.

Faster and faster.

She tugged at the clothing bunched over her head. Pulled it free. Saw her naked body flying in circles around a huge, grinning man. One of her outflung arms struck the refrigerator. She had no breath to scream at the pain. The twirling man stepped closer to the refrigerator.

Next time around, more than her arm would hit.

She tried to curl forward but the momentum kept her stretched and the edge of the refrigerator door struck her face.

Joe Horner spat in the sink and rinsed his toothbrush. He cupped cold water with his hand, drank some, and rinsed the toothpaste foam off his lips and chin. Putting away his brush, he saw a glob of striped paste and streams of spittle in the sink. Mom, he knew, would nag if he left it there. But she wouldn't see it before Mike came in to brush his teeth. Let Mike take care of it. He dried his mouth and hurried downstairs.

Nobody in the den.

Great!

He flipped through the channels to *Night Beat*, a cop show he'd only seen once, on a fabulous night when Jean was baby-sitting and she let him and Mike stay up late if they promised not to tell.

He sat cross-legged on the floor.

Maybe, if he was really good, Mom and Dad would let him see the whole show. After all, he'd been cheated out of the last one.

Fat chance.

'Not on a school night,' they'd say.

Well, if they stayed away long enough . . .

He sighed with disappointment at the sound of footsteps in the hall.

'Hey, Dad, this is a really neat . . .'

The man who stepped into the den wasn't Dad.

# Chapter Fourteen

Sam drove back toward Ashburg, listening to quiet music on the radio, his mind on Melodie and Cynthia and his new problem.

He wanted to see Melodie again. He wanted to look in her wide, eager eyes. He wanted to hear her voice. He wanted to hold her, and feel the warmth of her body against him.

Melodie, not Cynthia. Damn it, how could this happen? He'd thought he loved Cynthia, thought he wanted to marry her. It didn't seem right that suddenly, by accident, he should meet a woman who made him want to break away from her.

God, how could he do that to Cynthia?

'I'm not going to disappear,' he'd told her this morning.

'I've heard that before,' she'd answered.

Damn it, she *expected* him to dump her. As if she thought she deserved to fall in love with men and lose them. Life had taught her some nasty lessons: if Sam left her, he'd be adding his own.

He couldn't.

That's it for Melodie.

The pain of the thought made him want to jam on the brakes, whip the car around and speed back to the motel. He would take Melodie in his arms, kiss . . . *No!*

His clenched hands ached on the steering wheel.

I've chosen Cynthia, he told himself. I can't go back on her now. It's too late for that. In a few days, I'll forget all about Melodie.

No, I won't forget her.

But I can't have her. There's plenty of things you can't have in this world, and you go along with it because you don't have a choice.

I have a choice here, though. I could stop seeing Cynthia, make up excuses . . .

That's no choice.

I just can't do that.

I can't.

Why, damn it to hell, did I have to follow Elmer out there tonight?

He pounded the steering wheel. He was tempted to bash his forehead against it, and wondered if he was going crazy.

Then, up ahead, he saw a quivering red glow in the sky.

'My God,' he muttered.

His foot rammed the gas pedal to the floor.

Must be the Sherwood place, he thought as he sped up the road. There were only a few houses this far out on Oakhurst, and the Sherwood house seemed most likely.

Not surprising for an abandoned structure like that to go up in smoke.

Kids or a derelict could've broken in, started a fire. Or Glendon Morley, its owner, might've finally decided to sell it to the insurance company.

Had to be arson. Had to be.

Swinging his car around a bend, Sam saw the last house on Oakhurst Road – the home of Clara Hayes. It was okay. Then the Sherwood place came into view, its front shimmering with fireglow, red emergency lights streaking across it. The next house was a pyre.

As he raced toward it, he tried to think who lived there. He didn't know. Parking in front, he leaped from his car. He spotted

Berney near the tail of the hook-and-ladder truck parked in the yard, and ran to him.

'She's a goner,' Berney said.

'Whose place is it?'

'Horners.'

'They get out okay?'

Berney shook his head, his glasses flashing reflections of the blaze. 'Nobody's seen 'em,' he said. 'A neighbor down the road called in the alarm. By the time we got here . . .'

With a roar of crashing timber, a portion of the roof collapsed. Embers erupted into the red sky.

'Guess they cooked,' Berney said. 'Four of 'em. Two kids.'

'Maybe they weren't home.'

'Both cars in the garage.'

'Shit,' Sam muttered.

'Hasn't been a good day, not a good day at all.' Berney took off his glasses, and rubbed his eyes. 'You come up with anything on the Dexter business?'

'I'm still looking for Thelma.'

'Well, stick with it. She's as good a suspect as any, better than most.'

'Yeah.'

Berney held up his glasses. He squinted at the lenses, and blew on them. 'Damned ashes,' he said.

Sam turned away to watch the fire. The two white jets of water thundering into it seemed to have no effect. Eventually, though, the flood would knock the flames down.

Too late to save the house.

Much too late to save the family.

As he watched, another section of roof crashed down. The heat grew more intense on his face, and he turned away.

A small crowd was gathered beside the road, some folks chatting, most gazing up at the fire. He recognized a few of them: Basil White, Joan Trask, Cameron Watts. Was Clara Hayes among them? She'd been a good friend of Dexter, and Sam wondered if she'd heard about his death.

Everyone must know, by now.

As he looked for Clara, his eyes moved past the fire-red face of a teenaged boy. A familiar face. He went back to it, and his heart lurched.

Eric!

He shot a glance at every face near the boy, but didn't find Cynthia.

'See you later,' he told Berney.

'Right.'

The boy's eyes remained on the fire as Sam approached. He had the same, shiny eyes as his mother. The same delicate nose, and high cheekbones. Only the mouth looked alien to Sam – a long slit with almost no visible lips. Must be Scotty Harlan's mouth.

'Hi, Eric.'

The boy flinched. He looked at Sam, and took a step backwards, treading on a woman's foot.

'Ouch!' she cried.

Eric lurched away from her.

'Hell of a fire,' Sam told him.

Eric frowned, looking confused.

'Want a closer look?'

'The policeman told us to stay back.'

Sam gestured for Eric to come forward.

'You sure it's okay?'

'Sure.'

Eric stepped onto the lawn.

Turning away, Sam walked toward the hook-and-ladder. He stopped at its front. A moment later, Eric appeared beside him.

'The view's better from here.'

'Yeah,' Eric said, gaping at the blaze.

'I guess the people got killed.'

Eric wrinkled his nose. 'Yeah,' he said. 'Gross.'

'You didn't know them, did you?'

'I've seen 'em around. Joe, mostly. He was a jerk.'

'Not anymore.'

'Yeah.'

'Is your mother here?'

He shook his head, glanced at Sam, and quickly looked back to the fire.

'How'd you get here?'

'Walked.'

'Does your mother know?'

'She's not home. What're they gonna do with the bodies?'

'They'll bring 'em out, once the fire's cold. That won't be for a long time, though. How about a ride home?'

'No, that's okay.'

'Come on, Eric.'

He scowled up at Sam. 'I don't feel like it.'

'Why not?'

'Doesn't matter.'

'Are you mad because of last night?'

'Maybe.'

'Well, I can understand that. I'm sorry it happened, too. It was a hell of a way to meet. But can't we forget about that, and start over?'

'Why should we?'

'I'd like to be friends.'

'I don't need a friend like you.'

'Like me?'

'All you care about is messing around with Mom.'

'Eric, your mother and I . . .'

'Now you want to kiss up to me and get me on your side so you don't have to sneak around anymore behind my back. Well, screw you!'

'Eric!' Frowning, Sam reached for the boy's shoulder.

Eric knocked his hand aside, whirled around, and ran for the road. Sam decided to let him go. He wouldn't accomplish much by intimidating the kid. Better to work on him gradually, winning his trust a bit at a time.

He turned away. For a while, he watched the fire. Flames still reached out the windows. They burned inside the structure and clawed at the sky through the blazing skeleton of rafters.

Sam turned around, and scanned the crowd for Eric.

The boy was gone.

# Chapter Fifteen

Eric ran past the last house on the road, and ducked behind a telephone pole. From there, he looked back at the distant group of people watching the fire. Nobody seemed to be coming, so he raced to the side of the house. Keeping close to the wall, he walked through the grass to the back yard. Light from a kitchen window lit the lawn below it.

The old woman, he thought, might be looking out. Could she see him if he crossed the dark part of the yard by the graveyard fence? Maybe. He might be safer, though, staying close to the wall and sneaking under the window.

Eyes on the back door, he rushed past the steps and crouched against the siding. Though the window was high enough to walk past, he dropped to the ground. The grass was cool and slippery on his hands. The dew quickly soaked through the knees of his jeans. As he crawled beneath the window, he held his breath.

She was at the window, glaring down – he knew she was. Any second, she would fling open the window and reach down for him, grab him by the neck, drag him into the house . . .

That's dumb, he told himself. She couldn't reach down this far, even if she tried.

As soon as he was past the window, he scurried to his feet and ran. He didn't stop until he reached the corner of the house. Looking back, he saw only the lighted window and the deserted yard. He leaned against the wall, breathing hard.

Stupid to be so scared of an old lady, he thought. He could always outrun her.

Easing away from the wall, he studied the area ahead. A flowerbed marked the edge of the old woman's property. He would have to jump that, then race across a wide space to the garage of the Sherwood house.

He looked around the corner, toward Oakhurst Road. Seeing no one, he stepped into the open. Headlights appeared. With a gasp, he leaped back and pressed himself to the back wall. He waited, then looked again. The car was gone. Nobody was in sight. He sprinted across the grass. Dead leaves crashed as his foot hit the flowerbed. He cringed at the noise, but kept running.

Still nobody by the road.

Still nobody behind him.

He dashed behind the garage. Safe there, he walked slowly through the weeds, catching his breath. He peered around the corner. The side of the house blocked his view of the road.

He'd made it!

With a sigh of relief, he walked from the garage to the back porch of the house. He silently climbed its steps. The screen door groaned as he pulled it open. No longer afraid of being heard, he grinned at the sound.

What a great place for a Halloween party!

The porch floor creaked under his sneakers. He twisted the doorknob, and pushed the door open. He stepped inside.

Nothing moved in the dark kitchen. He walked slowly through it, and pushed open the door to the dining room.

The room smelled strongly of paint.

He entered, and shut the door. His eyes searched darkness so intense that he blinked to be sure his eyes weren't shut.

'Hello?' he whispered.

He waited, listening. The silence was so complete that he heard quiet ringing inside his head – a high-pitched hum as if his brain were a television with its volume off.

'Hello?' he whispered again. 'It's me, Eric.'

When no response came, he walked through the darkness with his arms outstretched, seeking a wall. With each step, he half expected to bark his shin or stumble. What if the floor suddenly ended, and he lowered his foot into nothingness!

Don't be a dope, he told himself.

He'd been in here before. There was no furniture to trip over, no hole in the floor.

Feeling the black air, he continued walking slowly until his foot struck an object. He stumbled forward, stepping on something with his other foot, losing his balance completely and falling through the darkness. The floor came from nowhere, battering his hands and elbows and knees.

'What are you doing here?' The voice was a low whisper, scratchy and hardly audible. It came from the blackness ahead of Eric.

'I wanted to see you,' Eric said.

'I told you to stay away.'

'But the fire. The house next door. I was afraid you might want to call off the party.'

'It won't be called off. Did you make the invitations?'

Eric nodded.

'Did you?'

'Yes.'

'You sent them to all your enemies, everyone who has ever punched you, or laughed at you, or spit in your face?'

'Well . . .'

'Answer me.'

310

'I mailed them to all the *kids*. What about grown-ups, though? There's a guy at school, Mr Doons. He's really mean to me. He made me do push-ups in piss. And Miss Major. I kind of got back at her, already, but she slapped me right in front of the whole class.'

'Slapped you? Why?'

'She said I was looking down the front of her dress.' Eric heard soft, hissing laughter. 'It was her fault, though. She kept bending over, and her dress was sort of loose, and she wasn't even wearing a bra.'

'Got a good look, did you?'

'Yeah, but she slapped me.'

'Go ahead and invite her.'

'What about Mr Doons?'

'Him too. Anybody you want, invite 'em. The more, the merrier.'

Eric grinned into the darkness. 'We'll really scare the hell out of them, won't we?'

'They'll never give you grief again.'

'I can't wait.'

'Won't be long, now.'

'Can you show me how you fixed the place up?'

'Not now.'

'Please?'

'Never beg, kid.'

Eric nodded, blushing. 'I won't again. I promise. Is it real scary, though?'

'Real scary.'

'Whatever I tripped on, was that part of the decorations?'

'Yeah.'

'Boy, this is gonna be the best Halloween party ever.

Maybe we can do it every year. You know, make it an annual thing.'

'Sure.'

'You won't go away again, will you?'

'I'm here to stay.'

'Great! Hey, maybe you and Mom can get back together again. Wouldn't that be neat? You could get married, and . . .'

'She doesn't want me.'

'I bet she'd like you fine, once she got to know you.'

'No.'

'You could at least try, Dad. Ask her for a date, or something.'

'You better get out of here. Make sure nobody sees you leave.'

# Chapter Sixteen

When Sam drove home, he saw Cynthia's car parked in front of his duplex. He pulled into the driveway, and hurried to his door. As he searched through his keys, the door swung open.

Cynthia smiled out at him. 'May I help?' she asked. She was wearing one of his big, flannel shirts. Her legs were bare.

Sam entered. He shut the door, and took her into his arms. 'That helps,' he said. 'A lot.' He pressed his mouth to her full, open lips. His hands moved down her back, stroked her buttocks through the soft flannel, slipped under the hanging shirt-tail and caressed her bare skin. He moved them upward, feeling the warm smoothness of her back. 'I thought we weren't going to see each other tonight.'

'I thought so, too,' she said, pressing herself tightly against him.

'What happened?'

'I heard about Dexter on the news. I thought you might . . . want some company.'

'Did you wait long?'

'I came over about nine.' She kissed the side of his neck. 'You smell like smoke.'

'I was at a fire.'

'A fire?' she asked, her lips tickling his neck.

He didn't want to tell her about the fire just now. He didn't want to think about it, or about Eric or Dexter, about the Sleepy Hollow Inn where he nearly let himself abandon Cynthia for a smiling blond with a badge on her breast. He wanted to forget it all, forget everything except the way she felt in his arms.

But he couldn't.

'A house burnt down, over on Oakhurst Road.'

She looked up at him, concern in her clear eyes. 'Whose house?'

'The Horners. Do you know them?'

'Lynn Horner? I met her at PTA.' She read the expression on Sam's face. 'Oh no.'

'I left before they went in for the bodies.'

'Did all of them . . .?'

'Apparently.'

'Oh geez.'

'I saw Eric at the fire.'

She stiffened. 'Eric? What was he doing there?'

'Watching. There were quite a few spectators.'

'He was supposed to be home.'

'I guess he heard the fire trucks and got curious. Fires have a way of drawing people. He said you weren't home.'

'You talked to him?'

'For a couple of minutes. He didn't seem too happy about it. I offered him a lift home, but he ran off.'

Cynthia sighed and shut her eyes. 'Damn it, I shouldn't have left him. May I use your phone?'

'Sure.'

She looked up at him. With a half-smile, she drew her fingertips along his cheek. 'I just wanted to be with you,' she said. Then she turned away.

Sam watched her cross the room. She bent over the phone, and dialed. For a moment, Sam looked at the pale slopes of her exposed buttocks. The view started to arouse him, so he looked away. He wandered into the kitchen, and took a beer from the refrigerator. Snapping open the top, he returned to the living room.

Cynthia hung up. 'He didn't answer. I guess I'd better go back.' She smiled hopefully. 'Want to come?'

'If you want me to.'

'I want you to.'

Sam drank half his beer on the way back to the refrigerator. He put the can away, and returned to the living room. Cynthia wasn't there. She came in from his bedroom, a moment later, wearing shoes, tan corduroy pants, and a white bra. As she walked, she put on her blouse. Sam opened the door for her. 'I'm awfully sorry about this,' she said.

'Don't be.' He clutched the back of her neck. She smiled with disappointment, and stepped out the door.

They took separate cars to her house, several blocks away. Inside, Sam waited while Cynthia wandered through the house calling out for Eric.

She came back, shaking her head. 'He's not here, Sam.'

'Has he done this sort of thing before?'

'Sneaked out at night? No. Not that I know of. Damn it, I trusted him. We had a deal that we'd tell each other, whenever we went out. You know, so the other wouldn't worry and we'd know where to get in touch. He isn't supposed to go out, at all, when I'm gone at night.'

'I guess the temptation was too great this time.'

'Yeah. Well, he was upset tonight. Maybe he did this to get even. Eric likes to get even. Of course, I guess he didn't know I'd find out.' She sighed. 'How about a drink? Let's have a drink, and give him a few minutes, and if he isn't here by the time we finish, we'll go out looking.'

'Fine with me.'

'A beer or a gimlet?'

'How about straight vodka with a slice of lime?'

'Aye-aye.'

They went together into the kitchen, Cynthia took glasses down from the cupboard, and Sam removed a quart of Gilby's from her cabinet.

'What upset Eric?' he asked.

'Well, we started off talking about you. Then it got around to his father. Eric seems to think I cheated him out of a dad by not marrying Scotty Harlan.'

'Does he know about Scotty?' Sam asked, surprised.

'You think I'd tell him that he's the product of a rape? He's got enough problems without having *that* laid on him. I just told him that we hardly knew each other, and got carried away one afternoon and that Scotty left town before he was born. Pretty much what I'd told him before. But he got all upset and kept saying I should've married the creep.'

'If he feels that way, maybe you should tell him the truth.'

'I can't.'

They finished making the drinks, and went into the living room. They sat on a couch.

'I think it'd help,' Sam said, 'if he got to know me.'

'You're probably right.'

'Why don't we plan something for Saturday? There's a football game at city college.'

'He isn't much for football.'

'What does he like?'

'Well, movies.'

'Okay. We'll go to the movies, then. He can pick what we see. We'll stop by the Pizza Palace, first, for supper.'

'All right.' She frowned into her drink, and took a sip. 'I just don't want him hurt again.'

'He won't be,' Sam told her. Suddenly, his heart began to race. 'Neither will you.'

She stared at him.

Sam's mouth went dry. He took a drink. His hand trembled as he lowered his glass to the table. He faced Cynthia. She kept staring. He saw fear and hope in her eyes as if she knew what was in his mind.

'How would you like to marry me?' Sam asked.

She raised a hand to her mouth. The fingertips pressed against her tight lips. 'Are you serious?' she asked through her fingers.

'I know this isn't a great time to ask. I'd planned to take you out for a fancy dinner . . .'

'You really want to marry me?'

'I've always wanted to, ever since we met.'

Her eyes sparkled with tears. 'It isn't . . . just because of Eric?'

'It's because of you.'

'Jeezus.' Her long fingers wiped the tears from her cheeks. 'What do you say?'

She couldn't say anything. Nodding, she threw herself against Sam and hugged him. After a while, she drew back. Smiling, she hugged him again. 'Cynthia Wyatt,' she said.

'Sounds good.'

'Sounds wonderful. Oh, Sam.'

'Huh?'

'I wish we could be like this forever.'

'We'd get stiff necks.'

Laughing, she kissed him. The front door opened, and she pulled quickly away as Eric walked in. She frowned at the boy. 'Where have you been, young man?'

'Didn't *he* tell you?'

'You're not supposed to leave this house, when I'm gone.'

He shrugged. 'I wanted to see the fire.'

'That doesn't matter. A rule's a rule.'

'I'm sorry,' he said.

'Go on up to your room.' .

He glared at Sam, and went up the stairs.

'I'd better have a talk with him,' she said.

'Maybe I should leave.'

'No. I won't be long. Why don't you fix yourself another drink? I'll be down in a few minutes.'

Eric was buttoning his pajamas when his mother knocked and opened the door. 'What do you want?' he said.

'I want to know what you think you're doing.'

'Going to bed.'

'Knock off the smart answers, all right?'

'I just wanted to see the fire.'

'How did you know there *was* a fire?'

'The trucks went by.'

'They wouldn't pass here, going to Oakhurst Road. They'd be going the other way.'

Eric scowled. 'I was taking a walk, and they went by.'

'So you were already outside?'

'Yeah.'

'Why did you leave the house?'

'I felt like it.'

'Where were you going?'

'Nowhere. I just felt like getting out.'

'You must've been going somewhere.'

'I wasn't. I just felt cooped up. It isn't fair. You can go out whenever you want, and I have to stay home.'

'I never just leave without telling you. Didn't occur to you that I might worry?'

'I didn't think you'd find out.'

'Well, I did.'

'Only 'cause I ran into that damned cop.'

'Eric!' she snapped.

'Well, it's true. If he hadn't told, you never would've found out.'

'You think that would make it all right?'

'What you don't know, won't hurt you.'

She gazed at him, looking stunned. 'You don't really believe that.'

'Sure.'

'You think it's okay to do something wrong, as long as you don't get caught?'

Eric nodded.

'You can't . . . Where on earth did you *pick* that up?'

He grinned. 'From you.'

'I never . . .'

'The way you sneak around, sleeping with guys. It's okay, as long as little Eric doesn't find out. What he doesn't know, won't hurt him. Isn't that so?'

'No!'

'Oh yeah?'

'I have every right to see any man I want. For Godsake, I didn't go on a date for ten years after you were born, and you have the gall to criticize my morals! Goddamn it, Eric . . .'

'You should've married Dad.'

'Your father was despicable and he probably still is, if, somebody hasn't killed him by now.'

'Go to hell.'

She slapped him.

Eric smiled.

She whirled away and left the room, slamming his door so hard its noise hurt his ears and nearly brought tears to his eyes.

Sam heard the sharp crash of the door, and grimaced.

What am I getting into? he thought.

He took a sip of icy vodka, wondering if he'd made a mistake. What if the kid doesn't straighten out?

Better have a long engagement. Very long. Make sure Eric isn't going to sour everything. If it looks bad, maybe everyone will be better off just forgetting it.

He expected Cynthia to come downstairs right away. He

grew restless as the minutes passed. Maybe he should've gone home, after all. Too late for that. He couldn't leave without saying good-bye, and if Cynthia was so upset that she didn't want to face him . . .

At the sound of quiet footsteps on the stairway, Sam got to his feet.

Cynthia came down the stairs, one hand gliding along the banister. She wore a white nightgown that Sam had never seen before.

'You all right?' he asked.

'This is our night, Sam. I won't let Eric ruin it.'

The gown floated against her body, transparent as gauze, as she slowly walked toward Sam.

# Chapter Seventeen

Eric lay in bed, wide awake. He heard his mother and Sam walk up the hallway, whisper words too quiet to understand. He shut his eyes as his door opened.

Soft footsteps crossed his room.

The side of his mattress sank. He smelled his mother's perfume, and her hand stroked his cheek.

'Honey?'

He moaned as if waking up. As the fingers caressed his forehead, he opened his eyes. 'Huh?' he said.

'I'm sorry we quarreled.'

'Me too.'

'I was just so worried when you weren't at home.'

'I'm sorry.'

'I love you so much.' She bent down, and kissed him. 'We'll try to do better, okay?'

'Okay.'

'Goodnight, honey.'

'Night.'

He watched her walk toward the open door. The light from the hallway passed through her nightgown, and made her look naked. He stared at her breasts as she turned to pull the door shut.

She's dressed like that for Sam, he thought.

The dirty bastard.

He's probably waiting in her room, right now, taking off his clothes.

If Dad only knew . . . *He's* the one who should be going to bed with her, not this damned cop.

Eric climbed from bed. He found his sneakers, and went to his door. He listened for a moment. Hearing nothing, he opened his door and looked out. The hallway was dark. It looked deserted.

He stepped out, and silently closed his door. He tiptoed along the hall to the head of the stairway. The house below him was dark. A few of the stairs creaked as he descended, but nobody came to check.

He hurried into the kitchen, and turned on the light. A paring knife lay on the counter beside a carved lime.

It might break, he decided.

So he slid a butcher knife out of its rack. Holding it behind his back, he rushed to the front door. There, he put on his sneakers.

He ran across the yard, gritting his teeth against the chilly wind that blew through his pajamas. As he ran, he glanced up at the windows of his mother's room. They were dark. Crouching by the front of Sam's car, he stabbed the side of the tire. The point didn't penetrate enough. He worked the knife with both hands, pushing hard against it. Suddenly, it rammed deep. Rubber-smelling air hissed into his face.

As the corner of the car sank, he crawled to the rear. He sat on the wet grass, feet against the tire. Leaning forward, be held the knife to the whitewall. He stomped his heel against its butt. The knife punched in.

Eric tugged the knife free, and stepped into the street. He sat down on the cold pavement, held the knife in place, and kicked. It went easily into the third tire.

He did the same to the final tire.

That'll fix you, he thought.

His jaw hurt from clenching his teeth. He opened his mouth wide, and tried to work out the tension.

Peeling the wet pajamas away from his rump, he looked up and down the block. He saw no one. He glanced again at his mother's windows.

They're too busy to see me, he thought.

It didn't matter, though.

Sam would know who'd done it.

Maybe the dirty bastard would get the message.

Eric ran back to the house. He entered its warmth, and took off his shoes. Picking them up, he walked silently into the lighted kitchen.

The knife blade was streaked with black from the tires.

If he put it back in the rack without cleaning it ... How could he clean it without making noise? Soap and water might not work, anyway. He'd need to use paint thinner, or nail polish remover, something like that. Rubbing alcohol? A whole bottle of it stood in the medicine cabinet.

Turning off the light, he left the kitchen. He held the knife behind his back, and went to the stairway. The hall above was still dark. He slowly climbed the stairs, cringing each time the wood creaked under his feet.

At the top, he looked down the hall. The door of his mother's room was still shut. He turned to the right, and tiptoed into the bathroom.

He locked the door. He flicked the light on, and opened the medicine cabinet. The rubbing alcohol sloshed in its plastic bottle as he lifted it down. He poured the clear liquid onto a wad of toilet paper. It soaked through, feeling strange on his fingers – burning and cool at the same time.

He rubbed it on the knife. The black streaks of rubber seemed to dissolve. In less than a minute the blade was sleek and shiny. He wiped it dry with more toilet paper, tossed both wads into the bowl and automatically reached out to flush. As his fingertips touched the handle, he realized what he was about to do. He pulled his hand away.

With the bottle back in the medicine cabinet, he picked up his shoes and knife. He silently opened the door, and walked up the hallway. He passed the stairs. He continued up the hall and put his shoes just inside his room. As he pulled the door shut, he heard a quiet gasp.

It came from his mother's room.

Heart suddenly hammering, he tiptoed to her door. He stood there, listening. From inside came muffled sounds of harsh breathing and moans and the squeaking bed.

He saw that the door was open a crack.

His heart pounded so hard that he felt dizzy and sick.

Stepping forward, he pressed gently against the door. The crack widened.

In the light from the windows, he saw them. Their tangled, thrusting bodies were dark against the sheets. He couldn't tell one from the other.

Pushing the door wide open, he stepped into the room. He walked toward the bed.

It was Sam on top, Mom under him with her knees up, hands clutching his back as his ass jerked up and down. She writhed, gasping and moaning.

Eric stopped at the foot of the bed. He gripped the knife so tightly that his hand ached.

Such awful sounds. Flesh pounding flesh. Wet, sticky noises. Grunts like wallowing pigs.

'Bastard,' he muttered.

'Eric?' gasped his mother. 'Oh my God!' Her hands pushed at Sam but he clung to her. 'No!' she cried.

Sam's body stiffened and jerked.

He quickly rolled off.

Mom squirmed over the sheet. Reaching down beside the bed, she picked up her nightgown. She pressed it to her body, sat up, and turned on the bedside lamp.

'*Eric!* Put down that knife!'

'He's not my dad,' Eric said.

'Put down that knife!'

He slashed the palm of his left hand. Blood spilled from the slit.

Mom screamed.

Sam lunged off the bed at him, smashing the knife from his hand and throwing him backward to the floor.

# Chapter Eighteen

They spent nearly two hours at Emergency, most of it waiting because an eighteen-wheeler rear-ended a passenger car out on the highway. Eric sat beside Cynthia, mute and staring.

When they finally got back to the house and put him to bed, Cynthia suggested that Sam go home.

'Eric's so upset,' she said. 'Maybe . . . I don't know . . . Maybe you'd better not stay tonight.'

'He's asleep now.'

'Maybe he is and maybe he isn't.'

'If you want me to leave, I will. But I don't think it'd be smart to reward Eric that way. You'd be letting him win, teaching him that it works to bust in on people, mutilate himself, slash tires . . .'

'I guess you're right,' she admitted.

They went to bed, then. For a long time, Sam couldn't sleep. He lay beside Cynthia, staring into the darkness, knowing that she was also awake. They didn't talk or touch. When Sam finally fell asleep, he dreamed he was awake.

He dreamed that Eric stood at the foot of the bed, knife ready. He was safe as long as Eric thought he was sleeping. But a heavy, bloated spider was scurrying down the wall. In seconds, it would creep onto Sam's face. He wondered, vaguely, how he could see the spider so well with his eyes shut.

They're open!

With a sudden grin, Eric dived onto him. The blade plunged into his stomach, stiff and cold.

He sat up, grabbing his stomach, gasping.

For a long time after that, he lay awake. He didn't want to fall asleep if it meant returning to the dream. So he kept his eyes open, and tried to think of something pleasant.

His thoughts drifted to Melodie Caine.

They were in the motel office, and she wore her white sweater and kilt. Sam shut his eyes to see her more clearly.

'If I'm supposed to be your deputy,' she said, 'I need a badge.'

He held it out to her.

'No, you have to pin it on me or it's not official.'

He tried to pin the badge to her sweater, his fingers trembling against her breast.

'Don't be nervous,' she whispered. She jumped and said 'Ouch!' as he stuck her.

'Are you okay?'

'I don't know.' She lifted her sweater over her full, milk-white breasts. A spot of blood shimmered above the nipple. 'You'd better kiss it and make it well.'

He pressed his lips to the wound, tasting the warm salty blood. Then her nipple was in his mouth. His teeth teased the springy column of flesh; his tongue flicked and circled.

'Oh, Sam,' she gasped. 'Oh, Sam, I love you.'

# Chapter Nineteen

Half an hour before classes began, the first floor hallway of the main building was nearly deserted. Eric stopped in front of the door marked MR DOONS, VICE PRINCIPAL. He glanced both ways. Nobody was nearby or watching. He crouched, slid an envelope under the door, and walked away.

Upstairs, he passed a couple of girls standing at an open locker. They paid him no attention. He walked by an open classroom.

What if Miss Major's door was open?

As he approached it, his heart started to pound, sending throbs of pain into his wounded hand.

Her door was shut.

He glanced back at the girls. Their backs were turned. He flipped open the cover of his English grammar text, and took out an envelope. Crouching, he dropped the envelope to the floor and pushed it toward the slot beneath the door.

The door sprang open.

Eric jumped back.

Miss Major looked down at the envelope, then at Eric. She planted her fists against her hips, and Eric realized she was wearing the same dress she'd worn the day he saw her breasts, the day she slapped him.

Her toe nudged the envelope. 'I assume it's for me,' she said.

Eric nodded.

Miss Major held out her hand. Her long fingers trembled slightly, and Eric wondered if she was afraid of him. Probably not. She looked angry, not frightened. 'Give it to me.'

He picked up the envelope, and laid it across her hand.

She turned it over. She ran it through her fingers. Her eyes fixed on Eric. 'I'll give you one chance. You can take it back now, unopened, and that'll be the end of it.' She held it toward him.

Eric's hand throbbed. The pain made it hard to think. He wanted to accept the envelope and get far away from Miss Major. But he didn't want to back down.

'What'll it be, Eric?'

'I guess I'll take it,' he mumbled, and reached for the envelope. As his fingers closed on it, she snatched it away. Her tight mouth smiled.

'You said . . .'

'I changed my mind. I just can't wait to see what it is that you're so eager to take back, now that you're caught.'

'It's nothing.'

'I'll just bet.' She slipped a finger under the flap, and slowly worked it up the envelope, ripping the seam. 'Well well well, what have we here? Not another rat, obviously.' She plucked out the paper and unfolded it. 'Join the fun,' she read in a mocking voice. With a frown, she read the rest in silence. She gazed at the paper for a long time, as if reluctant to meet Eric's eyes. Her face was red. Finally, she lowered the invitation. 'You're giving a party?' she asked.

Eric nodded. He smiled, trying to look embarrassed. 'I thought you might like to come, if you're not too busy. It'll be a bunch of kids and a few of my teachers and Mr Doons.'

'But why me?'

'Well.' He shrugged. 'I feel bad about – you know – what happened. I just thought maybe you could come and have a good time, and maybe we wouldn't have to be enemies anymore.'

'That's very thoughtful of you, Eric.' She looked again at the invitation. 'You're having it at the Sherwood house?'

'Yeah. We've got it all fixed up for the party. It'll be real spooky.'

'But it's abandoned, isn't it?'

'Oh, my mom's good friends with the owner.'

'Glendon Morley?'

'Yeah. He's gonna be there, too. So's my mom and some of her friends.'

'Sounds like you'll have quite a crowd.'

'Yeah. I hope you'll come. You can bring along a friend, too, if you want.'

She folded the invitation and slipped it into the envelope. 'We'll see,' she said. 'I'll try to make it, if I can. At any rate, I appreciate being invited.'

Eric smiled and shrugged.

With a friendly nod, she stepped into her classroom and shut the door.

Eric started down the hall. At first, he felt only relief at escaping her wrath. Then he thought of her embarrassment, and smiled.

He had really put one over on her. All his lies had worked. Moreover, she'd sounded as if she might actually come to the party. In triumph, he slapped his leg – and yelped as pain streaked up his arm.

# Chapter Twenty

'Are you all right?' Betty asked when he entered the station the next morning.

'Hanging in there,' Sam said, and yawned. He poured himself a mug of coffee. 'Cynthia's son cut himself, last night, and we took him over to Emergency.'

Betty frowned. 'I hope it wasn't too serious.'

'Took a dozen stitches,' he said. He sipped the coffee, and sat at his desk. 'How are *you* doing?'

'Managing,' she said. 'It isn't going to be quite the same around here without Dexter. He was . . .' She pressed her lips tightly together. Her chin trembled. She reached for a tissue and covered her eyes. Sam looked down.

He took small drinks of coffee, the steam burning his raw eyes.

God what a night, he thought.

Betty blew her nose. 'Anyway,' she said, 'I heard you were out at the fire.'

'Yeah.'

'They couldn't find the Horners.'

'*What?*'

'Apparently, everyone thought they were burnt. But the fire department searched through the rubble and couldn't find their bodies. So it looks as if they weren't home last night, after all.'

'Well, that's lucky. Where were they?'

Betty shrugged. 'Nobody knows. They haven't shown up. Chet's supposed to check the bus terminal and taxis.'

'Berney thinks they skipped?'

'He does. Hank Horner is now topping his suspect list.'

'He thinks Horner killed Dex?'

'Killed him, panicked, and sneaked out of town, last night, with his family.'

'Why would he burn the house?'

'So we'll assume he's dead.'

'We're not going to assume he's dead if we don't find the body.'

'Oh, you know *people*.' She made a weary smile. 'Horner probably didn't know any better. He figured, if he burnt the house down, we'd think he and his family got turned to ashes.'

'Not a very smart fellow.'

'Murderers aren't normally famous for their brains.'

'Has Berney come up with a motive?'

'Not yet. He's going over to Horner's office this morning. You're supposed to continue with the Thelma angle. Oh, a call came in for you, a few minutes ago.' She glanced down at the log book. 'A Miss Melodie Caine.'

The name slammed into him. His heart raced and his mouth went dry.

'You're supposed to call her right away.'

He swallowed. 'Did she leave a number?'

Betty read the number, and Sam copied it with a shaky hand.

He dialed from the phone at his desk. As he listened to the ringing, he nearly hung up; he could drive out to the motel, and get her message in person. The idea excited him, but he'd promised himself to stay away. He would hold to that promise.

I'm committed to Cynthia now, he thought.

For better or worse.

'Sleepy Hollow Inn,' said the low, familiar voice.

'Melodie, this is Sam Wyatt.'

'Good. I'm glad you got back to me so fast. I've got something for you, Sam. You know those people in room Four? Well, one of them – the man – made a telephone call after you left. He called from his room, so I had to put it through for him. Would you like to know the number?'

'I sure would.'

'Thought you might.'

Sam copied the number as she gave it to him. 'That's great, Melodie. Thanks a lot.'

'Hey, let me know how it all turns out, okay?'

'I will.'

'Take care, Sam.'

'You too.'

Her telephone clacked down. For a moment, Sam listened to the empty, desolate sound of the empty wires. Then he hung up.

'Got something?' Betty asked.

'Could be.' He flipped through the special directory listing its entries by telephone number.


A woman in jeans and a sweatshirt opened the door. Sam gazed at her dishwater-blond hair, her haggard, familiar face. 'Thelma?' he asked.

'I'm Marjorie,' she said.

Sam glanced at his note pad. 'Are you Mrs Doons?'

'That's right.'

'You look . . .'

'Thelma's my sister.'

'Twins?'

'We're a couple of years apart. If you're looking for Thelma, she's not in.'

'Is she staying with you?'

The woman nodded.

'Could I talk to you?'

'Come in.'

He followed her into the living room, and took a seat. 'I'm Sam Wyatt,' he said.

'You're here about Dexter.'

'Yes.'

'God, that was a terrible thing.'

'Where is Thelma?'

'She's spending the day in Dendron with our mother.'

Dendron again. As if fate were trying to drag Sam back there, back to the Sleepy Hollow Inn and Melodie. 'Your mother lives in Dendron? Could I have her address?'

'There's really no point in that. Thelma'll be home this evening. Why don't I have her phone you when she arrives?'

'I'd prefer to see her as soon as possible.'

Marjorie sighed. 'If you insist, then. It's 354 Tenth Street.'

'Thank you,' he said, writing it down. 'When did Thelma arrive in town?'

'Tuesday morning.'

'And she's been staying here with you?'

Marjorie nodded. 'If you think she had anything to do with Dexter's death, you're wrong. It's just an unfortunate coincidence that she happened to be in town this week. She's been back – oh, two or three times a year since she and Dexter split up. Nothing ever happened before. If she wanted to kill him, she had plenty of chances to do it before now. She was finished with Dexter the night she walked out on him.'

'Why did she come to town this week?'

'Tomorrow's my birthday.'

'She came in from Milwaukee to celebrate your birthday?'

'Oh, she hasn't lived in Milwaukee for years. She went there with Babe Rawls. They were only together for six months or so. He treated her shamefully – beat her up all the time and subjected her to . . . well, I needn't dwell on all the sordid details. Suffice it to say that she had enough of it, and left him. She's been living in Hayward for the better part of a year.'

'Do you know where she was Wednesday night?'

'She spent the night here.'

'Did she go out?'

'Why, yes. She went over to the Sunset Lounge.'

The Sunset Lounge. Sam had been there himself that night, with Cynthia. Of course, he hadn't been looking for Thelma then. At that point, he hadn't even known what she looked like. She might have been sitting at the next table.

'Did she go there alone?'

Marjorie shook her head. 'She went with Ticia Barnes.'

Sam raised his eyebrows.

'They're old friends,' Marjorie explained. 'Ticia used to live next door to us, when we lived on Seventh Street.'

'What time did Thelma leave for the lounge?'

'Oh, nine-ish. You can check with Ticia, if you wish. She picked Thelma up.'

'What time did Thelma get back?'

'I have no idea.'

'You said she spent the night here.'

'And so she did. Phillip and I hardly felt it necessary to wait up for her. We went to bed at our usual time. Maybe Phillip heard her come in, but I'm afraid I was dead to the world. I haven't the vaguest notion what time she came in. I know she was here, though. She joined us for breakfast in the morning.'

'What time was that?'

'Seven'

'And she didn't tell you what time she got home?'

'Not a word.'

'Did she say anything about what she'd done?'

'Oh, just that she and Ticia had a great time.'

'Did she say she'd met anyone?'

'No. But why don't you have a word with Ticia? I'm sure she can fill you in.'

# Chapter Twenty-one

At the ten-thirty 'nutrition break,' Eric headed for the school library. With all the kids running loose, it was the only place of safety. He'd discovered this sanctuary during the second week of school, after spending his nutrition and lunch periods in terror.

Nate Houlder had chased him, that day, threatening to beat the shit out of him.

Eric barely made it to the library door. He rushed inside, Nate hot on his tail.

'Hold it!' Mr Carlson had yelled, his voice booming through the quiet library.

Eric stopped, but Nate kept coming and grabbed his arm.

'Let go of him!'

Nate dragged him toward the door.

Mr Carlson's face turned bright red and he suddenly ran from behind the circulation desk, his corduroy jacket fluttering behind him.

Nate hesitated, then smirked as if he thought the librarian was a joke. He pulled Eric toward the door.

'Damn it, you little . . .!' Carlson's hand chopped Nate's forearm. Eric pulled away from the loose fingers.

'You *hit* me,' Nate snarled.

'I told you to let go of him.'

'Man, I'm gonna sue your ass.'

'Be my guest. In the meantime, get out of here.'

Nate glared at him.

Carlson shoved him.

'Hey, don't push me!'

'Get out of here.'

Nate turned away. 'I'm going, I'm going.'

'Not fast enough.' Following the boy, Carlson nudged his trailing foot sideways and tripped him. Nate caught himself on the bar of the door. As he left, he looked over his shoulder: 'Goddamn fag. You two deserve each other.'

Eric smiled, remembering the scene. By driving him into the library that day, Nate had done him a real favor. His life at Ashburg High had improved a lot since discovering the refuge: nutrition and lunch periods were no longer times of being chased, punched, and trash-canned. Instead, he could sit in the safety of the library, read, or join the others chatting with Mr Carlson.

Of course, it was still a problem getting there unscathed. As he walked past the other students, today, he kept a sharp eye out for Nate and Bill and half a dozen other guys with nothing better to do than torment him.

Glimpsing someone close to his side, he took a quick step away and looked around. Only Beth. She smiled slightly, her lips together in a way she'd started smiling since she got her braces.

'What happened to your hand?' she asked.

'Ah, nothing. I cut it on a broken glass last night.'

'Where're you going?'

'The library.'

'Me, too. No more snack bar for me.'

'You're not fat.'

She laughed softly. For a moment, her bright clear eyes met Eric's. Then she lowered them as if embarrassed. 'I'm not skinny, either.'

'Who says you have to be?'

'Oh, nearly everyone.'

'What do they know,' he said.

As they talked together, he sneaked glances at Beth. She was no taller than him, with light brown hair and a band of freckles across her nose and cheeks. He'd known her since she moved to Ashburg three years ago. She never made fun of his size or his mind, and she wasn't pretty enough to frighten him so they got along just fine.

'Are you going to the Halloween party?' Eric asked.

'Which one?'

'Which one?' He looked at her, frowning. 'The one at the old Sherwood house.'

'Do you think that's for real?'

'Sure. I got an invitation.'

'So did I, but I can't imagine the place will be opened for a party. It's been boarded up for years.'

'It'll be open tonight.'

'You sound awfully sure.'

'It just doesn't make sense for somebody to send out all those invitations and then not have a party.'

'I think it's just a gag,' Beth said.

Eric shook his head. 'Gee, I was hoping . . .'

'What?' She looked at him, smiling.

'I was kind of hoping you'd be there.' He reached for the library door.

'Wait. Let's not go in yet.'

Their eyes locked. He saw her blush, and felt heat rushing to his own face.

'Aleshia's having a party tonight.'

'She *is*?' Eric tried to keep his disappointment from showing. If Aleshia had a party, she wouldn't be at the Sherwood house. Not Beth, not Aleshia. How many others wouldn't show up? Maybe he'd be the only one . . .

'Eric, would you like to go with me to Aleshia's party?'

'Me?' He pictured Aleshia, lithe and smiling. At her party, he could look at her for hours, talk to her, maybe even somehow touch her, feel the warm smoothness of her skin. 'I'd sure like to . . .'

Beth shrugged. 'I know it's awfully late to be asking. You probably have other plans.'

'Sort of.'

'It's all right. I can ask somebody else.'

'No, don't. I'll go with you.'

'Really, you don't have to.'

'I want to. It's just that . . . I've got a problem about . . .' He sighed. 'I want to go to the Sherwood house.'

'What on earth *for*?'

'I guess because it's been shut up all these years. I've always wondered what it must be like inside. Haven't you?'

'A little, maybe.'

'And it just seems like such a great place for a Halloween party.'

'Great, like a boneyard.'

'Yeah, that's just the point. And another thing is, nobody knows who's giving the party. Like it's a big mystery. I'd like to go and find out.'

'I don't know.' Beth shook her head. 'I promised Aleshia I'd go to her party. I guess, if you really have to go to the other one . . . Well, maybe I'd better find someone else for tonight.'

'Oh, don't do that.'

'What about the Sherwood house?'

'It won't be much fun, anyway, if nobody else is there.'

Beth smiled, this time not holding back to hide her braces, this time beaming.

# Chapter Twenty-two

'What do *you* want?'

'I'm sorry to bother you again, Mrs Barnes . . .'

'Then don't. I'm quite busy. My daughter is having a party tonight, and I've got a jillion things to do.'

'I won't take up much of your time.'

She looked past him as if she half expected neighbors to be gathering in the street: 'You'd better come in,' she said.

Sam followed her across the foyer. In the living room, Ticia stepped over a vacuum cleaner and sat on the couch. She folded her hands in the lap of her Sassoon jeans.

'If it's about last night,' she said, 'I frankly don't see why my private life is any of your business.'

'It's not about that. Where were you Wednesday night?'

Her pale skin turned red. 'What are you implying?'

'You weren't home Wednesday night. I'd like to know where you were.'

'I fail to see what this has to do with anything.'

'It has to do with Chief Boyanski's murder. Now, please answer the question.'

She stared at her folded hands, her eyes blinking rapidly. 'All right,' she finally said. 'I have nothing to be ashamed of. I went to the Sunset Lounge.'

'Alone?'

Her eyes narrowed. 'You already know, don't you? Otherwise, you wouldn't be asking these questions.'

'I don't know as much as I'd like.'

'I went with Thelma. I picked her up at her sister's house.'

'What time?'

'Around nine.'

'When did you leave the lounge?'

'Midnight.'

'Did Thelma leave with you?'

She stared down at her hands. 'I really fail to see . . .'

'She didn't leave with you?'

'We met some friends. After a few drinks, we went our separate ways.'

'When did Thelma and her friend leave?'

'They left a little earlier. Eleven-thirty, maybe.'

'Who did she go with?'.

'You don't know?'

'I'm asking you.'

Ticia smiled. 'I do hate to disappoint you, but I don't know the man's name.'

'You and Thelma sat and had drinks with him for – what, two hours? – and you didn't catch his name?'

'He was at the bar. Thelma went to join him, while I stayed at the table with Elmer.'

'You were with Elmer Cantwell?'

'He doesn't know the man, either. We both thought it a trifle foolhardy of Thelma to go off with a stranger. Elmer was somewhat disappointed, too. I'm sure he'd joined us with the expectation of swooping away with Thelma. He hardly knew me, at that point.' Ticia smiled with satisfaction. 'I must say, however, his disappointment was short-lived.'

'You didn't see Thelma, after she left with the stranger?'

'Should we have?'

'Did you?'

'No, we saw neither hide nor hair of them after that.'

'Have you seen Thelma since then?'

'She phoned the next morning to say she'd had a wonderful time.'

'Did she mention what they did?'

Ticia grinned. '*Really*, Mr Wyatt. I think we can make certain assumptions on that score – no pun intended.'

Sam wasn't amused. 'Did she say where they went?'

'Somewhere private, I should imagine.'

'But she didn't say?'

'No, she didn't say. I think you'll have to ask Thelma about that.'

# Chapter Twenty-three

'Eric Prince?' Aleshia, walking with Beth during lunch period, rolled her eyes. 'He's such a simp. You certainly could've done better than Eric *Prince*.'

'I like him.' Beth dodged to safety as a boy raced by on the asphalt.

'I like Hostess Twinkies, for heaven's sake. That doesn't mean I have to date one.'

Beth shrugged and took a bite of her turkey sandwich. Mom had made it for her and used such a tiny speck of mayonnaise that the sandwich was too dry to eat. She managed to swallow the lump already in her mouth. 'There's nothing wrong with Eric,' she said.

'There's nothing wrong with Twinkies.'

'The guys just pick on him because he's smaller than they are.'

'If you prefer to think that, be my guest.'

'He's *not* a fag.'

Aleshia smiled. 'Is that a fact?'

'Everybody's a "fag" around here if he gets good grades and doesn't go out for football.' She tossed her uneaten sandwich. It vanished into a trash can, and thunked. 'Eric's just more sensitive than most of the other guys.'

'You must admit he's a trifle effeminate.'

'A little, maybe. Doesn't bother me. I mean, the guy hasn't got a father.'

'I always knew he was hatched.'

'I'm being serious. How can you expect a guy to act all tough and masculine when he's never had a father around to learn from?'

'Beats me. What're you going as?'

'We haven't decided. We're meeting after cheerleaders and going over some ideas. Do you know what you'll be wearing?'

Aleshia struck a pose, chin high, one eyebrow raised, fingers deep in her hair. 'Perhaps I'll come as myself, Aleshia, the divine one whose body lights men afire with pagan lust.'

'Lots of luck,' Beth said, and danced out of the way laughing as Aleshia kicked. Her shoulder struck someone. Her feet tangled. Hands flew and clutched her, pulling her down backwards. She landed on top of a sprawling boy.

'Hey, offa the merchandise,' he said.

Beth recognized the voice. Squirming onto her side, she saw the grinning, whiskered face of Nate Houlder.

'I mean, I know you're crazy about me but this is ridic . . .'

Her elbow dug into his ribs as she raised herself.

'Oomph! Jesus *Christ*!' He slammed her elbow away and she flopped onto him, her cheek against his scratchy chin, her breasts mashed against his chest, her hips inside his open legs.

Beth tried to push away, but he held her to him.

'Let go!'

'Nate Houlder!' Aleshia snapped.

Others had already gathered around, laughing and whistling and offering comments.

'Put it to her, Houlder!'

'Right on, right on!'

'Let her go!'

'Oaf.'

He bumped up against her, ramming his groin against her lap, bouncing her.

'Stop!' she cried.

'Have at it, Houlder!'

'Leave her *alone*.'

'Give her one for me!'

'Oooh baby,' Nate said. 'Oooh baby, I like it, I like it.'

'Teacher's coming!'

Nate suddenly flung her aside. She hit the asphalt, rolling against several feet as the crowd backed off. Through teary eyes, she saw Nate smash aside the spectators and disappear.

Aleshia and Mary Lou helped her up.

'All right!' shouted Mr Doons as he shoved through the ring of students. 'All right, break it up. What's going on here!' He clutched Beth's arm. 'What's going on?'

'Nothing,' she said.

'Yeah? How come you're crying?'

'Nate Houlder,' Aleshia said.

'He pushed her down,' said Mary Lou.

'No,' said a boy. '*She* pushed *him*. I saw it.'

'They were wrestling,' said a small girl in glasses.

'Okay, young lady, you come with me.' He pulled Beth by the arm.

'I didn't *do* anything.'

'Come along.' He pulled her through the crowd and led her across the asphalt yard.

Beth fought back her tears. Everyone was looking.

'Please,' she said.

'We'll discuss it in my office.'

There was a cold lump in her stomach. This can't be happening, she thought. She'd never been taken to the office before. She felt helpless and terrified.

They walked past one of the teachers, Mr Jones. He glanced at her, looking perplexed.

'You don't have to drag me,' she said to Doons.

He ignored her.

'I'm not a criminal.'

He pulled her up the back stairs and into the building. The hallway, at least, was deserted; students weren't allowed to wander inside during the lunch period. Halfway down the long hall, he opened a door. The paint on its frosted glass read MR DOONS, VICE PRINCIPAL.

'Inside,' he said, and let go of her arm.

She stepped into a carpeted room with a dozen empty chairs against its walls. Mrs Houston, a silver-haired secretary, looked up from her typewriter.

'Sit,' Mr Doons said. 'I'll see *you* later.'

Beth sat down, and Doons left.

Mrs Houston returned to her typing.

'Yeah, just like I was humping her. Should've been there, Bill-boy. The little twat didn't know whether to shit or go blind.'

Bill was glad he'd missed it. He'd been in classes with Beth, here and in junior high, and he didn't like the idea of Nate bullying her. She was a soft-spoken, cheerful girl. If Nate wanted to dump on someone, he should've picked one of the bitches. Plenty of them around.

'Why *her*?' Bill asked.

'Like I said, man, she bumped into me.' He grinned. 'She's what y'call your "target of opportunity." I mean, you can't just go up to a gal and throw her down – you'd be up Shit Creek without a canoe. But if she bumps into *you*, well now, that's different.'

'You shouldn't have done it. Not to her.'

'Christ on a hunchin' crutch, man, you turning into a fag on me? First, it's Bennett you're sticking up for, now it's this Beth. You lost your sense of humor?' He shook his head, looking disgusted. 'And here I was, just about to give you my plan that's one-hundred percent guaranteed to get you in the sack with Bennett.'

'I've already heard it: you hold her down, I . . .' He found himself unable to say, 'fuck her.'

'Fuck her?' Nate said for him. 'Nothing so crude, dingus. That'd be rape. We'd go to *el slammer* for that. No no no. What I've got in mind is seduction.'

Bill grinned as if he thought Nate was crazy. 'A plan guaranteed to work?'

'One hundred percent.'

'I'll believe it when it works,' he said, feeling a tight eagerness inside. Christ, what if he *could* somehow seduce Miss Bennett? 'Let's have it.'

'In the art of seduction, Billy, my lad, the trick is to get yourself alone with the seducee and let nature take its course.'

'Sure.'

Nate tilted back his head and shut his eyes. 'Our romance begins with a flat tire. You happen to be nearby and rush to the aid of the stranded motorist.' He opened one eye and looked at Bill. 'Get it?'

'Here comes Doons.'

'Oh shit! See you later.' Nate dashed away.

'Hold it!' Doons yelled.

Bill laughed, earning a fierce glare from the v.p.

'Stop! Get back here, Houlder!'

Nate kept running, and vanished around a corner.

'Prick,' Doons muttered. Then he fixed his eyes on Bill. 'Wipe that grin off your face, Kearny.'

Beth sat in the office, waiting. She breathed deeply, trying to calm herself, but the thought of facing Mr Doons was too terrifying. Her hands felt cold and numb. Goosebumps made the light hair on her arms stand up. Her cheerleading sweater, under her arms, was soaked with perspiration. Droplets even rolled down her sides, wetting her bra.

This was worse than waiting for a doctor's exam, and she'd thought nothing could be that bad.

Finally, the bell rang, ending the lunch period.

Won't be long now.

She pressed her hands between her thighs to warm them.

That creep, Nate. It was all his fault.

She heard voices, laughter, and banging lockers from the hallway.

What would happen if she just got up and walked out? Wouldn't help. Doons'd send a call slip to her next class – or go over, himself, and drag her out.

How? He doesn't know my name, does he?

He could find out easily enough.

Besides, sooner or later, he would see her between classes or something, and grab her. But maybe he'd forget about her, by that time.

Mrs Houston glanced at her. Beth smiled, but her mouth trembled. The woman returned to her typing.

She won't try to stop me . . .

The door opened and Mr Doons came in. 'Into my office, Elizabeth.'

He *does* know my name!

She got up. On weak legs, she walked ahead of him, past Mrs Houston's desk, and through the open door.

Doons shut the door. He stepped around a big desk and sat on a swivel chair. Leaning forward, he planted his elbows on the green blotter. 'Take a seat,' he said.

She sat on a folding chair across from him. Her chin trembled. She pressed her lips together.

'Now, Elizabeth, tell me what happened.'

'I was just . . . I was talking to Aleshia and I backed up and bumped into him.'

'Nate Houlder.'

'Yes.'

'Then what?'

'We fell down.'

'Houlder pushed you down?'

'We . . . just fell.'

'And he wouldn't let you up?'

'No. I mean yes. He held me down.'

'Why?'

'I don't know.'

'What did he do, then?'

'Nothing.' Her throat felt tight and achy. She tried to swallow, and almost gagged.

'Where were his hands?'

'Just . . . just holding me. I wanted to get up, but he wouldn't let me.'

'Where were his hands?'

'Behind me, I guess.'

'You guess?'

She nodded.

Mr Doons's eyes dropped briefly to her breasts, then returned to her face. His thumb and forefinger rubbed the flesh above his lip. 'Did Houlder touch you anyplace intimate?'

She shook her head.

'Your breasts?'

'*No.*'

'Your genital area or buttocks?'

'No,' she said, her voice husky and quiet.

'You don't sound very sure.'

'He *didn't!*' Tears came to her eyes. She wiped them off with her sleeve.

'I don't like liars, Miss Green.'

'He didn't touch me there!'

'I was told by a witness that he put a hand in your panties.'

'That's a lie!'

His face reddened. 'Are you calling me a liar?'

'No,' she sobbed. 'Not you. The witness. Whoever told you that.'

'It came from a reliable source. Why do you feel that you have to protect Houlder?'

'I'm not!'

'Is he your boyfriend?'

'No!'

'Then why did you let him put a hand inside your panties?'

'I didn't. *He* didn't.'

Doons sighed.

'He *didn't*!'

'Perhaps you just didn't notice. All right, Elizabeth. That'll be all. Have Mrs Houston give you a re-admit slip.'

# Chapter Twenty-four

After lunch, Sam drove out on Oakhurst Road. He slowed down, passing the Horner house. Only its chimney and half a wall remained standing. The rest of the house had fallen to a charred pile of debris.

Next door, the Sherwood house seemed almost cheerful.

Wouldn't be such a bad place, Sam thought, if somebody'd move in and fix it up.

Driving past the house of Clara Hayes, he saw the morning

newspaper on her front lawn. He wondered why she hadn't picked it up yet.

Across the road, he saw a group of brightly clad golfers on the green of the third hole. One of the men waved at him. Though he only glimpsed the man, he tapped his horn twice in greeting.

Then he tried to remember what he'd been thinking about before the golfer waved.

Something about the Sherwood house?

Wouldn't make a bad fixer-upper.

Maybe Morley could sell it to the Horners, if they ever showed up again. Assuming Hank isn't the one who killed Dexter.

Though Sam knew little about Hank Horner, he saw no reason to believe the man was involved. The burning house and disappearance of the family were certainly not proof.

Strange, though, that it happened the day after Dex got killed. Maybe a connection, but not the one Berney was hoping for. Maybe both men had the same enemy. Maybe whoever chopped up Dex . . .

Sam moaned as he again saw himself lift the toilet seat and look down at Dexter's floating head. He took a deep breath.

'Whoever killed Dex killed the Horners,' he said aloud. The sound of his voice drove the memories away. 'Burnt the house to destroy any physical evidence he – she – they – left behind. So where are the bodies? If they're not in the house . . .' He clucked his tongue as he thought. 'If they're not in the house . . .?' he repeated. 'Buried out back?'

He remembered what was 'out back' of the Horner house.

Oakhurst Cemetery.

Dendron could wait. If he didn't see Thelma this afternoon, he'd find her tonight.

Slowing, he swung the car into a U-turn and sped back toward the cemetery.

The wrought-iron gates of Oakhurst Cemetery stood open. Sam drove through, and followed the narrow road to the parking lot. Except for a black Coup de Ville and a pick-up truck, the lot was deserted. He parked and climbed out. Walking into the wind, he watched dry leaves tumble and skitter toward him.

The grass on the rolling fields looked bright green in the sunlight and he thought, with a pang of nostalgia, what a great day this would be for touch football.

A great day, but not a great place.

The door of the cemetery office opened, and a tall grayhaired man stepped out, his suit jacket flapping in the wind. When he saw Sam, his head tipped back and he smiled. He changed course, slightly, and approached.

'Wyatt.'

'Brandner,' Sam said, shaking hands with his old friend.

'What's a nice fellow like you doing in a place like this?'

'I was about to ask you the same thing,' Sam told him.

'Too windy for tennis. Perfect weather for a Bloody Mary, though. How about joining me?'

'Believe me, I'd like to.'

'Busy detecting, I presume.'

'Right.'

The smile left Brandner's lean face. 'Rotten about Dexter. I hear you're the one who found him.'

'Yeah.'

'He was a good man. I guess you'll be here Sunday for the interment.'

'Yeah.'

'Christ, it gets to me when a guy I know . . . Well, business is business, I guess. One of these fine days, I'm gonna chuck all this and buy me a bar.'

'Hope you do it soon.'

'How about a partnership?'

'Just tell me when.'

'I guess you must have plenty socked away, from all your graft.'

'A bundle. Right now, though, I've got some snooping to do.'

'Snoop away.'

'I know you wouldn't be caught dead here at night . . .'

'*Touché!*'

'But do you know if anything unusual happened here last night?'

Brandner rubbed his chin, and shook his head. 'You don't mean the fire, I take it.'

'The Horners' bodies weren't found.'

'You're thinking they segued into my bone orchard?'

'I'd like to find out. If they were murdered, the killer probably didn't move them far.'

'Why move them at all?'

'Don't ask me. If they weren't in the house, though, where are they?'

'Visiting Aunt Mary?'

'Do you want to come along?' Sam asked.

'Where?'

'I want to check the area in back of their house.'

'I suppose my Bloody Marys can wait.'

They walked, side by side, to the far end of the parking lot, then up a grassy slope, passing between well-tended grave sites.

'To think I used to play here as a wee child,' Brandner said. 'My cousin cured me of that. We were playing tag, one day, blithely scampering among the graves – did I ever tell you this?'

Sam had heard the story a couple of times before, over drinks, but he shook his head.

'She – my cousin – tripped in a gopher hole. She looked down the hole, and kept looking and looking. I said, "Hey, what're you doing?" The little bitch said, "There's somebody down there winking at me." '

'Did you take a look?'

'Are you kidding? I ran like hell, and wouldn't come near this place for a year. Christ, I still get the creeps whenever I see a gopher hole around here. And there're plenty. I often suspect the little buggers are carnivorous.'

'You'd better buy that bar soon.'

'Don't I know it. This business is not for the squeamish. Should've sold out when my father died.'

'Why didn't you?'

'A sense of family obligation, I suppose. Obligation gets to you every time.'

Ahead, through the trees and monuments, Sam saw the wrought-iron fence of the cemetery boundary. The dark chimney of the Horner house stood not far beyond it.

Brandner frowned. 'You think someone chucked their bodies over my fence?'

'Maybe buried them over here.'

'A logical place, I suppose.'

'Any recent graves over here?'

'Open ones? No. And I think Willie would've noticed if

someone had been digging. He's a sot, but he's not deaf and blind.'

'It's a big cemetery.'

'He makes regular rounds. He's *supposed* to, anyhow.'

They reached the fence. Sam looked through at the rubble. The wind carried a pungent odor of burnt wood.

With his back to the fence, he looked down its length. The gravestones, monuments, and clusters of trees and bushes offered plenty of places to conceal bodies or crouch, out of sight, to dig a hole.

'I hope you're wrong about this,' Brandner said.

'It's worth a look.'

They began walking alongside the fence, occasionally separating while one inspected the ground behind a tree or gravestone.

'If these Horners *were* murdered,' Brandner said, 'you would have to suspect they were done in by the one who killed Dexter.'

'I've thought of that.'

'Thought you might've. Has it also occurred to you that we're now directly behind the Sherwood house?'

'What about it?'

'Seems a bit funny, to me, that two families, right next door to each other, should get slaughtered.'

'Fifteen years apart.'

'How many mass murders have we had in Ashburg? Two. Fifteen years apart, but side by side. Seems funny to me. I think, if I were looking for the Horners' bodies – which I apparently am, thanks to you – I'd take a look in the Sherwood house.'

'I may do that.'

'Fine. Let's forget all this and . . . well well well.'

As Brandner crouched behind a tombstone, Sam rushed to his side. 'There were bodies here, all right,' his friend said.

On the grass by the tombstone lay a collapsed tube of pink latex.

'Live ones,' Sam added.

'In my experience,' said Brandner, 'corpses rarely use rubbers.'

# Chapter Twenty-five

Glendon Morley got up from his desk as a young couple entered his real estate office. At first, their appearance put him off.

The woman, though somewhat pretty, wore no makeup. Her thick brown hair was drawn back in a pony-tail, and she wore a loose, faded dress that looked home-made. She seemed clean, though. Glendon guessed that she wasn't a poverty-stricken gal from the hill country, after all – just an artsy-fart who wanted to look like one.

The man beside her was a giant, well over six feet tall with unruly black hair and eyes so intense that they made Glendon nervous. He wore a tan, corduroy jacket that badly needed to be pressed. Beneath it was a T-shirt decorated by a hideous, troll-like character. Printed below its leering face were the words, 'Trust Me.' He wore blue jeans, and a pair of Adidas running shoes.

'Mr Morley?' the giant asked, offering a hand.

'Yes, *sir*,' Glendon said. He shook the man's powerful hand, and smiled at the woman.

'I'm Harold Krug. This is my wife, Seana.'

'Pleased to meet you,' Glendon said. 'House hunting?'

Harold grinned. It was a one-sided, play-evil grin one might use to tease a child. 'I think we found what we want.'

'Excellent. Have a seat, won't you? Could I get you some coffee?'

'Yeah. Black for me.'

'How about you, Seana?'

'I'd prefer tea, if you have some.'

'Sure thing. Tea it is.' Leaving them at his desk, he stepped to the card table in the rear. As he poured the drinks, he tried to size up Harold and Seana. They were from out of town, he was sure of that. They dressed weird – kind of like college kids he'd seen at some of the JC football games. They didn't seem poor or stupid, but Harold obviously didn't earn his keep as a legitimate business man. Teachers? That had to be it.

'Where you from?' he asked, approaching with the tea and two cups of coffee.

'Maine,' Harold said.

'Whew. Long way from the home ground.'

Harold smiled and nodded. He was slouched in the chair beside Glendon's desk, a foot propped over his knee.

'And you're planning to settle down here in Ashburg?'

'For a while.'

Glendon handed the styrene cup of tea to Seana, the coffee to Harold. 'Couldn't pick a nicer little town. I've lived here all my life, myself, and I don't mind telling you wild horses couldn't drag me away from here. What do you do?' he asked Harold.

'I write books.'

'Oh?' He tried to keep his smile as he saw the chances of a sale sink away. 'What sort of books do you write?'

'Occult thrillers.'

'Oh? Like *The Exorcist*?'

'Something like that.'

'My daughter saw that movie.' He chuckled. 'It scared her silly.'

'I'm interested in the Sherwood house.'

'You're interested in buying it?'

Harold nodded, and poked a cigarette into his mouth. 'Okay if I smoke?'

'Sure. No problem. I'm a cigar smoker, myself.' He pushed a spotless, glass ashtray over the desk toward Harold.

'Thanks.'

'So, you plan to do a little first-hand research for one of your books, Harold?'

'Partly that.' The cigarette bounced in his lips. 'We hear it's in bad shape. Is it liveable?'

'Sure. No problem, there.'

'What's the asking price?'

Glendon told him.

Harold scowled through his smoke. 'Sounds reasonable enough. What do you think, Seana?'

She arched an eyebrow, and nodded.

'Most banks will want about fifteen percent down.'

'No problem,' said Harold, grinning.

The man's casual attitude toward the price encouraged Glendon. Maybe this was a writer with money.

'Well,' Glendon said, 'shall we go over and have a look-see?'

'Let's go.'

As they prepared to leave the office, Glendon asked, 'You do know what happened there?'

'Not as much as I'd like to.'

358

'How did you hear about it?'

'I've been corresponding with a fellow from your high school. The librarian there. Name of Nick Carlson.'

'Oh?'

'He says it's been deserted since the murders.'

'That's right.' Glendon turned off the lights, and held the door open. Harold and Seana stepped out. He locked the door. 'My car's just over there.'

They headed for the brown Fleetwood.

'Nobody in this town's too interested in living there, after what happened.'

'Sherwood was the high school principal?'

'Vice principal, I think. I tell you, this town was mighty shook up by the killings. Never did find out who did them, so I think about half the folks were just holding their breath, waiting for the killer to strike again. He never did, though. Whoever he was, he must've moved on.'

Glendon unlocked the passenger door, and opened it. 'Plenty of room in the front,' he said. They climbed in, and Glendon went around to the driver's door. 'Are you planning to write about the house, Harold?'

'I'm more interested in the atmosphere just now.' He made that play-evil grin again. 'I write better when I'm frightened. I like to scare myself.'

'Well, this place should certainly fill the bill.' Glendon started the car, and pulled away from the curb. 'Do you write, too, Seana?'

'Not I. One neurotic in the family is enough.'

'Will this be your first house?'

'We have one near Portland,' she said.

'Has it sold yet?'

'Oh, we're keeping it.'

'That's our home base,' Harold explained.

'So you're not planning to make Ashburg your home?'

'For a year or two.'

'Well, this'll make a dandy fixer-upper. Do a few improvements, you should be able to sell it at a nice profit. Your living in it should take the curse off, and folks won't be afraid to buy.'

'If we don't get butchered,' Harold added, eyes twinkling.

Glendon laughed loudly. 'Oh, I doubt you have to worry on that score.'

He swung his Fleetwood onto the driveway. Weeds had pushed through the loose gravel, and the yard was overgrown. He'd been careless, lately, about keeping the place up. Wouldn't have to give it any more thought, though, if these folks took it off his hands.

He would be proved right about his investment, too. Everyone had said he was crazy when he bought the Sherwood house at public auction – for next to nothing. He'd finally almost decided they were right. But if these Krugs bought the place, he'd be doing very well indeed. Nobody laughs at a 500 percent profit.

'Lawn needs some work,' he admitted, shutting off the engine.

'Needs a tractor,' Harold said.

Glendon laughed. 'At least you won't be bothered by noisy neighbors. You've got your graveyard out back, and the golf course in front. Mrs Hayes, over there, is an elderly lady who keeps to herself. And I'm sure nobody'll be building on the Horner lot for some time.'

They climbed out of the car. 'Electricity's not on,' Glendon said, and raised the lid of his trunk. He took out a powerful, battery-operated lantern. Then he led the way through the weeds. Smiling back, he noticed how the wind pushed Seana's dress against her body, molding it to her breasts and slim legs as if the fabric were wet. Not a bad looking woman, he thought, if only she'd fix herself up a bit.

He paused at the foot of the veranda. The banister's white paint was curling and flaking like the dead skin of a sunburn. 'She could probably stand a coat of paint,' he said.

Harold grinned. 'Looks just great to me.'

They climbed the steps. 'I guess,' Glendon said, 'if the place was all kept up neat and pretty, it wouldn't have that atmosphere you're talking about.'

'Very true, Mr Morley.'

'Call me Glendon, Harold.'

Harold nodded.

Glendon pushed a key into the padlock. 'We had to put some extra security on the place,' he said. 'Otherwise, there's no telling what might go on in here. Kids, you know. A few got in, a couple years back. Didn't do much harm, though. Painted up the walls a bit, is all.' He removed the padlock, and fit a key into the door's lockface. 'If you take the place, I'll send a man out and have the boards taken off the windows. Windows are all intact, by the way.'

He opened the door. Light from outside spilled into the foyer, and lit the foot of the stairway. 'We can leave the door open. Give us a little extra light.'

He frowned, stepping inside. The stale air smelled of paint. Had someone broken in again?

'Is it supposed to be haunted?' Harold asked.

'Everybody says so.' Glendon hadn't heard anything to that effect, but he knew the man wanted atmosphere, so he elaborated. 'They say the ghosts of the Sherwoods walk the rooms at midnight.'

'Hope so,' said Harold.

Glendon turned on his lantern. 'The living room's over here.' He led the way. The smell of paint grew stronger. In the entry, he shined his wide beam into the room. He gasped, took a quick step backward, and bumped into Harold.

'*Bars* on the windows?' Harold asked.

'Something's wrong here.'

The front door banged shut.

Whirling around, he glimpsed a pale figure at the door. He shined his light on the motionless shape of a man. A policeman? The uniform was dark with stains like dry blood. The face under the brim of the cowboy hat looked vaguely familiar. Old, wrinkled, womanly, sagging like a poorly fitted mask.

'Who are you?' Glendon muttered.

'Harry?' Seana gasped.

Harold grabbed her shoulder, and pulled her close to him. 'Is there a back way out of here?' he asked.

'Locked,' Glendon said. 'On the outside.'

One of the arms moved away from the silent man's side. The hand gripped a hatchet.

Seana groaned.

'No way out?' Harold asked.

'He's standing in front of it.'

'Give me that.' He yanked the lantern from Glendon's hand, and threw it toward the door.

'What're you . . .?' Glendon stopped his voice as the light crashed and went out. For a few moments, his eyes retained the beam's after-image. Then all he saw was blackness.

'Blind man's bluff,' whispered Harold. His voice wasn't close.

'Don't leave me!' Glendon cried.

Light blasted his eyes as the front door flew open. In the glare from outside, he glimpsed Harold and Seana on the stairway, heading up, *leaving* him!

'*Wait!*'

But then he saw his chance. The awful figure with the hatchet was gone. Had he run out?

Glendon sprang for the door.

It crashed shut in front of him.

He threw himself against it, clawing the knob, sobs shaking him as he realized that the man hadn't run out the door at all, but only hid behind it and now was coming at him in the darkness.

'No, please,' he cried. 'Don't. Please!'

Something brushed against his hair. He jumped, bashing his forehead against the door.

'Please,' he sobbed. 'Don't . . .'

Something smacked his back, just below the shoulder blade. It split him, burning. The *hatchet*! It pulled out. It went away.

'*No!*' he shrieked.

He tugged the door, but it wouldn't open. He felt a sharp jolt, heard a *thunk*. Pain ripped across his back. He could feel it, actually feel the hatchet head inside his back, wedged between his ribs, feel it rock as the man tried to pull it out.

His legs went numb.

He fell face down.

The hatchet went away.

Again, it chopped into his back. And again. Though the pain was a steady roar in his head, part of his mind seemed calm, almost rational. This must be Jim Sherwood, it told him. Jim's ghost? He thinks I'm a trespasser. If I can just explain I'm his old friend Glen . . .

Another burst of pain shook him.

The hatchet chopped and chopped in the blackness. It struck his back, his shoulders, his buttocks. Glendon wanted to shout for the man to stop.

His voice wouldn't work.

Who does he think I *am*?

A singsong voice from his childhood came back.

*I'm nobody, who are you?*

Harold pulled his wife by the hand through the blackness.

'What'll we do?' she whispered.

'Shhhh.'

He walked slowly, feeling the wall.

So hard to believe this was happening to them. Trapped in a deserted house by an ax-wielding maniac. He'd seen such situations countless times in the movies, read about them in so many books, written them himself more than once.

Incidental characters, in this circumstance, never survived. The main character, though, usually found a way to triumph. Didn't seem completely fair.

In his next book, he ought to handle it differently. Hell, though, *somebody* has to bite the dust.

Not us!

He found an open door, pulled Seana inside, and shut it. He felt the knob. Found a lock button, pushed it. The lock made a feeble click.

'That won't . . . He's got a hatchet.'

'I know.' Harold found the light switch, and flicked it. Nothing happened. He took a matchbook from a pocket of his corduroy jacket, flipped open its cover, and peeled out a cardboard match. He struck it.

In the shimmering light, he saw that they'd taken refuge in a bathroom.

Seana sat down on the toilet seat, and rubbed her face.

Harold stepped to the sink. He smiled nervously at himself in the medicine cabinet mirror. The reflection of his face, quivering with deep shadows, looked demonic. He quickly lowered his eyes to the sink. He turned a faucet handle. It squawked, but no water came.

'Can't flood him out,' he whispered, grinning.

He pulled open the medicine cabinet. Its shelves were bare. The flame singed his fingers. He dropped the match into the sink, and lit another.

A large tub. A shower curtain rod with metal rings but no curtain.

At the far end of the tub was the bathroom's only window. No light came through. A wrought-iron grate covered it on the inside. 'What are the *bars* for?' he muttered.

'To keep us in,' said Seana.

'This guy does plan ahead.'

'I'm glad you haven't lost your sense of humor.'

'It's always the last to go.'

'What'll we do?'

He shook out his match. Whispering in the darkness, he said, 'Did you bring your gun?'

'Oh, Harold.'

'No, I didn't think . . .' He jumped as something crashed against the door. '*Jeezus!*' Rushing through the darkness, he bumped into Seana. They both fell. 'Here. *Here.*' He pushed the matchbook into her hand. 'Light 'em for me.'

'What're you . . .'

Another blow shocked the door.

Harold scurried off Seana. Standing, be jerked open his belt. He tugged it off.

'Light.'

Seana struck a match. In its wavering glow, he saw a splintered gash in the door panel. He stepped to the side. The hatchet struck again, shaking the door. A corner of its head appeared. It hit again, spraying splinters, the hatchet head breaking through the door. Harold hooked his belt under it, looped over its top, and yanked. The hatchet sprang loose. He pulled it in.

'You got it!' Seana cried.

'Into the tub, quick!'

Grabbing the weapon, he rushed to Seana. He clutched her arm. The match went out. He pulled her toward the tub. They crawled over its side.

'Lie down,' he whispered.

'But . . .'

'He's got a gun.'

'You sure?'

'Yes.'

He pressed her to the bottom of the tub, and crouched at her head, hatchet ready. His heart thudded so hard he thought he might vomit. He took deep breaths.

They waited.

'Maybe he doesn't have bullets,' Seana whispered.

'I'm not going out there to find out.'

'What'll we do?'

'Wait.'

# Chapter Twenty-six

Driving away from the Oakhurst Cemetery, Sam recalled Brandner's suggestion: 'If I were looking for the Horners' bodies . . . I'd take a look in the Sherwood house.'

It seemed like a good idea.

He might, at least, make a quick tour of its outside – check the doors, see if anything seemed out of place. But as he approached the house, he saw the Morley Realty car parked in front. Not much point looking around, he decided, if Glendon's in the house. The real estate man would be certain to report anything he found amiss.

So Sam didn't stop.

Nor did he stop when he noticed, again, that Clara's newspaper still remained on her lawn.

He'd spent a long time at the cemetery. After a thorough search of the area near the north fence, he and Brandner made a quick inspection of the rest of the grounds. Along the way, he questioned Benny, the grounds keeper, and learned nothing of importance. The entire procedure had taken nearly two hours; if he met another delay, he might as well forget about Dendron and simply wait for Thelma to return.

He didn't want to wait.

He wanted to make the trip on the chance of catching Thelma at her mother's house. He wanted to make it, even if he failed to meet her.

He was very nervous.

I'm not going to stop, he thought. No reason to be nervous,

because I'm not going to stop. When I get to the Sleepy Hollow Inn, I'll just keep driving. I've got a job to do.

What about afterwards?

No!

Wouldn't hurt to stop and thank Melodie for the help. If it weren't for her call, you wouldn't have the first idea where to find Thelma.

I'll thank her by phone.

I can't see her again. Can't.

As the motel came into view, Sam's heart hammered so hard and fast he felt dizzy. He scanned the area, but didn't see her. He stared at the office windows. He turned his head, looking for as long as possible before he left the motel behind.

He hadn't so much as glimpsed her. The loss made him ache inside, like a child whose birthday was forgotten.

I can always stop on the way back, he told himself.

But I won't.

I'd better not.

Couldn't hurt to thank her, though.

Yes, it could. It could hurt a lot.

The house at 354 Tenth Street in Dendron looked small and well-kept. A picket fence enclosed its neatly trimmed lawn. A Honda Civic was parked in its driveway.

Sam stopped at the curb and climbed out. He hurried toward the front door, eager to conclude the hunt that had occupied so much of his time for the past two days. He didn't expect resistance. He expected her to play it cool, even if she were responsible for Dexter's murder. As he reached the door, however, doubts crept in. Should he notify the local police? He'd have to phone them, anyway, if it came down to an arrest.

That could wait.

For all he knew, Thelma had already returned to Ashburg.

He stood off to the side, as a precaution, and pressed the doorbell. He heard it ring. His hand lowered to his revolver.

The door opened and a petite, white-haired woman looked out at him. 'Yes?' she asked.

'Is Thelma here?'

'Why, yes she is. You must be Mr Wyatt.'

He nodded.

'Marjorie called. She told us to expect you, but we thought you'd be here ages ago.'

'I had some other business,' he said, wishing now that he hadn't delayed so long.

'Won't you come in?'

He followed her into the living room. Thelma, sitting in a rocker, watched him over the rim of a cocktail glass. Her half-shut eyes had the same lazy insolence Sam knew from her photo. She looked much older, though: thin, with a sallow complexion and harsh lines.

'I wasn't so hard to find, was I?' She smirked and took a drink. 'Mother, how about disappearing for a bit?'

'Would Mr Wyatt care for a drink?' asked the older woman.

'No, he wouldn't,' Thelma answered.

'There's no call to be rude, darling.'

'No call to be polite. This man wants to bust me for killing Dexter.'

'I'm not here to bust you,' Sam said.

'I'll believe that when I see it.'

'I just want to . . .'

'I know, ask a few questions. Good-*bye*, Mother.'

Looking peeved, the old woman scurried from the room.

'Okay,' said Thelma, 'what do you want to know?'

'Let's start at the beginning.'

'How about getting it over with? You've already got my story from Elmer and Marjorie and Ticia and God-only-knows who else.'

'I'd like to hear it from you.'

She sighed. 'Elmer's right about you. Okay. I get into town Tuesday afternoon, check in at my sister's house. Have supper with them, then make my merry way to the Sunset Lounge where I meet my old friend Elmer. We hoist a few, then take off in his Volvo, spread his blanket on the eighth hole of the golf course and go humpy-humpy. Okay? The automatic sprinklers go on, and we get drenched. Never fuck on a golf course.

'Elmer takes me back to Marjorie's, and I hit the sack. Wednesday, I meet Elmer for lunch. He takes me shopping, so I can pick up a few items for Marjorie. I eat supper with the family, then take off with Ticia for the Sunset. We meet Elmer there, and I meet Joe.'

'Joe who?'

'Joe Schmow, who the hell knows? So me and Joe go off together for a merry time.'

'When?'

She smirked. 'Eleven or twelve. I didn't clock out. Who knows?'

'Do you know where you went?'

'Not to the golf course, you can bet.'

'Where?'

'Here's the good part, the part you've been waiting for. You figure I went over to Dexter's place and chopped him up, right?'

'Did you?'

'Hate to disappoint you.'

'Where did you go?'

'Stiff City. Oakhurst Cemetery.' She swirled her ice cubes, and took a drink. 'You haven't lived till you've gone humpy-humpy in the graves. It adds a certain thrill. Makes it terribly exciting, like screwing in public without the scandal.'

'How long were you there?' Sam asked.

'Oh, an hour.'

'Nobody can prove you were there.'

'Only Joe. I'm sure, if it's necessary, we can dig him up.'

'You'd better hope so.'

She shook her head, smiling with one side of her face. 'I don't imagine it'll be necessary.'

'Why not?'

'Oh, I saw something that will interest you.' She took another drink. 'Guess what I saw.'

'Why don't you just tell me?'

'I'd have told you, long ago, if you hadn't insisted on my repeating all that useless trivia.'

'What did you see at the cemetery?'

'Not a what, but a who.'

'Okay.'

'I saw Dexter.' She licked her lips and took another drink. 'It was only by the purest luck that I happened to see him. If I'd been under Joe, at the time . . . Most men prefer it that way, do you?'

Sam didn't answer.

Thelma chuckled. 'They like to feel they're controlling the action, get insecure if the gal's on top. At any rate, Joe isn't that way. So I was merrily riding him along, and I happened to be facing that creepy old house where all those people got murdered – the Sherman house?'

'Sherwood.'

'At any rate, I happened to be looking that way and saw Dexter go in the back door.'

'He *entered* the Sherwood house?'

'That's what I said. He went in, and I didn't see him come out.'

'Are you sure it was Dex?'

'I couldn't see his face, obviously. But he was Dexter's size, and wearing a police uniform and Stetson just like Dexter's. Oh, it was him all right.'

'Why didn't you notify someone?'

'Why should I? His business is no business of mine. Especially now.' She sucked an ice cube into her mouth. It muffled her voice as she said, 'God rest his soul.'

# Chapter Twenty-seven

'Hey, jack-off!'

Bill ignored Nate's voice, and finished stuffing his books into his overflowing locker. He let go. As the books started to avalanche, he slammed the metal door. He turned to his friend. 'Doons catch you yet?'

'Doons couldn't catch shit if he tripped over it.'

'Where'd you hide?'

'The girls' locker room.'

'Sure.'

'I tell you, my dick's been hard so long I'm starting to take it for granite.'

Bill shook his head. 'You must've spent all afternoon thinking up that one.'

'Nah. I'm a natural wit.'

They walked up the crowded hallway, Bill watching as Nate collided with students in his way. Girls and smaller boys only. When boys larger than Nate drew near, he sidestepped out of range.

Bill followed him across the hall, curious until he saw a large-bosomed blond ahead. Nate altered course and walked into her.

'Watch it,' she snapped.

'I think you busted my arm!'

'Bull-twinkie,' she said.

Nate turned to Bill. 'Busted my arm. Get it? Busted?'

'Very funny.'

'What're you, still pissed off about your sweetie Beth? Or is it Miss Bennett? Look, it's time we get on the ball with Bennett, you know what I mean? It's now or never, do or die, shit or get off the commode. Hey hey, look who's here.'

Bill saw Eric Prince walking up the hall.

'Hey, dork-face,' Nate called.

Eric saw him, and stopped.

'Hey, dingle-berry, come here.'

Eric took a single step forward. Several students pushed past him.

Nate stopped in front of him. 'Trick or treat,' he said.

'I haven't got . . .'

'How much *have* you got?'

Eric shrugged.

'Well check, turd-head.'

He pushed a bandaged hand into a front pocket of his trousers, and brought out a comb and handkerchief.

'Try the other pocket.'

Wincing, he shifted a load of books to his left hand.

'What's the matter with your hand?' Nate asked.

'I cut it,' Eric said, reaching into a pocket.

'Sure. I bet you wore a hole in it jacking off.'

Eric's right hand appeared. He held it out to Nate, and opened it. 'This is all I've got,' he said.

Bill glanced at the nickels and pennies.

'That's all?' Nate asked.

'Yeah.'

'How'm I supposed to exist on such a pittance? Answer me that.'

'I don't know.'

'Keep it,' Nate said, and slapped his hand up. The change flew, several coins striking a nearby girl in the face.

'Come on, Bill.'

As they walked away, Bill looked back. Eric was still, standing where they'd left him, surrounded by talking, shoving, laughing students who passed him like a stream swirling around a rock. For a moment, Bill felt a little sorry for the kid. Then he saw a corner of Eric's mouth twist into a sneer. A chill prickled the back of his neck, and he turned away.

'Okay, so here's my plan for Bennett.'

'I won't let you flatten her tires,' Bill said. They went outside, and down the concrete stairs. 'Why don't we just forget about her?'

'Hey, you haven't heard my new plan, yet. What we do, we

374

get in my car and wait by the faculty parking lot. When she comes out, we follow her home. How's that sound?'

'I don't know,' Bill said.

'We'll hang back – she'll never be the wiser.'

'What'll we do when we get there?'

'What do you want to do?'

'Nothing.'

'Then that's what we'll do.'

'Then why go at all?'

'So we'll know where she lives, dildo.'

# Chapter Twenty-eight

From a distance, Eric watched the cheerleaders practice. He was still shaken up by his encounter with Nate, but he soon forgot about it as the girls leaped and twirled, and kicked their bare legs.

They all looked so beautiful.

Especially Aleshia. Her slim legs were golden in the afternoon sunlight. When she whirled around, her pleated skirt flew high, giving Eric glimpses of her thighs and green underpants. When she jumped, plunging her arms at the sky, her sweater slid up and uncovered her belly for an instant.

He knew she didn't wear bras to school.

If only she would jump higher . . .

Once, she did a cartwheel and the sweater dropped nearly to her ribs before she whipped to her feet and it fell again into place. He imagined her doing another cartwheel, this time her sweater sliding down all the way and uncovering her small, pale breasts.

He realized he had an erection. Glancing down, he saw it pushing out his corduroys. He folded his hands in front of the bulge, and turned his eyes toward Beth.

Though nowhere as pretty as Aleshia, Beth was fairly cute. Doing the cheers, she seemed more enthusiastic than the others. Compared to her, the rest of the girls looked lazy, almost bored.

Her arms snapped forward as the voices chanted, 'Push 'em back, push 'em back, waaaay back.' At the cheer's end, she bounded from the ground, arching her back, waving her arms, kicking her feet up high behind her. Eric looked quickly at Aleshia and found her in mid-air, her sweater up, her belly showing pale and smooth.

He imagined sliding his hands up her belly, up under the sweater where it was warm and dark, and taking her breasts in his hands, holding them gently, his palms barely touching the velvet skin.

'Hi, Eric!' Beth called, waving at him. 'We're almost done.'

He nodded and yelled, 'Okay.'

A few of the girls huddled around Beth. Eric guessed they were talking about him. He wished he could hear them, but they spoke quietly and the distance was great.

What if they'd seen his bulge?

How could he face Beth, after that?

The girls weren't giggling, though. Soon, they stopped talking and resumed practice.

Eric turned away. He walked along the side of the field, his back to the cheerleaders. Though he wished he could watch them, he didn't want to embarrass himself by getting another erection. So he walked along, listening.

'We are the Spartans, the mighty-mighty Spartans! Everywhere we go-o, people oughtta kno-ow, who we are *so* we tell 'em. We are the Spartans . . .'

He saw the football team ahead, running a scrimmage. The coach was there, so none of the jerks were likely to try anything with Eric. Just to be safe, though, he turned away and walked toward the school.

He glanced back at the cheerleaders and saw them in a line, kicking their legs high.

Finally, he reached the main building. He sat on the steps to wait for Beth. From there, he could barely hear the chants of the cheerleaders. He watched the girls dance and leap, but they were tiny now, their features less distinct. He found it difficult to tell one from another. Beth, the only stocky girl of the five, was easy to spot, but he couldn't make up his mind which of the others was Aleshia.

As he waited, the coldness of the concrete seeped through his pants. He began to feel as if he were sitting on a slab of ice. Raising himself off the step, he slid his grammar book beneath him. He sat on it. The book felt warm under his buttocks.

Opening his three-ring binder to a blank page, he began to doodle. He drew a revolver, but it turned out crooked, the barrel curving upward as if bent by Superman. His Bowie knife came out well. He inked in drops of blood falling from its blade. Encouraged by his success with the knife, he tried to draw a P-40 Kittyhawk. The fuselage looked good, but he had trouble with the wings and tail. He went ahead, regardless, and drew the shark's mouth on the engine cowling. When he was done, the combat plane looked lopsided but vicious.

On the back of the page, he drew an oblong and imagined it was a girl's torso. Aleshia's torso. He sketched breasts onto it. They were merely two circles with dots in the middle, but as his pen stroked the paper he could almost feel their smooth flesh.

Then he heard voices nearby.

The cheerleaders, done with practice, were wandering in his direction.

With a few swift strokes, he drew a nose between the breasts, a grinning mouth below them. He put ears on the torso, and a patch of scraggly hair on top.

'Okay, see you tonight,' Beth said, breaking away from the group. She headed for Eric, while the other girls continued around the side of the school.

Eric stood up.

'I hope you didn't mind waiting,' Beth said.

'No, it was fun.' He picked up his books, and saw that she had none. 'Do you need anything inside?'

She shook her head, smiling. 'I finished all my homework in study hall.'

'Wish I had.'

They started to walk.

'What've you got?' Beth asked.

'Homework? About six chapters of *Huckleberry Finn*. I fell behind this week.'

'You have Miss Bennett, don't you?'

'Yeah. Fourth period.'

'I've got her first. She'll be at the party, you know.'

'Aleshia's?'

'Yeah. She's the only teacher Aleshia invited. So, what do you think we should wear?'

'I don't know. What do you think?'

'It'd be neat if we could go as a pair. You know, like Laurel and Hardy or the Blues Brothers.'

'How about Tarzan and Jane?'

Laughing, she bumped him with her shoulder. 'That's awful. Besides, we'd freeze.'

'We'll be inside.'

'You go as Tarzan, if you want. I'll wear clothes.'

Eric frowned. 'Actually, I think we should go as something spooky. I mean, it's Halloween. We oughtta dress up as ghosts or vampires or something.'

'You're right,' Beth said. 'Any ideas?'

'I'd like to be something *real* spooky.'

'Like what?'

Eric shrugged.

'It'll have to be something simple,' Beth said as they crossed the deserted faculty parking lot. 'We haven't got much time.'

'Do you have some old, ragged clothes? An old dress or something you can wreck up?'

'I guess so.'

'Great.'

'What's great?'

'What's the scariest thing you can think of?'

She shrugged. 'I don't know. I haven't thought about it. A psycho, I guess. You know, like those guys that rape girls and torture them to death.' She wrinkled her nose at the thought. 'Wouldn't be much fun to dress like that.'

'What about the living dead?'

'Like *Walkers?*'

'I was thinking *Night of the Living Dead.*'

'I never saw that. I heard it's yucky.'

'It's great. Anyway, we can dress up like one of those – if you don't mind looking sloppy.'

'No, that's fine.'

'You want to?'

'Sure. I guess.'

'Okay. So wear a dress you don't need anymore.'

'Is that it?'

'I'll bring along some stuff.' He grinned. 'This'll be great.'

# Chapter Twenty-nine

Sam turned on his headlights as darkness lowered over the road to Ashburg. He was alone in the patrol car.

No need to bring Thelma back.

He believed her story.

She hadn't killed Dexter. She'd been in the graveyard with Joe, just as she claimed. In Sam's mind, the condom confirmed that. It might've belonged to anyone, of course, but its location fit her story. From the place where they found it, she would've had a clear view of the Sherwood house.

As he sped over the dark road, Sam recalled that Ruthie had seen Dexter drive away from home that night. Around ten-fifteen or ten-thirty, when she went out to her car for cigarettes. Dex might've been on his way to the Sherwood house.

Thelma had seen him there after midnight – seen him go in, and not come out.

What the hell was he doing there?

Off duty, but in uniform.

The bright neon sign of the Sleepy Hollow Inn pulled Sam's thoughts away from the case. He stared at the lighted windows of the office. The curtains were open. He glimpsed movement inside, but couldn't recognize Melodie. His foot left the gas pedal. It brushed against the brake and started to descend. As he approached the motel driveway, he slammed his palm on the steering wheel, sending a shot of pain up his arm. He forced his foot back to the gas pedal.

For a few moments, he watched the motel in his side mirror. Then he took a curve, and darkness replaced its bright lights.

He imagined Melodie at a lighted window, peering out and seeing his car pass by. Would she feel the same disappointment Sam felt now – the same hungry ache and longing?

Sam shook his head.

Forget Melodie.

Melodie . . . a *melodie that's sweetly played in tune*. What the hell is that, a poem?

'That's sweetly played in tune,' he repeated. 'As fair art thou, my bonnie lass, so deep in love am I, and I will love thee still, my dear, till a' the seas gang dry. Sure. Burns. Rabbie Burns. Till a' the seas gang dry.'

He hadn't thought of that poem in ten years. He'd memorized it in college – his junior year – for Donna. God, he'd been crazy about Donna. He'd recited the poem to her, one night by the river, and afterwards they made love together for the first time.

Good old Rabbie Burns.

The memory soured as he remembered Donna dumping him for that jerk, Roy. He'd warned her that Roy was a sadistic sicko, but she'd laughed it off. Claimed it was sour grapes.

Well, he hoped Donna never had to find out the hard way.

Funny he should think of Donna, after all this time. It was the poem – *a melodie that's sweetly played in tune*.

Melodie again.

I hardly know her, he told himself. Why can't I just forget about her?

Think about the case. Dexter. The Sherwood house. Why had Dex gone over there late at night? To meet someone? Then why in uniform? Must've gone on police business, or he would've worn civvies. There'd been no calls to the station that might've taken him there. Maybe someone called him at home.

Clara Hayes? She's next door to the Sherwood house. She and Dexter were old friends. Maybe she saw a prowler, something like that, and asked him to come over.

Sam remembered the newspaper – still on Clara's lawn at mid-afternoon today.

He hadn't seen her at the fire last night.

His foot eased the gas pedal down. Speeding around a curve, he saw a car ahead. As he gained on it, he switched on his flasher. The car pulled aside, and he shot past it.

He drove as fast as he dared, slowing at curves, picking up speed on the straight-aways. Finally, Clara's house came into view. Her porch light was on, and pale light showed through the curtains of her picture window.

Morley's car, he saw, was still parked in the driveway of the Sherwood house.

Pulling onto the road's shoulder, he stopped in front of Clara's place. He switched off his lights, killed his motor, and climbed out. A chilly wind blew against him as he hurried across her lawn. He picked up the *Clarion*. Walking toward her door, he slipped off its rubber band and glanced at the headline: CHIEF BOYANSKI SLAIN.

On the front stoop, hidden behind a shrub, was another newspaper. Sam picked it up and opened it. The Thursday morning *Clarion*.

He pushed the doorbell.

As it rang, he heard an engine start. The car in the Sherwood driveway backed up. It swung onto the road, still in reverse, and sped backwards.

'Hey!' Sam yelled.

With a crunch of metal and glass it slammed into the front of Sam's patrol car.

'Damn it, Morley!'

He leaped from the stoop and raced across the lawn.

Morley's car didn't move.

As he ran toward it, the passenger window rolled down.

'Morley, what the hell are . . .?'

Two quick gunshots crashed through his words. He dived for the ground. As he hit, Morley's car took off. He drew his revolver and snapped off four shots. Through the roar of his gunfire, he heard three slugs thunk into the car. The last missed. He took careful aim at the distant target, but decided not to shoot again. Too chancy.

Scrambling to his feet, he ran the final yards to his patrol car.

Though the front was smashed in, the engine turned over. He swung onto the road. Far ahead, Morley's car turned right. Sam floored the accelerator.

He tried the headlights. Dead. But the flasher and siren still worked.

As he raced up the road, he grabbed his radio mike. 'Car Five to headquarters.'

'Go ahead, Car Five.'

'I'm in pursuit of a brown Fleetwood, just turned right on Maple at Oakhurst. Suspect armed. Shots fired. Any units in the area? Over.'

Easing off the gas, he skidded around the corner onto Maple and spotted the car a block ahead. This was a residential street, cars parked along both curbs, the streetlamps widely spaced leaving deep swaths of darkness in the middle where the spinning red of his flasher made his only light.

His radio crackled. 'Car Three is responding. What's your ten-twenty?'

'Heading west on Maple, approaching Tenth.'

Yards ahead, a tiny white-sheeted figure stepped out from behind a parked car. Sam hit the brakes. He saw the ghost turn toward him and drop its grocery bag. A little witch grabbed the ghost's sheet and pulled.

Sam wrenched his steering wheel to the left.

The parked station wagon looked bloody in his flasher.

He flung up his arms.

Pain blasted through him, but only for an instant.

Chet Goodman, in Car Three, sped up Maple from the east until he spotted a car in the middle of the road. At first, he thought it was coming his way. Then he realized it wasn't moving at all.

Several yards in front of it, he stopped.

The car was nearly invisible beyond the glare of its headlights. He trained his spotlight on it. A brown Fleetwood.

He picked up his mike. 'Car Three to headquarters.'

'Go ahead, Car Three.'

'The suspect vehicle is stopped on Maple between Eleventh and Twelfth Streets. No sign of Car Five. I'll give him a minute to catch up.'

He aimed the spotlight at the windshield, and saw no one.

Removing his Browning from its clamp, he climbed from the car and crouched behind its open door. He pumped a cartridge into the chamber and aimed his shotgun at the Fleetwood's windshield.

'Trouble, officer?' asked a voice behind him.

He looked over his shoulder and a tall, smiling man shot him in the face.

# Chapter Thirty

'Yee gad!' cried the woman in the doorway.

Eric moaned at her. She shook her head, chuckling, and held out a tray of candy bars.

'I'm not a trick-or-treater,' he told her.

'You always dress this way?'

'I'm here for Beth.'

'Oh! You must be Eric. Please come in. Beth'll be ready in a minute.'

Eric entered the house.

'Martin!' the woman called.

A man with a dish towel came out of the kitchen. When he saw Eric, he made a face and said, 'Yuck.'

'This is Eric Prince, Beth's date for the party.'

'Hi, Eric.' Martin stepped toward him frowning with concern. 'You feeling okay?' he asked, shaking hands. 'You look like death warmed over.'

'It's just burnt cork,' Eric explained. 'And some Vampire Blood.'

'They're supposed to be corpses,' the woman said.

'The living dead.'

Martin nodded, pursing his lips as he studied the costume. Eric looked down at himself. The front of his dirty, torn shirt was untucked. His knee showed through a split in his slacks. Through a rent in the other leg, his thigh was visible. Maybe he'd ripped his clothes too much: he didn't want Beth's parents to think him indecent. He wished he hadn't torn the shirt away from his left nipple. The old sports jacket he'd bought at the thrift shop nearly covered it, though.

'I'd say you look very corpse-like,' Martin finally said.

'Thank you.'

At that moment, Beth came into the room. 'Oh wow,' she said. 'You look fantastic!'

'You, too.'

She shrugged. 'It's the best I could do. Did you bring something for my face?'

Eric took a burnt cork and tube of Vampire Blood from his pocket.

'We'd better get back to the dishes,' said her mother. 'You two have a good time.' To Beth, she said, 'Twelve o'clock.'

'Okay.'

'Have fun,' her father said. 'Nice to meet you, Eric.'

'Nice to meet you,' Eric muttered.

He watched them leave. Then he turned to Beth and smiled.

'You'd better fix me up,' she said.

'Now?'

'Might as well. Are my clothes all right?'

'Fine,' he said. Her white blouse was stretched tightly across her full breasts. Its sleeves left her wrists bare. Her green, pleated skirt hung below her knees. She wore old, scuffed loafers. 'It won't hurt to get 'em dirty?' Eric asked.

'We were just gonna give them to Goodwill. They're crummy old things.' She scanned Eric's outfit, grinning. 'Not as crummy as yours, but we can fix that.'

'Yeah,' he said, and blushed.

'Okay, how about doing my face?'

'Well,' he said, offering her the cork. 'You can use this to mess yourself up.'

'You do it.'

She stepped close to him. He smelled a mild, sweet perfume that made his mouth go dry.

'If you want,' he mumbled.

'I want.'

He brushed the charred cork lightly under her eye, but little came off. 'I need to burn it.' He lit a match, and held it to the cork. The charred stub caught fire. He puffed it out, and waited for it to cool.

Beth watched his eyes as he blackened her pale skin. He rubbed smudges under her eyes, heavy lines running down from the sides of her nose to the corners of her mouth. Her constant gaze made him nervous, at first, but soon he began to like it. He shaded her cheeks and chin. 'There.'

'Now the blood.'

Squeezing the plastic tube, he dribbled the syrupy red fluid onto the corners of her mouth. It trickled down her chin. Before a drop could fall to the floor, he smeared it with his fingers.

'More,' she said.

He squirted the blood onto his fingertips, and spread it over her mouth and cheeks and chin. Her skin felt slippery and smooth.

'There,' he said.

Beth took his hand, and wiped it on the belly of her blouse. 'Let's have a look.'

They went to a mirror over the fireplace.

'Fantastic!' she said. 'Boy, aren't we a pair?'

'Yeah. *You* look worse than *me*.'

Still gazing at the mirror, she messed up her hair until it stuck out in wild disarray and strands hung over her face. Then she did the same for Eric.

'That's better, huh?' she asked.

'Great.'

'Let's go.'

They went outside, and cut across Beth's yard to the sidewalk.

'Burrrr,' Beth said.

'Want my jacket?'

'No. Thanks, though. I've got work to do.'

'Hmmm?'

As they walked along, she tugged the front of her blouse out of her skirt. She studied the effect, then tucked one side back in. Picking up her skirt, she yanked the hem. It didn't give.

'Do you have a knife or something?' she asked.

'I have the one I used.' He took out a small pocket knife, opened a blade, and handed it to her.

'Oh, this is good.' She cut through the hem. Clamping the knife between her teeth, she tore a long rip up the front of her skirt.

'Just a minute,' she said. They stopped under a street light. Beth pinched the shoulder of her blouse, pushed the knife into the fabric to start a tear, then hooked her fingers into the hole and jerked. The cloth split. When she finished, her left sleeve hung off her shoulder, still attached to the blouse only at her armpit. 'How's that?'

Her shoulder looked round and glossy in the street light. 'Great,' Eric said.

'One more rip, I think.' She lowered her head, turning it as she studied her front. 'The question is, where?'

'Anywhere.'

'I don't want my bra to show. How about down here?'

'Fine.'

She gripped the blouse below her right breast, and punched a hole in it. Holding the knife in her teeth, she inserted both forefingers into the opening and pulled. The cloth burst open. The tear shot up her front, the taut fabric parting over the mound of her breast. 'Oh shit,' she said, gazing down at the black protruding cup of her bra. 'Now what'll I do? I can't go to the party like this.'

'You could.'

'Aleshia's mom'll be there. *And* Miss Bennett. Besides, all the guys would gawk and act like jerks. I'd better go back and change.'

'What'll your parents say?'

'Oh geez. I'll try to sneak in . . .'

'I have an idea. Let's trade.'

'Thanks, but I don't think my blouse will fit you.'

'I can just wear the jacket,' he said, taking it off. Looking up and down the block, he saw nobody except a group of distant trick-or-treaters. He started to unbutton his shirt.

'I can't take your shirt.'

'Just put it on over yours.'

'You'll freeze.'

Shivering, he handed his shirt to Beth. He put on his sports jacket. Its lining felt cool and slick against his skin. With shaking hands, he fastened the two front buttons.

Beth put on his shirt. 'Now we *really* look weird.'

'The weirder, the better.'

As they walked along, Eric rubbed burnt cork onto his neck and chest. Then he added Vampire Blood, squirting it onto his skin and letting it dribble.

'Want some more?' he asked.

'No thanks.'

He put it away. 'You know how to walk?'

Beth shrugged. 'Let's see you do it.'

'Like this, sort of.' He waddled, arms stiff at his sides, his mouth hanging open, eyes wide and staring. 'And you moan. See, the idea is, we're the living dead and we want to eat everybody we see.'

'Yum yum.'

Side by side, they lurched across the road. As they moved slowly up the block, a group of trick-or-treaters left a dark porch and crossed the lawn to the sidewalk.

'Let's give 'em a scare,' Beth whispered.

Ahead of them, a small girl in a Wonder Woman costume stepped off the sidewalk and stared. A cowboy drew his revolver. He fired, yelling, '*Pow pow pow!*' as his hammer clanked down. Eric and Beth stalked forward. The cowboy jumped out of their way, but Darth Vader blocked the sidewalk.

'What're you supposed to be?' he demanded.

Beth groaned, and reached for him.

He backed away, stepping on the toe of a bunny behind him. The bunny shoved him, snapping 'Watch it!'

Darth Vader ignored him. 'I'm not scared of you creeps.'

In a low voice, Eric muttered, 'We're gonna eat you,'

'Oh yeah? You and who else?'

'Me,' said Beth. 'Yum yum.'

'Go fuck yourselves,' he blurted, and dashed around them. He ran into Wonder Woman, knocking her to the grass. Eric stepped toward the girl, wanting to help her, but she squealed in terror and scrambled to her feet and ran away.

Eric returned to Beth.

She shrugged. 'Guess that didn't work out too well.'

'Creepy kid.'

When they met trick-or-treaters at the corner, they walked normally and had no trouble. They crossed the street. Ahead of them, a car stopped. Its rear doors opened and two figures climbed out. The car moved on.

'They must be for the party,' Beth said.

'Is that Aleshia's house?'

'Yeah. Come on, let's go into our routine.'

Stiff-armed and moaning, they shambled up the sidewalk.

# Chapter Thirty-one

'I don't know about this.'

'What's to know, jack-off? It's Halloween! We're just a couple of trick-or-treaters.' Nate drove slowly past Miss Bennett's house. At the end of the block, he pulled to the curb.

'Maybe we oughtta forget about it,' Bill said.

Nate shut off the headlights. 'Hey, what's the point in knowing where she lives if we're not gonna pay a visit? Come on.' Nate climbed out of the car.

Bill hesitated, then swung open the passenger door. As he climbed out, the cold wind hit him and he wished he'd dressed more warmly. He might, at least, have worn shoes and socks instead of sandals.

Nate opened the trunk and took off his jacket. He turned to Bill, arms out. 'How do I look?'

'Cold.'

'I can take it.'

Like Bill, he wore sandals, jeans cut off raggedly at the knees, and a sheath knife on his rope belt. While Bill wore a striped T-shirt that gave him some protection against the weather, Nate wore only an open leather vest.

'Catch this,' he said. He spread the flaps of his vest, and Bill saw a rough drawing of a skull and crossbones on Nate's chest.

'Didn't know you're an artist.'

'I'm a man of many talents.' He flipped a black patch down, covering his left eye. Then he reached into the trunk and took out two grocery bags. 'For our goodies,' he said, handing one to Bill.

Side by side, they headed for Miss Bennett's house. Her front porch light was on. A jack-o'-lantern grinned at them through her picture window.

'Now don't do anything dumb,' Bill warned.

'Dumb? Me?'

'We'll just ring her doorbell, and trick-or-treat, and that's all.'

'Sure.'

'I mean it.' Bill adjusted the red bandanna tied around his head. He touched the big, hooped earring that hung from his right ear, and wondered if he should pluck it off; he didn't want to look silly.

'What're you waiting for?' Nate asked.

'Do I look okay?'

'You look gorgeous. The baddest buccaneer that ever sailed the Seven Seas.'

Bill reached toward the doorbell.

''Cept your tool's out.'

Bill pressed the button. Then, though he knew Nate was joking, he touched his fly. He found it safely zipped.

'Had you worried.'

'Sure.'

The door opened.

Miss Bennett smiled out at them. Her face was smeared with soot. She wore a shapeless felt hat, a bandanna around her neck, a shirt of red flannel, and baggy brown pants held up by suspenders. A polka-dot patch adorned one knee of her trousers.

'Trick-or-treat,' said Bill and Nate.

'What have we here? A pirate and an exhibitionist?'

Nate made a crooked smile. 'Guess you're a tramp.'

She laughed. '*Touché!* A hit, a palpable hit. Come on in out of the cold. Do you like cider?'

'Sure,' Bill said.

They stepped into the house. Miss Bennett closed the door. As she turned away, Nate nudged Bill with his elbow and winked his uncovered eye.

'You boys must be freezing,' she said.

'We're tough,' said Nate.

They entered the living room. 'Have a seat. I've got hot cider on the stove. I'll be back in a jiff.'

Bill sat on the sofa, and watched her walk away. A polka-dot patch covered the seat of her pants. Nate winked again, and dropped into a stuffed chair near the corner. 'Still think this was a lousy idea?'

Bill shook his head, grinning.

'Got you to first base. Imagination and guts, that's all it takes.'

A hand reached from behind the chair and clutched Nate's shoulder. With a yelp, he leaped to his feet. As he whirled around, a black-clad Frankenstein monster rose into view. Nate backed away. 'Very funny,' he told the monster. 'You're a real barrel of yucks.'

It slowly stepped from behind the chair. Arms out, it lurched toward Nate.

Bill saw Miss Bennett in the kitchen doorway, shaking as she tried to hold in her laughter.

Nate continued to back away from the monster. 'Okay! A joke's a joke. Now knock it off!'

It kept coming.

'Damn!' He put up his fists. 'One more step, shit-head!'

'That's enough,' Miss Bennett said in a calm voice.

The monster's huge, misshapen head turned toward her.

'Sit down and be good,' she said.

It lowered its arms. It turned away and lumbered back to the chair where Nate had been sitting. With a quiet grunt, it sat down. It folded its hands and crossed its legs.

'Sorry if he scared you,' Miss Bennett said, coming in with two mugs of cider.

Nate smirked and snorted. He sat on the sofa beside Bill.

'Who are you?' Bill asked the monster.

The monster sat motionless, and said nothing.

'Who is it, Miss Bennett?'

'My friend, the Wretch.'

'Makes *me* want to retch,' Nate muttered.

'He's quite harmless, normally.' Miss Bennett set down the mugs on the coffee table.

Bill thanked her, and picked one up. Pushing a cinnamon stick aside, he took a sip. 'That's good.'

'It'll warm your bones,' she said. She crossed the room, and sat down on the lap of the Wretch. 'So, what're you fellows up to?'

'We're gonna pillage the town,' Nate said.

'Actually, we're going to a Halloween party, but that's not till later.'

'Same with us.'

'We're not keeping you, are we?'

'No. There's no rush.'

'You heading over to the Sherwood place?' Nate asked.

'One of my students is having a few people over.' She slapped one of the monster's hands as it slid up her thigh. 'There's a party at the Sherwood . . .?' The doorbell interrupted her. 'Excuse me,' she said. She pushed the Wretch's hand off her leg, and went to the door.

Bill heard her open it. A chorus of children's voices called out, 'Trick-or-treat.'

Across the room, the monster stood. It began walking slowly toward Nate.

'Okay, Wretch, knock it off.'

It raised its arms.

Nate jumped to his feet. 'Okay, asshole.'

The monster reached out for him.

Nate kicked. His foot shot toward the crotch, but a quick hand blocked his blow, gripped Nate's ankle and threw him backwards. He hit the floor, his head barely missing the coffee table.

Bill sprang to his feet, ready to fight, but the monster held up its hand. 'I've got no quarrel with you,' said a voice muffled by the mask.

'Lay off Nate.'

'I'm done with him.' The monster's hands fumbled with its mask then pulled it off.

Mr Carlson, the school librarian, frowned down at Nate. 'That was for yesterday, Houlder, for knocking her into the bushes.'

'You cocksucker,' Nate muttered. 'I'm gonna sue your ass.'

'I believe this falls into the category of self-defense.'

'What's going on here?' Miss Bennett asked, frowning as she entered the room.

'Houlder was just leaving.'

'Damn it, Nick!'

'Sorry,' he said. 'But Houlder had it coming.'

'An eye for an eye never solved anything.'

'It helps, believe me.'

'That's right, man,' Nate said as he got to his feet. 'You just remember that. 'Cause you're gonna pay.' He flipped open his vest and tapped the skull-and-crossbones drawn on his chest. 'See this? You're gonna look worse by the time I'm done. Count on it.'

'You scare me, Houlder.'

Nate's hand darted to the hilt of his knife. He unsnapped the sheath.

Bill grabbed his wrist. 'Come on, Nate. Let's get out of here.' He held on until Nate's arm relaxed.

'Yeah, okay. Let's go.'

Miss Bennett hurried ahead of them, and opened the door.

'Sorry about this,' Bill told her. 'But your friend did start it. Nate was just sitting there.'

She nodded and said nothing.

'Carlson started it,' Nate said, 'but I'm gonna finish it.' He stopped at the door and looked back at the blackclad man. 'You hear that, Carlson? I'm gonna finish it. An eye for an eye.'

'Just try it, Houlder.'

Bill tugged Nate's sleeve. 'Come on.'

They stepped outside, and Miss Bennett shut the door.

# Chapter Thirty-two

'So then Doons accused *me* of being Houlder's girlfriend.'

'Doons is a jerk,' Eric said.

'I hate him.'

'Me too.' He finished his plastic glass of punch, and saw that Beth was nearly done. 'You want some more?'

'Yeah. Good, isn't it?'

'Yeah.' He took her glass. 'I'll be right back.' She smiled, and Eric left her. He made his way across the living room, looking for gaps through the frantic dancers and watching the girls. They paid no attention to him as he weaved among them. Most had vacant looks in their eyes as if entranced by the loud music and the motions of their own jerking bodies.

Aleshia wore pink tights and a white tutu. Her shoulders were bare. A pearl choker hung at her throat, and she wore a tiara in her hair. Eric had never seen her look so beautiful. If only he were more like Eddie Ryker ... He watched Eddie dance. The tall, handsome boy wore no real costume – just a football jersey and jeans. He had a complacent smile. His eyes were on the ceiling – not even *looking* at her!

Eric bumped into someone.

'Jesus, Prince!' Mark Bailey scowled at him from under his helmet liner.

'Sorry, sir,' Eric said, and snapped a salute.

'Creep,' muttered Mark's partner.

Eric turned to her. Sue Diamond, the head cheerleader. She, too, was apparently dressed as a soldier. She wore a tiger-striped field bat, a drab olive jumpsuit, and a canteen on a web belt. Her jumpsuit was unzipped almost to her belly, showing a long V of bare skin and no trace of bra.

'Fuck off,' she said.

Eric hurried past, then looked back, wondering what would show if she bent down. She didn't bend down. Instead, she gave him the finger.

He finally reached the refreshment table. He stood in line behind a clown and a vampire. Nobody spoke to him. He waited, watching Elmer Cantwell dip punch from the cut-glass bowl for the vampire.

Elmer seemed to be dressed as the hunchback of Notre Dame. With his squat figure and bulgy eyes, he looked right for the role.

'Is that Aleshia's father?' Eric had asked when he first saw Elmer.

'No,' Beth told him. 'Her dad's never home. That's Elmer Cantwell.'

'What's he doing here?'

'He's a friend of Aleshia's mom. Ugly, isn't he?'

'Sort of.'

'Women are supposed to be crazy about him. I can't see it, though, can you?'

Eric had shaken his head.

'He must have something going for him, 'cause it sure isn't his looks.'

'Maybe he's rich.'

'Maybe.'

The vampire and clown were gone, and Eric looked across the table at the man. He saw the eyes lower to his bare chest, and stare. He fought an urge to pull his jacket shut.

'Two punches, please.'

Elmer grinned, showing his crooked upper teeth, and reached for the empty glasses. Eric held them out. The man's fingers stroked his hands. He squirmed, wishing Aleshia's mother was still at the punch bowl instead of this man.

Elmer took the glasses. He set them down, dipped into the punch bowl, and filled them with the frothy red liquid.

'I've seen you at the library, Eric,' he said in a whispery voice.

'You have?'

'Many times.'

'Where?'

'The public library.'

'Oh.'

'You have such lovely skin. A shame to hide it under such filth.'

'Oh.' He felt as if worms were crawling on his back. 'Thanks for the punch,' he said. He picked up the two glasses and hurried away. This time, passing through the dancers, he didn't even notice those around him. He found Beth still standing in the comer. Mary Lou, one of the cheerleaders, was with her.

'Hi, Eric,' Mary Lou said.

She was a slim redhead, dressed as a nurse.

'Hi.'

'Are you okay?' Beth asked.

'Sure.' He handed a glass to her.

'You look sick.'

'I'm the living dead.'

'What happened?'

He shrugged. 'Oh, that guy Elmer.'

'What'd he do?' Mary Lou asked.

'He's just a creep.'

'Do you know what he said to John? You know John? He's Dracula. He was in front of you. Did you hear what that crazy guy said to him?'

Eric shook his head.

'Get this.' Mary Lou glanced from Beth to Eric, her eyes bright and eager. 'He said, "You can suck me anytime, Count."'

'Good Christ,' Beth muttered.

'Gross, huh?'

'Is he . . . gay?' Beth asked.

'God, I guess so. But you know, he's supposed to be a real lady-killer.'

'Maybe he likes both,' Eric said.

Beth shook her head. 'I don't see why anybody'd be interested in *him*.'

'Haven't you heard? He's . . .' Mary Lou glanced at Eric, then back to Beth. 'Well . . . They say he's got an absolutely enormous *thing*.'

'Yuck,' Beth said.

'It's supposed to be – you know – gigantuous.'

'Do you think he and Aleshia's mom . . .?'

'Why else would he be here?'

'Boy,' Beth muttered. She wrinkled her nose as if disgusted.

Mary Lou turned to Eric. 'So look, what'd he say to you?'

'He said I've got nice skin.'

'Oh gross.'

As she sipped her punch, Beth's eyes lowered to Eric's chest, and lingered there. 'He's right,' she finally said.

Laughter burst from Mary Lou. 'You're a nut!' she gasped. 'God, what a nut!'

Beth set down her drink. Her mouth dropped open, her head tilted to one side, and she gazed at Mary Lou with wide, vacant eyes. Moaning, she raised her arms. She reached for the girl's throat.

'Hey!' Giggling, Mary Lou backed away.

'Gonna eat you,' Beth mumbled. 'Yum yum.'

Eric started to shamble alongside Beth. 'Gonna eat you.'

Mary Lou backed into John the vampire. She squealed as he threw his arms around her and nibbled the side of her neck.

'Wanta get Aleshia?' Eric asked.

Beth nodded.

They moved slowly across the room, moaning, bumping into dancers who ignored them or laughed or pushed them away. Then Aleshia was in front of them. Her head was back, her eyes half-shut and dreamy as she shrugged and flung her arms and twirled. They staggered past Eddie Ryker. He kept on dancing as if they were invisible.

'Gonna eat you,' Beth mumbled.

Aleshia paid no attention.

Eric saw specks of sweat on her upper lip, but her shoulders and chest looked dry. The tops of her breasts showed above her bodice. One hard downward pull would free them . . .

And every guy in the room would jump on Eric.

Beth grabbed Aleshia's arm.

'Hey!'

'Gonna eat you,' Beth said.

'Oh yeah?' Aleshia pulled free, grinning. 'Nobody eats me but Eddie.'

Beth gasped and burst into laughter.

With a harsh laugh, Aleshia resumed her dance.

Eric watched, sick with disappointment. Why hadn't he grabbed her? At least her arm, like Beth?

Shit!

He'd missed his chance. He'd chickened out.

'Want to dance?' Beth asked.

'I guess.'

# Chapter Thirty-three

'It's stopping,' Bill said.

Nate slowed down.

A block in front of them, the car containing Carlson and Miss Bennett backed into a space along the curb.

'That's gotta be the place,' Nate said.

'Yeah.' The house was bright, its porch light on, a green spotlight on the front lawn illuminating a stiff-armed motionless figure.

'Keep an eye on 'em,' Nate said.

Bill watched Carlson and Miss Bennett climb from the car. They turned toward the lighted house and strolled up its walkway. The solitary figure didn't move. A scarecrow, Bill realized as they drove slowly closer.

He saw a grinning jack-o'-lantern in the picture window. Beyond it, people in costumes were standing around, some dancing. 'Kids,' he said.

'And to think we weren't invited. What kind of asshole has a party and doesn't invite us?'

The screen door opened. Carlson and Miss Bennett entered.

'Pisses me off. What do they think we are, lepers? You got leprosy, dingus?'

'Nope.'

'Me either. The fuck-heads.'

At the end of the block, he turned the corner and parked.

'What're you doing?'

'What does it look like?'

'We're not going in.'

'Hey, we're trick-or-treaters. We'll just go up to the door and see what develops.'

'Bullshit. You want to get in there and wipe out Carlson.'

With a wink, Nate flipped the black patch down. 'Fuckin'-A right. We bad dudes, man. Pirates. Nobody pushes us around. We do the pushing.' He threw open the car door and leaped out. Running up the street, he cried out, 'Rape, plunder, pillage! Ho ho ho and a bottle of rum!'

Bill ran after him. 'Wait up!'

'Fuck you, slowpoke.'

'Hey, you kids!' yelled a woman.

Bill spotted her on the sidewalk with half a dozen children.

'Eat it, lady!' Nate called back as he cut across the corner lot.

She was still ahead of Bill. 'You creeps oughtta be locked up!'

'Up your ass!' Bill yelled.

'Right on!' Nate shouted from a distance.

Bill stayed on the road until he passed the woman, then he dashed over the sidewalk and across the corner yard. Nate, just ahead, jumped up and down waiting for him.

'Come on, dipstick!'

Side by side, they ran down the block.

'Rape pillage plunder!' Nate shouted.

Rock music blared from the house ahead. '*I'm dying to be your woman, I'm dying to be your guy, we're dying to be red-hot lovers – under the sunbeam sky.*' Nate sprinted toward the scarecrow. Its head was a painted grocery bag. '*Under the sunbeam sky sky sky.*'

'Yeeyah!' He crashed into it. The post snapped, and he drove the scarecrow to the ground. It came apart at the waist. Balls of wadded newspaper spilled out of its shirt and pants.

'*Dying to be lovers, dying to get high, dying to be your wonder-waker under the red-hot sky.*'

Rolling, he scrambled to his feet and rushed the door. The main door stood open.

'Nate!'

'Rape pillage plunder!'

'Don't!'

He flung open the screen door. A woman in an evening gown blocked his way. He smashed her aside.

Bill hesitated. He didn't want to follow Nate inside, wanted no part of the fight and destruction sure to come.

Eric was dancing with Beth, watching her and trying to imitate her moves when he saw a pirate plow into Mrs Barnes. The woman yelped and stumbled backwards. She hit the wall hard.

'*I'm dying to go down with you, I'm dying to feel your skin.*'

'Rape pillage plunder!' the pirate yelled.

Nate Houlder!

'*We're dying to be red-hot lovers – doing the sunbeam sin.*'

Nate charged across the room, smashing his way through startled dancers.

'Stop him!' someone shouted.

'Get him!'

Eddie Ryker reached out, as Nate rushed by, and grabbed his

shoulder. Nate whirled and slammed a fist into Ryker's nose. Jerking free, he lunged at the Frankenstein monster – Mr Carlson – who'd come in with Miss Bennett only a minute ago. Carlson landed a punch on his chin, but it didn't stop him. He threw himself against the man, grappled with him, drove a knee up into his groin. Carlson cried out and fell. Nate scurried over him. Reached the refreshment table. Elmer backed away, and Nate lifted the punch bowl.

'No!' Miss Bennett yelled.

He lurched toward Carlson, stumbled, and emptied the punch onto him. The red flood washed over his head and back, splashed off him and spattered those nearby.

Miss Bennett wrenched the empty bowl away from Nate. 'You idiot!' she snapped. 'You stupid goddamned idiot!'

'My *carpet*!' shrieked Mrs Barnes.

'Get him!' cried Aleshia. 'Everybody get him!'

Three of the guys from the football team – Mark Bailey the soldier, John the vampire, and an Indian – hit him at the same time. He went down in a pile of bodies.

'Go help,' Beth said, nudging Eric.

'They don't want me.'

'Go on. They'll think you're chicken.'

'Well . . .' He left Beth. By the time he reached the group, six boys were on Nate. Aleshia stood over them, giving directions. Her face was red and she was breathing hard.

'His leg,' she gasped. 'Get his other leg.'

Eric crouched and grabbed Nate's left ankle – the only visible part of his body.

'Okay, pick him up. Pick him up.'

'Let's call the cops,' said John.

'No. I've got a better idea. Get him outside.'

John and a cowboy climbed off Nate. The others lifted him.

'My carpet,' muttered Mrs Barnes.

'He'll pay for it,' said Elmer.

Eric walked backwards, still holding Nate's ankle. The foot was bare. Nate was panting, sobbing. His eyepatch hung around his neck. Blood trickled from his nostrils. The right side of his face was red and swollen. His chest bled from a dozen fingernail scratches.

'What're we gonna do with him?' Ryker asked.

'Get him outside,' Aleshia said again.

'I think the police should be notified,' Miss Bennett said as she walked behind the group.

'We'll take care of him.'

'He's been hurt enough.'

'We won't hurt him,' said Aleshia.

Somebody held open the screen door. They carried Nate outside, and down the porch steps.

'Okay,' Aleshia said. 'Strip him.'

'Yeah!' said the cowboy.

'All *right*!' said the Indian.

'Serve the bastard right,' said Ryker.

'Kids!' snapped Miss Bennett. 'I don't think this is the right way to . . .'

A wild cry of rage stopped her voice.

Eric dropped Nate's foot as he saw a pirate leap from behind a nearby bush.

'Bill!' Miss Bennett shouted.

The pirate glanced at her, but didn't stop. He dived onto the backs of three boys, throwing them forward across Nate's body, smashing them into those on the other side. A couple stumbled backwards and stayed on their feet, but the rest fell in a tangled mass.

'Boys!' Miss Bennett yelled. 'Boys, stop it!'

'Get him!' Aleshia shouted, jumping up and down.

Ryker and Bailey, the ones still standing, went for Bill. They grabbed his arms and shoulders, trying to drag him off the others.

Nate, no longer held by anyone, rolled over. He got to his hands and knees. He started to crawl.

'Boys!'

'Oh no you don't,' said Beth. She leaped onto Nate's back, driving him to the ground. She straddled him. She shoved his shoulders, trying to keep him down, but he rolled onto his back and snarled up at her.

'You,' he muttered. His hands flailed. Beth tried to catch them, but they clutched her breasts, squeezed and twisted. She shrieked.

Her cry of pain tore at Eric. He rushed forward and kicked. The toe of his sneaker caught Nate on the cheek. Nate cried out and grabbed his face.

He pulled Beth to her feet. She was crying softly. 'Are you okay?'

She shook her head, and stepped into Eric's arms. He held her. She felt soft and warm.

Bill lay on the ground, battered, keeping his eyes shut. If they realized he was conscious, they might start in again. Through the ringing in his ears, he heard voices.

Aleshia. 'Okay, get their clothes off.'

Miss Bennett. 'I'm calling the police.'

'No, let's go ahead and let them, Karen.' Who was that? Carlson, probably. The Wretch. 'It's harmless.'

'It's not harmless, its disgusting and degrading.'

'And appropriate. Christ, look what Houlder did to me. Not to mention the carpet.'

'Let's not spoil the fun,' said a quiet, whispery voice.

'Do what you want with them.' The unfamiliar voice of a woman. 'As far as I'm concerned, you can boil them in oil.'

'Let's take a vote,' Aleshia said. 'All in favor of stripping the bastards?'

Bill heard a chorus of *ayes* and *yeahs*.

'Opposed?'

'You're all crazy,' Miss Bennett said.

'The ayes have it.'

Hands began to tug Bill's T-shirt.

'I'm calling the police.'

'Not from my house. The party's over. If you're so eager to help these ruffians, go home and call.'

'Mrs Barnes, I don't think . . .'

'Maybe we should leave,' Carlson said.

'Yes. Maybe we should.'

His shirt was off. He felt the cold, wet grass under his back.

'Geez, look at this knife.'

'Take it,' Aleshia said. 'Take everything.'

He felt hands on his rope belt, on the button of his jeans. The zipper slid down. He raised his head, opened his eyes, and the soldier crouching near his head smashed him in the face with a helmet liner.

His jeans were jerked down his legs.

'What about his shorts?'

'Take 'em. Take everything.'

Someone pulled his underpants off.

'All *right*!' Aleshia cried.

He heard giggles from several girls.

'Tiny little critter,' said a boy.

'Nothing to brag about, is it?'

'Probably couldn't get it up if he had to.'

'You ever see one of these, Mary Lou?'

'Up yours.'

'Hey, get a load of this one.'

'I always knew Houlder was an eunuch.'

Laughter and giggles.

'Okay,' said Aleshia. 'Let's go back in and boogie.'

'Right!'

'No way. The party's over.'

'*Mom!*'

'You heard me.'

'But we only started!'

'It's over.'

'There's a party at the Sherwood house,' said a new voice. Who was that? Oh yeah. Prince. That little fart, Eric Prince. 'Why don't we all go over there?'

'Yeah!'

'Right! I got an invitation.'

'Who's giving the party?'

'Who knows?'

'Who cares!'

'Let's go!'

'All *right*!'

'What'll we do with these guys?'

'Leave 'em.'

'Yeah. But let's take their clothes. If they want 'em back, they'll have to come to the party.'

'Yeah, dressed as skinny-dippers.'

'Streakers.'

'A prick and an asshole.'

Bill heard laughter, and finally silence. Then a familiar voice said, 'We been screwed, dingus.'

'Yeah,' he muttered.

'We gonna let 'em get away with it?'

# Chapter Thirty-four

'Looks like we're the first here,' Doons said. He slowed, made a U-turn, and parked in front of the Sherwood house.

'Oh, I don't know,' Marjorie said.

'You see any other cars? How many? Nine? Ten?'

'Lay off her, Phil.'

'When I need your advice, I'll ask for it.'

'Tough guy,' Thelma said.

'Damn right.'

'Let's not argue,' said Marjorie. 'This is Halloween. We're supposed to have fun.'

Thelma snorted. 'I just hope there're some decent men at this thing.'

'Oh, I'm sure there will. It'll be fun. I've always wanted to see inside the old place, haven't you?'

'Hardly.'

Doons climbed out of the car, and opened its rear door.

Thelma scooted out first, reaching up a hand for assistance. He gave her a pull.

'What a dear,' she said.

'I know it.' He helped Marjorie out. 'Will that be all, ladies?'

'Oh, Phillip.'

'He's pissed 'cause he had to sit alone.'

'I should've come dressed as a chauffeur.'

'You look fine, darling.'

'I feel like an ass.' He jammed his hands into the pockets of his bib overalls. Marjorie had rushed out to buy them after he phoned about the party. She'd bought similar overalls for herself and Thelma.

Thank God, Doons thought, she couldn't find anyplace selling straw hats.

Three fuckin' hayseeds.

'You *have* to dress up,' Marjorie had insisted. 'It's a costume party.'

'The place looks deserted,' Thelma said, interrupting his thoughts.

'That's what I said.'

They started across the front yard, walking through its high weeds.

'You know what?' Thelma asked. Her voice was quiet and missing its usual sarcasm. 'I saw Dexter go in this place the other night.'

Marjorie gaped. 'Really?'

'Yeah. The night he was killed, in fact.'

'Oh my goodness!'

Doons snorted. 'How'd you happen to see that? Or shouldn't I ask?'

Thelma ignored him. 'I saw him go in the back door. And he didn't come out.'

Doons stopped near the veranda. He turned to Thelma. 'What are you, trying to scare us?'

'I just wanted to mention it.'

'You don't think . . .' Marjorie started.

'I don't know,' said Thelma. 'I told that cop about it, and he seemed awfully interested. He was so interested, in fact, that he didn't bother to pull me in.'

Doons blew air through his gritted teeth. 'Jesus Christ, Thelma, what're we doing here?'

'Going to a party.'

In a calm voice, Marjorie added, 'You're the one who, suggested it, Phil.'

'Well Jeezus, nobody told me this is where Boyanski got his ticket cancelled.'

'Don't worry about it,' Thelma said. 'It probably didn't happen here, anyway. Let's go in and have a good time.'

'Sure.' Doons didn't move.

With a smirk, Thelma hooked her thumbs into her overall pockets and climbed the front steps.

'This is crazy,' Doons said.

'Don't be a spoilsport,' Marjorie said. She took Doons's hand. Together, they followed Thelma up the steps to the front door.

'You planning to make me open it?' Thelma asked.

He reached for the knob. As his fingers curved around it, the door flew open. He jumped with alarm. Thelma gasped. Marjorie yelped and clutched his arm.

Inside stood a woman dressed in a long white gown. She held a lighted candle. Her face was in shadows. 'Phil?' she asked.

He managed not to sigh with relief as he recognized the voice. 'Barbara?'

'Boy, am I glad to see you. This place was giving me the willies.'

'Barbara, you've met my wife Marjorie. This is her sister, Thelma. Thelma, this is Barbara Major, one of the teachers from school.'

'Hello,' Thelma said.

'Nice to meet you. Come on in.'

'Anybody else here yet?' Doons asked as he stepped inside.

'See for yourself.'

The women entered and he shut the door. The foyer was dark except for Barbara's candle. They walked slowly over the hardwood floor, and passed through the entryway to the living room.

'Jesus Christ,' Doons muttered.

The candlelit room was deserted except for three gorillas hanging by their arms from wrought-iron window grates.

'Are they real?' Marjorie whispered.

'They're costumes,' said Barbara.

'Anyone in them?' Thelma asked,

Barbara shrugged. 'I haven't gone close enough to find out. They don't move, though. I think they're just stuffed. They sure give me the willies, though. I was about to leave when you guys came along.'

'Let's have a look,' Doons said.

'You look,' said Thelma. 'I'm getting a drink.' She started across the room toward a table at the far end.

'Not a bad idea.' Doons followed her, flanked by Marjorie and Barbara. He realized that he was walking strangely, rolling from heel to toe in an effort to quiet his footfalls. His stomach muscles felt tight. He kept his eyes on the gorillas.

They hung several yards apart along the left-hand wall, each in front of a different window. Their wrists seemed to be bound to the upper crossbars, suspending them well above the floor. Doons could stand on a chair, he decided, and pull off the headgear to see who – if anyone – was inside. But there were no chairs in the room. Only the table.

Thelma was already there. Doons flinched at the sudden noise she made dumping a handful of ice cubes into a plastic glass. 'Gilby's Vodka,' she announced. 'Whoever's throwing this bash has decent taste.'

'Eric Prince,' Barbara said.

'His mother must've bought the booze,' Doons said.

'Where *is* everyone?' Marjorie asked.

As Doons pulled three glasses from the stack, Barbara said, 'Eric told me he'd invited a whole bunch of people.'

'And we're the only ones dumb enough to come.' Doons quietly filled the glasses with ice from a plastic bag.

'It's early yet,' said Thelma.

Marjorie frowned. 'You'd think the host, at least, would be here.'

'You're right.' Doons turned around, eyeing each of the gorillas. 'He's probably in one of those monkey suits. Hey, Eric!' he called out. No answer came. None of the gorillas moved. 'Bet he is.'

'Wouldn't surprise me,' Barbara whispered. 'He's a spooky little kid.'

'What'll you have?'

'Bourbon and Seven.'

He poured Barbara's drink. 'How about you, honey?'

'Scotch and soda.'

He made it for her, and poured Scotch for himself. He sipped it, and immediately felt more relaxed. Comforting, he thought, to have a familiar drink in your hand. 'Well, shall we have a look at our three silent friends?'

'Help yourself,' said Thelma. 'I'm staying here at the comfort station.'

A dozen lighted candles stood on the floor along the wall. Doons crouched over one near the center gorilla. It clung to the floor with dripped wax. He pulled it free, and stood. Holding it high, he studied the gorilla's face. He was too low to see into the sunken eyeholes.

'Hello?' he asked.

No answer.

'Anybody home? Eric?' He pressed the thick, black fur of its leg. 'Feels like someone's in there.' He jabbed his fingers against it. 'Yoo-hooo. Hello in there. Speak now or forever hold your peace.'

Marjorie took a step backward. 'Maybe we should leave it alone.'

'Bullshit.' Doons reached up to the gorilla's groin and goosed it.

'Phil!'

Barbara laughed.

The gorilla didn't move.

Doons shrugged and took a sip of Scotch. 'Hell with it,' he muttered. 'Let's have a look at . . .'

A blast of rock music hit his ears. He swung around and saw Thelma on her knees beneath the table. The volume lowered. She got up and looked around. 'Radio,' she explained. She stepped aside and Doons saw a radio the size of a briefcase under the table. 'Now all we need are a couple of men. How about the monkeys?' Holding her drink high, she pursed her lips and danced toward the nearest gorilla.

Doons shook his head. 'You've always had a fondness for big apes.'

She made a loud, sucking kiss in his direction and continued to dance toward the gorilla at the last window. Doons watched. She looked ridiculous – vaguely repellent – shaking her shoulders and ass.

'What a sight,' he muttered.

Barbara smiled at him, as if sharing his opinion. For the first time tonight, he looked closely at her. She wore a red corsage above one breast. Her straps were red velvet, the rest of her dress white.

'Cinderella?' Doons asked.

'This is my old prom dress. Thought I'd come disguised as a kid.'

'You look beautiful,' Marjorie said.

'Nice,' Doons agreed. If enough people would show up, he planned to get her alone in one of the upstairs rooms. They'd do it on the floor or up against a wall. He'd ruck up her dress. She wouldn't have underwear on – she never did. It'd make the damned party worth the bother.

'Get on down,' Thelma said, tugging the leg of the far gorilla. 'Come on, hon. Get on down and boogie.'

It dropped from the window bars. Its feet thudded the floor. It stood in front of Thelma, crouching, arms out. A short length of rope hung from each wrist.

'Well well!' she said. She downed the rest of her vodka, tossed the glass over her shoulder, and stepped into the arms of the gorilla.

It lifted Thelma off her feet.

'My kind of guy!' she announced.

It carried her down the center of the room. She hung on, one arm hooked around the back of its neck, and waved as she passed Doons.

'Phil!' Marjorie whispered.

He looked at her and shrugged.

'Find out who it is.'

He didn't want to. But he couldn't let himself look like a coward in front of Barbara. 'Hey you,' he called.

The gorilla stopped. It stood near the opening to the foyer. All of Thelma but her dangling legs was blocked by the gorilla's broad, hairy back.

'Who are you?' Doons demanded.

'He's my gorgeous hunk,' said Thelma. 'Bug off.' In a softer voice, she said, 'Come on, hon. Take me to your tree. Bet you've got a banana for me, huh?'

The gorilla carried her from the room.

Doons heard her husky laughter in the foyer.

'Phil!'

'She's got what she wants. Why fight it?'

Marjorie hissed through her nose. '*I'm* seeing where they go.'

'Oh, for . . .' He stopped himself. If Marjorie followed the two, he would have a few minutes alone with Barbara. 'Go ahead, if you want.'

She hurried on tiptoes toward the front of the room, back hunched, arms flapping like a crazed tightrope artist about to fall.

Doons winked at Barbara. She took a small step closer.

Marjorie stopped at the wall and peered around it.

Barbara patted Doons's rump.

Marjorie looked back. She pointed upward.

'They're going upstairs?'

She nodded.

'You gonna follow them?'

Shaking her head, she pointed at Doons.

'You want *me* to follow them?'

She nodded and waved him forward.

He turned to Barbara. 'Want to come along?'

'Sure.'

They walked over to Marjorie. 'You really want me to go upstairs?'

'I'm worried, Phil. Heaven only knows who might be inside that suit.' She turned her eyes to the two gorillas still suspended from the window bars. 'Or in those.'

'I guess we'd better all go up together. I'm warning you, though, Marjorie – Thelma's gonna be plenty pissed if we interrupt her in the middle of a good ... an *intimate* moment.'

'We'll be quiet.'

Doons grinned at Barbara. 'My wife's a closet voyeur.'

'So am I.'

Doons led the way. He walked slowly up the stairs, lowering each foot with great care. In spite of his caution, every stair squeaked and groaned under his weight.

They were halfway to the top of the stairs when the front door swung open. Doons gripped the bannister and looked down. Aleshia Barnes, dressed in tights and a tutu, stood in the doorway grinning at them.

'Trick-or-treat, everyone!'

Doons pressed a finger to his lips.

Eddie Ryker came in behind her, followed by a group of kids in costume. 'Mr Doons?' Eddie asked. 'What's going on?'

'We just have to check on something. You kids go ahead and have fun.'

'Anything we can help you with?'

Doons pictured the whole bunch walking in on Thelma as she lay on the floor rutting with the gorilla. 'No,' he said. 'We'll take care of it. You all go ahead and start the party. We'll be down in a minute.'

# Chapter Thirty-five

Eric entered the house beside Beth, and saw the group on the stairway; Doons, Miss Major and a stranger. The unfamiliar woman wore bib overalls and a plaid shirt, like Doons. Probably his wife. Eric shook his head, astonished that the v.p. and teacher had both shown up. It was almost too good to be true.

'Where're they going?' he asked.

'Doing something upstairs,' said Eddie.

'*Doing* something?' asked John the vampire, wriggling his eyebrows.

At the top of the stairway, the group turned left and disappeared.

'Where'll we put the guys' clothes and stuff?' asked Mary Lou.

'We'll think of something,' said Aleshia. 'Hang onto them for now. Come on.'

They followed Aleshia into the living room. 'Holy shit,' she muttered.

'Wow,' said Beth.

Eric stared, gaping at the rows of candles on the floor along each wall, at the pair of shaggy gorillas suspended from the window bars, at the crudely painted drawings.

The drawings fascinated Eric. He saw a witch riding her broomstick across the ceiling – the witch naked, the broomstick a rigid penis. On a wall stood a black-hooded headsman, his bloody ax held high. Farther down the wall, a group of naked women were gathered in a circle munching parts of a dismembered man.

Eric walked along the wall, looking closely.

'Sick,' Beth muttered. 'Really sick.'

'Yeah.'

He took a few more steps and saw the red-painted Devil sodomizing a woman.

'My God,' Beth said. She turned away. 'Come on. Let's stay with the others.'

Ahead of them, the group had split up – half continuing toward the refreshment table, the other half veering to the left for a closer look at the gorillas.

'God, you don't think there's anyone in those things?' Sue Diamond squeezed the leg of the nearest one.

Mark Bailey pounded the leg with his helmet liner. 'Nobody alive,' he said, and laughed.

'Very amusing.'

'Looky here! Booze!'

'All right!'

'Better get some before Doons comes down.'

'Fuck Doons.'

'Thanks but no thanks.'

'*Look* at this! Scotch, bourbon, vodka, gin. Jesus H. Christ, we can all tie one on.'

'Man, I'd like to meet the guy that's throwing this party. I'd like to shake his hand.'

'I'd like to kiss him.'

'You don't know who the host is?' asked a whispery voice from the rear.

Whirling around, Eric saw Elmer Cantwell lurch through the entryway and hobble forward.

'It is I,' he said. 'Hop-Frog.'

'Hey, well, it's fantastic!'

'I'm pleased that you're pleased.'

'I thought you were the hunchback of Notre Dame.'

'Hop-Frog,' he said, scurrying toward them. 'Hop-Frog at your service.'

'You sure know how to throw a party.'

They walked slowly down the hall, Doons in the lead with his candle, the two women close behind him. So far, they'd passed two doors. Both had been locked. Doons had rapped quietly on each with no response.

'Should we try calling out?' Marjorie whispered.

'No,' Doons said. He came to the door with a splintery hole hacked into it. Crouching slightly, he peered into the gap. A face appeared. He yelped and jumped back, bumping into Marjorie. She grabbed his arm.

'Hey,' a voice whispered from behind the door.

Doons took a deep, shaky breath. 'Good Christ,' he said. 'You scared the . . .'

'You've gotta get us out of here.'

'What're you doing in there?'

422

'He nailed the door shut.'

'Who?'

'There's a maniac in the house.'

'Oh my goodness!' Marjorie gasped.

'I think he killed the real estate guy. Morley? This afternoon. He tried to get us. He has a gun.'

'You on the level?'

'Look, you've gotta help us get out of here.'

'This is a joke, right? A Halloween prank?'

'It's no prank, damn it. Look, somebody went by here a minute ago. A woman. I heard her laughing. Thought she might be with the killer, so I kept down.'

'That was Thelma.'

'She's with a guy?'

'A gorilla.'

'Shit! You may think this is funny, pal, but . . .'

'A guy in a gorilla suit.'

'You know him?'

'Haven't seen his face. He was here when we arrived.'

'Oh Christ. Have you got a weapon?'

Doons shook his head.

'You'd better take this.'

'No!' cried a woman behind the door. 'It's all we've got.'

'It's okay, honey.'

'Harold!'

'We'll be all right,' he told her. Then a metal object was thrust through the hole in the door. A hatchet head. 'Take it,' he said, pushing the hatchet out.

Doons took it.

The face of the man reappeared. 'That's all the protection we had, mister. We're counting on you.'

Doons nodded.

'Go get the bastard.'

'Maybe we'd better get you out, first, and . . .'

'It'd take too long. If you want to save that lady's skin . . .'

'Yeah. Yeah, you're right.' Doons swung around. 'One of you gals go for the boys. Get 'em up here quick.'

'I'm staying with you,' said Marjorie.

'I'll go.'

Barbara raced up the hall.

'Excuse me,' Eric said. 'I need to find a bathroom. I'll be right back.'

Nodding, Beth raised a glass of bourbon to her lips. She tasted it and shivered.

Elmer hobbled in front of Eric. 'Enjoying the festivities?'

'Yeah.' Eric kept walking.

'The fun has barely begun.' He reached for Eric's arm.

Eric sidestepped. 'Don't touch me.'

'It's my party. I touch whomever I please.'

'It's not your party, you liar. It's *my* party. *Mine!* And I didn't invite you.'

Elmer chuckled and rolled his eyes. 'My mistake.'

'Damn right.' Eric shoved him aside, and hurried by.

He left the living room.

Miss Major came running down the stairs. 'Quick! Get all the guys! We need help!'

'Fuck you,' he said.

'Eric!'

He stepped to the front door, and removed a padlock from his pants pocket.

'Eric! What're you doing!'

424

The latch was where he'd been told it would be, where he'd seen it as he entered. He flipped it over the metal hoop on the doorframe, and snapped the padlock into place.

'Eric!'

'Nobody leaves.'

Miss Major gazed at him, her eyes wide, her mouth hanging open. Then she ran into the living room. 'Help!' she cried out. 'Everyone! Upstairs!'

Doons blew out his candle and slid it into a pocket of his overalls. The hatchet was slippery in his wet hand. He reached for the doorknob, and slowly turned it.

This door was not locked.

He suddenly felt as if he would lose control of his bowels. He clamped his buttocks together and clenched his sphincter. He took a deep breath. Then he pushed the door open.

Marjorie screamed.

Doons stared. His sphincter let go. He began to whimper.

He saw naked corpses on the floor, some lying on their backs, others sitting with their backs to the far wall. Mutilated. A couple of small boys. A man he didn't recognize. Glendon Morley. An old woman with red pulp where her face should be. Two younger women. One was Thelma. She lay near the door, her torso slit open, a lighted candle imbedded in the coils of her exposed guts, another in her mouth, another protruding from between her legs. Every corpse held a candle in its mouth. Each woman had one in her vagina.

The gorilla stepped out from behind the door.

Still screaming, Marjorie ran up the hall.

Doons swung the hatchet, missed the gorilla by a yard, and ran.

# Chapter Thirty-six

Karen Bennett saw them walking along the shoulder of Oakhurst Road. Nate wore a big shirt. His legs were bare below its hanging tails. Bill wore pants, but no shirt. He hugged his chest as he walked.

She stopped beside them, leaned across the passenger seat, and rolled down the window. 'How about a lift?'

'Miss Bennett?' Bill asked.

'None other.' She unlocked the back door. The boys ran to it and climbed in.

'Ah, warmth,' Nate said.

Bill sighed.

'Can I take you fellows home?'

'We're going to the Sherwood house.'

'We're gonna fix their asses.'

'Besides, they've got our stuff.'

'Where'd you get the clothes?'

'Offa the scarecrow. Christ, I think my dick's got frostbite.'

'Nate!' Bill snapped.

'So sorry.'

'Did you come back just for us?' Bill asked.

'Couldn't leave you out in the cold, bare-ass and bleeding.'

Nate laughed. 'Hey, you're a decent lady. Who'd ever think you're a teacher?'

'Anyway, I got rid of Carlson, the s.o.b., and decided to come looking for you.'

'Did you call the cops?'

She shook her bead. 'They would've been tough on you guys. I figured you'd been through enough without that.'

'Hey hey hey!'

'You really want me to take you to the Sherwood house?'

'Damn right.'

'Dressed like that?'

'It's nothing they haven't already seen, the shit-eaters.'

'Nate.'

'Sorry. Hey, Miss Bennett, you wouldn't have a tire iron in your trunk?'

'I may be decent, but I'm not about to provide you with a deadly weapon.' She started driving. 'I'll go in with you, though. Maybe we can get back your things without resorting to . . .'

'You better not,' Nate said. 'What we're gonna do to those piss-buckets won't be fit for a lady's eyes.'

# Chapter Thirty-seven

Eric stayed near the front door, and watched the others start up the stairs. They all had candles. They made him think of a peasant mob in a Frankenstein movie.

Doons and his wife rushed down the stairs toward the group. 'Move it!' Doons yelled. 'Move it! There's a killer! Bodies! Oh my God, the bodies! Get down!'

He looked over his shoulder and gasped.

Eric looked. He saw a gorilla in the darkness at the top of the stairs.

Doons shoved his wife. She bumped into Aleshia, and Aleshia stumbled backwards against Eddie. They both fell into those below them. Doons, holding a hatchet high, made his way down through the sprawling teenagers. He pulled his wife along behind him. At the foot of the stairs, he shoved Eric aside and lunged for the door. He gripped the knob, twisted it, jerked. The door hit the latch and banged shut. 'A lock! Who locked the fuckin' door!'

'Eric,' said Miss Major.

Doons swung around. 'Bastard! Give me the key!'

Eric shook his head. 'Nobody leaves.'

Doons raised the hatchet. A shot blasted through the shouting. A hole appeared in Doons's forehead and a red mass splashed the door. Screams erupted. He fell.

Dropping beside him, Eric grabbed the hatchet. He leaped to his feet.

Mark Bailey reached for him. A shot sent his helmet liner spinning away, and he dropped.

Eric looked at the stairs. The gorilla stood in darkness at the top, the furry suit half off and hanging around his legs. He wore a stained uniform. He held a revolver in both hands. He fired. Eddie Ryker's throat opened.

He fired. The Indian clutched his chest and tumbled backwards.

John the vampire ran past Eric, cape fluttering. A shot exploded. His head jerked forward and he fell sprawling.

The girls kept screaming and wailing. Except for Aleshia. She shouted, 'Run! Run!' She rushed past Eric, and up the hallway beside the stairs. Beth followed her. Then Miss

Major, and Mary Lou, and finally Sue Diamond. Only Mrs Doons remained. She lay on the floor, holding her dead husband.

The gorilla kicked free of his suit and came down the stairs, loading his revolver.

'Use the hatchet,' he said, his voice muffled by the black gorilla head. 'Finish her.'

'Dad,' Eric muttered. 'Dad, you ... you weren't supposed to ... you *killed* them!'

'They're your enemies.'

'You weren't supposed to *kill* them!'

'Give me that.' He snatched the hatchet away from Eric. He went to Mrs Doons.

'No!' Eric cried.

'Shut up.'

Mrs Doons didn't look up. He split the back of her head.

'Let's get the others.'

'No.'

He holstered the revolver, and clutched a lapel of Eric's jacket. 'Don't snivel and whine. It's their night to snivel and whine. It's their night to pay for all the times they pissed on you.'

The side of the hatchet head pressed against Eric's pants, rubbed his penis.

'We're gonna fuck 'em. You want to fuck 'em, don't you? We're gonna fuck 'em all, and chop 'em up.'

Eric felt himself getting hard. 'I don't want to kill them.'

'Want 'em to tell? Wanta go to prison? I been there, been fourteen years – long as you been alive, almost. Know how I got there? Somebody told. Out in California. I slit her open but she didn't die like the others, and she told. Can't let 'em tell. Gotta chop 'em up.'

The hatchet went away. A hand touched him through his pants.

'First we're gonna fuck 'em.'

Eric stared at the face of the gorilla. The hand stroked the length of his erection.

'You'll like that, won't you?'

Eric nodded.

'When we're done, I've got a surprise for you. The best surprise of all.'

'Okay.'

He took a flashlight from his pocket. 'Come on.'

'Elmer,' groaned a low, quiet voice.

Elmer, under the table in the main room, curled closer to the transister radio. It was a large radio, but too small to conceal all of him. He tucked his legs against his belly.

'Elmer?' the voice called. It sounded weak.

He trembled.

He'd thought he was alone in the big, candlelit room.

'Elmer, help me.'

My God, he thought. The gorilla! The voice came from one of the hanging gorillas! He wanted to scurry from under the table and run. But where could he run to? That little shit Eric had padlocked the front door. The rear door, if he could find it, was probably also locked.

To find it, he would have to wander through the dark house. The gorilla with the pistol was out there.

'Elmer.' The voice was stronger now. 'Get out from under the goddamn table and help me.'

The voice, though muffled, sounded vaguely familiar.

Elmer got to his hands and knees. He crawled out from

under the table, and gazed up at the nearest gorilla. Its thick, hairy legs were swinging. The other gorilla remained motionless.

'Get your ass in gear and cut me down.'

'Sam?' Elmer whispered.

'Do it!'

Elmer nodded. He turned to the liquor table and picked up a bottle of bourbon. He hated to break it – the noise. Looking around, he saw a heap of clothing on the floor. He rushed to it, tossed aside a vest and striped T-shirt. Hanging from the rope belts of the cut-off jeans were two big knives. He slipped them out of their sheaths and hurried to the window. He looked up at the black gorilla. 'You're too high.'

'Climb the bars.'

'I don't know if I can.'

'You'd better give it the best try of your life.'

They found Sue Diamond curled in the corner of a hallway closet. She whimpered and covered her face as the flashlight shined in her eyes. 'Hold the light.'

Eric took the flashlight.

His father grabbed Sue's feet and dragged her from the closet. She kicked her feet free. She started to sit up. He kicked her in the face and she fell. The back of her head smacked the floor. She didn't move.

He knelt beside her and jerked down the zipper of her jumpsuit. It stopped at her groin. She wore black, lacy panties. He pulled open the jumpsuit, and Eric stared at her big, pale breasts. They jiggled as his father peeled the jumpsuit off her shoulders and down her back. The nipples looked smooth and pink, but they didn't stick out as Eric would have liked.

His father tugged the cuffs, pulling the jumpsuit down her

legs and off. He tore off her panties. Eric stared at the curly black tuft of hair.

'Go ahead, she's all yours.'

He ached, but he hesitated.

'Go ahead.'

'What about the others?'

'They're not going anyplace.'

'Can't I wait?'

'Suit yourself.' He handed the hatchet to Eric. Then he knelt between Sue's legs and opened his pants. 'I'll warm her up for you,' he said. He laughed quietly inside the gorilla head, and grabbed her breasts.

Grunting and moaning, Elmer tried to pull himself up the bars. Sweat dripped into his eyes. He tried to find a toe hold in the wall, but his feet slipped down. He let go. 'I can't . . . can't make it.'

'Bring over the table. Stand on the table.'

'Yeah!' He rushed to the table. It was laden with a dozen bottles, and two big plastic bags of ice. He lifted one end of the table, and pulled. Its far legs skidded and squawked on the hardwood floor. The table vibrated. The bottles shook and clattered together. One tipped. Elmer gasped and held the table motionless, but it fell. It burst on the floor.

'Oh Christ oh Christ,' he muttered. 'Now we're in for it!'

'Get that table over here!'

'I'll take the things off.' He set it down and reached for the two nearest bottles.

'It'll take too long. Don't. Just . . . just get it over here and cut me down.'

Elmer moaned. He looked toward the foyer, then around at the closed door to the rear.

'Hurry!'

He picked up the end of the table and again began to drag it toward the window. The bottles swayed and clinked. Another fell and exploded, but Elmer didn't stop.

'What was that?' Eric said.

'Who cares?' His father climbed off Sue Diamond. 'Your turn.'

'I don't want to.'

'Why not?'

'I want to wait.'

'What for?'

'Aleshia. The ballerina.'

His father nodded. He held out a hand. Eric gave him the hatchet. 'Watch this.'

Eric tried to watch. At the last moment, he shut his eyes. He heard a wet thud, and splashing sounds. More thuds.

'Let's go.'

Eric looked down. Sue Diamond's white skin was shiny with blood. She no longer had a head.

His father hurled it down the hallway. It vanished into the darkness, trailing black hair. A moment later, it crashed against something. It thumped once more, and was quiet.

They walked up the hallway.

The head lay near a shut door, looking up at them. The nose was smashed almost flat. Most of the front teeth were gone. The door had a red smear where the head struck it.

Eric stepped around the head.

His father stepped over it and pushed the door. As it swung open, Eric heard a quiet gasp from inside the kitchen.

They stepped in.

He swung the flashlight. Its beam lit the door to the back porch, safely padlocked shut on the inside. It shined on the linoleum floor, on cupboards and a sink, on a white-painted wooden door.

'The utility closet.' His father laughed softly.

They walked toward the closet door, and Eric's father jerked it open.

Aleshia sprang out at him. He drove a knee into her belly, the impact lifting her feet off the floor. She fell face down.

'This Aleshia?'

'Yeah.'

'The one you want?'

'Yeah.'

'Know what's funny?'

'What?'

'This is where I got Hester. Right here. Right where you're gonna get Aleshia.'

'Who's Hester?'

'Hester Sherwood. Lived here a long time ago. This is where I fucked her. Right here.' He rolled Aleshia over. Eric shined the flashlight on her. She was grimacing, gasping for air, clutching her belly. 'Right here on the floor.' He ripped her bodice down.

Standing on the table, Elmer sawed through the rope that bound Sam's right hand to the upper crossbar. When the rope parted, Sam's arm flopped down as if lifeless.

'How'd you get here?' Elmer asked, starting on the other rope.

'Crashed. My head . . .'

'You've been unconscious?'

The gorilla head nodded. 'I heard shots. Guess they brought me out of it. I saw you come running in.'

Elmer grabbed one of the bars, pressed himself against Sam, and cut through the rope. Sam's arm dropped. Elmer used all his strength to force him against the bars, but it wasn't enough, Sam's heels slid over the table top, pushed through bottles, knocked them to the floor. Then he was sitting on the table, straddled by Elmer. Elmer climbed off and jumped to the floor.

Sam continued to sit on the table.

'Now what?' Elmer asked.

'Help me to my feet.'

'Want her?'

Eric swallowed. He stared at Aleshia's small, pale breasts. The nipples stood rigid. 'Yeah,' he said.

His father tugged Aleshia's tutu down her legs. He peeled down her tights.

Off to the side, a cupboard door squeaked open. Eric swung the flashlight. In its beam he saw Beth. She climbed from the cupboard and stood up.

'Get out of here, Beth,' Eric said.

Her eyes widened and gazed at him with a dull stare. Her mouth dropped open. Her head tilted to one side, and she moaned.

'Beth.'

She staggered toward him.

'What the fuck is she doing?'

Eric shook his head.

His father gave him the hatchet. 'Chop her down.'

She shambled forward as if in a daze. Her face was streaked with burnt cork, smeared with Vampire Blood. Her thigh showed through the tear in her dress, and Eric remembered how she'd ripped her clothes to better look the part.

Her arm went behind Eric's back. He felt the pressure of her breasts against his chest.

'Chop her.'

He felt her warm breath on the side of his neck. Then her teeth. They bit into his neck and ripped. He shrieked. Beth jerked the hatchet from his hand and shoved him backwards.

Spitting Eric's blood and flesh, Beth lunged at the man in the gorilla head. She swung the hatchet, but he caught her arm and took it away. Roaring, he flung her to the floor. He raised the hatchet high.

Something huge and dark ran at him from the kitchen door. He turned, swinging the hatchet. It hacked into the dark thing's arm, and she heard a grunt of pain. But the dark thing – a gorilla – didn't stop. It smashed against the man and plunged a knife into his belly.

Screaming, he shoved the gorilla. It stumbled over Aleshia and fell. He pulled the knife from his belly. Threw it down. Raised the hatchet and stumbled toward the gorilla.

Beth crawled for the knife.

He kicked her in the side and she tumbled over, gasping.

The door from the back porch crashed open.

'That asshole's got an ax!'

'Oh shit!'

'Drop it!'

He turned toward Nate and Bill.

'Back off, monkey-face! I'm warning you!'

He staggered toward them.

Bill saw a knife on the floor. He dived for it, grabbed it, flung it toward Nate and rolled against the man's feet.

The man fell backwards, growling.

Nate leaped over Bill. His knees drove into the man's belly. The man screeched. Nate pressed the knife to his throat.

'Who is this fuck-head?' he said.

'Kill him,' said a girl.

'Beth?' Bill asked.

'Kill him.'

'Not me,' Nate said. 'I may be a shit, but I'm not a killer.'

# Epilogue

'He died in surgery.'

'What a shame.'

'Yeah. My heart bleeds. He should've been executed for the California murders, but they didn't have capital punishment back then. So he got life. Which came down to fourteen years and a massacre in Ashburg.'

'He won't kill anyone else.'

Sam nodded

'He murdered Clara Hayes and all the Horners so they wouldn't interrupt his party?'

'And because he enjoyed it, I suppose.'

'You didn't say, though. What about the third gorilla?'

'Cynthia.'

'Oh my God.'

'She was dead. He must've got her . . . I don't know, sometime that afternoon.'

'I'm sorry, Sam.'

'Well . . .'

Melodie lay her head against Sam's chest, and they sat in silence for a long time in her room behind the office of the Sleepy Hollow Inn.

# The Richard Laymon Collection Volume 1

## Richard Laymon

RICHARD LAYMON'S ACCLAIMED BEAST HOUSE TRILOGY

THE CELLAR

The deeper the tourists go into the Beast House, the darker their nightmares become. But the worst part is beneath the haunted structure. Don't even think about going into the cellar . . .

THE BEAST HOUSE

Bestselling author Gorman Hardy is looking for ideas for his next novel. Petite Tyler and her sexy friend Nora are looking for a wild time. Maybe Malcasa Point can provide both? On the other hand it is just the place to find pain, bestiality and death . . .

THE MIDNIGHT TOUR

Horrific events have made the Beast House infamous. For the full story, take the Midnight Tour. Saturday nights only. Limited to thirteen tourists. It begins on the stroke of midnight. You'll be lucky to get out alive . . .

'If you've missed Laymon, you've missed a treat' Stephen King

'A brilliant writer' *Sunday Express*

0 7553 3167 2

## headline

# The Richard Laymon Collection Volume 2

## Richard Laymon

### THE WOODS ARE DARK

In the woods are six dead trees. The Killing Trees. That's where they take them. Innocent travellers on the road in California. Seized and bound, stripped of their valuables and shackled to the Trees. To wait. In the woods. In the dark . . .

### OUT ARE THE LIGHTS

The Vampire movie came first, then the story of the Axeman. This was the horror movie series to end them all. Cinema buffs admired the grainy, amateur camera work – it suggested the action was the real thing. But it couldn't be – could it?

'If you've missed Laymon, you've missed a treat' Stephen King

'A brilliant writer' *Sunday Express*

'This author knows how to sock it to the reader' *The Times*

0 7553 3169 9

**headline**

Coming soon in the **Richard Laymon**
Collection and available from your bookshop
or *direct from his publisher*.

FREE P&P AND UK DELIVERY
(Overseas and Ireland £3.50 per book)

Volume 1:                                          £7.99
The Beast House Trilogy

Volume 2:                                          £7.99
The Woods Are Dark & Out are the Lights

Volume 4:
Beware! & Dark Mountain                            £7.99

TO ORDER SIMPLY CALL THIS NUMBER

**01235 400 414**

or visit our website: www.madaboutbooks.com

Prices and availability subject to change without notice.